SUSHI
SERIES

SINGLE SASHIMI

BOOK 3

Camy Tang

ZONDERVAN.com/
AUTHORTRACKER
follow your favorite authors

Single Sashimi

Requests for information should be addressed to:

Zondervan, *Grand Rapids, Michigan 49530*

Library of Congress Cataloging-in-Publication Data

Tang, Camy, 1972-
Single sashimi / Camy Tang.
p. cm.—(Sushi series; bk. 3)
ISBN 978-0-310-27400-1
1. Chinese American women—Fiction. I. Title.
PS3620.A6845S56 2008
813'.6—dc22

2008010802

Published in association with the Books & Such Literary Agency, 52 Mission Circle, Suite 122, PMB 170, Santa Rosa, California 95407-5370. www.booksandsuch.biz

Interior design by Michelle Espinoza

Printed in the United States of America

---

08 09 10 11 12 • 24 23 22 21 20 19 18 17 16 15 14 13 12 11 10 9 8 7 6 5 4 3 2 1

SINGLE SASHIMI

Also in the Sushi Series

Sushi for One?

Only Uni

To Stephanie Quilao and Sarah Kim
Thanks for your ideas, inspiration, and information.
Venus and this story would not exist without you.

ONE

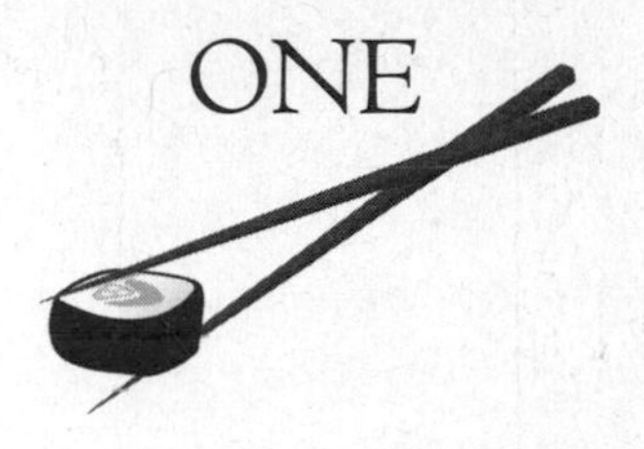

Venus Chau opened the door to her aunt's house and almost fainted.

"What died?" She exhaled sharply, trying to get the foul air out of her body before it caused cancer or something.

Her cousin Jennifer Lim entered the foyer with the look of an *oni* goblin about to eat someone. "She's stinking up my kitchen."

"Who?" Venus hesitated on the threshold, breathing clean night air before she had to close the door.

"My mother, who else?"

The ire in Jenn's voice made Venus busy herself with kicking off her heels amongst the other shoes in the tile foyer. Hoo-boy, she'd never seen quiet Jenn this irate before. Then again, since Aunty Yuki had given her daughter the rule of the kitchen when she'd started cooking in high school, Jenn rarely had to make way for another cook.

"What is she cooking? Beef intestines?"

Jenn flung her arms out. "Who knows? Something Trish is supposed to eat."

"But we don't have to eat it, right? Right?"

"I'll never become pregnant if I have to eat stuff like that." Jenn whirled and stomped toward the kitchen.

Venus turned right into the living room where her very pregnant cousin Trish lounged on the sofa next to her boyfriend, Spenser. "Hey, guys." Her gaze paused on their twined hands. It continued to amaze her that Spenser would date a woman pregnant with another man's child. Maybe Venus shouldn't be so cynical about the men she met. Here was at least one good guy.

Trish's arms shot into the air like a Raiders' cheerleader, nearly clocking Spenser in the eye. "I'm officially on maternity leave!"

Venus paused to clap. "So how did you celebrate?"

"I babysat Matthew all day today." She smiled dreamily at Spenser at the mention of his son.

Venus frowned and landed her hands on her hips. "In your condition?"

Trish waved a hand. "He's not that bad. He stopped swallowing things weeks ago."

"I'm finally not wasting money on all those emergency room visits," Spenser said.

"Besides, I got a book about how to help toddlers expect a new baby." Trish bounced lightly on the sofa cushion in her excitement.

"And?" It seemed kind of weird to Venus, since Trish and Spenser weren't engaged or anything. Yet.

Trish chewed her lip. "I don't know if he totally understands, but at least it's a start."

A sense of strangeness washed over Venus as she watched the two of them, the looks they exchanged that weren't mushy or intimate, just ... knowing. Like mind reading. It made her feel alienated from her cousin for the first time in her life, and she didn't really like it.

She immediately damped down the feeling. How could she begrudge Trish such a wonderful relationship? Venus was so selfish. She disgusted herself.

She looked around the living room. "Where is—"

"Venus!" The childish voice rang down the short hallway. She stepped back into the foyer to see Spenser's son, Matthew, trotting down the carpet with hands reached out to her. He grabbed her at the knees, wrinkling her silk pants, but she didn't mind. His shining face looking up at her—*way* up, since she was the tallest of the cousins—made her feel like she was the only reason he lived and breathed. "*Psycho Bunny*?" he pleaded.

She pretended to think about it. His hands shook her pants legs to make her decide faster.

"Okay."

He darted into the living room and plopped in front of the television, grabbing at the game controllers. The kid had it down pat—in less than a minute, the music for the *Psycho Bunny* video game rolled into the room.

Venus sank to the floor next to him.

"Jenn is totally freaking out." Trish's eyes had popped to the size of *siu mai* dumplings.

"What brought all this on?" Venus picked up the other controller.

"Well, Aunty Yuki had a doctor's appointment today—"

"Is she doing okay?" She chose the Bunny Foo-Foo character for the game just starting.

"Clean bill of health. Cancer's gone, as far as they can tell."

"So that's why she's taken over Jenn's domain?"

Trish rubbed her back and winced. "She took one look at me and decided I needed something to help the baby along."

Jenn huffed into the living room. "She's going to make me ruin the roast chicken!"

Venus ignored her screeching tone. "Sit down. You're not going to make her hurry by hovering." She and Matthew both jumped over the snake pit and landed in the hollow tree.

Jenn flung herself into an overstuffed chair and dumped her feet on the battered oak coffee table.

Venus turned to glance at the foyer. No Nikes. "Where's Lex?"

"Late. Where else?" Jenn snapped.

"I thought Aiden was helping her be better about that."

"He's not a miracle worker." Spenser massaged Trish's back.

"I have to leave early." Venus stretched her silk-clad feet out, wriggling her toes. Her new stilettos looked great but man, they hurt her arches.

"Then you might not eat at all." Jenn crossed her arms over her chest.

Venus speared her with a glance like a stainless steel skewer. "Chill, okay Cujo?"

Jenn pouted and scrunched further down in the chair.

Venus ignored her and turned back to the game. Her inattention had let Matthew pick up the treasure chest. "I have to work on a project."

"For work?"

"No, for me." Only the Spiderweb, the achievement of her lifetime, a new tool that would propel her to the heights of video game development stardom. Which was why she'd kept it separate from her job-related things—she didn't even use her company computer when she worked on it, only her personal laptop.

A new smell wafted into the room, this one rivaling the other in its stomach-roiling ability. Venus waved her hand in front of her face. "Pffaugh! What is she cooking?"

Trish's face had turned the color of green tea. "You're lucky *you* don't have to eat it. Whatever it is, it ain't gonna stay down for long."

"Just say you still have morning sickness."

"In my ninth month?"

Venus shrugged.

The door slammed open. "Hey, guys—*blech.*"

Venus twisted around to see her cousin Lex doubled over, clenching her washboard stomach (Venus wished *she* could have one of those) and looking like she'd hurled up all the shoes littering the foyer floor.

Lex's boyfriend Aiden grabbed her waist to prevent her from nosediving into the tile. "Lex, it's not that bad."

"The gym locker room smells better." Lex used her toes to pull off her cross-trainers without bothering to untie them. "The *men's* locker room."

"It's not me," Jenn declared. "It's Mom, ruining all my best pots."

"What is she doing? Killing small animals on the stovetop?"

"Something for the baby." Trish tried to smile, but it looked more like a wince.

"As long as we don't have to eat it." Lex dropped her slouchy purse on the floor and walked into the living room.

Aunty Yuki appeared behind her in the doorway, bearing a steaming bowl. "Here, Trish. Drink this." The brilliant smile on her wide face eclipsed her tiny stature.

Venus smelled something pungent, like when she walked into a Chinese medicine shop with her dad. A bolus of air erupted from her mouth, and she coughed. "What is that?" She dropped the game controller.

"Pig's brain soup."

Trish's smile hardened to plastic. Lex grabbed her mouth. Spenser—who was Chinese and therefore had been raised with the weird concoctions—sighed. Aiden looked at them all like they were funny-farm rejects.

Venus closed her eyes, tightened her mouth, and concentrated on not gagging. Good thing her stomach was empty.

Aunty Yuki's mouth pursed. "What's wrong? My mother-in-law made me eat pig's brain soup when I was a couple weeks from delivering Jennifer."

"*That's* what you ruined my pots with?" Jennifer steamed hotter than the bowl of soup.

Her mom caught the *yakuza*-about-to-hack-your-finger-off expression on Jenn's face. Aunty Yuki paused, then backtracked to the kitchen. With the soup bowl, thankfully.

"Papa?" Matthew's voice sounded faint.

Venus turned.

"Don't feel good." He clutched his poochy tummy.

"Oh, no." Spenser grabbed his son and headed out of the living room.

Then the world exploded.

Just as they passed into the foyer, Matthew threw up onto the tiles.

Lex, with her weak stomach when it came to bodily fluids, took one look and turned pasty.

A burning smell and a few cries sounded from the kitchen.

Trish sat up straighter than a Buddha and clenched her rounded abdomen. "Oh!"

Spenser held his crying son as he urped up the rest of his afternoon snack. Lex clapped a hand to her mouth to prevent herself from following Matthew's example. Jenn started for the kitchen, but then Matthew's mess blocking the foyer stopped her. Trish groaned and curled in on herself, clutching her tummy.

Venus shot to her feet. She wasn't acting Game Lead at her company for nothing.

"You." She pointed to Jenn. "Get to the kitchen and send your mom in here for Trish." Jenn leaped over Matthew's puddle and darted away. "And bring paper towels for the mess!"

"You," she flung at Spenser. "Take Matthew to the bathroom."

He gestured to the brand new hallway carpet.

Oh no, Aunty Yuki would have a fit. But it couldn't be helped. "If he makes a mess on the carpet, we'll just clean it up later."

He didn't hesitate. He hustled down the hallway with Matthew in his arms.

Venus kicked the miniscule living room garbage basket closer to Lex. "Hang your head over that." Not that it would hold more than spittle, but it was better than letting Lex upchuck all over the plush cream carpet. Why did Lex, tomboy and jock, have to go weak every time something gross happened?

"You." Venus stabbed a manicured finger at Aiden. "Get your car, we're taking Trish to the hospital."

He didn't jump at her command. "After one contraction?"

Trish moaned, and Venus had a vision of the baby flying out of her in the next minute. She pointed to the door again. "Just go!"

Aiden shrugged and slipped out the front door, muttering to himself.

"You." She stood in front of Trish, who'd started Lamaze breathing through her pursed lips. "Uh ..."

Trish peered up at her.

"Um ... stop having contractions."

Trish rolled her eyes, but didn't speak through her pursed lips.

Venus ignored her and went to kneel over Matthew's rather watery puddle, which had spread with amoeba fingers reaching down the lines of grout. Lex's purse lay nearby, so she rooted in it for a tissue or something to start blotting up the mess.

Footsteps approaching. Before she could raise her head or shout a warning, Aunty Yuki hurried into the foyer. "What's wron—!"

It was like a Three Stooges episode. Aunty Yuki barreled into Venus's bent figure. She had leaned over Matthew's mess to protect anyone from stepping in it, but it also made her an obstacle in the middle of the foyer.

"Ooomph!" The older woman's feet—shod in cotton house slippers, luckily, and not shoes—jammed into Venus's ribs. She couldn't see much except a pair of slippers leaving the floor at the same time, and then a body landing on the living room carpet on the other side of her. *Ouch.*

"Are you okay?" Venus twisted to kneel in front of her, but she seemed slow to rise.

"Venus, here're the paper towels—"

Jenn's voice in the foyer made Venus whirl on the balls of her feet and fling her hands up. "Watch out!"

Jenn stopped just in time. Her toes were only inches away from Matthew's mess, her body leaning forward. Her arms whirled, still clutching the towels, like a cheerleader and her pom-poms.

"Jenn." Spenser's voice coming down the hallway toward the foyer. "Where are the—"

"Stop!" Venus and Jenn shouted at the same time.

Spenser froze, his foot hovering above a finger of the puddle that had stretched toward the hallway. "Ah. Okay. Thanks." He lowered his foot on the clean tile to the side.

Aiden opened the front door. "The car's out front—" The sight of them all left him speechless.

Trish had started to hyperventilate, her breath seething through her teeth. "Will somebody do something?!"

Aunty Yuki moaned from her crumpled position on the floor.

Smoke started pouring from the kitchen, along with the awful smell of burned ... *something* that wasn't normal food.

Venus snatched the paper towels from Jenn. "Kitchen!" Jenn fled before she'd finished speaking. "What do you need?" Venus barked at Spenser.

"Extra towels."

"Guest bedroom closet, top shelf."

He headed back down the hall. Venus turned to Aiden and swept a hand toward Aunty Yuki on the living room floor. "Take care of her, will you?"

"What about me?" Trish moaned through a clenched jaw.

"Stop having contractions!" Venus swiped up the mess on the tile before something worse happened, like someone stepped in it and slid. That would just be the crowning cherry to her evening. Even when she wasn't at work, she was still working.

"Are you okay, Aunty?" She stood with the sodden paper towels. Aiden had helped her to a seat next to Lex, who was ashen-faced and still leaning over the tiny trash can. Aside from a reddish spot on Aunty Yuki's elbow, she seemed fine.

Jenn entered the living room, her hair wild and a distinctive burned smell sizzling from her clothes. "My imported French saucepan is completely blackened!" But she had enough sense not to glare at her parent as she probably wanted to. Aunty Yuki suddenly found the wall hangings fascinating.

Venus started to turn toward the kitchen to throw away the paper towels she still held. "Well, we have to take Trish to the hospital—"

"Actually ..." Trish's breathing had slowed. "I think it's just a false alarm."

Venus turned to look at her. "False alarm? Pregnant women have those?"

"It happened a couple days ago too."

"What?" Venus almost slammed her fist into her hip, but remembered the dirty paper towels just in time. Good thing too, because she had on a Chanel suit.

Trish gave a long, slow sigh. "Yup, they're gone. That was fast." She smiled cheerfully.

Venus wanted to scream. This was out of her realm. At work, she was used to grabbing a crisis at the throat and wrestling it to submission. This was somewhere Trish was heading without her, and the thought both frightened and unnerved her. She shrugged it off. "Well . . . Aunty—"

"I'm fine, Venus." Aunty Yuki inspected her elbow. "Jennifer, get those Japanese Salonpas patches—"

"Mom, they stink." Jenn's stress over her beautiful kitchen made her more belligerent than Venus had ever seen her before. Not that the camphor patches could smell any worse than the burned Chinese-old-wives'-pregnancy-food permeating the house.

At the sound of the word Salonpas, Lex pinched her lips together but didn't say anything.

Aunty Yuki gave Jenn a limpid look. "The Salonpas gets rid of the pain."

"I'll get it." Aiden headed down the hallway to get the adhesive patches.

"In the hall closet." Jenn's words slurred a bit through her tight jaw.

Distraction time. Venus tried to smile. "Aunty, if you're okay, then let's eat."

Jenn's eyes flared neon red. "Can't."

"Huh?"

"*Somebody* turned off the oven." Jenn frowned at her mother, who tactfully looked away. "Dinner won't be for another hour." She stalked back to the kitchen.

Even with the nasty smell, Venus's stomach protested its empty state. "It's already eight o'clock."

"Suck it up!" Jenn yelled from the kitchen.

It was going to be a long night.

Venus needed a Reese's peanut butter cup.

No, a Reese's was bad. Sugar, fat, preservatives, all kinds of chemicals she couldn't even pronounce.

Oooh, but it would taste so good . . .

No, she equated Reese's cups with her fat days. She was no longer fat. She didn't need a Reese's.

But she sure wanted one after such a hectic evening with her cousins.

She trudged up the steps to her condo. Home. Too small to invite people over, and that was the way she liked it. Her haven, where she could relax and let go, no one to see her when she was vulnerable—

Her front door was ajar.

Her limbs froze mid-step, but her heart *rat-tat-tatted* in her chest like a machine gun. Someone. Had. Broken. Into. Her. Home.

Her hand started to shake. She clenched it to her hip, crushing the silk of her pants. What to do? He might still be there. Pepper spray. In her purse. She searched in her bag and finally found the tiny bottle. Her hand trembled so much, she'd be more likely to spritz herself than the intruder.

Were those sounds coming from inside? She reached out a hand, but couldn't quite bring herself to push the door open further.

Stupid, call the police! She fumbled with the pepper spray so she could extract her cell phone. *Dummy, don't pop yourself in the eye with that stuff!* She switched the spray to her other hand while her thumb dialed 9–1–1. Her handbag's leather straps dug into her elbow.

Thump! That came from her living room! Footsteps. *Get away from the door!* She stumbled backwards, but remembering the stairs right behind her, she tried to stop herself from tumbling down. Her ankle tilted on her stilettos, and she fell sideways to lean against the wall. The footsteps approached her open door.

"9–1–1, what's your emergency?"

She raised her hand with the bottle of pepper spray. "Someone's—"

The door swung open.

"Edgar!" The cell phone dropped with a clatter, but she kept a firm grip on the pepper spray, suddenly tempted to use it.

One of her junior programmers stood in her open doorway.

TWO

What are you doing?" *Translation: You better have a good reason for invading my home or I'm going to break both your kneecaps.* Venus's fingers twitched around the pepper spray, but she resisted and lowered her arm.

It was dark except for the light from her living room, but she could see his chipmunk cheeks glowing red. "Oh! Venus."

She spoke slowly and distinctly. "Why are you in my house, Edgar?"

He recovered quickly, flashing a wide and insincere smile. "I had some sensitive material for you and didn't want to leave it outside, so I checked for a spare key. I found it under the doormat."

She bit her tongue before she could exclaim a very un-Christianlike word. "I don't leave a key under the doormat."

Edgar smoothly handed her a key. "Well, I found one."

She snatched it away. A copy, probably made at Home Depot. She'd changed the locks herself when she first moved in, and she didn't even *have* a generic copy. She certainly wouldn't be stupid enough to leave one outside her condo. Edgar was lying through his teeth—but how had he gotten a copy of her house key?

At work, she kept her purse in her locked desk drawer ... but the lock was flimsy, and she hadn't gotten around to getting it replaced. She shuddered at the vision of Edgar poking through her purse when she'd been out of her office. *The weasel had stolen her key and made a copy.* And she couldn't prove it.

What was worse, her home alarm system had broken the night before—waking her out of a sound sleep—and she'd arranged for the repairmen to arrive *tomorrow,* when she would meet them during her lunch hour. She couldn't even say Edgar had tampered with her alarm, because it hadn't been activated.

She would change the locks ASAP. "Why are you here?" She hadn't even realized he knew where she lived.

"I needed to drop off some reports you have to look at before the meeting tomorrow morning."

"Where are they?" She cast a pointed glance at his empty hands.

"I left them on your desk."

"It couldn't wait until tomorrow morning? Why would you come all the way to my condo?"

"Yardley sent me here."

The CTO? Was he in on this or was that a lie? Venus's lips pinched as if she'd eaten a Lemonhead. She bent to pick up her cell phone before she could say something she'd regret.

"Hello?" The operator's reply was staticky—drat, the fall had broken her phone. "No, I'm fine, operator! No, really! It's a coworker. Thank you!" She closed her phone with a snap, then wondered if she should have reported Edgar's break-in instead of exonerating him.

She glanced down at the key in her hand. She couldn't prove he'd made this copy. She couldn't prove she never left a copy under her doormat.

She glared at him where he stood, relaxed stance, smiling in a way that made her grind her teeth. She stalked closer to him, reveling in the fact that her height and her heels allowed her to look down on him slightly. His smile never wavered, but his irises contracted. She intimidated him, although he was smart and strong enough not to show it.

When she'd been the fat girl, she'd never received this kind of nervous reaction from any man, no matter how much of a rage she was in—mostly because they'd always overlooked her as inconsequential. One of the perks of being tall and thin was the way her anger made men uneasy.

But what could she say? What could she prove?

"Move, Edgar. I need to get into my condo." *To find out what you did, because I doubt you'd admit it.*

He didn't flinch at her rude tone, although he bared more teeth. He gave way with gallantry that mocked her even as it seemed to defer to her.

She didn't look back at him as she entered her home. "Goodnight." She slammed the door shut and bolted it with some violence.

She could smell his sickly cologne and a sweaty man smell. Ugh, disgusting. She started to peel off her shoes . . . No, wait. The dummy had walked on her sanitary floors with his shoes on. She'd have to clean them again. She rubbed her arms as she headed to her kitchen, limping from her tortuous heels. The Febreze spray bottle was under the kitchen sink.

Ahh. Drenching the living room made her feel much better. She cast her eye around. What had he done?

The couch didn't look like he'd sat on it, but then again she doubted he'd wanted to wait for her to return. Her *People* and *Star* still lay on the coffee table, neatly stacked on top of *InStyle*, *Vogue*, and her gaming magazines.

In a corner of the living room sat her treadmill—she had to remember to get the worn belt replaced eventually—and in the other corner was her desk—actually, a sleek vanity table she used as a desk, since she didn't have the square footage for a real one. A manila folder sat on a corner—Edgar's all-important reports. A few bills she'd carefully stacked earlier on the opposite corner were now askew.

A chill slid down her throat to nestle against her heart like a shard of ice.

Her laptop cords had been neatly laid out, ready for her to plug in the computer, but the cords were twisted. Her lamp had been knocked at an angle. A few pens had fallen out of her pen holder onto the floor.

He'd touched her personal things. She wanted to grab everything and throw them in a pan full of bleach and water. She shot a few more sprays of Febreze to get rid of his smell—later, she'd grab the Lysol and wipe everything down.

He'd rifled through her files—the hanging folders in their open crate under the desk were crooked and spread out instead of standing in the neat, straight order she always left them, flush against the back of the crate.

He'd probably sat in her one-thousand-dollar ergonomic chair too, with his nasty sweaty behind. *Ewwww.* She made a mental note to douse it with Lysol later.

Edgar had been looking for the Spiderweb.

That sliver of ice in her heart suddenly became a drenching of ice water.

The door to her bedroom stood ajar instead of closed. She poked at it with the Febreze bottle to make it swing open.

The impression of his behind still lay in her snowy white down comforter where he'd sat on the bed. Other divots in the comforter showed where he'd also laid things.

Venus squirted the spray bottle as she walked further into the room. Her fingers twitched, ready to tear the comforter off the bed and wash the cover pronto, but first she had to make sure the Spiderweb was safe. She snapped on the light, then did a hairpin turn around the open door to reach her closet.

The sliding door was cracked open. She swallowed. She dropped the spray bottle to pull the door open with both hands.

Her clothes had been shoved to the side, revealing her fireproof, anti-theft, digital-lock safe bolted to the floor (and the wall) in the corner of the closet. He couldn't have gotten in, could he? She dropped to her knees and checked the safe door. Still locked.

But there were fine scratches in the steel. Maybe with a penknife? She wasn't sure whether to grind her teeth or shout in triumph. She unlocked the safe.

Oh, praise God. Venus snatched up her laptop and hugged it to her chest.

A *plop* came from the bathroom. She froze.

Edgar might have had an accomplice. She should have checked that the house was clear before opening the safe!

She shoved the laptop back in and locked the door. She twisted around to glance at the bathroom door. Ajar. She darted toward the bed. Her aluminum baseball bat lay under the edge on this side, thankfully. She wobbled to her feet—which hurt like crazy, stupid shoes, but she wasn't setting foot on the Edgar-contaminated hardwood until she'd done some serious Lysol-ing—and bent to retrieve the bat.

Armed, she approached the bathroom. What if he had a gun? She could honestly say she might choose to die before giving up the combination to the safe. Besides which, the laptop was also password protected with the best encryption program money could buy.

She poked open the door. A rushing water sound. Water? Someone had definitely been in here, but it looked empty now. She peeked in the shower just in case. Not that she really expected some spy in a white wetsuit to be hiding there, but better safe than sorry.

The water was filling the toilet tank. She opened the top and peeked in. Something was wrong with the plunger inside. Rats. She'd have to fix—

Wait a minute. Oh, gross!

Edgar had used the toilet.

The smell of bleach, Bounce, and Lysol relieved her as she snuggled under the comforter, the cover still warm from the dryer. She curled into a fetal position.

She still felt violated. Only her family had ever been inside her condo. She didn't even like electricians or the cable guy invading her home. Her postage stamp-sized living room prevented her from having anyone over after work, even if she'd been close enough friends with her coworkers to suggest it. She'd gotten this condo on purpose because of the small size. No entertaining. No one here but herself.

This was her shell. Here she could relax, soak in the silence, let her guard down. No one complained about her neatfreakness (Lex), or her nonfat foods (Jenn), or her exercise regimen (Trish). Here she could be as weird as she wanted to be.

But Edgar had been here. That was like someone else trying on her socks and then giving them back to her.

Oh, God. Even in her head, it sounded more like a sob.

She flipped on the light and grabbed her Bible from the bedside table. She needed to read the Old Testament. Order and rules. Everything exactly so. God's perfection and commandments.

She started in Exodus chapter twenty-five, the plans for the tabernacle. The lists of materials soothed her. "Blue, purple and scarlet yarn and fine linen; goat hair; ram skins dyed red for cloth—"

Rrring!

What? That was the phone. She looked at her alarm clock. It was almost midnight. Caller ID said it was her dad.

Oh, no. She pushed the talk button. "Dad, what's wrong?" She gasped her words because she'd started to hyperventilate.

"I, um ..." He cleared his throat. "I need you to pick me up."

"Where are you?"

"Just on Lawrence Expressway."

"On the side of the road?"

"At the corner of Lawrence and Homestead."

"What happened?"

"Nothing, nothing. I got into a small fender bender."

"So small you can't drive your own car away?"

He harrumphed a little more. "It's kind of cold, honey. Can you pick me up soon?"

Venus sighed, torn between a gusty sigh or a barely suppressed scream. "I'll be there in ten minutes."

"*Small* fender bender?" Venus gaped at the crushed pulp that used to be her father's car. At least he—and probably the motorcycle cop who had stayed with him—had managed to push it onto the side of Lawrence Expressway, out of the way of the rare car traveling this late at night.

"He came out of nowhere." Her father frowned and scratched his reddened cheeks, which had been smacked hard by the airbag.

"Dumb young kids with their fancy big trucks, roaring all over the highway . . ."

"Well, at least you're okay." Venus rubbed her stiff shoulders, but it didn't help the tension filling her chest like a water balloon about to burst. At least the policeman had stayed with her father, although the poor guy looked bored standing a few yards away near his motorcycle.

"Did you already call a tow truck?" There was no sign of the truck Dad had hit, so the other guy must have had his car towed and then taken off himself.

"Yeah."

She joined her father against a chain link fence on the side of the road. They stood there in silence while an occasional car sped down Lawrence Expressway.

"Good thing there weren't too many cars out this late at night."

He grunted.

"Working late?"

"Crunching numbers for your grandma."

Oh, the bank.

"I saw your mother at the bank today."

This time, she grunted. "I thought Grandma gave her a position that doesn't require her to be there." Especially after the last fiasco involving a few thousand dollars she "borrowed" from a bank client that had to be replaced before he figured out what had happened.

"She's in human resources now. She was turning in some papers."

"Let's hope she doesn't screw that up, like she did everything else."

"Venus." His stern voice made her pout, and she didn't look at him. "She's your mother. You don't talk about her that way."

"She hasn't been your wife for seventeen years, so I don't understand why you'd care how I talked about her."

He sighed, a low, reedy breath. "It's because I owe a lot to your grandmother."

"Yeah, well, Grandma kept you on at the bank after the divorce because she likes you more than she does her own daughter."

"Venus." His voice had become a growl.

"Sorry." But she wasn't. "So did you talk to Mom?"

"She seemed in a good mood."

"That means she'll be in a bad one tomorrow." Her mother, the emotional yo-yo. Charming one moment, angry and insulting the next. Mom had been that way for most of Venus's childhood.

He sighed but didn't reprimand her again, even though she knew she deserved it.

"I didn't think you'd be up so late when I called you."

"I was cleaning."

He shifted his weight and looked at her. "Why were you cleaning so late at night?"

She knew it was going to alarm him, but maybe it would make him feel more comfortable to worry about her rather than think about his accident. "I came home tonight and the front door was open. One of my junior programmers was walking out of my condo."

His eyes suddenly blazed hotter than a sword-maker's fire. "What was he doing there?"

"He said he found a spare key under the doormat, and the CTO had sent him by to give me some sensitive papers that he didn't want to leave outside."

"Why do *you* think he was there?"

She'd kept her emotions at bay as she scrubbed the toilet, mopped the floors, disinfected all the door handles, drove here to find her father. But now the pain started in her gut, the feeling of being stabbed over and over with a carving knife. "I think he was looking for the Spiderweb."

Her father grew very still. "How would he even know about it?"

"Jaye and I have been working on it for years. It's a small industry—maybe word leaked out somehow."

"Well, does it matter? Patent is pending—"

"All they have to do is make something similar that won't infringe on the patent. It's done all the time."

"You had it locked up, right?"

"Of course." She was her father's daughter—she'd even bought the same brand of fireproof safe that he had. "But I think he tried to get into the safe."

"He didn't succeed?"

"He didn't."

A thoughtful, tense silence. Her father's worry for her was almost a tangible thing that wrapped around her.

"What are you going to do?" he asked.

She stared up at the night sky, at stars dimmed by the nearby street lamp. She had to be rational, not fly off the handle the way she wanted to. "I can find out easily if he was telling the truth or not."

"And if he wasn't?"

"I don't know, Dad. This company is like the Google of game development. It's only going to get bigger, whether I'm there or not."

"Do you want them to go big by stealing your proprietary program?"

Maybe it was the dust and dirt from standing beside an expressway, but a headache started throbbing behind her eyes. "It's not even completed yet. I'm not ready to start my own company yet."

"I keep telling you, you'll never feel ready to start your own company." He thrust his hands in his pockets. "You just have to do it."

Maybe he was right. "Besides, if Oomvid makes me Game Lead in fact—rather than acting Game Lead—there's a good chance I would sell them the Spiderweb. Why would they try to steal it?"

"Are you sure they're going to hire you as Game Lead?"

"I've seen all the candidates. I'm the best out of all of them."

Her dad snorted. "Does Oomvid really want the best? Or just whomever they happen to like?"

She didn't want to think about it.

She didn't have to—the tow truck arrived. After the wreck got sent to the garage her father used, they waved at the relieved policeman, and she drove her dad home.

He paused after getting out of her car. "What are you going to do tomorrow?" Always have a plan. He'd taught her that.

"I'll see if Yardley really sent Edgar to my condo."

"And then?"

"And then ..." What could she do, short of turning in her resignation? "I'll poke around, see what else he's been up to."

Dad sighed and looked grave.

"I'm not going to just quit, Dad. I'm acting Game Lead, and I'm not going to throw that away."

"You're *acting* Game Lead; Yardley's an *established* Chief Technology Officer. There's a big difference between them." He walked up the driveway and let himself into his townhouse.

Venus wasn't about to admit he might be right.

"I don't like the face of this Goobermonster."

Venus handed the sketch to her administrative assistant as they hurried down the carpeted hallway toward the boardroom. "Tell the design team to make him less like Barney and more like *Aliens.* He should make the consumer want to shoot him into tiny pieces, not sing along with him."

Her admin, a young Asian girl right out of college, handed her another file. "Jaye can't find the bug the testers complained about."

"Schedule a meeting so the testers can demonstrate what they do to make the video game crash."

"The testers have said they're too busy."

Venus stopped and planted her stiletto heel. Her admin halted and swallowed as she gazed up at her.

Venus frowned. The girl didn't have to tremble as if Venus was going to eat her. It didn't help that this particular admin was petite and frail-looking. "Tell the testers we pay them to help us make the game better, not to dictate to me if they have time or not."

She turned and continued toward the boardroom. "If I have to go into the basement to roll some heads, I will." In this male-dominated business, she wouldn't let anyone be impertinent to her—certainly not a posse of uppity testers. Most testers she'd worked with at other game development companies had been nice guys—this particular group was like a high-powered laser rifle shot to the rear end.

She stumbled a little on a bump in the carpet. Her world tilted on its axis before it righted itself with agonizing slowness. Too little sleep, too much caffeine. She needed to be alert for this meeting. "Tell Edgar's programmers that the Angoramonsters' mass attack on level five is too slow. They need to speed it up a bit."

The admin wrote the memo down and nearly tripped flat on her face as she struggled to keep up with Venus's long stride. "They just finished the Inca Death Mine set for level nine."

"I also wanted the Vampire Spike Field ready. Where's that?"

The admin swallowed again. "They didn't mention it."

Venus ground her teeth. Edgar's group kept "neglecting" to tell her if they were behind schedule—yet another small way some of the men under her flouted her authority. "If they needed more time, I could have reallocated resources or rescheduled the Smelly Werewolves design for a later date."

The admin remained silent.

Venus would have to go down herself to get things done. She could never win with her admin choices—the female ones jumped every time she sneezed, which made them ineffectual at relaying Venus's instructions to the men who worked under her. However, whenever Venus hired male admins in the past, they backstabbed her at the first opportunity, speculating that she'd warmed a few beds to get where she was.

This particular admin wasn't bad—just intimidated by Venus's height. Also possibly green at the way Venus garnered attention from a certain Korean American programmer, who looked like the hero of the girl's favorite Korean soap opera. Venus wasn't the most sensitive person, but she'd have to be blind to not notice how the admin straightened her posture and smiled more when Jin Hoo came to report to Venus.

She hadn't yet found anyone she wanted to have a relationship with, and it wouldn't be a programmer—she never dated someone who worked under her. When she'd been fat, they hadn't been interested in her, anyway. When she lost weight, she wasn't interested in them because they'd acted so differently toward her, and that galled her. But no one knew she'd never had a significant relationship with any man, they just assumed she couldn't have reached the age of thirty and still be a virgin.

Venus always gently brushed off Jin Hoo before he could make any overtures, like she did all her coworkers, but he never seemed to lose that just-been-slammed-in-the-face-with-a-sledgehammer look when he saw her. He never noticed the pretty little admin right outside her door.

Well, Venus could at least do something about that. With her hand on the boardroom door, she turned to her admin. "While I'm in my meeting, take the new design specs to Jin Hoo."

The girl's eyes sparkled like the Chopard earrings Venus had coveted in her latest *InStyle* magazine.

"I'll be busy with the meeting all afternoon and you deserve a break. Leave your notes on my desk and then take the rest of the day off." Hopefully with Jin Hoo at her side, if the girl had an ounce of female persuasion in her.

The admin looked like she wanted to kiss her. "Thank you, Venus."

"Wish me luck." Venus opened the boardroom door, ready to face Goobermonsters in Armani suits.

"You want me to do what?"

Venus bolted to her feet and stared down the length of the oak conference table at Ed Mandley, VP of Marketing and the biggest idiot she'd ever worked with in all her years as a video game programmer.

Ed skewered her with dark eyes under his bushy gray brows. "This isn't negotiable, *Miss Chau*."

She hated it when they called her Miss Chau. It delineated her from the rest of them—the VPs in designer suits who sat on either side of the table. Her Versace business suit had masculine lines, but the feminine curves underneath didn't. And those curves were all they saw, sometimes. Like now. They saw "brainless woman," not "competent programmer."

Venus took a sharp breath through tight nostrils. "The game heroine already has an improbable size C cup. She can't possibly do all the flips and aerials in the fighting sequences with a larger chest size."

Ed's gaze didn't waver. "The testers wanted a more sexually appealing character— "

"The testers are only supposed to be looking for software bugs and trying to make the game crash. They are not the product's focus group."

"On the contrary, our marketing department values their input highly." The VP of Manufacturing, a thin man in a burgundy tie to her left, spoke up timidly.

"The testers do nothing but stare at a gaming monitor for twelve hours a day. Of course they'd want more stimulating eye candy." *In lieu of a real social life ...*

"The testers are an important part of your team, Venus." Ed cleared his throat and smoothed his Italian silk tie.

Venus flexed her jaw. He always found something in her to criticize, possibly because she'd spilled champagne down the front of his suit when he'd made drunken overtures to her at the last milestone party. "Lara Croft has been done already. We've gone through considerable effort to distinguish our heroine from Tomb Raider. A larger chest will only decrease our market impact."

"For crying out loud, it's a minor physical detail, not a complete overhaul of the game."

"It's not minor." A woman's body was never minor. Venus didn't eat tofu and nonfat frozen yogurt for something minor. She didn't run on her treadmill or take those killer spinning classes for something minor. She liked being healthy, and she worked hard to keep herself healthy. She didn't appreciate men who wanted a sex kitten instead of a strong, likable heroine for the game.

"Venus, we have duly noted your suggestion but overruled you." Yardley, the chief technology officer, attempted to be both firm and conciliatory in his tone, but Venus wasn't in the mood.

Ed smirked.

"You hired me because of my expertise in the gaming industry and my understanding of the market trends." Venus stabbed her manicured finger at him. "What is the point if you keep overruling me? First it was her name—and I still firmly believe 'Tweety' is the biggest mistake the gaming world will ever know—"

"Market research indicated—"

"Then it was her height—a five-foot-tall woman looks ridiculous taking on some of the monsters you wanted."

"The testers thought she looked too masculine—"

"Now you want me to give her a chest so large she'll cut herself with her sword." Venus planted her hands on her hips. "We spent thousands to fine-tune realistic video graphics. You're throwing it all away with these impossible—"

"People don't want reality, they want fantasy." The Chief Financial Officer, silent until now, thumped the table, making his portfolio jump. "They want escape. We give them that escape with a woman they'd want."

"This will turn the game into the same kind of thing that's already glutting the market. With nothing to distinguish it, your sales aren't going to meet projections."

"The decision is made, Miss Chau."

Venus stared at the sea of closed, hard, male faces. She'd hit this invisible wall countless times, and it still slammed her like a crack to the head with a baseball bat. *Calm down. You are in the middle of a meeting with all the VPs and the CEO. Stop shrieking like a spoiled child.*

Her hands touched the table. At least she wasn't trembling. *Be professional.* She sat down with a hopefully neutral expression.

Despite her outburst, she knew she'd been doing a stellar job as acting Game Lead. In her report, she had put a good spin on some of the delays her admin had told her about, and she knew she could get her programmers to kick into gear and get the projects done by the deadline she'd set.

As they continued with the meeting, she glanced at Yardley. He hadn't looked her in the eye since she entered the room. He probably knew she'd corner him to find out if he'd really sent Edgar to her condo last night.

"Lastly, we have some news from the Board of Directors." Yardley straightened his tie.

Venus and the VPs of Product, Manufacturing, Sales, and Marketing looked at each other. News? Something more for them to do, probably.

Yardley cleared his throat. "Miss Chau has done an amazing job the past several months as acting Game Lead for the Tweety project. Because of her work, we are ahead of development schedule and due for our next milestone soon."

He'd never praised her before. Her gut started to gurgle. Did this mean what she thought it did?

"As you know, the Board of Directors decided not to hire outside the company for the new Tweety Game Lead."

They'd decided that weeks ago. She'd been working overtime and pushing herself to prove to the VPs that she could do the job—and better than the previous Game Lead, in her opinion. She knew she had it in her to be the best Game Lead the company had ever seen.

Was this her chance? Had her earlier outburst ruined her chances? But the Board had made this decision in their own meeting, before this one had even started, right?

"Miss Chau, we applaud you for keeping things running smoothly for our new Game Lead, and we know the transition will be seamless because of you."

Something inside her flash-froze, with harsh cracks radiating from her breastbone.

"Our new Game Lead has distinguished himself in his … er … current position." Yardley accidentally glanced at Venus and blushed as he looked away. "He's, um … worked here for more years than most programmers. We'll announce it today to the company. We've chosen Edgar Smiley …"

Venus had turned into a finely chiseled ice sculpture, about to shatter into a thousand shards and hopefully nail a few of those arrogant executives in their Italian-suit-clad behinds.

Edgar. They'd hired one of her junior programmers to replace her.

THREE

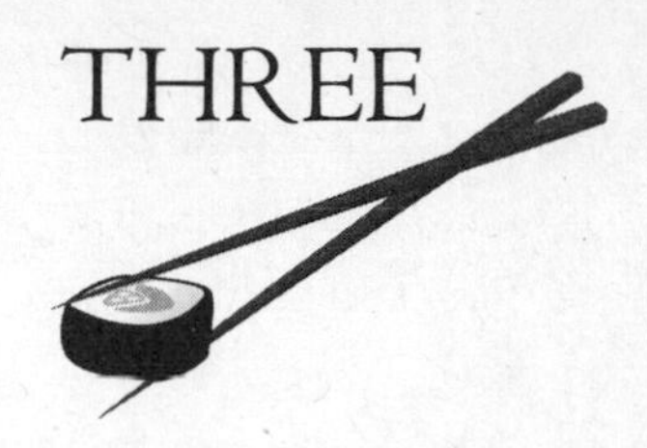

Venus could always count on her cousins turning up on time for food. Two cars entered the parking lot of Moon Pearl Restaurant just as Venus stepped out of her Beamer.

The September chill in the evening air didn't faze her as she steamed toward the restaurant doors. She'd suppressed her frustration—barely—all day, but her insides boiled like Chinese hot pot soup. She really needed to vent to her cousins.

"Reservation for four," she said in Cantonese to the hostess.

Lex came up behind her as the woman looked down at the reservation book. "Hi there. I brought Trish. You made reservations?"

"I'm upset, not stupid." Venus wasn't in a mood to wait to be seated.

"Well, duh." Trish waddled through the door, her hands at her back. "You never want to go out to Moon Pearl because of the MSG and the oil and the— "

The hostess glanced up at Trish. She blushed and stopped talking.

Venus glanced around the restaurant, about three-quarters full. Jenn walked in the door just as the hostess grabbed four tattered-edged menus.

"This way." The hostess seated them at a square table near the back of the restaurant. A busboy deposited a steel pot of guaranteed poor quality jasmine tea.

Jenn started pouring tea into the small porcelain teacups. "So Venus, tell us what happened."

"They hired my junior programmer to be Game Lead." Just saying it made her want to cry.

Lex sucked in her tea the wrong way and started coughing.

Jenn swatted her on the back. "You're kidding. Why would they do that?"

"Do they want you to quit or something?" Trish's eyes had gone round like the small dishes for chili sauce that she'd been passing out from the kiosk on the table.

"I can't think of any other reason." Venus brushed her fingers to the side of her teacup, but the tea had made it too hot to touch. "If I quit—versus if they fire me—I forfeit my stock shares."

"Who did you offend?" Lex shot her with a narrow look.

Venus sat up straight in her shabby velvet chair. "I didn't offend anybody."

Jenn's face remained carefully neutral while Lex and Trish both rolled their eyes.

Okay, maybe it wasn't so unreasonable a question. "They hired me as Programming Lead, and I did such a good job they made me acting Game Lead for three months. I did an even better job than the previous Game Lead. Why would they want me to leave?"

"I don't know, your winning personality?" Lex said.

Venus's glare should have pulverized her on the spot, but Jenn intervened. "Did you ask the CEO why they made that decision?"

"I tried, but he shot out of the meeting like a phaser burst."

"Venus, you're with us now. Normal-speak, please." Trish winced as she rubbed her back.

"I talked to his admin to try to make an appointment with him, but she said he was booked. I think he told her to give me the runaround."

"Coward." Lex frowned.

Jenn lightly backhanded her arm to chastise her, then turned to Venus. "So what are you going to do?"

"Right now, I want to eat. Where's the waiter?" She craned her neck to try to catch someone's eye, but they all ignored her.

"This place is terrible. Why do you like eating here?" Trish stretched side to side.

"They have the best beef chow fun with black bean sauce on the planet, and I need comfort food badly." She waved her arm, but the skinny waiter a couple tables down seemed to deliberately keep his eyes on the floor as he scooted around the chairs. Her stomach growled. She hadn't eaten lunch and she'd skipped her fruit and yogurt this afternoon. Any minute now, she was going to start slurping down the red chili seeds in oil that sat in a small container on the table kiosk.

Finally, the hostess saw Venus's gyrations and turned to speak sharply to a waiter lounging by the cash register. Great. Of course they'd get the one slacker waiter in the restaurant.

"Whatchoo want?" He dug out a scuffed writing pad from his back pocket.

They ordered. Venus threw in a dish of *dau miu*, sautéed pea greens, to appease the guilt nagging at her for her carb- and fat-laden meal.

"Ha!" Lex chortled. "You can't even eat junk food when you're upset."

"Vegetables keep me regular," Venus growled.

"Don't talk to me about regularity." Trish pouted. "This baby is throwing my whole system out of whack."

"So." Jenn leaned forward onto the glass-topped table. "Are you going to quit?"

"If you want to enact revenge, you can leave in the middle of a big project." Lex gave a feral grin.

"I can't quit. I need the money."

Lex's look was a cross between *Are you kidding me?* and *Are you stupid?* "You have tons of money."

"Jaye and I want to start our own company, and we're still working on that development tool. I can't be unemployed and live on nothing while we're completing it. Who knows how long it'll take? I also might need the money for starting up the company, if we can't get investors."

"Oh." Trish chewed the inside of her lip. "When is your software going to be ready?"

Venus pressed the heel of her hand into her forehead. "I think Oomvid tried to steal it."

"*What?*" Lex exploded.

Jenn laid a hand on Lex's arm, but spoke to Venus. "What do you mean?"

"Last night, I came home and my door was open. You know that junior programmer who's replacing me?—he was coming out of my condo. He said he'd come by to drop off some 'sensitive' papers, so he looked under the doormat and found a key."

"Yeah, right." Lex crossed her arms. "Did he really give you the papers?"

"Actually . . ." Venus sighed. "After the meeting today, the CFO asked if I'd gotten the folder that Yardley had Edgar drop off at my place. So apparently Edgar was telling the truth about the papers."

"Did he take anything?" Trish asked.

"I think he went through my desk, and there were scratches on my safe showing where he might have tried to break into it."

All four of them got very quiet. The babbling conversations from other tables in the restaurant swirled in between them, mixed with the clinking of utensils and the calls of waiters to the kitchen.

"Think about this logically," Jenn said. "Why would they try to steal your program, and then make you quit?"

"The Board of Directors met yesterday afternoon. They'd already decided on Edgar as the new Game Lead before he was at my home last night."

"So they want you to quit," Lex said, "but they wanted a shot at getting your software before you go. Because they were probably scared you'd turn in your resignation right when you got the news."

"I would have, but . . ."

"Why in the world would you want to stay at such a creepy place?" Trish started handing out the long plastic chopsticks from the holder at the table.

"Because they're paying me a lot." Venus took her pair and wiped them down with her paper napkin. Her dad always taught her that she couldn't be too careful when the chopsticks were sitting out at the tables like this, but she soon figured out it wasn't just her dad's sense of cleanliness—everyone wiped their chopsticks and spoons when they were taken from the table kiosk.

She saw the waiter swing into view, making a determined beeline toward them. Finally. "Food's coming."

The waiter dumped the plates onto the table, splashing the women with hot grease from each of their entrees before whisking away.

"Hey, we need more tea . . ." Trish raised the empty teapot, but he'd already darted out of earshot.

Jenn scowled. "I don't care how upset you are. Next time, we're going to Union or Golden Dragon. This place is the armpit of Chinese restaurants."

Venus didn't think she'd want to come back here for another few years—this was her grease quota for the decade. But oh, that smelled so good.

"Jenn, you pray." Lex nudged her.

Jenn's husky voice gave a long, heartfelt grace. Venus bowed her head but didn't listen very closely. Something about wisdom for Venus and protection from food poisoning.

"Amen."

Venus savored the salty black bean sauce dripping from the soft rice noodle, the tender strips of beef, the slices of perfectly sautéed green bell pepper. Ahhh. Ambrosia.

"Can't you stay there only until you finish the software, and then bail?" Trish dug into her salt-and-pepper fried pork chop.

"I was thinking about that." She licked a drop of sauce from her chopstick. "Since I'm no longer acting Game Lead, I'll have more time on my hands. I could ignore their blatant message and stay on for six more months."

Jenn slurped her wonton soup. "They won't like that."

"Who cares? They shafted her!" Lex violently speared at her Hong Kong-style noodles, causing crispy deep-fried pieces to fly into Jenn's soup.

Jenn scooped up the noodle bits. "But is it safe to stay there considering that one guy—Edgar?"

"Yeah, is that going to be okay? Is he still going to be after your software?" Trish rubbed her lower back again.

"I moved my computer into a safe deposit box today." Venus sucked up a fat rice noodle.

"Am I the only one who thinks this is nuts?" Lex gave her an incredulous stare. "How can you work with those guys knowing they tried to steal from you?"

"I don't know if it's all of them. It could just be Edgar and Yardley. Yardley knew I was going to be passed over, and in case I quit, he sent Edgar to steal the software, or find notes on it, or something."

"You don't have notes lying around, do you?" Trish's brow wrinkled.

"Of course not. Why do you think I insisted on getting a condo with a fireplace? In sunny California?"

Lex spoke with her mouth full. "For once, I'm glad you're even more paranoid than your dad."

"Are you going to be able to work, considering they passed you over like that?" Jenn bit into a pork dumpling from her soup. "Ugh, too much ginger."

Venus stalled by taking some *dau miu*, slender stems and leaves from an English pea plant sautéed with garlic and oyster sauce.

She should be used to being on the outside—the lone woman looking in—but she had thought she'd finally earned their high opinion. Now, she'd be a company team player, and yet not. How could she not be working toward a common goal with her programmers and the other managers? How could she be a programming team leader while plotting her departure from the company as soon as possible? "I'll do what they want. I'll play the quiet little woman, doing my job, keeping my mouth shut. Finishing that program."

She shoved some pea greens in her mouth. Hmm, not bad. Heavy on the garlic but tasting like usual—similar in flavor to young broccoli. "In the meantime, I need to decide which designers and animators to interview, which angel investors to target."

"For angel investors, you could ask Grandma." Jenn snagged some *dao miu.*

The three of them turned to stare at her.

Jenn froze, a pea leaf sticking out of her mouth. "What?"

"Ask Grandma? Are you nuts?"

Jenn chewed and swallowed. "You're the one who's nuts if you're not going to get her advice and help. She's got connections like Imelda has shoes."

"But … Grandma?" Granted, Grandma was a notch higher than Mom, but she still wasn't high on her favorite persons list. Grandma's nagging about her singleness had gotten worse since they'd all turned thirty—with Venus, there were pointed jabs about her putting her work before her obligation to provide grandchildren to her parents. Grandma always found some way to try to manipulate her to going on a date or meeting some boy. Venus hated being manipulated, least of all by the family matriarch. She wasn't about to do anything she didn't want to do.

"You know, Jenn's right." Trish shrugged. "Grandma would know the angel investors who are more likely to want to back you."

Lex pointed at Venus with her chopsticks. "None of us, except Jenn—"

"Don't point with your chopsticks," Jenn interjected.

Lex put the chopsticks down. "None of us get along with Grandma very well, but she's always willing to help if she can. She thrives on being useful."

Venus frowned. "Sure, she's willing to help. *For a price.*"

Lex and Trish both looked down at their plates.

"Exactly." She couldn't believe Lex and Trish, of all people, would encourage her to go to Grandma for help. Especially after Grandma had tried to bribe Lex with a new apartment in exchange for dates with her friends' sons and nephews, and after Grandma had practically disowned Trish for not marrying her creepy ex-boyfriend, the son of some rich bankers in Japan.

"But think about it." Jenn snagged more pea greens. "Do you really want to waste time with disinterested investors? Grandma can help you be more efficient in going about everything."

Jenn was right, but Venus didn't want to admit it. "I don't like talking to Grandma. I always feel she's judging me and I'm not good enough."

"You do?" Trish's confused look scrunched up her face. "But she's been nicer to you than she is to any of us. I mean, she takes Jenn for granted a lot of the time, and she clashes with Lex, and right now she's not even speaking with me. She at least *smiles* when she talks with you."

Jenn nodded. "She seems ... approving when she talks with you."

"Actually ..." Lex swirled the noodles on her plate. "It's been since you lost weight."

Venus scowled. "Everyone started treating me differently since then." The programmers who had been her "buds" were suddenly hitting on her, the managers and VPs had suddenly been all predatory smiles, the women—whom she'd never really gotten along with anyway—were suddenly catty and vicious.

Originally, she'd been so happy when that stomach virus and her stomach sensitivity in the six weeks afterward had made her lose so much weight so fast, and she'd worked *hard* to lose even more and keep it off. She'd been overlooked and invisible as a fat, brilliant programmer, and she thought that her new body would make her more visible and appreciated for her abilities.

But the slender Venus that emerged hadn't had the new beginning she envisioned—she'd received sexual innuendos instead of respect. Ironic that now she hid herself behind tailored, nearly masculine clothing much like what she wore when she'd been overweight.

Jenn twirled a lock of her long, straight hair. "I think Grandma actually respects you more since you determined to lose weight and you actually did it, which is why she treats you better than any of us."

"I wanted her to respect me *before* I lost weight. I'm still smart, still good at my job. I won all those gaming tournaments in college." Why hadn't she been good enough then?

"The thing is, Grandma has always been beautiful." Trish sighed. "Like your mom, Venus. She tends to notice beauty more than success."

So much like her mom, and yet so different. Grandma was both beautiful and a successful businesswoman, for all her other faults. Mom was only beautiful.

Trish looked up at her. "You have to admit, you did change after you lost weight."

"What do you mean?"

Trish hesitated, but Lex answered for her. "You were always efficient and aggressive, but you were nice occasionally. Now you're just efficient and aggressive."

"I had to be aggressive. No one listened to the fat girl if she didn't speak up." She ignored the part about not being nice. She *was* nice. Occasionally. To her cousins, at least.

"But now you're so much more into your career than you ever were," Trish said.

"Exactly." Lex grinned. "You're not just *driven*, you're *maniacal.*"

"I'm not—"

"I actually think Venus is a lot like Grandma," Jenn said.

"What?" Venus rounded on her. "I am nothing like Grandma."

"Actually—" Lex put up her hands. "No, don't have a cow. Think about it. You're both beautiful, elegant, smart, and pushy."

"I am not pushy."

"You're aggressive," Jenn corrected. "So is Grandma."

Venus stilled. They couldn't be right. They couldn't. Grandma was ruthless and cold and selfish. Okay, Venus admitted she could be ruthless when it came to work, but not with people. Well, not people she cared about. She didn't count Mom or a few of the cattier cousins because they didn't care about her either.

"Think of it this way." Trish leaned closer. "Even if we're all not crazy about Grandma, you can't ignore the fact that she'd be happy to help you. Isn't that worth it? For your business?"

"Yeah, can't you suck it up for an hour and pretend to be nice?" Lex gave a cheeky grin.

Venus glared. Lex just grinned wider.

"I'll think about it." Like for two nanoseconds before throwing the idea in the wastebasket.

Lex exhaled in disgust and sat back in her chair. Trish rolled her eyes.

Jenn wisely kept her head down. "So you're going to stay at your company and work on your own startup at the same time?"

Trish gave her a quizzical glance. "Are you sure you'll have time to do that? You're *always* at work."

"I was acting Game Lead—"

"You were always at work at your last company too, and you were only Programming Lead there."

"I'll ... I'll make time." She looked down at her plate. Had she already eaten all the pea greens? She had to stop or she'd eat too much. She set down her chopstick. But she'd already eaten all that chow fun, why not a little more? No, she already had to run an extra half hour on the treadmill tomorrow. Yes ... no ... yes...

Stop arguing with yourself. She shoved her plate away with unnecessary force and tried to ignore the way her mouth craved more food, like a wild animal in itself.

"Oh!" Trish sat up.

"What? Are you okay?"

"I think so, I ..." Her brows knit and her head tilted to the side.

She suddenly inhaled sharply, and her face paled to the color of Jenn's won ton dumplings. She breathed in short gasps. "Guys, my water broke."

FOUR

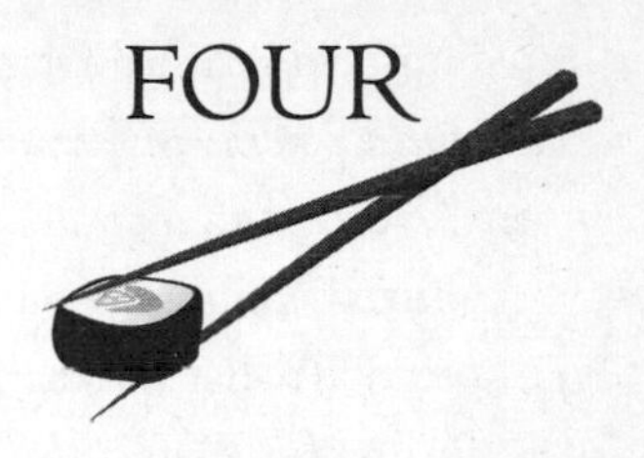

Venus peeled through the gates into her neighborhood and skidded into her parking slot. Even though the nurses had said the baby might not come for another few hours, she didn't like being away from Trish, even just to get clothes for them both.

She reached into the backseat of her convertible and grabbed Trish's bag that she'd picked up—already packed and ready. She stowed it in her trunk and then raced up the stairs to her own condo.

Keys, keys ... Her bag had never seemed too small before, but she couldn't seem to get her hand in deep enough to grab her k—what was that?

A shadow moved away from her door.

Her heart gunned in her chest like her car engine. Were they back to try again? She moved her fingers in her bag and grabbed the pepper spray.

"Hello, darling."

Venus's heart went from 300 horsepower to a hard, slow slamming against her ribs. "Mom. What are you doing here?"

Her mother's slim figure stepped into the circle of light from above the door. She laughed, a tinkling sound that grated down Venus's spine. "You know, I've never visited your home before. You've been here how long?"

"A few years."

She gave a chiding smile. "You never invited me over."

Venus crossed her arms. "I don't invite anyone over." *This is my space, and I don't want anyone in it, least of all you. And you come waltzing up here as if all those years of emotional abuse never existed.*

Unfazed, her mother laughed again. Venus gritted her teeth at the fake sound. "What do you need?" More money? Usually Mom went to Grandma for that.

"I just came by to say hello." She touched Venus's arm, and her numerous rings grazed her skin—warm, but hard metal. She smiled that serene, China-doll smile, her deep plum lipstick perfectly drawn over her full lips. She looked like Grandma, although softer in her beauty. Venus recoiled inside.

"I'm only running in to get clothes, and then I'm leaving again." She still didn't move closer to the door. Once she opened it, Mom would invade her home, and much as she'd like to, she couldn't slam the door in her mother's face.

"Oh." The powdered cheeks sagged a bit as Mom frowned, but she immediately smiled again so her wrinkles wouldn't show. "Well, let's have lunch tomorrow."

"I'm busy."

She pouted, her artfully made-up eyes smoky and soft in the darkness. "You're too busy at work."

"I would think you'd be busy at work too." Venus kept her voice low-pitched under the subtle dig at her mother's penchant for ditching work because her boss was her mother, Venus's grandmother.

Mom's face became a plastic mask with a neutral smile. "I'm not as busy as you are, apparently." Her eyes narrowed. "I saw your father at the bank a few days ago."

"That's what Dad said."

Bitterness glittered from her eyes. "I also heard you picked him up after his accident last night."

The same whining argument as before. Her mother's jealousy over how much time she spent with Dad made her want to scream. "He called me at midnight. Who else could have picked him up?"

"So you'd pick him up at midnight but not have lunch with me?"

"It's different." Why was Mom always so illogical and unreasonable?

Her mother huffed and tapped her pointed leather sole. "So, you won't spend time with me unless I call you at midnight from the side of the road? Great."

"Mom, it's not like I cut out on you in order to spend time with Dad."

"You have before." She crossed her arms and rubbed her silk jacket sleeves. She looked alone and hurt, but Venus knew by now it was just a manipulation tactic.

"What else am I supposed to do at Christmas? I can't be in two places at once."

"You always like being with him more than me."

"I hardly spend time with either of you because of work." However, her mother's accusation was true. Venus spent much more time with Dad, who had loved her even when she'd been fat, had praised her and believed in her. Unlike her silly, fashionable, irresponsible mother, who had harped on her in private and ignored her publicly because she was ashamed of her overweight daughter. She'd acted the part of the caring mother once Venus lost weight, but Venus knew her mom's selfishness by then and wasn't about to be taken in by a suddenly loving demeanor. Their relationship had become more strained, more cold on her side and complaining on Mom's side.

"Probably going out now to have dinner with him." She sniffed.

Venus stared at the stucco ceiling (ugh, there were huge cobwebs up there! She had to clean that right away) and tried not to give way to the long, blood-curdling shriek that was itching to burst out of her throat. "Mom, you are so paranoid!"

"Well, where are you going, then?" She flung her hands out.

Venus hesitated. Trish was still her niece, but Venus really didn't want her mom tagging along to the hospital. It was stressful enough waiting while Trish huffed and puffed in labor (or whatever it was she learned in those classes), but to have to deal with Mom's whining at the same time would make her ready for a straitjacket.

Still, she'd be *livid* if she heard about the baby from someone else, because she knew how close Venus was with Trish.

"Trish is in labor at the hospital." She heard the sound of a missile whistling downward and crashing into its target. *Kaboom!* The sound of her inner peace blowing to smithereens.

Mom gasped, looking so comical it was almost fake. She grabbed Venus's arm, and her rings bit into her skin. "We should go see her!"

"Ow! Leggo!" She yanked her arm away. "I came to get clothes for tomorrow. I'm going to spend the night at the hospital with her."

"Well, I'll wait for you." She stepped away so Venus had a clear shot to her door. She toyed with the fantasy of running inside and locking her mother outside. Coward.

"Why don't you go to the hospital and I'll meet you there?" Hope blossomed in her heart.

Mom's smile was as sweet as Japanese White Rabbit milk candy and completely insincere. "No, I'll drive with you."

Venus stalled as she opened her front door. Hardly anyone had been in her home except her cousins and her dad, all on rare occasions. And in a few days, she'd had a slimeball and her mother inside. She squeezed her eyes shut. Her heart was being torn into with some multi-pronged fork. She pushed open the door and deactivated the alarm.

Mom practically elbowed her aside to see her condo. "Oh ... this is nice."

Venus made quick work of packing her clothes, her vanity kit, and lots of her gossip mags to read in the waiting room. All the while, her mom commented on everything she saw.

"What a nice couch ... although it's a bit low to the ground. And don't you think it would look better with gold stripes along the white?

"What a gigantic television! Is that a flat panel? How much did you spend on that? Do you really need that huge TV just for playing your video games?

"You still play your video games, don't you? Or did you finally give that up? It made you a nice chunk of change while you were in college, and a little bit of fame too — but from the wrong kind of people. Who cares about all those grungy gamers, after all? Why couldn't you have caught the eye of some handsome promoter, instead?

"Do you still read those *People* and *Star* magazines? Really, Venus. I'm ashamed you have such plebian tastes ...

"Is that a Gucci suit? Now, that's handsome. Although it's a bit masculine, don't you think? I'd try it on, but it's probably a bit loose on me.

"What lovely shoes! You like Dolce and Gabbana? I don't care that much for them. They just don't look good on my feet. Do they look good on yours? Well, you have such long feet ..."

"Mom, let's go," Venus barked, holding open the front door, her bag in her other hand.

Mom twittered as she walked out, her heels clicking on the tile floor. "Such a nice color scheme ... although it would look better with a few bright red accents, don't you think? With some black thrown in? And your place is so *small!* How can you live in this teacup —

"Oh, your top is down?" Mom pursed her lips as she stared at Venus's convertible. "I'll drive — "

"I have to drive so I can go to work tomorrow. If you want, you can take your car — "

"No, I'll ride with you. Spend some girl time with my girl." She skipped to the other side and opened the door.

Girl time with my girl? Oh please. The last time Mom had wanted "girl time," she actually had wanted Venus to go shopping with her at Neiman Marcus so Venus could pay for an insanely expensive pair of shoes for her.

The sooner Venus got to the hospital, the sooner she could foist Mom off on one of the other aunties who might be there. Jenn had called her mom, so maybe Aunty Yuki was there. And Trish's parents had said they'd pick up Grandma before heading to the hospital. Venus would even welcome stern Grandma over her critical, talkative mother. Well, she might not be so elegant after a ride with the top down. Maybe she could take the freeway ...

She turned the key. The engine roared to life ... then sputtered and choked as it died. *Nononono.*

"What's wrong?"

"I don't know." She turned it again. Nothing. She kept turning, and nothing kept right on happening. She glanced at her gas gauge.

"I'm out of gas." She'd had an eighth of a tank when she drove into the Chinese restaurant parking lot, and she'd made a mental note to fill up before she got home. But with Trish's labor, going to Trish's house to pick up her things, then heading here, she'd completely forgotten about it.

Noooo. Not now. Couldn't her car have run on fumes for just a little while longer?

"Just call triple A. They'll bring you some."

"I guess so." Waiting for triple A? With her mother? She moaned.

"Oh, don't be so glum, darling." Mom rubbed her arm. "Think of it this way—more time with me!"

Venus discovered she was no match for Aunty Marian, Trish's mother. Trish still hadn't delivered, and Aunty Marian sent everyone home from the hospital despite protests they could all camp out in the waiting room.

Aunty Marian glared at all of them. "I'd like you all to be *awake* when the baby finally does come."

Even though Venus had gotten home at two a.m., she still woke up at five.

Staring at the ceiling made her aware of the cobwebs wafting in the corners. Well, if she couldn't sleep, no use staying in bed doing nothing.

Same-o, same-o: Throw on her exercise clothes, thirty minutes on the treadmill. Shower. Turn on the coffeepot. Dress.

Bible reading. Sitting at her one-person breakfast table, same as always, with a cup of organic coffee with organic soymilk. Following the Bible in a Year reading plan.

She stared at the worn cover. Had her quiet times become rote, like the rest of her routine? Were her quiet times like her one-person table—just her, no God? That same sense of stagnation now settled in her gut, as if there really was a weedy pond lying there. Did her faith stink to God too?

But Venus didn't know how to revive it. She read the Bible and prayed, every day, at the same time. She didn't think God would want her to *stop* reading or praying. She did what the Word told her to do—how could it not be enough?

She was tired of being told she was never enough.

She read the assigned passages, but the words reminded her of winter leaves raining down. Touching her, sliding off, gathering at her feet.

When finished, she slammed the book closed with more force than necessary, and it slid into her coffee cup. A brown waterfall poured onto her pristine linoleum.

Aaack! It had splattered on the wall, on the underside of the table, the legs of her chair . . .

As she grabbed the roll of paper towels from the kitchen counter, her cell phone rang. The wall clock said six-thirty. Who in the world would call her at this hour? Oh, Trish must be having the baby.

She dropped a few sheets to blot up the coffee, then raced to her purse, sitting on the end table in the living room.

Drake Yu.

She gasped—or tried to, but her chest had become a steel corset. Her heart thudded like a blacksmith's hammer. Why would Drake call her after . . . what, five years? Six?

Well, it explained who'd dare to call so early. Drake knew her schedule better than most of the CEOs she'd worked for. She flipped the phone open. "Hi, Drake."

"Venus."

That deep voice, slightly husky, slurring his words just a little, skipping over vowels. Just the sound made her remember his figure at the end of the meeting room table, long fingers fiddling with his fountain pen, the funny twitchy way he'd adjust his tie—usually blue, his favorite color—just before he intended to close down some discussion.

"Are you finally going to start your own company?"

"What?" Darn it, she hadn't been able to keep that from exploding out of her mouth. She cleared her throat. "What are you talking about?" How did he know? She ignored the "finally" that was almost a compliment, considering who it was coming from.

"You were thinking about it when you worked for me."

"Why, are you interviewing for CEO?" *Not that I'd ever hire you.*

"I figured you'd be Chief Executive Officer yourself."

Had she revealed part of her hand? Well, who cared if she did. "No, I don't have the personality for a CEO. I need to hire one who will help get me funding. I intend to focus on operations."

"I heard that Oomvid passed you over for Game Lead."

Crunch! Venus's molars collided, and pain stabbed into her jaw like needles. She unclamped her teeth slowly. "Did they announce it this morning?"

"On the Web."

A pause while she massaged her jaw and salvaged her pride. "Why are you calling, Drake?" She hated having to ask him, but she wanted to get back to her routine. She still had her prayers to do, and she had lots to pray about today.

"I've come out of retirement temporarily."

So soon? He'd retired last November. Not that she was keeping up with him, but she'd happened to read about it somewhere.

He paused a long moment, as if he expected her to say something. She didn't respond, instead grabbing more paper towels.

"My younger sister has started her own company, a Web-based virtual community. Bananaville is like Secondlife, but family-friendly."

Secondlife had exploded in recent years. The virtual world was essentially a gigantic multi-person game where people's virtual selves interacted with other virtual people. There were "islands" for interaction and entertainment, and residents could create their own islands, plus buy, sell, and trade with other residents.

She was intrigued in spite of herself. A Secondlife exclusively for children and parents would be interesting, provided they could get the right corporate sponsors to host their own "islands" within the game. Venus mopped up the majority of the coffee, then crouched down to swipe at the underside of the table and the wall.

"Are you okay?"

"What?"

"You're breathing ... unusually hard."

Venus gave a last grunt as she wiped the chair legs. "If you must know, I'm cleaning my kitchen while I wait for you to get to the point."

A soft exhale. "Same old Venus."

She tossed the towels in her trash can. "You have thirty seconds to—"

"I want to hire you for my sister's company."

"What part about 'starting my own company' did you not get?" She pulled out the bottle of Lysol and a bucket, then went to the coat closet to get the mop.

"I'm guessing you won't be at Oomvid much longer, and I only want to hire you for a few months."

"Doing what?" She splashed some Lysol into the mop bucket.

"Chief Technology Officer."

She froze. The Lysol bottle slipped. She grabbed for it and dropped the cell phone with a clatter.

"Venus?"

She snatched the phone up. "I'm here." She capped the bottle. "I've never been CTO. You know that."

"I've also seen you at work and know you'd be a good one."

"You're saying"—she turned on the faucet to fill the bucket halfway—"you'd hire me, without proper credentials, based on how I worked for you five years ago?" She wet the mop.

"I talked with some of your other employers."

"Are you stalking me?" She started mopping one-handed, awkwardly jamming the mop head into her chair leg.

"You have a reputation for being difficult to work with, Venus."

Whoa! Now, that was blunt. She stopped mopping, feeling her nails press into the wooden handle. "I am n—" She swallowed. "I am demanding of my team, and I get the job done on time. Every time."

"It will be hard to find someone else to work for, especially if you're going to set off on your own in a few months."

No kid gloves for Drake. She shouldn't be surprised—he'd always been that way with her, and she with him. "That's just your opinion." Except a nauseating gurgle in her stomach told her she knew it was true.

"How much are you hoping to earn? How long are you willing to work to earn it?"

She sniffed and didn't answer him. She'd been acting Game Lead at Oomvid—she could demand a high salary at her next position. Provided people *wanted to work with her.*

He named a figure that made her cough. Drake ignored her gurgling. "I'll pay you that for twelve months of your time, Venus."

"You're trusting me not to drive your company into the ground?"

"I know you wouldn't. It's not your nature."

Drat, the man knew her too well.

"I can help you with the logistics of starting your own company."

She snorted.

He sighed. "Venus, don't be stupid."

"I like being pig-headed." Her tone was sweeter than her organic Hawaiian white honey.

"I've started four successful companies, and I helped my sister start this one. I might actually know something about it."

Sarcasm. That was new. "And you'd help me?" Sure, he'd help her. He'd help her right into a minefield. "Why?"

"Because I want you to work for me."

She heard in his voice that resonance that was almost a growl, that titanium-hard determination to get what he wanted. And he usually got what he wanted.

Not this time. Last time had been enough. She wasn't about to confess he'd scarred her for life, but she didn't care if it was a choice between Drake and McDonalds—she'd choose french fries. "I don't want to work for you again, Drake."

"I know you don't."

A Zippo lighter sprang to life in her chest, searing her breastbone. "So why are you pushing this?"

"Because I also know you're wrong."

"I'm not wrong very often." *Not when it comes to you.*

"You will be a brilliant CTO, and you and I will work together very well."

That Zippo lighter was warming her core, but not searing her. No, she wouldn't be turned by his compliments, because he'd paired it with a statement she completely disagreed with. "This conversation is ended, Drake." She snapped her phone shut.

She stared at it, lying in her open palm. Then she noticed it was shaking. She set the phone down on the counter.

She'd never work for him again. It would take an act of God.

Venus kicked her office door shut and plopped into her chair. Slipping off her heinous shoes—new, absolutely gorgeous, and already feeling like a spike thrust into her heel, even though it was only noon—she propped her feet up on her desk and dialed Lex. "Hey. How's she doing?"

"Same as the last time you called. She's still not dilated enough."

"But it's been over eighteen hours."

"Tell me about it." Lex sighed.

"Hey, are you in trouble for taking off work today?"

"Naw. SPZ lets me take personal days at a moment's notice, and my boss knows about Trish and the baby."

Lex's company, SPZ, had such a laid-back atmosphere compared to most of the companies Venus had worked at. Oomvid took the cake. Edgar had thrown a fit when she'd asked for time off this morning so she could go to the hospital.

Venus sighed as she squelched a burp from the green monster in her gut. She may have to put up with more inflexible policies, but she was also paid a lot more than Lex. "Who's still there at the hospital?"

"Trish's parents are still around. I think they went for a walk together—they've been almost like newlyweds the past few months, have you noticed? Anyway, Grandma's somewhere harassing the nurses. Oh, and your mom's still here too."

"My mom?" Venus drew her feet down and sat up.

"Yeah ... she's been pretty nice, talking to me."

"I never said she couldn't be charming when she wanted to." She just never used it on her daughter unless she wanted something.

"Well, she's actually been encouraging. She told me your birth was pretty long too, and that I shouldn't worry about Trish; the doctors and technology are better these days than when she was pregnant, yadda yadda yadda."

A brisk knock at the door, and her admin poked her head in. "Venus, Jaye's programmers have a problem. They need you now."

"Lex, I'll have to call you back." She headed up a couple floors to where the programmers' cubicles crowded the office floor like *Tetris*, and just as colorful. Computer science guys tended to have the weirdest, funnest, wildest games for their desks. No simple basketball hoops over the trash cans for these guys. They had Space Invaders jaws over their trash, which chewed up any incoming bogeys that the sensors detected.

"Hey, Venus." She caught a bright pink and green Nerfball in the shape of a pair of antlers that was thrown at her. It had "Down with Ms. PacMan!" written on it.

She threw it back to her senior graphics designer. "You'll get in trouble, brandishing that in here." The gamers still slavishly devoted to old-school vintage games would lynch him. Or at least spill soda on his keyboard.

"Bring it on." He growled and struck an Incredible Hulk pose.

She hurried to the back of the large room, past more cubicles. Men stared at her. They usually did, *now*. They hadn't even seen her before the weight loss, despite the fact there had been more of her to see.

A part of her slumped in the cynical observation that she had to work her tail off to earn respect whether she was fat or skinny, only to find she didn't get it either way.

She entered a cluster of cubicles inhabited by her programmers. "What's up, guys?"

"Check it out." Jaye—a senior programmer, one of her oldest friends, and her secret business partner—pointed to another programmer's screen. They all crammed into the cubicle to look.

While staring at the screen, Jaye jostled her elbow and whispered, "Venus."

She turned her head slightly. "What?"

"Yardley came to talk to me today."

Cue the creepy, urgent music from *Saw*. "About?"

Jaye pressed his lips together for a second. His breath whistled through his large Roman nose. "Said we might have a new development tool to work with. Something that will integrate all areas of game development, be compatible with all programs."

Venus stared ahead but didn't see the monitor anymore. "Did he say where that tool was coming from?"

"No. Evasive about it, but seemed pretty certain we'd have it in a few weeks. Clear he didn't know I'm working on it with you." Jaye cleared his throat. "You wouldn't want to give Yardley our—?"

"Are you high? Of course not. We're partners in this." They had been the Dynamic Duo ever since they thought up the Spiderweb years ago, when they'd been working together at a startup company.

"Thought so." He turned to glance down the aisles between the cubicles. "Wanted to give you a heads-up. Don't like where this is headed."

"I'll try to fix it."

"Might not be able to fix this one, Venus."

"So, what do you think?" One of the junior programmers turned and stared at Venus through his green Lennon glasses, waiting for an answer.

She'd completely missed the problem they'd been showing her on the screen.

"Venus!"

She was almost glad for the interruption, until she turned to see Edgar hustling down the aisle between cubicles straight for her. Lovely.

"Hi, Venus." His round face pulled into a childlike smile. She almost couldn't tell how false it was. "Where are the weekly update reports?"

"I gave you the ones I drew up from last week."

"Where are this week's?"

"That's your job now, Edgar." She pitched her voice like Vietnamese iced coffee—sweet and bitter at the same time.

His smile stayed in place, but his hand came up to finger his thick, curly brown hair. "I, ah, just sent you an email."

"About?" She rested her weight on one hip, keeping her face neutral.

"Let's go to your office so I can show you. It's all in the memo."

"I'm taking care of something here. I'll join you in a minute." She turned back to the gaggle of programmers.

"I need you now, Venus."

His tone had been light, but the words made her shoulders slam out and back into steel rods. She felt a growling deep in her gut, a tiger that wanted to come roaring out of her mouth. He had *not* just reprimanded her in front of her programmers. She turned to him.

Her gaze should have blasted him colder than arctic winds from a frozen tundra. He kept smiling, although his hazel eyes seemed to glow like coals.

They stared each other down, him with steam and fire, her with chilly disdain. Her feet were killing her, but at least her stilettos raised her five-nine stature above Edgar's average height.

"I could reassign one of your programmers." His smile still had that gentle, reasonable curve that belied the fireballs coming from his eyes.

She heard soft intakes of breath from the programmers behind her, unwilling witnesses to the showdown. This particular group was a fantastic team, one of the best she'd ever worked with. Any reassignment would be a demotion for the unlucky guy.

She had frozen into an ice statue, vibrating with the resonance of her anger. The resonance grew louder, and she started to visibly shake. If she didn't do something, she'd shatter into a million pieces. "You'd do that, would you?"

"I would." That soft, childlike smile. She wanted to slap it off his face.

"I'll go with you." Her voice had gone low and dark. She leaned in close enough for his expensive cologne to clog her lungs, for his pupils to dilate as she blocked out the light from the windows that surrounded the entire floor. "But if you order me or threaten my programmers again, I'm going to break your nose."

His smile didn't change. He wasn't afraid because he didn't believe her. He only saw a woman with too much pride and arrogance for his taste.

His loss.

She turned and led the way down the aisle. He was probably staring at her rear end, but she didn't want him in front of her—didn't want to watch his confident swagger. She might be tempted to connect her pointed toe into his behind.

Back at her office, she sat at her desk to check her email. He followed and closed the door, his hands in his pockets, a picture of leisure.

He'd sent it right after she'd left her office. *Re: Responsibilities. Venus, this is Edgar.*

Well, duh.

I'm very excited to have you on board and know that with your help, we can take the company to the next milestone ... Yeah, yeah. She skimmed the feel-good fluff.

Detail of your responsibilities: Weekly update reports . . . scheduling programming projects . . . liaison between programming managers and VPs . . .

Everything she had been doing as acting Game Lead. She looked up at him.

"What do you think?"

"I think you're on crack."

His smile widened, but his eyes grew harder. He suddenly looked ages older than his twenty-odd years.

"I'm doing the exact same things I did as acting Game Lead, in addition to my normal duties as Programming Lead."

He spread out his hand in a conciliatory gesture. "Well, you do everything so well— "

He was an idiot if he thought she'd buy that line. "In case it didn't occur to you, I am no longer acting Game Lead. You are. Ergo, these duties should fall on you."

Edgar shoved his hands back in his pockets and turned to stare at something on the ceiling, releasing a long sigh. "There's always a transition phase— "

She was going to smack him if he kept using that voice, as if talking to a six-year-old. "I gave you my latest reports and schedules. You have everything you need to take over smoothly." *Just try to talk your way out of this one, slimeball.*

He turned his focus back to her with that horrible, simple smile. "Venus, Venus." His condescension shuddered down her back like the Banshee Demon's screech in level three. She jerked in her chair as he continued. "As Game Lead, I have many duties assigned to me, and it's my job to delegate."

"These particular duties belonged to both me and the former Game Lead, and now to you." *What makes you so much more special than either of us?*

"Yardley has given me *other* things more pressing."

Oh, excuse me. His smugness, exuding from him in waves, made her cough. "Since your new responsibilities are so important to your reputation, I'm sure you want to make sure these things are all done well, and you'd want to take them on yourself to ensure that." Edgar was all about how he looked to others. She was sure to appeal to his vanity.

"You're so encouraging, Venus." His smile actually showed teeth, now, but the way his mouth opened, they looked like fangs. "But that's why I'm delegating those duties to you. I know how capable you are. I can trust you to do the job and do it well."

"Not if I have to take up the reins as Programming Lead again. I'm sure you remember all the things you had to do as one of my *junior programmers*, don't you, Edgar?" She couldn't stop the hardness of her voice as she spoke.

The moron chuckled. "You're more than capable, Venus."

That was it. Her ire erupted like Diet Coke and Mentos. "Well then, why aren't you *capable* enough to handle the duties I did as acting Game Lead, now that you *are* Game Lead?"

His amiable mask cracked. He gurgled in his throat. "I have *other* duties—" His smile was strained now, and it looked like he was opening and closing his fists in his pants pockets.

"Like what? Golfing, online poker, surfing the Web?"

"It's from Yardley, and you don't have clearance to know." His anger flashed out at her like a poisoned dart.

"I have a right to know since I'm taking over all the responsibilities you're too *incompetent* to do yourself."

He sputtered a few moments, his breathing coming hard and heavy. "Yardley is going to hear about this." Saliva showered through his clenched teeth. He turned and whipped open her office door.

She shot to her feet and toward the door. "Feel free." She slammed the door behind him and almost caught his suit jacket.

She started pacing the small floor space. She was breathing too fast; she needed to calm down. She tried staring out her one small window into the company parking lot, but she saw Edgar's new Lexus parked across two stalls in the shade of the only tree in the entire lot, and it made her want to go down and key it.

She couldn't work for him. She'd commit homicide first. And she'd like it.

But she wasn't ready to start her own company.

Like she'd even have the time to work on the Spiderweb with all the extra junk she'd have to do for Edgar.

She was drawn to the window and Edgar's double-parked sedan like someone who couldn't stop picking at a scab.

Did she and Jaye have the guts to start their own company, to strike out on their own? She'd always been able to count on others in her team to support her, to help her take the brunt of any mishaps. She always took responsibility for her team members—that was her job—but she'd never been in a position where everything rested solely on her shoulders. As a cofounder of her own company, she'd fall on her own. And to rise, she and Jaye would need a good team—how could they find the right people? They didn't have the contacts. How could they keep from making any mistakes in judgment?

They needed someone with more experience and with contacts. Someone like Grandma.

She couldn't believe she was considering it.

Grandma was such a cool customer. Venus couldn't quite make her out. She didn't like when Grandma pushed her—Venus delighted in defying her, actually—but other than that, she didn't really know her. She supposed Grandma didn't really know Venus either.

Going to Grandma for help was playing with fire. Venus didn't like taking the risk of whatever Grandma would demand in exchange. She didn't like being bullied. But did she have a choice? Staying here while she worked on her own project wasn't going to fly. They intended to work her like a dog or force her to quit.

Her back snapped like a whipping ruler. She didn't like being manipulated. She determined the course of her own life. She made her own decisions.

Problem was, they had the upper hand.

Is this what they wanted? To lose her? Weren't they shooting themselves in the foot? She'd improved productivity when she'd stepped into acting Game Lead. Did they really think she'd continue all her duties without the title?

She'd face Yardley. He'd always struck her as reasonable and competent—until yesterday's decision, at least. She'd lay out her duties, tell him what Edgar told her. Ask him if he really expected her to do this. Facing him that way was more aggressive than even she liked to get, but she couldn't cower in the corner while they screwed with her life like this.

And if he didn't give her the answer she wanted to hear? Was she willing to quit?

She took a deep breath, feeling her lungs stretch and fill, tightening against her ribcage, pushing against her diaphragm.

Yes. She was willing to quit.

FIVE

Yardley's admin looked up at Venus over the large flat-screen computer monitor on her desk, her kohled and turquoised eyelids blinking slowly. Insolently. "I'm sorry, Venus, Yardley's down in meeting room B with some investors."

Okay, not the best time to walk into a meeting. "How about afterward?"

"He's scheduled to meet with Edgar at four, right after the meeting."

The admin had given her the runaround yesterday, but Venus wasn't in the mood to play that game today. She strode around Tiffanie's desk and peered at the schedule on the screen.

"What are you doing?" Tiffanie tried to blank the screen, but not before Venus caught sight of an eBay auction she was watching.

Venus stared hard at her. "You're the reason Yardley sent that memo about not doing eBay during business hours. I thought it was strange . . ."

"I don't . . . this is the first time." But Tiffanie's eyes blinked so rapidly, one of her fake eyelashes came loose at the corner.

Venus crossed her arms and looked down at her with as stern an expression as she could muster. "Schedule me for ten minutes before Edgar. He can wait."

Tiffanie sullenly grabbed her mouse and made the appointment.

"No, don't send it to his PDA right now." The last thing she needed was for Yardley to be forewarned he was about to be attacked. "Send it right at four, when my appointment is scheduled."

She turned to wait in one of the chairs situated around Yardley's office, then checked herself. She'd walked through Human Resources and past a few VPs' offices to get here. They might warn Yardley she was waiting for him here.

She'd waylay him as he got out of that meeting.

She marched out the way she came and headed downstairs to meeting room B. She turned the corner and—wait a minute, the meeting room door was open. She peered inside.

Empty.

What? What was the time? Three forty-five. They'd ended early. That meant Yardley would be walking the investors out the front door. She hustled toward the lobby.

No one. She turned to the receptionist. "Did you see Yardley?"

"He went upstairs."

"Back to his office?"

"No, he was talking with one of the VPs and they mentioned stopping off at the third floor."

She hustled up the steps. Halfway, she took off her killer heels and ran the rest of the way, grimacing as she slipped them back on at the third floor landing. She burst into the hallway and walked at a fast clip around the offices. Edgar's office, some empty ones, the copy room, the lunch area, her office ... No Yardley.

One of the interns was copying something at the copier. "Did you see Yardley?"

"He got a call just as he stepped off the elevator. I think he headed toward his office."

Back into the stairwell, up another flight of stairs. Her steps dragged as she got onto the landing. Too much walking in new shoes. She'd treat herself to a soak in her foot massage spa tonight ... oh wait, Trish was still in the hospital. She glanced at her cell phone. No text message from Lex. Still in labor? What was she carrying, twins the size of melons or something?

She ran back down the hallway toward Yardley's office. His admin caught sight of her and called out, "He was here, but he just went back downstairs."

This was not happening.

Her cell phone rang. She considered ignoring it—talking to Yardley was more important. She hustled back toward the elevator (no stairs for her this time), but the incessant ringing finally made her reach into her jacket pocket and pull it out.

Yardley.

"Hello?" Why would he be calling her? Not that she was complaining.

"Venus, where are you? I've been looking for you. We need to talk."

She stood there, in front of the elevator doors, wondering if she wanted to cry, scream, or faint.

"Venus?"

"I'll meet you in my office."

"Good, I'm headed there now."

She strolled into her office hopefully looking composed and unruffled and not as if she'd just run up and down the stairs. She sat at her desk and discreetly slipped off her shoes. "I made an appointment with you at four, but this is good timing."

Yardley sat in one of the leather chairs opposite her and smiled that blinding, I'm-a-Harvard-grad-and-I-want-you-to-know-it smile. "I wanted to talk with you yesterday, but I was too booked."

He could have had Tiffanie email her to set up a meeting today, but she didn't mention that glaring fact. "What did you want to talk about?"

"You mentioned you made an appointment—what did you need?" He smoothed his Italian silk tie—burgundy, today.

"Edgar mentioned he had extra responsibilities from you that didn't allow him to do the normal functions of his new position." There, that was somewhat tactful.

"He does have some new responsibilities, yes."

"Then you're aware he's forcing me to continue doing everything I did as acting Game Lead, in addition to my old duties as Lead Programmer?" She pinned him with a hard look.

He shifted in his seat. "I was aware some of his duties were necessarily delegated, yes."

"So you're expecting me to do the job of two positions without an increase in pay, and without a promotion." She crossed her arms and sat back in her chair, although her heart was pounding in her ears by now. No need to let him know that being so confrontational made her armpits sweat and her legs quiver. *Never let them see you as anything but strong.*

Yardley didn't look away from her, exactly, but he didn't make direct eye contact with her. More like eye contact with the file drawers directly behind her desk. "We chose Edgar because he's very good at what he does—"

"I have yet to see him do anything. I seem to be expected to do his job for him."

He continued nodding and smiling at her file drawers. "Edgar's destined for great things, just like his father—"

"His father?" She raised her eyebrows.

"Ah ... we're old college buddies." Yardley scratched his thinning yellow hair.

Venus stared him down. "It's a bit dangerous to foster nepotism in the company."

"Oh, it's not nepotism. We're not related."

Venus couldn't understand why he was nodding his head. But now she could understand why they'd promoted Edgar. "Regardless of why you gave Edgar Game Lead, is this what you're asking me to do? I don't intend to work for peanuts, Yardley." Whoa, that was strong, even for her. She crossed her legs tight to still her trembling and hoped Yardley couldn't see.

"That's partly why I wanted to talk to you today, Venus."

This better be good. "What about?"

"Ah ... I heard ... It came to me ..."

Telling her CTO to *spit it out* probably wouldn't go over well.

"I found out ... you're working on a software program."

The temperature in the office dropped ten degrees. "Where did you hear that from?" She laughed, but it came out sounding brittle even to her ears.

"Edgar talked to one of your old programmers from your last company, what was his name?"

Dan.

"Ben? No ... Tom?" He leaned forward and rested his elbows on his knees. Venus didn't trust the light in his eyes. "Anyway, he mentioned he'd seen you working on a certain software that would revolutionize game development. A development tool that was compatible with design software, animation software, motion capture data, programming software."

"You can check my computer." She swiveled her laptop around. "There's nothing on it like that."

He opened his mouth, then closed it again. Venus wondered if he had been about to mention her computer setup on her desk at home—wires and cables, but sans laptop—which he wasn't supposed to know about.

"Here's what I'm offering, Venus." He touched his hand to her desk. She wanted to reach for her bottle of Lysol and spray his hairy fingers. "That program could help us a lot. You know that. It would take us to our next milestone months ahead of schedule, and the investors would be fighting for the privilege to throw money at us."

As acting Game Lead, she had taken them to their previous milestone ahead of schedule *without* that program, but Yardley had conveniently forgotten that.

"Venus." He made eye contact with her again, his baby blues reaching out to her with sincerity and a touch of arrogance. "If you sell us that program, I'll make you our new VP of Programming."

He had asked Edgar to steal it.

Her CTO had asked a junior programmer to break into her home and steal her software.

This was not happening.

What also wasn't happening was her cousin's baby.

Lex flung herself into the plastic waiting chair next to Venus. "They gave her another epidural."

Venus put down her magazine. "Another one? Why? Didn't the first one work?"

"They gave it to her too early. It's already worn off."

"She's going to be okay, right?" Venus could barely voice the question. An emptiness echoed in her head, behind her eyes. Trish wasn't in danger, was she? Sweet, fun Trish?

"I think so." Lex's voice was soft.

They sat in silence. The murmur of the waiting room washed over them. Venus forgot to breathe through her mouth and caught a whiff of hospital smell—antiseptics mingled with sweaty children's bodies from a few other families waiting for their own mothers. She wondered if in the future she ought to carry a bottle of Febreze or Lysol in her car.

Neither Venus nor Lex were huggy types, but she reached for Lex's hand, squeezing it. Lex squeezed back so tightly, Venus's bones creaked.

Lex suddenly let go. "Aiden." She leaped up and darted toward her boyfriend, who'd just entered the waiting room.

Venus liked Aiden. Quiet and controlled, he complemented Lex's craziness. He was a bit too sensitive a person for Venus—she tended toward causticness, and sometimes surprised him with the things she said—but he always treated her with respect. He saw Venus, the person.

The two of them stood talking, Lex slim and athletic (Venus would *kill* for hip bones like hers), Aiden lean and fluid in his motions. The volleyball player and the runner. Made for each other.

No one was made for her. Because even if the perfect man found her, she wasn't sure she'd be able to trust him. In the past, she'd been one of the guys—aggressive by necessity of her gender, but valued (she thought) for her abilities. Now she was never sure what men wanted from her—it seemed like they only saw her as a sex object. She hoped there were some who didn't, but she couldn't tell. All of it made her too cynical to ever be in a relationship.

And after seeing Trish's torturous labor, she wasn't really sure she wanted to do the whole "get married and have babies" thing. Although, granted, Trish had skipped the "get married" part.

She admired Trish. Bubbly, ditzy, determined Trish, pregnant with her ex-boyfriend's baby, yet plowing forth as a single mother. She'd decided on this before the engagement, before she and Spenser even started dating.

She had more guts than Venus had ever had.

Trish had been in too much pain—she hadn't wanted anyone in the room with her except Jenn and Spenser. So Venus sat out here, no help to Trish's parents, not willing to sit next to Grandma to be quizzed or nagged, and not wanting to sit next to her mother, who still remained with them in the waiting room.

She tossed aside her gossip mag and crossed her arms. She should pray. It was so hard, especially after a long, stressful day, to just stop her mind from thinking and be able to focus on anything that didn't involve graphics and game controllers. She knew God was there, but it seemed jarring to drop everything, to *stop* and talk to Him.

Dear God. She cleared her throat. Refolded her hands. Shifted in the seat. *Dear God.*

You already said that.

Dear—um ... Please watch over Trish. Please help the baby come soon. Without too much pain. Or problems. Please don't let Trish ... She didn't want to say the word, as if saying it would make it come true. *Please keep her safe and, uh ... alive. And the baby too. Amen.*

Her prayers were horrible, but even more so in times of need, like now. She figured God didn't mind, since He listened to her prayers every morning.

Wasn't prayer supposed to make her feel better? She only felt more agitation in her body. It had suddenly, fully dawned on her that Trish's life was in danger. Her wonderful, fun-loving cousin Trish. They didn't always get along, sure, but she wouldn't trade their friendship for anything.

Her cousins were all she had.

Her chest tightened, making it hard to breathe. Trish would be okay, right? Venus had to be making something big out of nothing. So why did her relatives look so somber? She pressed her hand to her sternum, feeling her heart beating against the bone.

She couldn't even pray for Trish properly. Since when had praying become so hard? Hadn't she had an easier time of it when she first became a Christian in college?

She'd done a lot of things differently then. Maybe that was it. She'd gone to weekly Bible studies in addition to church, studying the Bible and soaking in all that she could. She'd attended college group, worshiped with complete abandon, felt at ease with both the guys and girls ... because she'd been fat. She had recognized it, even back then.

The guys had thought of her as one of them—androgynous. The girls had been friendly with that hint of pity, that relaxation in their smiles because she wasn't more competition for the cuter guys in the group.

She still read her Bible every day, she still prayed (badly) every day, still attended church every week. But it didn't have that same enthusiasm, that same spark.

Since when had her faith turned into a smelly, stagnating pond?

Lord ... maybe through all these troubles at work you're trying to tell me something. But I'm not sure what.

In the meantime ... There's just so much going on at once right now. Please take care of Trish. I'll bother you later with all my other stuff.

She was sure that made God just giddy with anticipation.

She pressed her forehead into her hand.

Someone sat beside her. She caught a scent of . . . Mom's perfume. Expensive and elegant.

Her eyes snapped open. She raised her head, already feeling her shoulders knot like sailor's rope.

Mom grabbed her hand, lying loosely in her lap, before Venus could snatch it away. "It's okay, darling."

"I'm fine, Mom." She sat straighter in the uncomfortable plastic chair.

"I saw her earlier. She's fine, you know."

Venus didn't answer, but her mother's voice had such a strange confidence. It eased the pain in her chest a little, despite the fact she didn't want it to. She didn't want her mother's comfort.

"She's just like how it was when I had you. First babies typically take longest."

"It's over twenty-four hours, Mom. How can that be normal?"

"You took thirty-six."

Did she know that already? She must have. Mom must have told her at some point in her life, right? Why couldn't she remember that? "You were in labor for thirty-six hours?"

"It started around midnight, so I was awake for about two days straight." Despite the horror of her words, Mom's face seemed serene. Pleasantly reminiscing, even.

"Did you even have strength to push?"

She laughed, and this time it wasn't that brassy tinkle she usually had. "By that time, I was begging you to come out."

They lapsed into a silence more comfortable than any she'd had with her mother in a long time.

"Anyway." Mom patted her hand, then released it and stood up. "I just wanted to tell you that what Trish is going through is fine. You looked worried."

"Yeah . . . th-thanks, Mom." Her mouth almost couldn't form the words, she'd rarely said them.

Mom moved back to sit with Trish's parents. She chatted with them with such ease—sweet smiles, nonstop mouth, animated hands.

And the worry lines on Aunty Marian's face disappeared, and Uncle Arvin flashed one of his winning smiles at his younger sister.

How strange to see Mom useful, rather than whiney, flighty, and irresponsible. No, that was mean. Her mom was always like that—charming, putting people at ease with effortless energy.

Venus didn't have any of that charm. But she had lots of organizational skills, and a keen mind for business. Rather like...

She saw Grandma sitting on a seat, as elegantly dressed as her daughter, flawless makeup even after hours in this waiting room. Her still-slender figure relaxed as best she could against the chair, cool and collected.

Ruthless, nagging, manipulative. Always getting her way. Ruling her family like a queen over a small country. Running Grandpa's bank as smoothly as if she'd founded it herself.

No, Venus wasn't like Grandma.

And yet, Venus had to admit there were times when she envied her. Grandma's constant poise and command, her sharp mind, her focused energy.

Grandma wouldn't have gaped at Yardley after his astounding suggestion this afternoon. She'd have given him a decided answer in a heartbeat, and it would have been whatever was best for her career.

Whatever answer that was. Venus didn't know.

Yardley had told her to think about it, then sauntered out of the office as if he already knew she'd take his offer. Arrogant twit. She wouldn't be bullied *or* bribed.

Every cell in her body rebelled at giving Yardley the Spiderweb. Look at what he'd already done—since he couldn't steal it, he'd tried to buy it from her. And she couldn't forget the tiny fact he gave her the boot, too, *after* trying to steal it from her. No way could she stay there and work under him, no matter how much he offered for the Spiderweb.

But... a VP.

How much power would she really have? They already treated her like a second-class citizen because of her gender, or her looks, or both. And they could fire her at any time, in which case it would all be for nothing.

Her own company was the only way to go. She needed to talk to Grandma.

Right now, before she changed her mind.

Okay, one step at a time. And remember to breathe. Don't want to faint before you even get to her. Avoid the toy truck and the Highlights *magazines on the floor. Wouldn't be good to fall flat on your face and knock yourself out.*

"Grandma?"

She barely heard herself, but apparently Grandma heard her. Red lips parted in a wide smile. "Sit, Venus." *Come into my lair, my pretty . . .*

Venus gave herself a mental slap. *Focus.* "I had a question—"

Spenser burst into the waiting room. His hair looked like he had blow-dried it upside down, pink splotched his pale face, and he still wore his surgery room smock. He was also grinning brighter than a pulsar.

"It's a girl!"

SIX

I am so tired of people saying I got off easy!" Trish, sleep-deprived and recently delivered mother, had the wild eyes and hair of one of the three Furies, and looked like she would bite someone's head off if they came within three feet.

Venus didn't blame her. Twenty-eight hours of labor wasn't exactly a cakewalk, even if it wasn't close to the horror stories everyone was telling her about.

"Everyone" had expanded to Spenser's mom, who arrived with his son Matthew, and Jenn's mother. The crowd in Trish's hospital room made Venus ease out into the hallway, but some nurses rushing past compelled her back into the room, squeezed close to the doorway. She forced herself to breathe deeply, to not hyperventilate. She was very happy for Trish, but she also wanted to go to a quiet place and recover from the stress of the waiting room, the noise of all these people.

And she needed to talk to Grandma.

That probably stressed her out the most. To have to approach her to ask for something, to wait for what she'd require in return. It was like asking Tony Soprano for a favor.

Venus also didn't do "humble," "contrite," or "biddable" very well. If Grandma asked her to do something heinous, Venus wouldn't be able to hide what she really thought of the idea. And that probably wouldn't go over too well.

For now, she had to wait. Grandma was busy with Trish, who was holding the baby and trying not to fall asleep. It was kind of cute to see Trish smiling at the baby and dozing at the same time.

And was it just her, or was that baby kind of ugly? Red and wrinkly, and everyone kept saying she looked like Aunty so-n-so or Uncle what's-his-face, but Venus didn't think she looked like anyone alive that she knew.

"What are you going to name her?" Aunty Marian touched her granddaughter's ear.

Grandma straightened. "Oh, you can't name her yet."

"What do you mean?" Trish's eyes popped open. Despite her tiredness, she was wide awake at Grandma's statement. Venus sighed. Grandma might be back on speaking terms with Trish now that the baby was here, but Trish wasn't about to kowtow to her after months of the silent treatment.

Grandma had on her "Let's be reasonable" face. "We have to call the *bonsan* in to tell you what letter the baby's name has to start with."

"I'm not even Buddhist. Why would I want the priest in, telling me what to name *my* baby?"

Uh-oh. Trish's weariness had ratcheted her temper up a notch. Venus started squirming her way around people toward the bed.

"But he has to bless the baby." Grandma seemed genuinely confused why Trish wouldn't follow the same tradition she followed with all the aunties and uncles, the same tradition the other cousins in the family followed with their children.

"I'll get my pastor to bless the baby, and I'll name—"

"Grandma." Venus grabbed Trish's foot under the blanket to make her shut up. "Trish is really tired. We should let her rest."

On the other side of the bed, Venus's mom just had to stick her nose in. "I was in labor for thirty-six hours and didn't need to rest."

Trish opened her mouth, but Venus pinched her toe hard. Trish gave a soundless yelp and subsided.

"Mom, why don't I take you and Grandma home." It wasn't a question. She speared her mother with a look that dared her to rebel.

Mom flung her hands up, ringed fingers sparkling. "Fine, fine."

Grandma, however, gave Venus a speculative glance. She never offered to take Grandma home; she usually waited for someone to ask her to do it. And half the time, she had the excuse she was going back to work. A strange smile played on Grandma's lips as she gathered her purse and said good-bye to everyone.

Venus ignored her mother's huffing and puffing when she put up the convertible top for Grandma, after refusing to do it for her yesterday. "Mom, is your car still at my place?"

She paused in fluffing her short, permed hair (which Venus didn't understand, considering there was no one around to see her). "No, Jenn drove me over to get it, and she drove to my apartment with me so she could take me back to the hospital."

Venus paused, one foot inside the car and one foot out. "Aside from that, you've been at the hospital the entire time?"

Her mother's head, visible above the top of the car, halted before she squeezed into Venus's miniscule backseat. "Of course. Where else would I be?" She flashed an "I'm such a compassionate aunt" smile before ducking into the car.

Venus caught the smirk on her grandmother's face as she flipped the passenger seat back into place and eased herself in.

Who knew Grandma had a sardonic streak?

She drove Mom home while listening to her swing between gushing over the baby and grousing about Venus's tiny car.

"That's why I'm taking you home first, Mom." Oops, did she lay the sarcasm on too thick on that one?

"Well, your place is so close. You could have dropped me off there to wait for you while you took Grandma home."

What was the deal with Mom wanting to spend so much time with her all of a sudden? Her mother had turned into one of those clingy Jellyfish Monsters from the video game who would lock her in a death grip and suck her face off.

By the time they arrived at her mom's apartment, Venus's foot itched to give her an extra boost out the door. Well, not *really.* No matter how annoying her mother got, she couldn't truly want to cause her physical harm. But she wouldn't feel badly over a few bruises.

Something inside her twinged as she watched Mom amble toward her apartment complex gate. A daughter shouldn't despise her mother, no matter how unmotherly she'd been for most of her life.

But she'd only become halfway kind to Venus once she'd lost all that weight, not before. And that was hard for any daughter to take. As if to mock her thoughts, her mom gave a cheerful wave before she closed the complex gate and disappeared.

Venus drove away. Now was her chance. Her chest tightened and butterflies fluttered inside—she took a deep breath. In the darkness of the car, somehow Grandma seemed more approachable. *Don't screw this up.* "Grandma, I need some advice."

"I'm always happy to help you, Venus." Her mild voice held a thin, sardonic ribbon.

Venus almost didn't continue. She wouldn't be talked down to, not by anyone, especially Grandma. Except she needed her help, so Grandma was entitled to some condescension. She damped down her temper. "I'm thinking of starting my own game development company."

"What's your product?" Her voice had changed. Suddenly Venus heard the crisp, confident thread of steel that made her so good at running the bank.

"I have a good idea for a game, but more than that, a friend and I are working on a development tool that will enable all aspects of a game development team to access all other areas—the Spiderweb unites design, animation, and programming."

"I'm assuming there's nothing like this tool out there, in any other versions?"

"It's been tried by other companies, but ours is more comprehensive. There's nothing close to it out in the market."

"You don't want to partner with any other game development companies out there already? It would be the easier option."

This was a test. Venus knew it somehow. Yardley's arrogant face flashed in front of her, as well as the faces of the other VPs. She blinked it away. "No. For the Spiderweb, I'd want my own company, my own game." *I think, anyway.* But she needed to sound confident for Grandma, or she'd rip her idea to shreds. "I'll succeed or fail on my own."

"You're going to quit your current company?" There seemed to be a brighter tone to Grandma's voice. Venus must have passed the test. She couldn't be sure because it was dark and she wasn't about to take her eyes off the road to peer at her grandmother's darkened face.

"I'm strongly considering it." Probably. Maybe. Why couldn't she just make up her mind?

"Do you have enough money?"

Venus hesitated. Here again was the quandary. Before she could formulate her answer, Grandma spoke again. "Do you need—"

"No, I'm not asking you for money." She made her voice firm. "I still need time to set things up so that I can present to an angel investor. I might work for another company while hiring people, finishing the Spiderweb, designing the game demo."

"Then what do you need from me?"

"Angel investor recommendations."

"Is your business plan drawn up?"

"I'm working on it now." It wasn't totally a lie—she had a generic template on her computer at home, and a few lines written in it. "I'm not sure if I'll need it, because I have an open invite from a friend at EA to show them our demo when it's done."

"I have to admit, I'm not as familiar with the gaming industry."

Okay, one—Grandma was actually admitting to imperfection, and two—did that mean she couldn't help Venus? "Most gaming investors want to see a good game demo rather than a business plan. Once we finish the Spiderweb, we'll work on that. I have a game idea that's unique enough to stand out in the current market, and what will really sell it is how little time it took to create the demo because of the Spiderweb."

Grandma was silent. Had she offended her with her explanation of the gaming industry? No, Venus wouldn't second-guess herself. She wasn't going to waste her time or Grandma's if there wasn't anything she could do for her.

"You've given this a lot of thought." Grandma sounded faintly surprised.

"I wouldn't jump into this on a whim." Venus wasn't her mother.

"No, I wouldn't think you would."

What? A compliment from Grandma? Venus must be hearing things.

"I have one friend in the gaming industry. His name is Hudson Collins."

Hudson Collins??? The "ungettable get"? The most prestigious, respected investor in the video game industry in the entirety of northern California? Everything Hudson chose to pursue turned to gold, so he had gained an almost magical reputation with video game publishers. If Hudson decided to back a particular project, doors opened like the thieves' cave in the *Arabian Nights.*

If Venus could show Hudson her demo, he'd instantly realize the potential of both the game and the Spiderweb. And they'd be set.

"I could speak to him about you."

"You would?"

Venus waited for the other shoe to drop. What would Grandma want in exchange? These days, since Venus had turned thirty, Grandma nagged a lot about dating. Although come to think of it, she'd backed off once Trish announced she was pregnant.

Still, what had Jenn said? Her theory was that Grandma was feeling her age, and grandchildren—and great-grandchildren—were her immortality. She also thought Grandma's only Christian friend, Mrs. Matsumoto, had said something that hit too close to home, which was why Grandma chose to persecute the four cousins—the only Christians in their family.

Venus steeled herself. Who would Grandma want her to meet and possibly marry? (Because she was sure Grandma's imagination did not stop at dating.) She hoped it wouldn't be anyone totally dweeby. Geeks she was okay with — she worked with geeks.

"Here's what I'll do for you, Venus. I'll mention your company to him. When you're ready, and not a second before" — Grandma's voice rang like a unsheathed *katana* sword — "I'll introduce you to Hudson."

Meaning, don't take this opportunity and mess it up with incompetence or inadequate planning. "I won't embarrass you, Grandma."

Grandma started — Venus saw it out of the corner of her eye. Then she turned to Venus and laid a hand on her leg. "I'm glad we understand each other." But there wasn't a threat in her voice. It was more like ... admiration. Did Grandma actually *approve* of her?

She turned into Grandma's driveway and waited while she got out. Venus suddenly saw that yes, she was moving a bit slower than normal. She still favored her right hip — Lex had noticed that a year ago and pointed it out to them.

Grandma leaned down to speak to Venus. "You're smarter than anyone else in the family, you know. I think you can do this." She swung the door closed.

Venus could only gape. The air stopped in her throat as if a hand had cut off her esophagus. She watched Grandma walk up to the front door, unlock it, and let herself in. Only then did her throat open up, and she sucked in a whooshing breath.

Who had kidnapped her grandmother and replaced her with this *nice* woman?

Maybe her cousins were right. Maybe Grandma did relate to her because they were alike on some level. She'd felt comfortable talking business with her. They'd known exactly the deeper meanings behind what was said.

Maybe, with Grandma's help, her company could succeed.

Only after she backed out of the driveway did she realize Grandma hadn't yet told her what she expected in return.

SEVEN

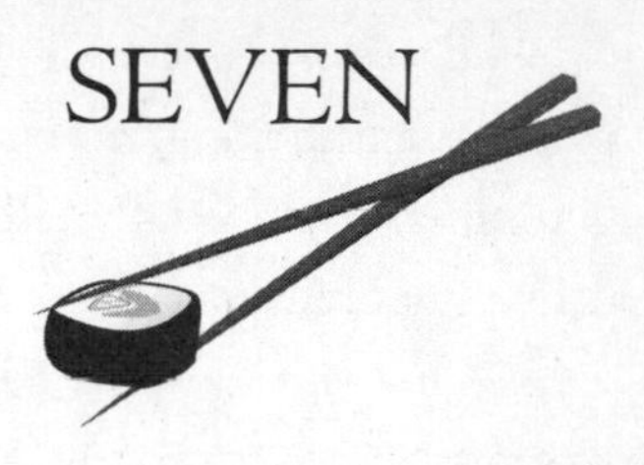

She took a sick day for the first time in three years.

She knew because she inputted everything into her PDA (people kept telling her to switch to a Blackberry or Treo or something like, but she couldn't resist the cute phones that kept coming on the market) and her last sick day had been three years, two months, and eight days ago.

Yardley might expect an answer if he saw her, and she wasn't ready to give him one. She needed time to think.

The night before, a quick call to the admin's voice mail took care of it. Venus took her shower (she couldn't stand a dirty body in clean sheets), then turned off her alarm before going to bed.

She still woke up at five.

Exercise. Shower. Coffee. Dress in jeans and a T-shirt. Bible reading...

Interrupted by her phone. *Brrrring!*

She shouldn't answer it. She wasn't going into work today, and who else would call her at six thirty in the morning? *Brrrring!*

Actually, even her admin didn't come in that early.

Well, she was in the middle of First Kings and whoever it was could just wait until she'd finished. *Brrrring!*

Oh, for goodness' sake, this was driving her nuts. She picked up the handset and checked caller ID.

"Hi, Grandma. Isn't it a little early?"

"Oh, I knew you'd be up."

Venus stifled a groan. "What do you need?"

"I don't *need* anything, but I'd like you to do something for me."

The music from *Jaws* cued up in her head. Oh, boy. Here it comes. Grandma would finally tell her what she demanded in exchange for delivering Hudson Collins to her.

"What is it?" Venus tried not to sound like she was grimacing. Except she *was* grimacing.

"Why don't you come over for breakfast?"

Grandma loved to prolong the suspense. Sometimes she could be as melodramatic as Trish. "Can you give me a hint about what you'd like to talk about?"

"I heard Drake Yu wants you to work for him."

"What?" How had she found that out?

"I'd like you to take him up on his offer."

Venus stood there speechless. She knew her mouth hung open, but she couldn't get her jaw to close. She had turned into a statue of gelatin—stationary, senseless.

She had vowed it would take an act of God for her to work for Drake again.

Or an act of Grandma.

Without makeup, Grandma looked almost human. Still beautiful, more earthy and natural than usual. But she'd already had her first cup of coffee, being an early riser like Venus.

No, not like Venus. She wasn't like Grandma. "How did you know he wanted to hire me?" Venus leaned against the marble-topped island in Grandma's kitchen and stared her down.

Grandma calmly sipped her second cup of coffee. "I heard about it from Mrs. Nishimoto. Her son works for one of your old companies and heard that Drake Yu was inquiring about you." She set her cup down, her face completely reasonable, which made Venus feel like a drama queen in comparison. "I didn't know for certain he wanted to hire you, but because of his inquiry, I guessed he might. At the time,

I didn't think it was important because you were in line to become Game Lead at Oomvid, and I knew you wouldn't consider becoming CTO at a smaller startup."

Venus opened her mouth, then closed it. Grandma didn't know she'd rather do a knee-knocking presentation in front of a million people — in her underwear, even — than work for Drake again. Grandma would naturally recall a job opportunity when Venus said she was thinking of quitting Oomvid.

"I didn't even know you knew Drake."

"I know his family."

Ah, yes. The Yu family was one of the branches of the Triumvirate, one of the largest and most successful venture capital firms in the Bay Area. Of course Grandma would know them — they were both in money. Large quantities of it.

"Anyway, I talked to him about you — "

"You talked to him? Grandmaaaaa ..."

"Let me clarify." Grandma's eyes narrowed, and she set her hand on her hip, making her stiff cotton nightgown billow out. "I spoke to his father, who suggested I talk to Drake."

"Oh." She couldn't complain if Grandma had gone through his father.

"Drake said he'd called you a few days ago."

"He did. Earlier than I would have liked." Similar to a *certain person* who'd also called before normal business hours. Venus glowered at the kitchen clock. Seven fifteen.

Grandma waved a careless hand. "Oh, you're always up."

"I hadn't even finished my coffee. I wasn't exactly in the right frame of mind to decide my future at six thirty in the morning."

Grandma shrugged. Not her problem. "When I spoke to him, he indicated he'd still like you to work for his sister's company, even though you're going to start up your own game development company. He knows it's only a temporary position for you."

Grandma had gone through an awful lot of trouble about this. Venus regarded her through narrowed eyes. "Why do you want this?"

She flung her hands up in disgust. "Want? I'm trying to find you a job. Do you see any benefit in this for me?"

Venus wasn't one to be intimidated by her grandmother's apparent frustration. Grandma could go into dramatics like the best of them in order to get her way.

Sure, Grandma was helping her. But why? Offering to help her with Hudson, calling Drake...

Wait a minute, why Drake? Venus didn't buy that it was just because she'd gotten wind he was going to offer Venus a job. After all, his sister's company was only a small startup.

"Are you *matchmaking*?"

Grandma's hand flew to her chest and her shoulders drew back. "Me? What in the world made you jump to that conclusion?"

Even Grandma's nose quivered with her indignation, but she didn't fool Venus for a second. Drake Yu, CEO of four successful startups, oldest son of Paul Yu, one of the most respected venture capitalists in California, if not the entire United States.

What's not to like?

"I didn't like working for Drake, Grandma."

"Why ever not? You're both smart, handsome—did he not see you before you blossomed?"

Blossomed? Was that how Grandma saw it? Venus only remembered a week of puking because of the stomach virus, followed by six weeks of trying to keep *jook* rice gruel in her ultra-sensitive stomach, not *blossoming.* The *blossoming* came weeks later after her new exercise program and stricter eating had kicked in.

"He saw the before and after, Grandma."

"Oh." Her shoulders sagged a little, then snapped back into place. "Well, now you're even more improved. The two of you should work wonderfully together."

"Because we're both smart and handsome? Grandma, what are you smoking?"

She frowned at Venus, her eyes betraying her confusion, but aware that Venus was mocking her somehow. "You both have excellent work ethics. I should know. Are you going to refuse to work for him just because I like him?"

Put that way, it sounded completely idiotic for her to object. "I didn't like working for him—"

"That was years ago. You don't know if he's changed for the better. And where else are you going to find a good, yet temporary job while you start up your business?"

"Am I even going to have time to work on my own business while I'm with Drake's company?"

"His sister's company."

"Fine, his sister's company. As CTO, even of a small startup, I'm going to be working the same hours as I did before."

"I'll sweeten the deal for you."

Venus crossed her bare feet, chilled by the tile floor. Or maybe the calculating look in Grandma's eyes.

"If you work for Drake—yes, yes"—she held up a hand when Venus opened her mouth—"I *know* you didn't like working for him, but listen to me. I want you to help him out, as a favor to his family from ours."

Suddenly Venus felt like a guppy in a *koi* pond. This was bigger than her own plans—this involved the Sakai family, the Yu family. She could see a glimpse of what Grandma wanted, why she wanted this.

"In return, I will invest money in your company *and* tell Hudson Collins that I've invested."

"What?"

"No strings." Grandma met her eyes directly. "No rights to the Board of Directors."

"You don't invest in gaming companies. It won't impress Hudson." It would, actually. Grandma didn't invest in companies very often—not even her own children's companies—and her financial stamp of approval would go a long way toward garnering Hudson's curiosity, at least, although it wouldn't necessarily snag his deeper interest. But Venus wasn't stupid—if Grandma was in a bargaining mood, so was she. She would milk this as far as Grandma would let her.

Grandma's eyes flattened and her mouth pinched. She regarded Venus a long moment, but Venus didn't break eye contact, didn't waver in her gaze.

"Fine." Grandma turned to the refrigerator and opened it. "I'll also introduce you some time in the next few months so you can pitch the idea to him." She set an egg and a plastic container of cantaloupe onto the counter. "I can give you fifteen minutes with him."

Yes! "Agreed."

Grandma straightened with a carton of soymilk. The disgruntled look on her face indicated she regretted not bargaining more.

"And that's only conditional on if I like Drake's terms," Venus continued.

Grandma went back to preparing her breakfast. "I'm sure you'll find it to be more than acceptable."

Working for Drake. Venus suppressed a shudder. He was ruthless—she could even say he was more ruthless than Grandma. Venus had never submitted to him and he'd hated her for it. His about-face surprised her and yet didn't—if he knew Venus was the only one who would get the job done, he'd put aside personal preference and hire her, especially if it was only for a few months.

Plus, maybe he'd changed. She'd heard about his unexpected heart attack last year—he was still young, only about forty—and while he'd recovered well and could have worked for a few more years, he'd retired when he sold the company. The Drake she remembered wouldn't have given up his high-powered lifestyle to go into early retirement. He thrived on the frantic, busy pace of a startup company. Yet he'd announced it—and this coming out of retirement was for a family member, not for himself, so it wasn't really getting back in the full swing of things.

So really, maybe it wouldn't be so bad to work for him. She wouldn't have to see him that much, right? She rarely saw her CEO except at meetings.

"Well, what are you waiting for?"

"Huh?"

Grandma made a shooing motion. "Go get dressed. Go talk to Drake. Put on something nice."

"What do you mean?" Venus opened innocent eyes. She spread out her arms and looked down at her jeans and T-shirt. "I can't interview for Chief Technology Officer in this?"

Grandma folded her arms and glared. Really, sometimes Grandma needed to lighten up.

"I will invite you to the bank's Christmas party if you'll change into something expensive and feminine before you go to see him."

Grandma was still bargaining? "Fine."

Her sudden smile shot a crossbow bolt into Venus's gut. "Good. None of those manly business suits."

Oooh, she'd been suckered. That's what Grandma had been after. "Expensive and feminine." She eyed her grandmother with ire. "That was low, Grandma."

The smile widened, as if to say, *Be careful if you want to play with the big dogs.* "I'll be happy to buy you something for the Christmas party. It's more posh than some of the ones you're used to."

"I can buy something myself, thanks." No way would she let Grandma dress her up like a Barbie doll.

"Well, I need to eat breakfast, and you need to go home to change." Grandma plugged in her egg cooker. "Remember ... expensive and feminine." She eyed Venus with a look as sharp as a ninja star. "Don't disappoint me."

EIGHT

Bananaville was a complete circus.

Venus entered the front door to the office building leased by Drake's sister for her company, Bananaville, and was smacked hard by the sheer volume. It sounded like she'd walked into a zoo where the animals had all escaped and were having shouting matches.

She draped her trench coat over her arm and approached the receptionist's desk, a little dizzied by the red, fuchsia, and yellow stripes. She peered over the high counter to catch the receptionist's eye.

The girl in her early twenties glanced up at her, then continued chattering on the cell phone glued to her ear. She focused on her computer screen and clicked here and there.

Venus stood there, listening to her chatter. Something about the mall and some cat named Lisa who was trying to be all that but who totally didn't have "it," whatever "it" was. Venus felt about a hundred years old.

The clicks started to fall into a pattern. Reminded her of . . . a game controller. Was the girl playing a *game?*

Venus grabbed the edge of the counter and leaned way forward to see the computer screen. Despite her height, she almost had to hop up and plant her ribcage on the high counter in order to catch a glimpse.

She moved too fast for the receptionist to hide her screen. She saw some space game before the screen went dark.

Rather than straightening, Venus leaned further over the counter until she was almost nose to nose with the girl. "Please get off the phone."

The smoke-and-silver smeared eyelids blinked, and her mouth stopped in surprise.

"Darla?" The tinny voice sounded from the phone.

"Don't make me repeat myself, Darla." Venus speared her straight in the eyes, and fear pooled in the girl's green gaze.

"Call ya back." The girl closed the phone and shrank in her chair, still staring at Venus.

Venus backed off. No need to completely unglue the girl—she'd gotten her point across. The noises coming from the back rooms of the building had increased, if possible. "Tell Drake that Venus Chau is here to see him." She discreetly pulled at her frilly silk blouse to straighten it from its trip over the counter. The lace at the collar and cuffs had been her only concession to Grandma's admonition to be *feminine.* She'd needed this pantsuit to face Drake—she wasn't about to appear in a skirt. She didn't think she even had a skirt suit.

Darla picked up the phone and dialed. "Drake, uh ..." She cupped the mouthpiece. "I'm so, so sorry, w-what was your name again?"

"Venus Chau." She flexed a muscle in her jaw.

"Venus Chau is here to see you ... Yes, sir." She hung up. "He said to head back to his office. Did you, uh ..." She bit her quivering lip. "Did you want me to escort you?" Her wide eyes pleaded, *Please say no, please say no...*

"What's his office number?"

Darla gave a rather loud sigh of relief. "112."

Venus skirted the receptionist's desk and plunged into the madhouse behind.

Once she turned the corner, the noise reached deafening levels. It sounded like a few parakeets screeching at a dozen monkeys, who were screaming back. She headed down the long hallway, lined with open doorways.

"Excuse me, who are you?"

The peevish voice sounded behind her. She turned to see an Asian woman's head popping out of a doorway.

She must be Drake's sister. She had his wide, square jaw and small mouth, his prominent nose—larger than the average Asian button nose—and long eyes that slanted up at the corners like a paintbrush tip. Right now, the eyes were narrowed and the mouth turned down.

"I'm Venus Chau. Drake called me." She approached with her hand held out.

The woman ignored it. "Drake's girlfriends all know not to bother him at work." The acid in her tone burned the air between them.

Venus bit her tongue and drew blood. She withdrew her hand and focused on drawing a thin breath through her pinched nostrils. "I'm here to discuss the position of CTO."

The woman started, but recovered quickly and sniffed. "Now I remember." She flicked her eyes dismissively over Venus's person. "You're too young. CTO is a big position." As if Venus were six years old. Why was she so antagonistic?

Venus drew herself up to her full height—aided by her Sergio Rossi stiletto heels—but stopped short of clamping her hand on her hip. This was the founder, after all. "Why don't you escort me to his office so we can discuss this?" Her words came out more clipped than she wanted them to—she hated showing her temper.

The woman gave a short exhale. "Fine." She pushed past Venus and headed down the hallway, oblivious to the chattering, cackling, screaming, and yelping coming from the other rooms. Drake's sister's lack of concern made a knot of worry kink at the base of Venus's neck. This kind of noise was normal?

As they approached the center of the hallway, Venus realized the noise came from *one* room—the break room, stuffed to capacity with all women. One of them, a blonde in pink, turned and saw Venus's escort. "Oh, Gerry, you have to do something!"

Nice to finally know her name.

The woman became a porcupine, exploding with spikes. "About what?"

Her wary tone didn't dissuade the pink lady. "Angeline's boyfriend just broke up with her over the phone. She's going hysterical."

Gerry closed her eyes. "Oh, for goodness' sake."

Venus strained her ears and heard one particular screech louder and longer than the others. The rest of the chorus seemed to be either consoling in loud voices or shouting suggestions about what the unfortunate girl should do.

Venus could honestly say she'd never seen anything like this before. For one, they were *all women.* For another, they were *all talking.* Her first reaction was complete and utter speechlessness.

Her second was a raging headache from standing outside the doorway listening to so many high-pitched voices. The pain seemed to leech from her ears to her eye sockets.

A good, sharp whistle would quiet a room of arguing men (not that she'd had to do that, except for one time when her programmers had gotten into an argument over who had nabbed the last Dr. Pepper without replacing the case). A piercing sound would be drowned out by this crowd, or failing that, might cause more hysterics.

Gerry seemed torn between marching Venus to her brother or quieting this fiasco in her break room. She didn't look like she particularly relished pushing her way in there, although they might part the waters for her, being the founder and all.

Venus took a deep breath. Then she took a deeper one, because suddenly it seemed like there wasn't enough air in the building. She turned to Gerry. "Mind if I handle this?"

Gerry shrugged. "I don't know what you think you could do."

She shoved her trench coat and purse at Gerry, then plunged in.

Her toes got smashed by a few heels, but she also stabbed a few herself as she struggled to inject herself into the throng. Muscles honed at the gym pressed aside tall bodies, short bodies, skinny bodies, fat bodies. All female bodies, all talking, either to the unfortunate Angeline or each other. What was this, break time for the entire company?

She reached the small circle gathered around the girl, who sat at the break room table crying her mascara off. A mound of gray-smeared tissues listed beside her elbow. For such a little thing, her wail carried sharper than a fireman's siren.

"Whaaaaat am I going to doooooooo withoooooooouuuut hiiiiiiiim?"

Venus elbowed around an elderly woman patting Angeline's shoulder, placing herself almost in front of the girl. She panted a little, partly from the trek this deep into the room, and partly from the unnerving press of bodies around her. She jabbed out her elbows to make the women around her back up a step.

Grabbing Angeline's shoulders, Venus shook her hard. Hard enough that the girl's head flung around wildly, threatening to snap off. She didn't shake her long, but it was enough to make her stop shrieking.

"Knock it off!"

It was like a gunshot. The women close enough to see gasped, but were silent. The women farther out noticed the sudden hush and shut up themselves.

Angeline stared at her with eyes the size of eggs and a mouth open so wide Venus could see her silver fillings. Taking advantage of her shock, Venus pulled her from the chair. Angeline responded like a rag doll.

She was surprised when the crowd parted and let her walk Angeline out the break room door. In the empty hallway, she marched past a wide-eyed Gerry, then herded Angeline into an empty office and slammed the door. She dumped the girl into a chair, then leaned forward, resting her hands on the chair arms and getting into the girl's face.

"Work. Is for. Work." Angeline's eyes started to mist over, so Venus grabbed her jaw and shook it a little. "No, you are going to stay with me. Work is for work. You do not bring your home life to work."

Angeline opened her mouth and loosed the beginnings of a wail.

She never got more than a fraction of a second into it, because Venus, still clenching her jaw, ruthlessly shut her mouth. A faint *click* sounded in the office. Venus could hear a murmur outside the closed door, but no one dared to knock at it. Angeline's eyes darted toward the doorway—freedom from this madwoman!—but Venus pulled her face back toward herself.

"You do your work at work." She impaled Angeline with a look sharper than an acupuncture needle. "Even if your personal life is screwed up. Do you understand me?"

Angeline's lower lip quivered, but she gave a half-hearted effort at a nod.

"And if you absolutely can't work, you go home. You do not disrupt the entire company to deal with your home problems. We do not pay you to have group therapy sessions in the break room."

Angeline relaxed a fraction. "Go home?"

Venus didn't know if she was a slacker or not, but she wasn't about to create a habitual truant. "And if you don't do your work, you stay as late as you need to the next day to finish it." Venus's glare promised retribution if she didn't get the job done.

Angeline blinked, and her mouth turned down. "Oh."

Venus straightened, partly to ease her lower back, which had started to ache from the bent over position, and partly to give herself some air from Angeline's sickly sweet perfume. "Now, go to your office—"

"I only have a cubicle." The girl stuck out her bottom lip. "And they *promised* me—"

No griping, not on her watch. "Go to your cubicle, hang your jacket over the opening, and fix your makeup."

The reminder that she looked less than lovely—looked pretty hideous, truth be told—awakened Angeline's strength. She exerted herself to straighten her back, wipe her cheeks, compose her expression. She smoothed her hair, which had turned into Medusa's snakes from the wild trip through the break room.

Venus covered Angeline with a kind look. "I know this is hard. Take some time to calm down. Arrange to go out to lunch today with some friends." She opened the office door. "Go."

The girl bolted like a mouse scurrying out of a cage.

As Angeline's figure sped past Gerry, still standing in the hallway and still holding Venus's trench coat and purse, Venus noticed the relatively empty break room. "Where did everyone go?"

"Back to their desks." Gerry's low growl made Venus suspect the woman had something to do with how fast that occurred. Her glance at Venus seemed to accuse her of causing the ruckus.

The nerve of the woman. What was her problem? Venus retrieved her coat and purse from her. "Does this happen often?" She kept her voicc overly mild.

Gerry's face colored a shade a little lighter than her plum lipstick. "No."

Liar. "It must take you from your other work to deal with things like this."

Gerry's lips disappeared in a taut line. Her gaze flickered to the open office door with a brief flash of guilt, possibly for not taking charge. "Drake's office is just around the corner." She walked past Venus down the hallway.

Venus didn't mind not being thanked for stepping in—she suspected Gerry rarely thanked anyone—but the fact that things like this were probably too frequent caused her some concern. Gerry seemed a capable woman—why wasn't she handling these employees? Well, technically it wasn't her job—she was the founder, not the company policeman.

That would be Venus's job, if she took it. And she'd just proven she could do the job well.

So why was Gerry so peeved about it? Shouldn't she be pleased Venus had shown her abilities?

Venus kept her head high as she followed Gerry, ignoring the looks from the women in the offices they passed—some frightened, some angry, some cautious, some speculative. She'd never dealt with women well, and this entire situation had burned a hole in the pit of her stomach.

She noticed that although the din of the break room had dissipated, there were still two clamoring voices. Female. They rose in volume as she and Gerry turned the corner of the hallway.

They were coming from behind a closed office door. Number 112.

Oh, brother.

"She's *always* taking lunch early—"

"*She's* always leaving work early—"

"How can you expect me to get my work done when she's *never* around—"

"I've stayed *so* late to make up for things she leaves unfinished."

Gerry's stride checked as they approached. Her mouth pulled down further (if that were possible) and she hesitated before knocking.

"Come in."

She reached toward the doorknob slowly, touching it as if it were a slimy toad. The door swung open.

Two agitated women stood at the two far corners of his desk, as far away from each other as they could, and as close to Drake as they dared. He was leaning away from both of them.

He turned to her. As soon as Venus saw him, she forgot about them, forgot about Gerry's disapproving presence beside her.

His gaze was like a splash of ice water over her entire torso. Her first breath was a soft gasp, cold going through her throat, as if she were standing on a glacier. His eyes, lighter brown than most Asians, still penetrated her like a winter wind, but it no longer held that knife edge it used to have. Pockets dug under his eyes, and lines had appeared around his firm mouth—Venus couldn't be sure if they were normal or caused by the two harpies haranguing him.

And then those eyes lightened—brightened, she almost believed—and his lips parted. "Venus."

That husky growl resonated in the depths of her stomach. His words broke the paralysis that had seized her. "Drake."

The two women looked like they wanted to snap at her to wait her turn, but the sight of Gerry stopped them from doing anything more than fire sizzling darts at her from their heavily made-up eyes. They could be Snow White and Rose Red—similar in face, opposite in coloring. The first thing Venus noted was that their skirts were *way* too skimpy for the workplace. It made Venus feel overdressed in her black pantsuit.

Drake turned back to the girls. "Ellen, Annie—"

"What do you intend to do about the unfinished code?"

"I'm not letting her pin that on *me*—"

"Hey!" The exclamation burst from Venus like a whip. "Let him finish speaking." She couldn't believe they'd interrupt their CEO that way. Even in the smaller companies she'd worked for, she had never let her programmers be so disrespectful of upper management.

She'd shocked Drake, too, because he had that neutral expression he wore when he was trying not to show he was unsure of something. Gerry blinked and wore a similar mask.

Her outburst had been a reaction to Gerry's incomprehensible antagonism and the fiasco she'd just diffused. She felt like she worked here already when she'd only come in to talk to Drake about it.

The girls were quiet—more confused and surprised than silenced—but Drake still hadn't said anything. His eyes found Venus, and she thought he had a pleading intensity in his gaze. It didn't surprise her, considering his frustration in dealing with them when she'd walked into the office.

Fine.

She turned to the girls and gave a polite smile. "I'm Venus Chau. I have an appointment to discuss the CTO position with Drake and Gerry. I'm sure you understand—"

Snow White burst out, "He needs to make a decision about—"

Rose Red shook her head. "I'm not taking orders from *her*—"

"I have an appointment." Venus was louder than both of them, plus she had a good six inches on them because of her heels. "Thank you, ladies." She opened the door for them and stood waiting.

Her assertive confidence shocked the girls so much, they didn't even bother to ask who she was to be giving orders. Snow White's cheeks burned like neon cherries, while Rose Red had paled so much, her dark eyeliner made her eyes stand out like disembodied orbs. They stumbled in their strappy sandals as they hurried out. Venus closed the door behind them.

Gerry didn't even wait for the door to fully close. "Drake, you never told me how young she was. She's completely unsuitable." She'd become all bristles and indignation.

Both Venus and Drake gave her identical looks of *Are you high?*

They spoke at the same time. Venus pointed toward the closed door. "Did you see what I did with Angeline"—while Drake motioned, also. "Did you see what she did with Ellen—"

They both stopped. Venus suddenly felt like her heels were too high and she'd topple in another second. Drake looked at his desk blotter.

Gerry had reversed her attack, now shifting her weight from foot to foot.

Drake sighed. "Venus, did Gerry bother to introduce herself?"

He knew his sister pretty well.

Gerry crossed her arms. "How was I supposed to know she wasn't one of your girlfriends—"

"Gerry, no girlfriend has ever come to see me at work." He sighed again, scratching the back of his head. His hair had become a swirl of salt and pepper, still kept short, emphasizing his long temples where the hairline looked like it might recede in a few years but never did.

He rose and walked around the desk, touching his sister's elbow in a gesture so gentle, he suddenly turned into a stranger. Drake had never been soft in the years she'd worked for him. "We discussed this. You were on board with Venus yesterday." His voice, too, had become like a chenille throw. It did strange things to her stomach.

"That was before I'd met her."

"Has she done anything today that you object to?"

This was awkward. Venus moved toward the door.

"No." Gerry spoke calmly, albeit grudgingly. "I suppose we'll give it a trial run."

Well, it was better than nothing.

Drake guided Gerry toward the door. "I'll talk to you later."

Gerry left, and he closed the door behind her.

Venus lifted her chin as she faced him, meeting his eyes directly even though her heart had started to pound like *taiko* drums in a fast, complex rhythm. “Drake— ”

He took a long stride toward her, pulled her into his arms, and kissed her.

NINE

She thought she saw stars.

Firm and pliable, his lips pressed into hers. Strong. He was strong. His mouth was strong, and yet seemed to give strength rather than take it.

He wore the same scent. Something expensive. A thread of musk, a shimmering ribbon that reminded her of showering gold, a woodsy hint like a bamboo forest. She remembered whiffs of it as they passed each other in hallways, or eased around each other in bustling meeting rooms.

His arms around her pulled her close, holding her lower back with firmness but not captivity. Warm. His hands were warm. Burning, almost.

She felt every brush of his fine wool suit, the fold of her silk blouse crushed into her shoulder, the soft touch of his lip at the corner of her mouth. She wanted to reach her arms around him, fold him into herself.

This is Drake Yu.

She shoved him away.

The air shuddered through her throat as if her lungs had forgotten how to breathe. His scent lingered around her face, warm where it whispered against her cheek. Her legs wavered on her narrow stilettos.

He was looking at her, but she couldn't raise her eyes from the blue and gray carpet, her breathing low and hard. She didn't want to face him yet.

A bolt of lightning had blasted through her and fried her circuit board. She could almost smell the smoke from burned wires. Everything that had happened since she walked through those doors had culminated in a huge electrical explosion.

No, stop thinking like that. You have to forget about it.

"Venus, I'm sorry."

Her fried circuit board started sizzling. She raised her head. "What am I supposed to say in response to that?" she snapped.

His eyes were too calm. Shouldn't they be more animated—er, agitated than that? His placid expression made it seem as if he grabbed and kissed women in his office every day of the week.

"With Ellen and Annie ..."

His quiet voice only made her start to tremble more.

"Thank you. I've been harassed all day. I've never worked with so many women ..."

Grateful. He'd kissed her because he was grateful. She'd run with that. She'd ignore the hollow *tang* of an empty brass cauldron in her chest. "You're welcome." She bent to pick up her coat and purse, which she'd dropped when he ... *Stop thinking about it.*

"Do you need a moment?"

So compassionate, his tone. Airy and silky like a mohair shawl. She took a deep breath, then rose to face him again. "No." It sounded confident enough to her ears.

He seemed to think so too. He transformed from this unnerving, magnetic stranger to the old Drake—businesslike, efficient.

She could be that too. She had to be.

He gestured to a chair across from his desk. "Sit."

She sat. Her legs stopped quivering.

Drake pulled a manila folder from his desk drawer. "Let's talk business."

Just like that. She swallowed and tried to look unemotional, professional. Neither of which she was feeling at the moment.

"Here's the business plan." He handed her a leather portfolio. She skimmed it as he talked. "Gerry's idea for Bananaville is a virtual world specifically designed for children, teens, and their parents. Several large corporations have agreed to sponsor large 'towns' in Bananaville with thousands of interactive games for kids, teens, parents, and both. Our parent–child competitions have been especially successful."

"Who creates the games?" She flipped a page.

"Either the company hires someone, or they hire us. We do some of the games ourselves, some we contract out."

"Do the sponsors participate simply for a corporate presence in the virtual world?"

"No, some have been holding weekly or monthly sweepstakes and competitions. It also lowers the tipping point for the Bananaville users to use the sponsors' products once they've interacted with their virtual town and played a few games."

"Do you sell advertising space?"

"Some, but most sponsors want an interactive town. It draws in more traffic."

"How's security against predators?"

"Tight. Our security manifest is the last half of that section." He pointed toward the section she was flipping through. "We also have pen-pal stations, stations for learning about different states and countries, science stations, history stations—we're still developing games for them."

Venus kept flipping. The concept was good. One of the largest consumer bases was parents, and a virtual world that encouraged family interaction was sure to garner more approval than objection. She had enough knowledge of the market to know this would be big in a few years, depending on the sponsors and the level of security.

And if she could get the employees in line. "Let me guess. Gerry only likes to hire women, ergo that shot me to the top of your list?"

He nodded and grunted. No apologies, no embarrassment.

"That's part of your problem. Female dynamics at work are different from male dynamics, and the gaming industry is male-dominated. You have to treat the employees differently."

"You seem to know how." He nodded toward the closed door, referring to Snow White and Rose Red.

She met his gaze. "Not really. I've worked with men so long, I'm more comfortable with men than women. Are you sure you want to hire me?"

His mouth quirked up. He'd always been impressed with, yet at the same time surprised by, her candor—some things hadn't changed. "I wouldn't have asked you if I wasn't sure."

"I'm just giving you a way out."

"Getting cold feet?"

"No. I just want you to know upfront where I'm coming from."

"Another reason why I want to hire you."

"Gerry ..." She hesitated, but then decided she needed to bring it up. "Gerry doesn't seem to like me at all. Are you sure she's okay with this?" She raised her eyebrows at him.

He sighed, his fingers massaging his forehead in a familiar gesture. "She's under a lot of stress. Her husband had an affair, so she divorced him last year and she's raising her kids alone. He managed to take a big chunk of their shared bank account."

That was awful. She'd be cranky too, if that happened.

"This company is important to her. She's a bit wary of change. She likes being in control of things."

And she wasn't able to control things very well, apparently, which probably galled her. That explained her reaction to Venus after she'd stepped in and taken care of the ruckus in the break room. "Be straight with me. Am I going to have to fight to prove myself to her?"

Drake didn't answer at first. Then he looked her in the eye. "Gerry's not a people-person. But she's logical and fair."

Meaning, she might eventually get over this unreasonable assumption that Venus was too young to be able to do a good job.

"It would only be for twelve months?" she asked.

"Or until you can find a competent CTO to replace you."

"You want me to do candidate screening too?"

He shrugged. "I wouldn't trust anyone else to do it. You'll get an assistant to help you."

"Fine." She could deal with that.

He rose. "I'll give you twenty-four hours to decide."

She rose, as well, juggling the business plan, her purse, and her trench coat. "When would you want me to start?"

He lifted an eyebrow. "Yesterday."

"I'll call you when I've made my decision." She hesitated, then held out her hand.

Bad move. He took it, a warm glove over her fingers, and he wouldn't let go. His eyes, glowing like dark amber, burned into hers, but she was too stubborn to look away.

"Venus, are you going to be able to work with me?"

Said the spider to the fly.

She pulled her hand away. "If I have to."

His eyes darkened at the insult. Something inside her darkened too. She had to remember that this was still Drake, and she wouldn't allow him to take advantage of her ever again.

She headed toward the office door. "It's only for twelve months." She exited and shut it behind her.

She almost got into three accidents on the way home.

Really, how could anyone expect her to pay attention to the road after what had happened?

A car horn blitzed by her as she narrowly avoided sideswiping a minivan, too intent on crossing two lanes in order to make her exit to look and see who she might hit.

Okay, four accidents.

To be honest, rarely had anything upset her so much that she couldn't drive. As she pulled into her parking slot, her hands rattled against the steering wheel. *No, stay with me until you can get inside.*

She got out of the car, then dropped her keys as she fumbled for her alarm button. *Breathe. Deep. In. Out.* The excess oxygen made her see spots. She kept her head above her heart as she knelt to pick up her keys—the last thing she needed was to pass out.

She made it up the stairs and into her apartment. Kicking off her shoes, she leaned back against the closed door, then slid to the floor, heedless of her silk pants.

The quiet of the apartment calmed her body, but her head whirled like a pinwheel. She touched the cold tile floor with her palms, needing the solid feel, the chill of the stone, the smoothness of the surface. *My place. My home.*

Here, she didn't have to wear stilettos. Here, she didn't have to be on guard and on top of things in order to prove herself to her male coworkers. Here, she didn't have to be strong and independent. Here, she was herself, the real Venus, the girl she'd always be—Daddy's little girl, a competitive gamer, an obsessive housekeeper. Here, she was safe in her clean, neat world.

Not quite safe. Memories of what had happened invaded—here, where she was vulnerable.

She was more affected by what had just happened than she wanted to be. What did it mean?

No, it didn't mean anything. She'd heard him—he'd had girlfriends. He'd also said he was grateful. Well, he hadn't said it, but he'd implied it. He was also the kind of man who would forget any type of episode in order to get the job done. And he obviously expected that of her too.

He was attracted to her. Very few things surprised her, but that had come out of left field. Considering their rocky parting when she'd quit his company years ago, and the fact that he'd never been attracted to her before, even when she went from fat to fab while working for him, his attraction now confounded her.

But lots of men had been attracted to her—after she lost weight. She usually despised them because they only saw her face and figure. It was the main reason her business suits were masculine cut and dark colors.

Drake had seemed to value her as an employee before she lost weight, but he'd been like the rest of them after—she'd never been a person to any of them; she'd just been an asset who had suddenly become more useful to them. So while they were attracted to her, she had yet to find one worthy of her good opinion.

She'd never been attracted to anyone like this before. And to Drake Yu, of all people.

She wasn't going to lie to herself—she'd enjoyed the kiss. She'd never enjoyed a kiss ever, in her entire life. Guys hadn't wanted to kiss her before the transformation, and she'd had to avoid unwanted ones after.

Did it mean something that she was attracted to Drake, even if it was only physical?

No, she didn't have time for a relationship, and not with this man. Not when she was working for his sister's company, not when he'd betrayed her. He'd done it once—who was to say he couldn't do it again? He might be changed, but he might not be changed either. She didn't want to risk figuring out which was true.

The comforting smells—bleach, Lysol, Febreze, and a hint of citrus from her perfume—had loosened the tightness around her neck like a collar slipping a notch. The sight of the simple furniture and simple colors—even the corner of her *Vogue* magazine hanging over the edge of the glass coffee table—calmed her with its familiarity. She got to her feet. She had to change.

She picked one of her powersuits, black with dramatic gold metal braiding, paired with one of her most expensive shoes—a gold python pump from Christian Louboutin. She made up her face and hair with more care than usual. After all, she wanted to go out in style.

She'd sweep in to Oomvid, type up her resignation letter, leave it on Yardley's desk—or his admin's, if he was busy—and exit the building like a royal procession. He'd be surprised—he'd be furious, possibly—but she would be her usual cool self. She never brought private things from home to work, not in all the years she'd been working in the game development field, not in any of the startups she'd been at. She'd walk in and walk out with head high, proud and elegant, and everyone would stare as she left.

Her only regret was her programming team, but she'd email Jaye later today.

At the front door again, she paused to take another deep breath. This was it. She would refuse this golden opportunity at Oomvid, which while not the most moral company, was the fastest growing in the Bay Area, and risk her own startup. And in between there, work for her ex-boss, handsome and ruthless. Oh, yeah—no problem.

She opened the door and took the plunge.

TEN

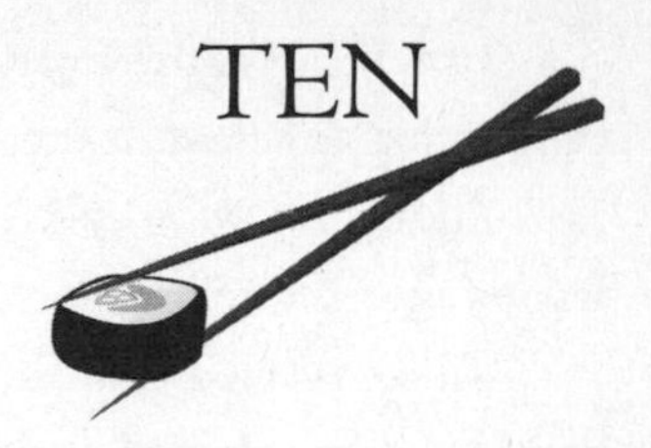

God had given Venus the perfect Operations Manager.

A slim girl—*hapa,* Venus guessed, from her half-Asian, half-Causasian features—walked into Venus's new office at seven thirty the next morning. "Hello, Miss Chau. I'm Esme Preston, the Operations Manager and your assistant." She gave a sweet smile and held out her hand.

Venus automatically shook her hand, glad for the interruption in the middle of poring through the policy and procedures manual. She'd been at work since six, and the fine print was making her eyes cross.

Esme held a leather folio, flipped open, and she whipped out a pen. "What can I do for you today?"

"Please sit." Venus waved her into the seat opposite the desk.

Esme perched on the edge of the padded chair, a picture of eagerness. Her half-Asian features gave her round face a youthful glow.

Venus didn't want to be hopeful, but Esme's folio and pen gave her an air of efficiency. *Just once, Lord, can I please have a halfway competent assistant?* "What are your normal responsibilities as Operations Manager?" No sense stepping on toes first day on the job.

Esme rattled them off in a quiet yet cheerful tone. They discussed responsibilities Esme wanted to keep, wanted to give to Venus, and wanted to share.

"Later this morning, I'll need you to get some things for me."

Esme immediately picked up her pen and lifted the folio.

"I need a company organizational chart and roster. I also need a programming schedule, and a list of work orders and projects we're in the middle of. I want to know what's upstream in the pipeline. I also want a meeting schedule."

Esme scribbled, smiled, and stood up. "I'm getting coffee. Would you like me to get you a cup?"

"Oh. Uh ... yes, thanks. You don't have to, though." She had been leery of asking her assistants for things like coffee because they weren't paid to run beverages for her. Plus they probably wouldn't have kept up with the demands of her addiction.

"I don't mind at all." Esme took Venus's empty cup and exited the office.

She'd just finished the policy and procedure manual when an alarm blasted through the air. Fire? What was going on?

She grabbed her purse—too dangerous leaving it—and opened her office door to an ear-throbbing honking. Several employees headed toward the back of the building, so she went that way too. Well, she couldn't complain that her first day was uneventful ... wait a minute.

No one was heading out the door. Instead, they clustered into a large room at the back of the building that was filled with cubicles. One largish cubicle seemed to be the focal point.

Another meltdown? More hysterics? Who broke up with whom this time? Was she going to have to handle two employee gatherings in a week?

"There you are, my pretty ... just a little closer ..."

"You can get him!" "Take him out!"

Huh? What was going on? If Venus didn't know better, it sounded like someone playing a video game. Or in a street fight.

"Rip his head off!"

Hmm, the employees were pretty bloodthirsty wenches.

Venus shoved her way through the crowd until she got to the cubicle causing all the fuss. The woman at the computer suddenly cried, "Aha! I got him!"

Cheers rose from her adoring fans.

Venus stared in perplexity at the computer screen and the woman, who was pulling a Rocky Balboa with her arms in the air. She raised her voice above the congratulations. "What's going on?"

The atmosphere flash froze. The good thing was that the noise level dropped as fast as the temperature.

The woman crossed her arms in front of her ample chest. Venus couldn't help staring—she had corded forearms as large as ham hocks. "Who are you?"

"Venus Chau."

"Venus?" The woman brayed, revealing a chipped front tooth. "Your name is Venus?"

The room was suddenly bathed in blood through Venus's narrowed eyes. "Why don't you tell me your name before you start making fun of mine?" A few juvenile "Oooohs" rose from the audience.

The woman sneered. "Nice to meet you, Venus. I'm Xena!" The room exploded with laughter.

She had dealt with the worst in male arrogance and immaturity. From college interns to crotchety old geezers who could barely use a computer. From arrogant testers to arrogant programmers to arrogant CEOs. This little troublemaker was small beans.

Xena was tall—but she slouched, and Venus was taller. She moved forward, pressing into Xena's personal space, close enough to see the pockmarks on her sagging cheeks and smell the hair gel keeping her crinkly, ash-colored curls tight against her head. Xena's arch smile stayed in place, but Venus could see her pupils dilate.

"I am your new CTO. The next time you cause a company-wide disruption like this, you're fired."

Xena's smile melded into a sneer. "I'm protecting this company."

"Excuse me?" She wasn't sure she really wanted to know.

"I get rid of predators who try to get into Bananaville."

Ah, that explained the violent exclamations from the other women. "Good for you. I don't care." Venus pressed closer. "You are disrupting the work day, and that stops now."

"Venus, what are you doing?" Gerry barked from behind her.

Venus didn't turn around immediately. She stared down Xena with her best—or worst, depending on how you think about it—stink eye. Then she turned to talk to Gerry. "I'm breaking up a—"

"Hester is our best security watchdog." Gerry's mouth pinched and her shoulders had turned into stiff clothes hangers. "You shouldn't keep her from doing her job."

Venus's neck kinked in reaction before she could suppress it. She smiled so she could bare her teeth. "I wasn't keeping her from doing her job. I was telling her how to help everyone else do their jobs better."

"What?" Gerry looked more annoyed than curious.

"The alarm? Who set that up?"

"It's always been there."

"It's distracting."

Gerry turned into a bulldog. "I see nothing wrong with it. It's not your job to change the work culture I've set up."

Venus's hands went to her hips. It made her seem larger, which worked with both Gerry and the wide-eyed crowd of witnesses. She kept her words polite, but each one rang like an unsheathed dagger. "Let's not discuss these things in front of everyone. Why don't we talk in my office?"

She waited for Gerry to move. Gerry stayed put.

Venus shifted her weight to one foot. She certainly had time to wait. She kept eye contact with Gerry, who started to flick her gaze around the room. Venus kept steady.

Finally Gerry turned and walked out. Venus followed. The crowd followed them with their eyes, some frightened, some gleaming with anticipation of good gossip.

Once in her office, she made sure the door was closed and didn't allow Gerry to speak. "If you question my authority in front of people again, I will walk. *You* hired me to get your operations in order. If you're going to undermine my authority in front of the people I'm supposed to be managing, you're only hurting your own company."

"You're a stranger. You don't understand the company policy and culture—"

"I understand your policy perfectly. And your culture is Bohemian and unorganized. If you keep allowing your employees to be distracted, you'll continue to miss your milestones and fall further behind schedule. Doesn't that matter to you?"

"I won't have you bullying my people."

The way she said it made Venus think she had been about to say, *my family.* Suddenly, she got it. That was how Gerry saw these women. That was why she ran her company like a matriarch—love and control. Approval and micro-managing. Venus was like ... the ex-husband's new wife.

Venus held Gerry's gaze. "In a year, your company will flop, no matter how brilliant your idea is—and yes, it is brilliant. But it'll all be wasted if you don't get your operations working efficiently."

Gerry's mouth had opened, but she paused at the word "brilliant." "You think it's brilliant?" She tried to keep a stiff-necked demeanor, but her eyes had become beseeching, like a child's.

"I've been involved in games or game development for most of my life, so I know what I'm talking about. You're not just another Web-based company—you're filling a gap in the marketplace."

Gerry had become quiet. Still distant, but not as prickly. Venus realized her acrid personality had arisen from insecurity. After all, she wasn't a fresh, straight-out-of-college engineer anymore—she was in her late thirties, and this was her first business venture. She had everything riding on this.

"Look." Venus leaned back to perch on the edge of her desk. "I'm going to be making changes. It's my job. You have to trust me to know what I'm doing. Drake wouldn't have hired me if he didn't think I could bring you back on schedule."

Some of her old belligerence appeared in her frown. "I won't have you threatening my employees." A mother hen, protective of her children.

"They're my employees, too, now. I don't use threats lightly. If they don't respect me, then I can't bring this company to your next milestone. Which is more important to you?"

She swallowed. "Hester has been here since the beginning."

"If Hester doesn't recognize me as her boss—if she fights me and ends up pulling your company down—are you going to thank her?" Venus didn't like being so hard on loyal employees, but she had to establish dominance, like the leader of a wolf pack, or she'd be torn apart.

"Listen ... I'll talk to her."

"I want to be there when you do."

"What? Why?" A tic worked in Gerry's neck.

"If you see her by yourself, it will seem like you're sneaking around behind my back, and Hester won't have any reason to listen to me."

Her gaze dropped, and her anger melted into acceptance. "I suppose you're right."

"I'll be the bad cop, if you like. But she has to toe the line. No more alarms, no more distractions."

Gerry glanced at her watch. "I have a conference call. I'll email you when I'm going to talk to her."

Venus held her gaze. "You promise? "

Gerry's eyes were honest and firm. "I promise."

They understood each other.

After she left, Esme knocked and came in. "Here's everything you asked for." She laid a neat pile of folders on her desk.

"Th-thanks." Venus flipped through them. Everything she'd wanted in less than an hour, including a few charts she hadn't asked for that related to the organizational chart. She straightened and hoped she didn't look too shell-shocked. "Thank you. This is wonderful." *You're wonderful!* The most competent, intelligent assistant she'd had yet.

Venus worked for another half hour before Esme suddenly burst into the office.

"Oh!" She clutched some folders to her chest. "I'm sorry, I didn't think you'd be in here. I thought you'd be in the meeting ..." She bit her lip. "I'm so sorry, I would have knocked if I'd known."

"What meeting?"

Although Esme's face registered apprehension and apology, there was a gleam in her eye that reminded Venus of a snake before it struck. She shook her head. How ridiculous. Esme was genuinely upset at disturbing her.

"Didn't anyone tell you? There's always an upper management meeting at nine on Fridays." Esme's rosebud lips bloomed into a pink O.

Venus shot to her feet. "Where?"

"Meeting room number 113. Next to Drake's office."

Venus grabbed her notepad and flew out the door.

Esme's anguished voice followed her down the hall. "I'm so sorry I didn't think to tell you ..."

Venus opened the meeting room door to find four other people around the table. "Sorry, I didn't know about the meeting until just now."

Gerry was back to her normal displeased self. "No one told you? I assumed you knew when we spoke earlier."

Venus resisted the urge to smack her.

Drake motioned to the other two women. "Venus, this is Julie and Carolyn, VPs of Marketing and Sales. This is our new CTO, Venus Chau."

She nodded at the two women, who were probably the cornerstone of Bananaville's income, expanding user numbers and soliciting the sponsors who paid for the opportunity to reach those users.

They discussed odds and ends, mostly bringing Venus up to speed with marketing campaigns, user numbers, and sponsor lists.

"Last on the agenda." Gerry consulted her notes. "I'm going to ask you to do something a bit unusual, but you know I've always supported a whole life approach to work."

What? Whole life approach? Venus didn't have a clue what that meant.

"I wanted us to not only be developing this great product, but to be able to fully understand and experience the worlds of our consumers."

Was Gerry asking them to become testers? Bananaville had hoards of testers—all ages, from five to fifteen—to tell them how the games were, and Venus wouldn't know the first thing about what would appeal to an eight-year-old. Her video game companies had all marketed to mature audiences.

"We have our family lives, it's true. I know you two"—Julie and Carolyn—"have children, but I still think it would be a good idea to interact with slices of our consumer base."

What? Children?

"So." Gerry cleared her throat. "I've decided that since we're marketing to children, we all need to have some experience with our target audience."

Experience? As in, what—she wanted Venus to adopt a child? Become pregnant? Maybe she could borrow Trish's baby. She suppressed a snicker.

Gerry didn't notice. "I'd like to have each of you do volunteer work with either children or youth."

ELEVEN

Volunteer work? With *children?*

Gerry's eyes darted around, not making contact with anyone. "I know this is taking time away from our home lives, but Drake and I agreed it will help us to do our jobs better."

Venus's jaw dropped, and she had to quickly snap it shut before someone — namely Drake — noticed. *Drake* agreed to this? Venus couldn't even picture him in anything other than an Italian suit. Working with children, being *playful*?

"Drake also thinks it will impress the investors that we volunteer with children outside of the company, considering the nature of the product we're selling."

Now that made sense — a dog and pony show for the investors. But ... children? Venus didn't mind kids, but it had galled her that she had been so *bad* at babysitting. Possibly due to the fact that six-year-olds liked playing Pokémon, which bored her, and got upset when she won.

"Okay, that's it for today." Gerry rose from her seat.

A touch on Venus's shoulder. She started, then looked up into Drake's face. Gerry and the two VPs were already heading out the door.

"You okay with this?" he asked softly.

"Sure, cavorting with children is how I like to spend my one day off a week." She busied herself with gathering her stuff, which was hard to do since she'd only brought a pad of paper and a pen.

Long, slow exhale. "Venus — "

"No, really, I understand the reasons why."

"Neither of us have experience with younger consumers."

"True." They'd both worked on various games for adults only.

He didn't give her a pep talk, didn't try to justify himself, didn't even ask what she intended to volunteer for. She knew he wanted to say those things, but he knew she didn't want to talk about it. She felt both comforted and alarmed at the realization that he knew her so well.

She shot to her feet, pushing her wheeled chair back. Unfortunately, he had passed behind her at the moment she stood up.

Her chair jerked to a halt, catching the back of her knees, flinging her torso toward the table. She thrust her hands out to catch herself.

He grunted, then suddenly his hand was on the small of her back, as if to steady her.

It burned like a hot iron.

She whirled to escape his touch, but it only brought her face to face with him instead. His eyes—so familiar and yet so unfamiliarly calm, a still, amber-colored lake. The fire, the energy, the barely contained forcefulness were gone. Had his early heart attack done that for him?

A faint smile creased his mouth. "I asked you the wrong question yesterday."

She didn't reply. She couldn't. His look wiped away her brain cells like 409 on grease.

"Venus, I don't know if *I* can work with *you.*" His eyes glowed, enveloping her with warmth.

He wanted her.

She shook her head. "I don't want this." She did, but she didn't. She couldn't trust him.

"We're both married to our work and not other people. You'll only be here for—"

"All you see is the outside." The bitterness had risen up, like ramen noodles foaming in starchy boiling water. "You never saw me when I was fat even though I saved the company's butt a couple dozen times. Then later, you only saw me because you could use me, because you had a pretty girl you could ask to join clients and investors for a drink after work ..." Her throat closed. The humiliation of the memory still made her shudder, even years later.

He looked away. "I was different then. The company was everything."

"I was different then too." Too willing to please her high-powered boss, too anxious to be accepted as a vital team member and not the token female. All too happy to do what he suggested ... until the client's sexual overtures had turned her stomach. And Drake's anger the next day: *"You mean you didn't sleep with him? We might have lost the account."*

She'd quit that very day.

"I'm sorry, Venus."

His quiet voice had the effect of a thunderclap. Her body jerked. He had never apologized, even when she'd shouted at him the day she quit. He'd been stoic and hard, arrogant in his assertion she should have done it for the company, in his assumption that she slept around.

No, he hadn't shown remorse then, but it radiated from him now, like lapping ocean waves. It crumbled her memories of him, water washing away the sand to reveal something hidden underneath. But not buried treasure, something uglier—the bitterness had become such a part of her, it seemed that was all she had in her heart now.

"What am I supposed to say? That I forgive you for trying to pimp me out to the client?" Her accusation was horribly churlish in the face of his regret, but she couldn't stop herself.

His eyebrows raised, then his lip curled slightly. Surprise and disgust at the hardness he saw in her—exactly what she felt about herself at the moment.

"Let's just forget it." She grabbed her paper and pen from the table. "The past never happened. That ..." She stumbled over the word. " ... kiss never happened. We're professionals trying to make this company successful. That's it."

She walked out.

It would have been a magnificent exit if she hadn't tripped over the threshold.

Venus started when Trish opened her apartment door. "Uh ... you're looking better."

Trish gave a weak smile, making the bags under her eyes more pronounced. "Oh, that's nice." She turned away as Venus entered the apartment.

Lex already sat in a chair in the living room. Behind Trish's back, she pointed and mouthed, *loopy.*

Well, duh. Two a.m. feedings and all that.

"Shh ..." Trish's mom, Aunty Marian, stood in the living room swaying back and forth, baby Elyssa in her arms. "We're trying to get her to go to sleep."

"Trish could use it."

"I meant the baby."

Lex chortled. Trish propped her hands on her hips. "What do you mean?"

Venus shrugged. "You look like death reheated in a broken toaster oven."

"Venus!"

Lex laughed harder. "No, tell us what you really think."

"I'm only kidding." On impulse, Venus walked up to Trish and pulled her into a hug. She hadn't hugged Trish in a long time—she was pleasantly squishier. "You do look tired, but you also look very happy. More so than I've ever seen you."

She didn't understand how that could be, but there it was. Trish—flighty, a little ditzy, always active and outgoing—radiated a tired but peaceful happiness she'd never worn before. It made Venus feel young and inexperienced in comparison, something so different from her normal relationship with her cousin.

Trish smiled. "It's so different. But it's also really nice. And hard."

Lex slouched deeper in her chair. "They never say babies are easy."

Venus dropped a stack of magazines on the coffee table. "*Vogue, Entertainment Weekly,* and *InStyle,* just as you asked."

Trish dove for the stack. "You're done with them?"

"These are last month's issues. Where's Jenn?" Translation: Where's the food? Venus dropped into the couch and looked at Lex. "And why are you here so early?"

Lex scowled at Venus. "I'm not always late."

"That is *such* a lie."

Lex's scowl transformed into a cheeky grin. "I got the last Diet Coke in the fridge."

"Ah, man!" Venus leaned back on the couch. "I totally needed one."

"Shh ..." Aunty Marian raised her eyebrows at them.

Venus mimicked a buttoned lip. "Sorry."

"Why did you need a Coke?" Lex tilted her head and eyed Venus. "You only intake artificial ingredients when you're stressed."

"Yeah, what happened with Oomvid?" Trish looked up from flipping through an issue of *Vogue.*

Wow, she really needed to get them up to speed. When she mentioned Grandma's offer, both Lex and Trish gasped.

"What?"

"Oh, come on. Even you can see that's a big deal." Lex skewered her with a hard look.

Venus hadn't really wanted to think much about it, partly because Grandma had been so ruthless to both Lex and Trish in the past, and she felt a bit guilty that she seemed to be getting off easy.

"I wonder why." Trish stared off into space, a frown between her eyes.

"It's obvious why. She wants me to get together with Drake, just like she wanted you to get together with what's-his-name, the creepy artist."

"Kazuo," Aunty Marian supplied.

Venus glanced up. She'd almost forgotten she was there. "It's all part of Grandma's obsession with more great-grandchildren."

"Her immortality," Trish said softly.

They all fell silent. Finally, Venus said, "Well, at least she's not as threatening as she was with you guys. It's strange, but I'm not about to complain."

"Go on, what happened after that?"

Venus continued, then finally told them about Gerry's idea that day. At the end, both of them exploded into a torrent of giggles.

"Hush, you two." Aunty Marian jiggled Elyssa, who had started squeaking.

Trish snorted through her hand over her mouth. Lex cackled softly. "You? With kids? I've got to see that."

Venus frowned and crossed her arms, burrowing into the throw pillows. "I'm fine if I can talk to them, but half the time I don't understand what they're saying."

Lex stilled and stared at Venus with furrowed brow. "Does it have to be children? How about teens?"

Venus perked up. "As in, able to string together coherent sentences and discuss something other than Pokémon? Gerry did mention youth."

"See, that's perfect." Trish smiled, although her face still had that gray, weary cast to it. "Does your church have a youth group?"

Venus winced. "It's kind of large. Like, over one hundred teens."

Lex choked. "You're kidding!"

"My church has several thousand members. They have—I don't know how many services on Sunday."

"Don't you want a church where people at least know your name?"

Venus bit her lip. "Well ... the church encourages people to get involved in ministry and get into Bible study groups, but I dropped out of the small group I was in. I was too busy at work ..."

"You'll have to make time, now." Trish crossed her arms and peered down at her.

"My church happens to need help with their youth group." Lex flashed a wide smile.

Venus and Trish both stared at her. "Really?"

"They need a female staff worker to step up to the plate. They've had a plea in the morning bulletin every Sunday for the past few weeks."

"How many teens?"

"There aren't more than fifteen or twenty teens gathered together after service each week."

"Perfect." Trish leaned down to slap Venus's knee.

"Trish!" Aunty Marian frowned at her as Elyssa erupted in a wail.

"Oh ..." Trish reached for her baby and nestled her against her. Amazingly, Elyssa quieted to fussy grunts. Trish's face reminded Venus of a hibiscus flower, rosy with orange blushes, sweet and delicate.

Venus watched her, and something in her melted a little, like Hawaiian shave ice on a hot day. She supposed kids weren't *that* bad. "Lex, do you know what they want the youth leaders to do?"

Lex shrugged. "There's youth group meetings on Saturday nights. They also have Sunday school once a week, but I think that's a separate teacher."

"Are you glued to your church now?" Even in a few short days, Trish had perfected the "mommy sway" as she stood there rocking Elyssa.

"Not really. I picked it because they start on time, they're biblically based, and they're only a few miles away from my home."

"And it's so huge you disappear in the crowd." Lex stretched her arms. "No chance of that at my church. It's small enough that everyone knows everyone."

Venus sighed. Disappearing wasn't so bad. At her mega-church, she didn't stand out—she could leave quickly after service and enjoy the rest of her Sunday on her own, a rare time to relax. Still, she'd rather volunteer for a twenty-person youth group than plunge in with a one-hundred-person youth group.

"Fine." She poked around in her purse and got out her PDA. "Who do I talk to?"

To: venus7876@gmail.com

From: thejayeman@yahoo.com

Subject: Life at Oomvid without you ...

Sucks! Still haven't replaced you, even after a week. Edgar had to take over responsibilities, but not organized enough. Everything behind schedule. Programmers upset the company made you leave, have been slacking on purpose to make Edgar mad.

Asked Edgar innocently about new software he'd mentioned. Told me to go render a forest or something.

How's working for the D-man? Never told me why don't like him.

Been working on the Spiderweb. How's your side coming?

Jaye

P.S. Emailing from home. Nancy and the baby say hi.

P.P.S. You left a copy of *People* in the break room.

To: thejayeman@yahoo.com

From: venus7876@gmail.com

Subject: Re: Life at Oomvid without you ...

Thanks for the update, Jaye. Bananaville is good. The company concept is a good idea, and they have a gold star sponsor list if I can get their technology solidified. Do you remember TrekPaste? Bananaville is about the same size. It's very different from working at Oomvid.

Drake and I have been getting along. We're professionals, even if we didn't part so well. We had different work styles, and we clashed one time too many. That's why I left. Now, he's learned to give me latitude in my job. Things are going smoothly.

I haven't worked on the Spiderweb lately. Bananaville's founder has asked us all to do volunteer work with kids in the consumer demographic (stop laughing), so Lex mentioned working with her church's youth group. I talked to the youth leader yesterday and intend to start at youth group meeting on Saturday night.

Tell Nancy hi. Tell the baby to sleep and let Daddy watch *24*.

Dump the *People* magazine, it's old.

Venus

Venus walked into Santa Clara Asian Church on Saturday night, and realized she looked like a schoolmarm.

She wasn't exactly geeky. She had on pale linen slacks and a black Ann Taylor top. Her shoes were black Italian leather with solid two-inch heels. Muted elegance, much more casual than her business suits.

However, everything about the teen girls sparkled—hair pieces, shirts, jeans, flip-flops. Sequins or glitter or crystals or rhinestones. As soon as she walked into the social hall, little twinkles from the girls' ensembles zapped her.

She felt so *old.*

She also felt gargantuan. Her height and heels made her tower over all but a few of the older high school boys.

The older kids gathered in clusters talking while the junior highers played tag at the back of the social hall. Well, a form of tag that involved somebody's grungy sneaker being thrown around and picked up by various people. *Ewwwww.*

A short Asian man approached her. "Are you Venus?"

She recognized the voice from the phone. "David?"

He stuck his hand out and smiled, and he suddenly looked like he was about fourteen years old. "Nice to meet ya."

"You're really young to be youth director." Oh, that was kind of rude.

He laughed. "Shh. I told the church board I was twenty-one."

Heat whooshed up her face. "Sorry, you probably get that a lot."

"I grew up in this church. Trust me, I'm used to it by now." He motioned to a willowy Asian woman who was setting up a portable projector and laptop. "Kat, come here. Venus, this is Kat, my wife."

Kat smiled and spoke with a soft Chinese accent. "Nice to meet you. Thanks for volunteering." She sounded just a tad relieved in the way she said that, which cued the creepy stalker music in Venus's head.

"Do you speak Chinese?"

"Mandarin. You?"

"Cantonese." Well, no conversing in Chinese with her. Shucks. Venus would have liked to practice on someone other than a waiter.

Kat made a helpless motion with her hand. "Keiko, our other female staff worker, had her hip broken by—I mean, she broke her hip a few weeks ago, and she hasn't been able to come. We really could use another woman with the high schoolers."

"You work with junior high?"

Kat nodded.

David waved over two other Asian men—one tall, slender, and about Venus's age, and the other stockier and about ten years older than herself. "This is Ronald and Herman."

"Hi." She shook hands with both.

Ronald seemed quiet, but Herman looked like he had Mexican jumping beans in his pockets. He was in constant movement. "Sorry we can't stay, we still have to practice for worship tonight." Herman gestured to the front of the room, with a battered upright piano and a guitar in a stand.

"Sure." As they moved away, Venus turned to David. "So, what do I do now?"

"We're almost ready to start. We're waiting on one more person. It's kind of weird." He smiled. "You were the second person to call me this week wanting to work with the youth group."

The creepy stalker music in her head morphed into *Twilight Zone.* No way. What were the odds? She had to stop thinking the world revolved around her—

The door to the social hall opened, and Drake walked in.

TWELVE

"What are you doing here?" she rounded on him.

He froze, one hand still on the door handle. His eyes bugged out of his head. "Venus?"

"No, Pluto. What are you doing here?"

He closed his eyes, released the door handle, and pressed his fingers to the heavy crease between his brows. "Don't tell me."

"Then I won't. I was here first."

David's eyes shone white behind his glasses. "What? You're not both staying?"

Drake sighed. "Venus— "

"I already work with you. Why would I want to spend more waking hours in your company?"

"Venus, don't be childish." He said it in a soft voice.

She started. Her back unkinked as it pulled out to full length, but then the quiet reprimand in his eyes made her feel like a spoiled brat. She didn't like the nauseating suspicion that he might be right.

David looked thoughtful. "Actually, Drake called me first."

"We're both staying." Drake's voice held that tone she remembered from meetings, the "I have decreed this so it shall be done forthwith" firmness.

Both David and Kat heaved sighs that came all the way up from their diaphragms. Then David turned toward the room at large. "Everybody, form two lines!"

Well, guess they were starting.

Kat had nipped out, and now came back with a baking dish filled with green Jell-O. *Huh?*

Venus stalked away from Drake and stood near the wall, shifting her weight from foot to foot. The girls gave her weird looks but didn't say anything as they passed her to form two lines in the open area at the back of the social hall.

David had set up two chairs at the head of each line. A few older teen girls loitered disdainfully near the back, a few boys had started giving each other noogies, and some of the junior high girls were standing in line and braiding each other's long, silky hair.

"Venus and Drake, you guys get to sit." David grinned, a full set of gleaming white teeth.

Not a good sign. Venus sat slowly.

Kat placed the baking dish on the floor in front of her, then ran out of the room again. Oh, it was fruit Jell-O ... except those pieces of fruit were extremely round.

"Okay, everybody take off your shoes and socks!"

What? Gross. Venus opened her mouth to protest, but then closed it. *Be a team player.* She took off her shoes and crossed her ankles.

Kat came back with another baking dish, which she set in front of Drake.

Her stomach cramped. She had a bad feeling about this, but she couldn't even fathom what was going to happen next. The ceiling could open and a spaceship appear for all she knew.

Kat placed a large empty bowl to the side of each baking dish.

"Okay, guys, it's Jell-O Toe-jams!"

What? She and Drake whipped their heads toward each other. His face looked as horrified as she felt.

The junior high girl who stood directly behind Venus started to moan. "Ewewewew!"

"Yeah, honey, I feel that way too."

Venus heard the girl giggle. Well, at least she was amusing.

"Here's what you do. Each person pick up one marble with your foot, drop it in the bowl, and then run to the back of the line. The next person sits down and does the same thing. First team with all the marbles out wins. Clear as mud?"

Clear as green Jell-O.

"Okay, ready, set, go!"

Venus squeezed her eyes shut. She couldn't do this. Put her *foot* in that? That was a *baking dish!* She couldn't put her foot in a baking dish.

She stuck her foot out but couldn't get herself to lower it into the Jell-O. She peeked at it. Ooooh, it was so disgusting a concept she didn't know if she wanted to throw up or ... throw up.

The kids behind her had unformed their line and crowded around her to watch and yell. "Come on!"

Clunk! Drake stood up and limped to the back of the line, trying not to get his Jell-O foot onto the sturdy carpet too much.

If he could do it, she could too, right? She plunged her toes in.

"Aaack!" That was totally *cold!* And *slimy!* Oh my gosh, this was gross! She flapped her hands as she moved her foot around in it.

Unfortunately, years in stilettos had cramped her toes. She couldn't get them around the slippery marble. Each one she grabbed kept sliding away from her.

"She's not going to get it." "Come on!" "Faster!"

The junior high girl behind her cheered, "You can do it!"

Finally! She pulled her foot up—rats! She dropped the marble.

Several boys groaned.

The marble was a tad easier to grab on the carpet. She finally dropped it in the bowl and barely had time to get out of the chair before the junior high girl plopped her tiny little behind down. Venus folded in half to get her shoes out from under the chair—no way was she letting those get dirty.

Ugh, her foot was slimy. She tried to hop-skip toward the back of the line.

Those young kids were tons faster at this Jell-O thing than she had been.

The lines had become big blobs of people, so in leaning against the wall in the back and never moving forward, she managed to skip her next turn. Some older teen girls winced as they saw her sticky bare foot and stayed back there with her in order to remain Jell-O-free.

Smart chicks.

Drake, on the other hand, took his place in the other team's people blob and got another turn at the Jell-O Toe-jam. He didn't smile, exactly, but his eyes lit up like a child getting a red envelope at Chinese New Year's.

He seemed so young. So juvenile. So un-Drake. Venus couldn't believe her eyes.

"What's your name?" one of the teen girls asked. She flashed her blue-smeared eyelids.

"Venus."

Their eyes widened so much, one girl's fake eyelashes loosened. "That's really your name?"

She sighed, remembering hateful years in high school as the big girl with the ridiculous name. "Yup." Teased by girls like these—cute, slender, made-up, feminine.

But they didn't know that. She forced a wider smile. "What are your names?"

"Mika." "Sarah." "Rachel."

Names seemed to suddenly undam their mouths, and they began chatting away. "So are you going to be our new high school youth leader?"

"Keiko's been gone for so long."

"She broke her hip, you know."

"But it totally wasn't our fault—it was Steve's fault."

"We were playing Toilet Bowl Tag, where if you get tagged, you have to get on your hands and knees until somebody sits on you and flushes you, and then you're unfrozen."

"It's a really stupid game."

"Anyway, Steve sat on Keiko, but he slipped and broke her hip."

Ouch. "Is she okay?" Should Venus have signed some kind of personal injury waiver?

"Oh, yeah." Mika waved her hand. "She broke her arm before too, but that was Timmy's fault."

Whaa?

"We have a winner!" David had his hands in the air.

Her team lost, naturally. By a landslide. A couple boys gave her mean looks. She tried to feel disdainful, but she couldn't—when she'd been rising as a video game competitor in her teens and early twenties, she'd been told by enough people, "It's only a game." She knew that sometimes, it wasn't just a game. It was the competition, the sense that only a factor or two kept her from doing better.

Factors like squeamish youth leaders with sticky Jell-O feet. How was she going to get this off?

Kids started streaming out the social hall toward the bathrooms to clean up. David stood wincing at the carpet. Luckily, it was that industrial strength short gray stuff, like in office buildings, so the Jell-O only formed small dark specks here and there.

Kat lightly backhanded his arm. "You forgot to lay down the plastic garbage bags."

Venus and Drake, both still with greenish toes that they tried to keep off the floor, stared at the sticky mess. The kids had walked around, although most of the mess spread out from the two demolished baking pans.

"My sister's got a steam cleaner," Drake said. "She lives ten minutes away. I can run over and get it."

"She won't mind?" David glanced at the clock. Venus did too. Seven thirty.

"No. She just used it yesterday when the kids spilled Kool-Aid."

Gerry owned and used a steam cleaner? Maybe the woman was as compulsively sanitary as Venus. Maybe she wasn't so much prickly as wanting to clean every doorknob with antiseptic wipes or wash her hands every five minutes or spray Febreze before she entered a room. Not that Venus needed to spray Febreze in *every* room.

Drake turned and hop-skipped out of the social hall. "I'll clean up and then go."

"Venus, you can clean up too." David pointed out the social hall doors. "Do you know where the bathroom is? We'll start the worship as soon as the kids get back, but you can just slip in after we start."

Girls crammed into the bathroom like Vienna sausages in a can. A couple had their limber legs propped up on the sink counter with the water running full blast over their toes.

Yuck. Something about feet in washbasins made her stomach curl.

Didn't the church have a kitchen?

Venus limped further down the hallway, walking on her heel. She turned the corner—and ran smack dab into a junior high girl. The poor kid had been pulling a flamingo, but Venus sent her sprawling across the carpet.

"Oh! I'm sorry." She limped to her side and helped her up.

"That's okay." Her cheeks had turned a ruddy pink, especially when she glanced sideways at a cluster of high school boys who'd already finished washing their feet and now loitered around talking. Otherwise, she looked fine.

Venus peeked into the kitchen. Rats, even the kitchen sinks were clogged with green-toed kids.

She waited until they'd finished—after all, she was the adult here, right? Finally it was just her and the girl, each at one of the two kitchen sinks. She wasn't going to stick her foot in the basin—she'd dislocate her hip even if she wanted to try—so the paper towel dispenser on the wall above it was a welcome sight.

At first, the girl tried to hook her leg over the edge of the large stainless steel sink, but her legs were too short and she had to unhook herself or else dangle from the edge. She leaped up to grab a paper towel from the dispenser, but the next piece had been jammed inside.

"Here." Venus handed her a wad of paper towels.

"Thanks."

"What's your name?"

"Rebecca."

"I'm Venus." Rebecca's eyes widened. Before she could say anything, Venus said, "Yes, really."

Venus took a long time cleaning her nasty foot—sticky and utterly black on the bottom despite her efforts to keep it off the floor—because, well, she was neurotic. But it seemed Rebecca was stalling, since she'd cleaned up her tiny foot several times already.

"You're missing worship." Venus could already hear music from the social hall.

"That's okay." Rebecca swiped again at her foot. "Herman's leading today."

"You don't like Herman's songs?"

Rebecca shrugged. "Chris and Eric usually lead, but Chris is in Japan on vacation with his family, and Eric's at his cousin's wedding."

Venus tossed her paper towels and slipped her feet back in her shoes. "I'm done. Are you ready?"

Rebecca sighed, but tossed her shredded paper towel and followed Venus out. The young girl hadn't brought her shoes, so she dirtied her feet as soon as she started walking.

By the time they returned to the social hall, the lights had been turned out and music drifted from the doors, which were cracked open. She and Rebecca slipped inside and sat in the back row.

Herman and Ronald played a rollicking worship song, one that she'd seen Sunday school children do with hand motions, but the kids sat lifeless. The song sounded kind of tinny with just a guitar and piano.

And Herman had a *terrible* voice.

Venus wasn't a singer, but her back twitched at every off-key note. Kat sat at a small table near the front, where the projector flashed the worship lyrics on a pull-down screen. She moved the PowerPoint slides forward as the song stumbled on. The kids sat back in their chairs, numbly watching the PowerPoint as if it were TV.

After the song ended, she leaned close to whisper to Rebecca, “Chris and Eric come back when?”

“Not for two weeks.” Rebecca sighed a mournful sound.

Venus wished she’d had a steam cleaner near church so she could miss this caterwauling. Drake had totally lucked out.

Come to think of it, she hadn’t even known he was Christian. How had he heard of this youth group, this church? And why would he go to a church instead of a community center or something like that?

The torture ended just as Drake walked into the social hall and sat next to her. “Where’s the steam cleaner?”

“In my car. I figured we’d probably clean up after youth group, and I didn’t want to leave it lying around anywhere.”

“Do you know what we’re doing next?”

He shrugged.

How weird to be here, together, both completely clueless and doing something so far removed from work. Him seeing her in this awkward situation was *almost* okay because he didn’t look all that comfortable either. The lack of usual polish in both of them made her feel like they’d entered some alternate universe.

David got up to make a few announcements, one about a video game competition in a few weeks. Interesting! Venus and Drake looked at each other with raised eyebrows.

He leaned closer. “It’s probably something kid-friendly like *Super Mario*.”

“When’s the last time you played?”

“Last week with my nephew.” A smug smile pulled at his mouth, and his eyes were half-lidded.

“I played a couple weeks ago with my cousin’s kids.” For about ten minutes, until they started whining and crying at how Venus wouldn’t let them win, and so her cousin told her to stop playing against them. She only played kids’ games at family gatherings, where sitting in front of the PlayStation with the children was easier than nipping around, trying to avoid both Grandma and her mother.

They stared each other down, dogs asserting dominance in the pack. Finally she held out her hand. "You're on."

He shook it. "I still owe you."

She'd trounced him at a company party years ago, playing ... *Halo? SOCOM?* She couldn't remember. It was the first time he'd noticed she worked for him despite her presence at weekly department meetings.

David finished his announcements. "One last thing. Meet our new youth staff workers, Venus and Drake. Stand up, guys."

Aw, man. Venus stood and tried to smile, but the kids only turned, gaped, and then sat back.

Well, what was she expecting? A standing ovation?

"Okay, high schoolers go with Herman, junior highers stay here."

Kids started tromping out the social hall doors. Venus caught David's eye, and he motioned for her and Drake to go with them.

They gathered in pews at the front of the main church sanctuary. When she joined Lex at church, it seemed like a closet compared to Venus's church in San Jose, but now with the pews empty, the walls echoed with the teens shuffling into the room, laughing and joking. Like soldiers in an uneasy truce, Venus and Drake sat together in a pew just behind the last row of kids.

Herman started handing out a sheet of paper. "We're lucky to have Venus with us today, guys. Okay, separate into small groups and work through the questions. Girls with Venus, guys with me and Drake."

Wait a minute! All by herself while the other new staff worker got to team up? That wasn't right. She wasn't exactly experienced at this.

Drake rubbed salt in the wound by giving her a jaunty wave as he rose to follow the guys to the other side of the sanctuary.

She was going to *pulverize* him at *Super Mario*.

The three girls she'd met earlier led the way as they collected in the seats beside and in front of her. Okay, only six girls. She could handle six girls. The high schoolers were heavy on boys, since Drake and Herman had at least twenty guys on their side of the room.

Luckily, the girls were chatting—howling, really, about how fattening the double mint chocolate chip mocha was at the nearby coffeehouse—so Venus could scan the sheet of paper. Only five questions. Hey, even better! This would be a breeze. This was like Bible study, only with fewer questions to work through. She didn't like the fact she hadn't had time to answer the questions herself beforehand, but these seemed rather straightforward. It was for teens, after all. How hard could it be?

She cleared her throat. "Okay, guys."

They kept talking. "I saw him put *five pumps* of chocolate in it!" "Well, that's because you got the mucho grande size." "Did not! It was just a medium."

"Guys."

"It's even worse if you order the triple fudge brownie one. They have chocolate syrup they pour on top of the whipped cream."

"Guys!"

One girl stopped mid-sentence, her mouth hanging open.

"I'm Venus."

Silence.

"Tell me your names," she prompted.

They looked at each other with wide eyes, biting their lips. Okay, maybe Venus's tone had been a bit harsh. She was too used to dealing with programmers, not hormonal teen girls. She just hoped they wouldn't start crying. "I already know Mika, Sarah, and Rachel. How about you three?"

"Naomi." "Karissa." "Stephanie."

"Great. Okay. Uh ... turn to Matthew chapter eight, verses twenty-three to twenty-seven."

The girls seemed a bit slow to grab Bibles tucked into the slots on the backs of the pews—due to a few inputs into the not-yet-finished chocolate syrup conversation—but eventually they turned to the right page.

"Who wants to read?"

The few girls still talking went dead silent.

Well, that was a way to shut them up. "Anybody?"

Six pairs of eyes stared blankly at her.

"Nobody wants to read?" *She* certainly didn't want to read.

Finally, Mika sighed. "Okay, I'll read."

The passage was when Jesus calmed the storm on the lake—short and sweet. "Okay, question one: What happened when the disciples were in the boat?"

Nobody said a word.

Venus stared at each of them. This was kind of a no-brainer. No one wanted to speak up? These girls knew each other—they weren't strangers, they weren't shy. They had plenty to talk about when it was chocolate syrup.

"Anybody?" *Bueller? Bueller?*

No bites.

"Oh, come on." Venus glared at them. "Tell me you're not complete idiots."

Their eyes had popped open wide, and a few of their mouths had followed. Maybe she shouldn't have called them idiots first day on the job.

"Uh ..." Rachel bit her lip. "There was a storm?"

"Right. Next question: Why were the disciples afraid?" That seemed kind of elementary.

"They thought they were going to drown."

"Good. Question three: What did Jesus do?" *What?* "Oh come on. Who comes up with this stuff?"

The girls giggled, but too late Venus realized she probably shouldn't have said that. For all she knew, Herman came up with the questions himself. She coughed. "Ahem. Well?"

"Uh ... what was the question?" Stephanie twirled her hair, reminding Venus of her cousin Jenn.

"What did Jesus do?"

"He calmed the storm."

"Question four: What should you do when you are in a storm?"

"Go inside?"

Venus stifled a laugh and almost choked. She hacked and gagged for a minute while the girls gathered around her with anxious expressions.

"Are you okay?"

"Do you want me to get you some water?"

"There's Kleenex in the kindergarten Sunday school room."

"I think it's locked."

"You don't have tuberculosis, do you?"

"Of course she doesn't."

"I'm learning about it in history class."

"I'm okay," Venus croaked.

"Oh, I have a history test on Monday!"

"I have a chem test on Tuesday."

"My chem test was last week."

"I'm taking bio this year instead of chem."

"Who do you have? My brother has Mr. Kawanami."

"Oh, tell me again who you have for English? Do you have Mr. Jennings?"

These chicks talked faster than an auctioneer. "Guys!"

They stopped as suddenly as if she'd slapped duct tape on all their mouths, all at once. Twelve eyes stared at her for a moment, then one of them—Karissa?—blossomed into a grin.

"So ..." She leaned forward, eyes bright like black crystal. The other girls followed suit until Venus had twelve ears straining toward her.

"So ..." Karissa repeated, "are you and Drake dating?"

"He's sooooo cute."

"He's kind of old."

"Yeah, but aside from that, he's sooooo cute."

"I want Nick to look at me the way Drake looks at you."

"Ew, Nick's Mika's brother!"

"So? He's cute!"

"How long have you been going out with Drake?"

"Are you going to marry him?"

"Ooh, your kids will be really good-looking."

"Guuuuuyyysss!" Venus's hiss sounded louder than their rapid-fire questions. She cast a nervous glance across the sanctuary at the boys' group.

Drake stared back at her.

Oh, God, please won't you have mercy and just strike me down dead?

"Ooh, hey!" Karissa punctuated her squeal by leaning even more forward until she was almost hanging off the back of the pew. "Can we be your bridesmaids?"

THIRTEEN

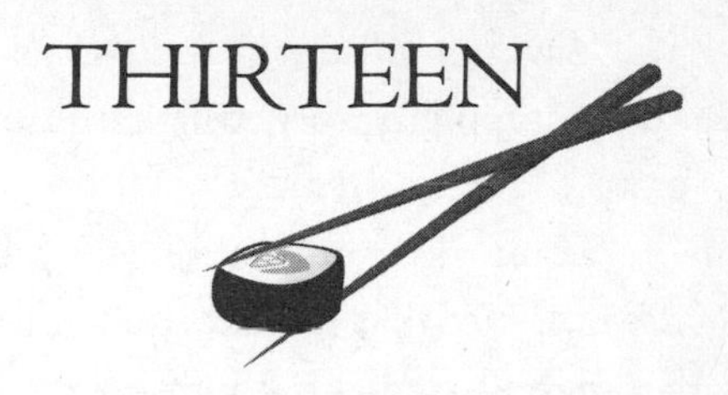

Who was she kidding? She was terrible with children—with anyone under legal age, in fact.

The church youth group hadn't been *that* bad. At least David and Kat had threatened—er, said, "See you next week!" when they all left last night. They had also seemed a little worried about letting her go, almost as if they expected her to hightail it out of the country.

Venus pushed back her plate. "That was great, Nancy." She loved when Jaye and his wife invited her over for dinner. Being second-generation Indo-American, Nancy's cooking had that sizzle of authenticity, tempered with health-conscious California flavor.

Jaye's wife dimpled and got up from the dinner table. "Did you want more?"

"No."

"Still can't picture you working with teens." Jaye scooped up the last of his *palak paneer* with a piece of flatbread.

"I'm not the Wicked Witch of the West."

"You're close."

"Oh, shut up. They said hello to me at church this morning." Although she suspected a couple of them had worn Wonderbras today. Was that her impact on those girls—inducing breast envy? "Besides, me working with teens isn't as mind-boggling as Drake working with teens."

"Think it's more believable, actually."

Venus sat back in her chair. "*Et tu, Brute*?"

"Saw him once with his sister's kid. Much better with kids than you. Although surprised he's at a church. Didn't think he was religious." Jaye looked away.

Venus tried not to raise her eyebrows. Jaye rarely brought up the R-word. Not that she talked about God much to him. "I asked him last night. He said his sister went to church there and knew they always needed more youth staff." Who woulda' thunk Gerry was Christian? Not Venus. But Drake had also mentioned how Gerry had been going since her divorce, and that it had seemed to help her.

Nancy swooped in and removed Jaye's empty plate. "Go ahead and work, guys. I'm going to clean up. But Jaye"—she motioned with her head toward their son—"will you take him so I can clean up that mess?" Jaye Junior had gotten more food on himself, the floor, and his tray table than inside his tummy.

Jaye swiped at Junior's mouth, while the baby started squalling and pitching his head back and forth. "Come on, dude ... doesn't like it when we wipe his mouth," he explained to Venus.

Mental note: wipe her own child's mouth early and often to develop good sense of hygiene. It could work, right?

"Got the bugs out of the Spiderweb? No pun intended." Jaye tried to get at a piece of carrot that Junior had shoved up his nose.

"Not yet. I still can't figure out why the tool won't work with the MoCap data you got for us. I'll work on it. It depends on how much time I have in the next month. I've only been at Bananaville for a few days."

"Need more data to test it. Guessing it won't be a good idea to use the MoCap studio at Oomvid."

No, they certainly couldn't use her former employer's equipment to test software they'd tried to steal from her. "Options?" They'd been lucky to get the original data from some friends who had worked at a studio and done the sessions for them for free, but the friends had since left the studio.

"Rent someplace. Got friends who might know the guys who own that small one in South San Francisco."

"I've been thinking about the business side. Grandma said to be prepared, and she meant more than just the demo. So I've done some market research on our game idea."

"Unique enough for the market?"

"We're both going to have to see if we can hear anything about what's in the pipeline. Right now, the all-female cast isn't a completely unique idea, but has audience appeal. We need a good designer and animator."

Jaye screwed up his face, but Venus couldn't tell if it was because he was trying to get pureed squash out of Junior's hair or because he was thinking of where they could find a good animator.

"Whoever we choose has to be top notch. We don't want to get into that same fiasco that ProvoTech did a few years ago." Fiasco was a nice way of putting it. ProvoTech had hired someone who turned out to be a complete amateur, and the time wasted had made ProvoTech the laughingstock of the entire game industry for months.

Jaye groaned. "Remind me of my year in purgatory, why don't you?"

"I told you not to work for them."

"Already used up your quota of 'I told you so's."

"So how are we going to find an animator who's both legit and good?"

Jaye finally cleaned his son's dinner off his person. "I'll do some research. Got to be a few who'd make good team members."

They spent a few minutes chatting about other things until Nancy could take Junior from him. They spent the next few hours on work. Jaye tested the program that Venus had brought with her, making comments on problems.

After they were done, they ended up playing *SOCOM: Disaster* against each other, as usual. Nancy didn't mind because unlike Jaye, Venus could hold a conversation while playing.

"Ha ha!" Venus took out one of Jaye's men. "So, how's Jaye's mom?"

Standing beside the couch and watching, Nancy gently rocked Junior. "Not so well. She insists she's okay, but his sister says she's moving slower and she's a little unsteady on her feet."

"She still won't move out here?"

"Nope. It would make it so much easier. Jaye's sister went to the doctor last week because she's always tired. Doctor said it's stress because she has her kids, and then she has to go over every day to check on Mom. At least here, we and his brother could split the time."

Venus had a fleeting thought about her own mother, and what she'd have to do when she needed more care. The family would expect her to care for her mom, even if said mother had been a royal pain for most of her life.

She blew up a tower. "Ha!"

"Do you miss it? The gaming competitions?"

Venus positioned herself to take out the fort wall. "No." She rarely talked about those days. Usually she changed the subject, but maybe because she wasn't working for a game development company at the moment, she felt more comfortable answering Nancy's questions.

"But you won so much money, everyone loved you."

"Everyone hated me. They wanted to beat me." Venus also suspected they'd hated her because she was a girl, she was overweight, *and* she'd beaten them, but she couldn't exactly prove it. "They were all relieved when I retired. And then I got a job at TrekPaste and met Jaye."

"And the rest is history." She laughed and bounced Jaye Junior. "Jaye says you've worked for your boss before."

"Drake? Yeah, at TrekPaste. We both worked for him."

"You must enjoy working for him."

Jaye snorted.

"What?" Nancy sounded confused.

"At TrekPaste, I got into a fight with Drake and quit."

"A fight?"

"We disagreed about ..." What could she say? She couldn't blurt out the truth that she'd thought he had the morals of a sociopath. " ... respect. It was his company, so I quit."

"That's a bit extreme."

"Even for you," Jaye piped up.

"Not really. I have to work for people I respect, but who also respect me. He didn't respect me, plain and simple."

"He didn't respect you? Why'd he hire you?"

He'd hired her because he had admired her programming abilities. She'd been promoted because they recognized her leadership abilities. But he'd stopped regarding her as just a programmer as soon as she shed all that weight, because suddenly she wasn't just his employee; she'd become someone he could use. Venus laughed off Nancy's question. "He respected me until he got a taste of my temper."

She trounced Jaye, as usual.

"Why do I bother?" Jaye flung his controller down.

"You say that every time."

"You're even *talking* the whole time we're playing."

"It's that extra X chromosome." Venus got up, gave Nancy a kiss on the cheek. "Thanks, Nancy. Great dinner."

"You don't come over often enough, Venus."

"I'm usually too busy. Like your husband."

Nancy rolled her eyes. "At least it's better than when he was working for startups."

Venus pulled on her trench coat. "Jaye, I'll try to get the bugs worked out by the end of the month."

"Kind of fast. Sure you'll have time?"

"Pretty sure." She paused at the doorway. "I'll get Bananaville's technology together in no time."

Monday was not the day for her coffeemaker to give up the ghost.

The smoke rising from it clued her in. She yanked the plug out and turned on the fan over the stove before the smoke triggered the fire alarm. Great. It was only a few years old.

And now she had to *drive* while uncaffeinated.

She almost got into two accidents on the way to work. Well, three if she counted the incident at the light. She was in the right turn lane, there weren't any cars coming, and she expected the Honda in front to make the right turn, so she gave a little gas. Then she had to jerk to a halt when she realized the Honda wasn't moving.

See? She drove terribly without coffee.

She'd just turned on her car alarm when Esme came racing out of the doors into the parking lot. "The Web director just quit!"

Venus stopped, wobbling a little in her four-inch heels. "Now?"

"I just got in, turned on my email, and there it was. She sent it on Sunday."

Venus had a fire to put out, and she hadn't even entered the building yet. "Where's Drake?"

"He's not coming in today." Esme skipped next to Venus to keep up with her longer stride. "He had to take his mom to the doctor."

"Is Gerry out too?"

"No, she's in and she's a bit upset."

That was an understatement. She heard Gerry's raised voice as soon as she opened the glass door into the lobby area.

The first thing she saw was the backside of a tall, gray-haired man in a fine blue suit. At seven thirty in the morning? Why didn't anyone do things during normal business hours? He hovered near the receptionist's desk while Darla smacked her gum and listened to the telephone. She kept her eyes glued to her computer screen, and Venus already knew she was playing a computer game while on the phone. "Sorry, she's not answering her phone. You'll just have to wait."

This was too much like *déjà vu.* Venus approached the man and stuck out her hand. "Venus Chau, CTO. Is there anything I can help you with?" She pasted a smile on her face while dreaming of coffee. *Another few minutes.*

He shook it. "Bruce Whittaker. I'm here to see Gerry Yu." He winced as Gerry's voice rose a notch. Venus wondered who she was yelling at. Luckily, the bend in the hallway prevented them from hearing her very clearly.

"Please sit down, Mr. Whittaker, and I'll get Gerry for you." She turned and headed out of the lobby area and down the hallway, trailed by Esme.

A sharp rap on the door stopped Gerry's hollering. Venus entered without waiting. "Bruce Whittaker is here to see you."

Gerry's hair had turned into a bird's nest, possibly from pulling at it. Venus didn't really blame her.

The cowering website programmer standing across from her desk had smudges under her kohled eyes and gray tears running down her cheeks. Venus pulled a tissue from the box on Gerry's desk and handed it to her. The programmer—Venus couldn't remember her name—honked her nose.

"Gerry, what's wrong?"

She waved a hand at the programmer. "She almost crashed the system this morning."

"But I didn't," the girl sobbed.

Venus exhaled slowly. "Gerry, it's not the programmer's fault the Web director quit."

Gerry's face paled as if she'd dipped her face in rice powder, but she didn't respond.

"You should maybe freshen your lipstick before you see him," Venus said.

Gerry looked a little lost, possibly because she might not have remembered who Bruce Whittaker was. "He's waiting in the lobby?"

"Yes. He looks like he's been waiting a few minutes already."

That shoved Gerry into action. She smoothed down her hair, grabbed her purse from under her desk, and headed out to the women's restroom.

The frightened programmer stood there sniffling and looking from Venus to the empty desk and back again. Venus pointed out the door. "Go on back to work." The programmer scurried out.

Esme sighed. "Wow, you took care of that so well—"

"I'm not done yet." She marched out to the lobby and approached Mr. Whittaker. "Gerry will be out momentarily. We apologize for the wait." She turned to Darla with a glittering smile. "Darla, sweetie, can I see you for a quick moment?"

Darla stopped mid-chew, giving Venus a nice view of her pink gum smashed against her molars.

"Close your mouth, dear."

She closed it. "But the desk— "

"It'll only be a minute." Venus showed more of her teeth.

Darla rose slowly, like a guillotine victim mounting the steps to her doom. Which wasn't too far from the truth. Venus followed closely behind her into the hallway. "My office, dear."

The three of them entered Venus's office. Esme closed the door, and Darla jumped at the sound.

Venus didn't sit down. She stood in front of her desk and took full advantage of her heels to look down at the hapless girl. "The next time a man in a three-thousand-dollar Versace suit walks into the lobby, you do *not* play computer games while he's standing there."

"I wasn't— "

Venus stopped her with a finger in her face. "Don't. Lie. To. Me."

Darla closed her mouth and started to shake.

"You also don't call Gerry when both you and the man in the three-thousand-dollar Versace suit can hear her all the way in the lobby. You get your lazy butt up off that chair, and you go to Gerry's office to let her know that a man in a three-thousand-dollar Versace suit is waiting to speak to her."

"I didn't know he had on a three-thousand— "

"You treat every person who walks through those doors as if they have on three-thousand-dollar suits. You will also get rid of your gum." Venus grabbed her trash can and held it in front of Darla's face. She spit it out. "And you will start dressing like a receptionist. None of this stuff." She flicked at the faux pink fur glitter shell top, which Darla had paired with a black leather miniskirt and black boots.

Darla's cheeks turned as pink as her top. "I can dress the way I want to."

Venus brought her face close. "Sure you can. And I'll speak to Drake and get you sacked within the hour."

Darla sniffed and raised her chin. "Gerry and Drake are my cousins."

No wonder they kept this little tramp. "Good. Because there shouldn't be nepotism in a company, anyway."

Darla's eyes glazed over. "Nepo … po …"

"Nepotism. Hiring one's relatives. Bad business practice." Venus crossed her arms.

Darla looked both confused and frightened, and not sure what she was confused or frightened about.

"Get back to work." Venus was about to grab the door handle, but Esme anticipated her and opened the door for her. Darla shuffled out.

Esme closed the door behind Darla, then clapped her hands together. "You were wonderful!"

Her enthusiasm startled Venus, but after a second, she gave a small smile. "Thanks." She would have been more friendly, but her annoyance at Darla didn't quite take the place of French Roast. She dropped her purse on the floor. "About the Web director—let me get some coffee, and I'll look into it."

Esme followed her to the break room. "I haven't told anyone else about it yet except Gerry."

"Who just told everyone—oh, man!" The coffeepot was empty. Venus resisted the urge to bang it against the counter. *Deep breath. Just make more coffee. Just a few more minutes.* She reached in the refrigerator for the bag of Starbucks. "The other programmers probably already know by now. I'll talk to them about taking up the slack for the next few days. Who's next in charge?"

"Lisa."

Oh, no. "The girl Gerry was chewing out?"

Esme bit her lip and nodded.

Venus filled the pot with water. "I'll give her a few minutes and then talk to her."

"I, umm ... might have a solution?"

Venus poured the water in, then switched on the coffeepot. "I'm all ears. Got a Web director up your sleeve?"

"Uh ... actually, my friend Macy is a Web director, and she's looking for a job."

Venus whirled and stared. She remembered to close her mouth after a second. "You're kidding me."

"No."

"Is she good?"

Esme smiled. "She's very good."

"Tell her to send her resume—"

"I have it, actually. I'll email it to you."

The smell of coffee rose from the pot. Venus had to stop herself from hovering over the machine to suck up the fumes. "I'll look at it today." Could this be the answer to her problem, so easily taken care of? "Thank you *so* much."

She grinned. "Glad to be able to ease some of the stress from today."

Esme had been invaluable last week. She'd told Venus of problems immediately, fixed the ones that she could, efficiently did everything Venus asked her to, and never seemed annoyed when Venus was feeling peevish. "Esme, I couldn't have asked for a better operations manager."

It came out of her in a rush. She wasn't used to dealing with women so well—aside from her cousins, who loved her almost because they had to.

"Thanks." Her smile grew brighter.

"Where did you work before here?" Venus dragged her eyes away from the pot. Coffee in a few minutes, coffee in a few minutes...

"A small startup. It died after only a few months." Esme peeked up at Venus with shining eyes. "I heard you worked for Oomvid."

Her favorite subject. "I did."

"You were laid off?"

"No, I quit." And good riddance.

"You quit?" Esme's mouth hung open, exposing her pearly bottom teeth.

"Um ... yeah."

"Why would you ever quit Oomvid?" She said it in a tone like asking someone why they'd tear up a winning lottery ticket.

Venus paused to pick her words. The gaming community was dangerously small, and even though Bananaville wasn't a game development company, some of these programmers could switch over to the dark side one day. "I wanted the opportunity to be CTO, and I also was tired of a large company. I missed the environment of a small startup." Hey, that actually sounded rather good.

"But ..." Esme bit her lip again, making a cherry-red mark. "But it was *Oomvid.*"

"It was Oomvid, not Mecca." Ooh, her tone had been a bit sharp. "I thought and prayed a lot before deciding to quit." Did ten minutes count as praying a lot?

"Oh, well if you prayed ..."

Wow, Esme was Christian? "Do you go to church?" The coffeepot burbled, signaling the end of Venus's pain and torture. She grabbed a mug from the cabinet and poured it to the brim.

She slurped some from the edge. *Bliss.*

Esme's eyes brightened. "Oh, yes. I go to—"

"Darling!"

Venus nearly spit out her coffee. She turned to the break room doorway, where a figure in cream wool and ostentatious pearls sashayed inside.

"Mom! What are you doing here?"

FOURTEEN

I came to see my daughter!" Mom struck a pose in the middle of the break room, which would have been rather funny if it hadn't been in the break room of *her* company.

"It's a little early for you, isn't it?" Luckily, it was early for most—although not all—of Bananaville too, and the break room was empty except for her and Esme.

"Hello, dear, I'm Venus's mother, Laura Sakai." Mom's eyes had lighted on Esme, and the look in her mother's eyes made Venus gnash her teeth.

Mom used to have the same look at family parties when she greeted Venus's skinnier, prettier cousins. Not quite embarrassed of her gargantuan daughter, but not quite acknowledging familial ties with her either. Obviously admiring the other girls while trying to ignore the fact her own daughter disappointed her.

And even when that daughter became skinnier and prettier (although still not as stick-thin as aforementioned cousins), she disappointed her mother because she didn't suddenly turn into the compliant half of a picture-perfect mother–daughter duo that Mom had wanted all those years. No, Venus wasn't about to suddenly fall in with Mom's idea of how a good daughter would make *her* look.

Hence the exuberant charm exerted for Esme, who dressed in flowy feminine dresses instead of power suits with masculine lines, who stood a good six inches shorter than Venus (ten inches shorter than herself in heels), who was only twenty-five, and who had the sweet and pleasing demeanor Venus had never perfected.

"So how do you like working for Venus?" Mom's question seemed innocent, but Venus read the bite behind her words. *How difficult is it to work for Venus?* Why did Mom seem to want to embarrass her so often?

Esme, however, didn't fall for it. "Oh, she's wonderful! So efficient and organized." She gave a bright smile to Venus. "I haven't worked with anyone so professional in any of my other jobs."

Mom's sugary expression faltered.

Was she serious? Venus tended to intimidate her coworkers or incite cattiness. Esme seemed to actually *like* her. "R-really?"

Esme rolled her eyes. "I can't begin to tell you the kind of incompetence I've had to put up with."

That sounded like something Venus would say. Sunlight flickered into the dark room that was her heart. "I enjoy working with you too." What a strange feeling. She was getting along with a woman who wasn't one of her cousins.

"Well, it was nice to meet you, dear." Mom's voice cut into their fuzzy-wuzzy moment, slicing with its hard edge. "Venus, I need to talk to you."

"Fine. Let's go to my office." She turned and walked out, sipping her coffee. She did *not* want to face her mother unloaded.

Mom followed her out. "What do you mean, 'fine'? That's so rude. I thought I raised you better."

"You didn't raise me, Mom."

She sniffed. "You *chose* to live with your father."

"Because Dad never made me feel unworthy just because I was fat." She flung open her office door.

"I never made you feel unworthy." Righteous indignation, but more affronted rather than hurt by her words. Venus had no illusions about how much her mother loved her.

"You also never visited me at work or called me to go to lunch until *after* I'd lost weight." Venus shut the door behind her mother.

Why did she keep revisiting the old argument? Why did it still sting? Why couldn't she just let it go? This was completely illogical, and Venus was never illogical. Well, mostly never.

"Mom, let's just forget it. I'm glad you came by to see me." Would God forgive that lie if it was meant to make her mom feel better? Good intentions counted, right? Do unto others—she'd want someone to lie to her.

Mom's mouth still pinched, but she perched on the edge of the chair across from Venus, who sat behind her desk.

"So, Mom, what are you doing today?"

"Obviously not as much work as you." She sniffed.

Venus counted to ten. Then she did it again for good measure. "Did you want to go to lunch today?"

"No, since you're so busy."

Venus dug her nails into her thighs under the desk. "Mom, I really am busy. My Web director quit this morning, I had to reprimand an employee, and it's not even eight o'clock yet. If you're going to be difficult, you can leave now and I'll call you tonight." As soon as the words left her mouth, she realized how they sounded. Oh, no.

Mom's nostrils flared, her bosom heaved, and her back was so straight, Venus wondered if it would snap like a ruler. But she exhaled long and hard through her nose, then settled back into her seat. "I came by to ask you about a dinner party I'm throwing in a couple weeks."

"When?" Venus opened her PDA.

"Saturday the seventeenth."

Venus's stomach burbled like a sulfurous hot water spring. Oh, brother. This was going to totally hack her mom off. "I can't. *Yeh-yeh's*—I mean, Dad's father's seventieth birthday party is that night."

"So your father's family is more important than me?"

Here we go. "Mom, it's Grandpa's *seventieth birthday.* It's a big deal in Chinese culture."

"Because obviously your Chinese side is more important than your Japanese side."

Sometimes, Venus wondered who was the child and who was the parent. "I don't have time to discuss this, Mom. Did you have anything else you needed?"

"For a Christian, you're terribly mean to your own mother!" Her voice broke.

Venus squeezed her temples with her thumb and fingers, but her nails bit into the skin. She wanted to laugh and scream at the same time. Her selfish, hypocritical mother talking to her about God.

Honor your father and mother.

No, she didn't want to think about it. She didn't want to remember that verse. Sometimes she wondered if she'd spent most of her life—post-divorce, anyway—avoiding that particular commandment. It simply wasn't possible. Her mother was too much. "I'm not arguing with you, especially about a religion you know nothing about." After all, wasn't a mother supposed to love her children?

"So now you're saying I'm stupid!" Her voice rose past the whiney stage straight to hysterical. "My own daughter calling me names!"

"Mother—"

"After all I've done for you! I bore you in my body for nine months. You gave me terrible back pains and even worse, you gave me *varicose veins*!"

Venus winced at the shriek in her voice. Everyone in the building could hear her. "Mom!"

"And all I get is your smart mouth. Well, you certainly didn't get that from me. And you didn't get your hips from me either, thank goodness. No one can blame me for giving you bad genes—you got that all from your father!"

What? "Mom, everyone can hear—"

"I don't care if they hear me! They all need to know I have an ungrateful daughter who can't even come to a small dinner party. She'd rather spend the evening with an old man—"

A brisk *knock, knock* was the only warning before the door opened. Drake walked in. "Venus, I—oh, hello Mrs. Sakai." His face blossomed, and Venus's heart blipped in response even though he wasn't even looking at her. "I'm Drake Yu. I don't know if you remember me, but my mother introduced us at your mother's last Christmas party. It's so nice to see you again. You're looking well."

Mom preened and actually batted her eyelashes. "Why, thank you." Gone was the harpy of only a few seconds ago. Venus wanted to hang her head in her hands. Her mother switched moods faster than an Intel processor.

Drake touched her elbow and raised her to her feet. "I'd love to introduce you to my sister, who's the founder of the company ..."

Behind her mom's back, but visible to Drake, Venus opened her eyes wide and made a neck slashing motion with her hand. *Bad idea.*

" ... right after I get you comfortable in my office. Here, let me get the door. Can I get you some coffee? There's a wonderful Vietnamese coffee shop across the street. Let me get, uh ..."

Venus mouthed to him, *Darla.*

" ... Darla to get us some while we chat. How have you been the past year? My mom says she sees you in Japantown every so often ..." The door to her office closed behind them.

Venus deflated and plastered herself over the surface of her desk. This wasn't happening. This wasn't happening. This wasn't happening. It wasn't bad enough the Web director had quit, but she had to deal with her mother at this insane hour of the morning, only to be rescued by Drake of all people. She hadn't even finished her first cup of coffee. She really needed chocolate.

She opened her stash drawer and took out her 72% dark chocolate bar, but the bitterness made her tongue curdle. This just didn't cut it.

She forced herself to swallow more coffee instead. She'd love some Vietnamese coffee, sweet and strong enough to melt your teeth ... *No, you have more self control than that.*

The door suddenly opened and Drake walked in. "The drama queen has left the building."

"So soon?"

"Bruce Whittaker was walking out of Gerry's office just as we got into the hallway, and the two of them decided to go for coffee together."

Oh, the gray-haired man. "Excuse my ignorance, but who's he?"

"Potential investor, friend of my father."

"Ah."

Drake dug into his pocket and handed her a small orange package.

Reese's peanut butter cups. Venus almost swooned. Her mouth began to water like a bubbling mountain spring. She closed it, but that made her breathe through her nose, and the chocolaty peanut butter scent filled her sinuses and her lungs with a sugar buzz. "I don't eat chocolate."

"You need this." He dropped it on the desk in front of her.

Defying her brain, her fingers felt the crisp ridges along the edges of the packaging. "I don't eat Reese's — "

"Now you're lying."

"— anymore." He remembered? "A lot has changed. It's been six years."

"It's been five years and five months since you walked out of my office, and you were so upset with me that you left an entire box in your desk drawer."

Oops. Busted.

"You look like you're going to bite into it without unwrapping the package."

That wasn't too far from the truth. She sighed, then ripped it open.

It melted on her tongue. Salty and oh, so sweet. A little sticky, but not gooey. She groaned. She hadn't had one in *years.*

Without even asking her, Drake reached out and broke off a piece from the other cup. Popping it into his mouth, he asked, "So, that's your mother?"

She groaned an entirely different groan.

Venus couldn't look away.

Josh, a tall high school boy, clutched his stomach with one hand while the other still held the half-eaten slice of pizza. Except it was no ordinary pizza—this one had gobs of dried red pepper flakes piled on top of it. Sweat streamed down his face, and he grimaced as he chewed.

Herman sat next to him, the instigator of this agonizing "game," wincing as he gathered the courage to take a bite of his own pizza, also loaded with red pepper flakes.

First one to finish won.

The high school kids gathered around, cheering and laughing. They loved challenging Herman because he was up for anything. Including excruciating bites of food that would probably melt his intestines tomorrow.

Leaning against the wall next to Venus, Rachel huffed. "He's supposed to be my date for the Monster's Ball, and now he's going to be too sick to go! I'll kill him!"

Naomi tittered. "If the pizza doesn't kill him first."

"You actually have a Monster's Ball?" Venus studied Rachel's face to see if she was just pulling her chain.

"Well, it's just a ball where the girls dress up and the guys dress grungy." Naomi sighed, echoed by a couple of the other teens.

"And it's in a couple weeks?"

"The weekend before Halloween."

"Do you guys dress as something?"

"We try." Sarah gave a sigh that came up from her gut and emptied her lungs.

"Oh, ignore her." Rachel flapped a hand in her direction. "She's still peeved her mom wouldn't let her go as a belly dancer last year."

Venus's mouth dropped open. "Belly dancer? I don't blame her."

"It was only *three inches.* Three little inches of midriff."

"Tcha! It was more like seven or eight."

"Besides, at least you can go." Mika looked down, not meeting anyone's eyes. There was a thread of hurt in her voice that silenced the other girls, as well.

"Your parents won't let you go?" Venus didn't know what to say. She wasn't used to dealing with drama like this. Her mother's drama didn't count—most of the time, that was like spaghetti thrown at a wall. Her mother would hurl all kinds of things at Venus to see what would stick, what would provoke a reaction.

"My mom won't let me go to any dances."

"Her mom hates men," Naomi piped up. "Ow!"

Sarah had smacked her in the arm. "Dummy. You don't know if Mika wants somebody else to know that."

"Oh."

"No, it's okay." Mika had that distant look and tone that Venus recognized, trying to pretend the issue wasn't that important when in reality, it ate at her heart like battery acid. "She's been like that since Dad left."

Silence descended among them, surrounded by the cheering of the other kids as Josh and Herman ate themselves to death. The girls fiddled with their earrings, their bracelets, their rings, with stray threads on their fashionable tops, with strands of their hair. What should she say now? Venus's panic was like a silent scream in the midst of their non-chatter. She didn't have a clue on how to be warm and fuzzy.

Jenn. Her cousin was always encouraging and sweet and everything Venus was not. She'd pretend to be Jenn. "It's okay—" She put her hand on Mika's shoulder.

She shrugged it off. "No, actually, it's not okay."

The girls seemed to be all holding their breaths.

"It totally sucks." Mika spoke in a throbbing whisper. "Sometimes I just hate her for being so unreasonable. And she's so bitter and selfish and she just doesn't listen to me."

Hmm, that sounded familiar.

"And Pastor Lester always says for us to do our best to honor our parents, because that's the only commandment with a promise attached."

There it was again. The commandment had popped into her head the past few weeks at random times. "How do you honor a parent you can't even respect?"

"Exactly!" Mika's breast heaved.

Venus didn't want to encourage a griping session, but she also knew she was supposed to have some kind of answer, wasn't she? After all, she was a youth leader, and she'd read through her Bible twelve times. Shouldn't she know how to answer her, rather than asking an angst-filled question?

"It's so hard." Mika sighed. "And I've been trying so hard. But I keep getting into fights with her."

Venus couldn't even say she was trying. This fifteen-year-old girl embarrassed her with her passionate heart. Venus's faith was simply stagnant—she treated her mother the way she'd always treated her.

"Do you still want to go shopping with us tomorrow?" Naomi asked.

"Naomi!" Rachel hissed.

"It's okay." Mika sniffled. "I can at least go shopping. It's one of the few things she'll let me do."

Venus doubted Mika's mom was that restrictive. She had realized in the past few weeks that these girls liked to exaggerate.

"Venus, you want to come with?" Naomi asked.

"Me?" She looked around at their fresh, young faces. "I don't know a thing about ball dresses." She hadn't gone to her own prom, much less any other dance in high school.

"But you're always dressed nice." Rachel fingered her Banana Republic blouse.

After that first night at youth group, she'd dressed both for potential mess and with a little more style. Problem was, her closet consisted of suits, workout clothes, and loungewear she'd never walk out of her house with. Her designer jeans had cost several hundred dollars, her tops were mostly separates to go with her suits.

But they must have thought she looked okay. Maybe it was the fact the price tag on her back probably topped these girls' allowances for an entire year. "I guess ... if you guys really want me to."

"Yes!" Naomi clapped her hands. "You can help us pick out something really sophisticated."

Maybe all those fashion and gossip mags she loved weren't just mind candy—she could use the style guides to help these girls look their best.

The one person who really knew fashion was her mother.

No. No no no. She wasn't even going to consider that. She hadn't spoken to Mom—or rather, her mom hadn't spoken to her—since that day at work weeks ago. Mom wouldn't even want to see her.

No, that wasn't true. Usually her mother's moodiness ensured she didn't hold grudges for very long. If Venus proffered an olive branch, Mom would probably leap at it.

Honor your father and mother.

She'd stopped telling herself to shut up by now because it hadn't been working. It had also occurred to her that the voice might be God and not just some secret place in her head.

"Can my mom come too?" The words flew out of her mouth before she could change her mind.

The girls looked thoughtful.

"She's really good at fashion. Better than me. She'd love helping you guys." And she realized that it was true. Her mother would delight in helping each girl look stunning in just the right dress for her.

"Okay." Naomi's eyes were as luminous as Mikimotos. "I could use help because I have such big hips." She sighed and looked down at her teeny weeny torso.

Venus had never been that small, and never could be, with her bone structure. She wisely looked away before she did something dumb. Like smack her.

"I'd like to meet your mom," Mika said.

Oh, Lord, I hope this isn't a mistake.

Meanwhile, at the table, Josh shoved his last bite into his mouth and collapsed onto the floor.

FIFTEEN

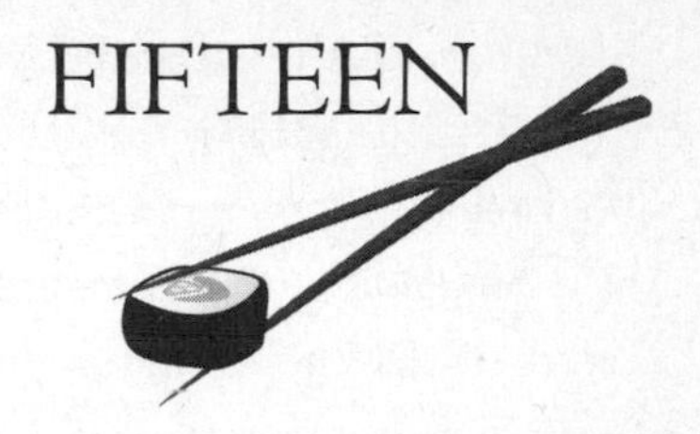

What Mom had lost out on in Venus's four years in high school, she made up for in two hours at Valley Fair Mall.

After church on Sunday, luckily, a group of boys from the youth group decided to go to the mall. Herman and Drake agreed to go, as well, which helped Venus out because she had no idea how to legally squeeze six girls into her little Beamer.

Valley Fair was packed, as usual, but they found parking. The girls in Drake and Herman's cars had been instructed to meet them at Tiffany, where Venus arranged to meet her mom. She suspected Mom would arrive early so she could do a little jewelry shopping beforehand. Sure enough, when Venus entered the store with the collected girls, a sales associate had just handed her mother a baby blue bag.

"Hello, darling. I picked up a little something. Want to see?"

The teen girls stopped their awed ogling at the glass cases and suddenly scrambled around them, as if the blue box was a magnet. Venus noted the pained expressions of the sales associates, so she hustled the girls outside the store first.

Mom delighted to show the girls the "little something"—a sapphire and diamond pendant. Venus's breath caught in her throat and stuck there painfully—not at the sight of the jewelry, but at the fact it probably cost a few thousand dollars and Grandma paid her mom's Visa bill way too often.

"Now." Mom put the bauble away. "Let's get started. This is going to be so much fun!" She beamed at the teens, the very picture of a way hip mother.

What was the point in disillusioning them?

Oh, she shouldn't be so catty. Mom had been extremely gracious about the invite to shop with six teenage girls. In typical Mom fashion, she'd pretended the argument hadn't happened. Beautiful in a flowered dress, Mom radiated maternal warmth to the girls. It contrasted the ugly scene Venus anticipated when unresolved things between them would blow up.

Why worry about it now? Mom was happy and in a good mood.

They headed down the mall, but Mom turned into a store only a few shops down from Tiffany. "Let's start here." She disappeared inside before Venus could hurry and stop her. Despite her normal languid stride, Mom could book it when doing something she enjoyed.

Venus skirted the few girls between them and lowered her voice. "Mom! This place is too expensive for these girls."

"Don't be ridiculous. Amadea's is my favorite shop. I bought that gown for Grandma's Christmas party here. They'll find wonderful dresses for their little ball."

She was doing it again—her "earplug syndrome." Well, no harm in letting the girls look around. They'd realize they couldn't afford anything pretty quick and ask to leave.

Naomi and Sarah gave a few soft squeals as they pawed through a few gowns on the rack. Rachel circled a mannequin in a cream duchess satin wedding gown.

Mika held back, her hands behind her, gazing at the gowns hanging from the wall with a look that reminded Venus of . . . herself. Fifteen years ago, in a shop like this one, with her mother. Mom had dragged Venus along while she tried on dress after dress for some party. Venus had no ball to go to, and a figure too large to wear most of the clothes with any style.

Venus approached the girl and gazed up at a gauze gown. "Too bottom-heavy."

"What?" Mika looked at her as if she'd just insulted the Queen.

"The dress. It's made for a woman with an apple shape—or rectangular. See? The belt gives the illusion of a nipped-in waist."

"I think it's pretty."

"Oh, it is. But for you ..." She pulled her over to a mannequin with a pale rose bridesmaid gown. "These satin roses"—she pointed to the blooms dotting the off-the-shoulder straps and lining the edge of the V-shaped bodice—"draw the eye toward your face and make your shoulders and bosom look larger."

Mika giggled. "The only thing that could make my boobs bigger is a water bra."

A saleswoman coughed behind her. Oh, no. Was she going to scold them for fingering the merchandise? Venus turned, head high and gaze icy, ready for a setdown, but she relaxed as she realized the woman's open smile enveloped Mika. "What would look really good on you is this." She pointed to a gown on the wall, a stunning beaded halter top gown with flowing lines draping down.

Mika sighed.

"When you get married," the saleswoman whispered, "you'll look great in something like this. The beads draw the eye, and you don't have to wear a water bra to keep it up." She winked.

Venus couldn't stop the smile cracking her cheeks as Mika drank in that gown. It was a sight to—

She stopped and stared at another gown on a mannequin next to it. "Is that a Marchesa?"

The saleswoman glanced up, her dark eyes sparkling. "We just got that in."

The cream gown had the signature romantic lines of sinuous fabric, but with ruby gems along the shoulders, in a delicate pattern at the waist, running down the skirt in narrowing swirls. The soft fabric and the twisting design would compliment Venus's hourglass figure.

Sure. If she had a few thousand dollars to burn.

"Try it on." Mika tugged at Venus's sleeve.

"No." She glanced up at the girls, who had stopped their window shopping and now stood around in a cluster in the middle of the store. The other sale associates, less friendly than this one, had gathered near the back of the store, shooting *Begone, you infidels!* looks at the teens, while an older woman chatted with her mother at the far corner. "Let's go somewhere you guys can afford."

She walked over and tapped Mom's shoulder. "We're going to another store."

Startled eyes met hers. "Why?"

"I told you already, Mom. These teenage girls can't afford these dresses." *Please, God, help her to get it this time. I don't want to get into an argument with her right here in the middle of Amadea's Boutique.*

Mom laughed, a tinkling sound that usually spelled doom for Venus in some way or another. "Don't worry. I'll buy their dresses for them."

"Mom!" Venus started at her own sharp tone, then lowered her voice. "That's inappropriate. You don't even know their parents. They won't accept that." And Grandma would fly through the roof at the Visa bill.

Storm clouds gathered in Mom's gaze, but Venus sparked some lightning in her own. "We're leaving now. You can stay if you want." Venus whirled away. "Come on, chickies."

She thought she heard a collective sigh of relief from the sale associates near the back, but didn't stop to freeze them with a White Witch glance the way she wanted to. She needed to get the girls out before Mom got it into her head to verbally promise them dresses without their parents' approval.

They paused outside Amadea's, where her mother hustled up. "You didn't have to get snippy."

Venus met her with a neutral gaze to mask her burning desire to strangle her. "Sorry, Mother. Let's go, girls."

Jessica McClintock had a better selection for their pocketbooks, and louder colors to appeal to their more youthful tastes. The girls darted from rack to rack, squealing over fabrics, designs, and nuances of shade, and Mom darted and squealed right along with them (well, okay, Mom didn't exactly squeal, but her coos were close enough).

Mika tried on a few dresses, but the brighter the gown, the more depressed she seemed. Venus wavered between asking her what was wrong and letting her deal with it on her own. In Mika's place, Venus knew she would want to mourn in peace, but other girls might not. She already knew she wasn't like most women, but she also didn't have a clue what another woman would do.

Mom finally made the decision for her. She sidled up to Venus and whispered, "Mika seems a little down, dear."

"Her mom won't let her go to the Monster's Ball with the other girls."

"Oh, that's terrible. Why don't you go talk to her? And if trying on dresses makes her feel worse, take her out to some other shops. Jewelry shops are always good." Mom's smoky purple eyeshadow had creased with the concern in her eyes.

That was a great idea. There was a small crystal jewelry shop with pretty but inexpensive pieces just down the way. "Thanks, Mom. I'll do that. I'm ... I'm glad you're here." Otherwise, Venus might have wasted time vacillating over what to do.

Her mother's smile rivaled the rhinestones in the girls' gowns, and she patted Venus's arm. Then in a flash, her attention turned back to Sarah, who had exited the dressing room with a slinky emerald satin number.

"Mika." Venus took her aside. "I'm going to the jeweler's a few stores down. Want to come with?" She almost didn't recognize herself—a few weeks in the youth group, and she sounded fifteen.

Mika's face lit up like a Swarovski figurine. "Sure."

They spent a few minutes looking at crystal earrings and necklaces set in gold and silver filigree. A little too antique-y for Venus, and apparently for Mika too—she flitted through the shop once and then stood by the open door, ready to leave whenever Venus was.

Once outside, Mika headed back the way they'd come. "Can we go back to that one store? With the wedding dresses?"

"The super expensive one? Why?"

"Do you think they'd let me try on that dress?" Her footsteps faltered. "They're awful snobby ..."

"Not that one girl." Venus grabbed Mika's arm and pulled her along. "Let's do it." And maybe she'd get up the courage to slip into that Marchesa.

The saleswoman from before greeted them as they entered. "Hi there. I didn't introduce myself before—I'm Jasmine. I was hoping you'd come back to try on those dresses."

A few of the other sale associates hung back near the dressing room doors with neutral expressions but half-lidded eyes. Venus shoved a poker down her spine and stared them down the way Audrey Hepburn would put a peon in his place in *Roman Holiday.* "We'd love to."

Jasmine collected the beaded halter top gown she'd pointed out before. Mika looked like she'd rip the dress from Jasmine's hand, until she realized the saleswoman was waiting for her to enter the dressing room.

She emerged timidly, like a little girl playing dress-up. Venus gasped. The dress was a little too large for her, and a bit too long, but Jasmine pinned the back for her and then spun her in front of the large mirrors.

Mika had aged five, ten years. Lucy Liu couldn't look more stunning in the rose-kissed cream dress, glittering with crystal beads. The halter and the flowing skirt gave more balance to her small chest and wider hips, making her body blossom.

Mika stared at her image, then screamed.

Venus and Jasmine laughed, although Venus glanced out the open doorway of the shop and saw a few passer-bys peer inside. One tired looking mother smiled at the sight of Mika lifting her skirts and twirling like Cinderella.

Venus had never cared much for dresses—she liked stiletto heels for the height and power they gave her, but she always wore pants powersuits and slacks, which straightened her curves. Skirts made her feel weak and too *feminine.* Now, watching Mika—her shoulders straighter, her chest lifted, her neck elongated and as delicate as a Lladró figurine—Venus was reminded of the mysterious world of feminine beauty, its allure, and the inner confidence it gave. Mika, in a beautiful dress, had seen and fully realized the beauty in herself—inside and out.

Venus, on the other hand, had only the outward beauty. She wasn't beautiful inside, she'd never been beautiful inside—even in her younger days, she'd been aggressive and hard-nosed. Now, she was aggressive, hard-nosed, and bitter.

She liked not being chubby and invisible anymore—she had vowed never to be invisible and overlooked ever again. But at the same time, a part of her despised the fact that she desired and liked something so shallow as her own physical appeal. Also, her new body hadn't done the miracles for her career that she thought it would—men took her less seriously, not more.

Which was why she sat on the couch to the side of the mirrors, watching Mika model like a superstar, rather than jumping into that Marchesa dress the way she wanted to. As if making her outsides look beautiful and feminine was somehow wrong.

A soft rustle, the *tink* of crystal beads, and Jasmine appeared at her side holding the dress she'd been trying not to think about. "Did you want to try this on?"

It shimmered. Venus drooled over every Marchesa gown in her fashion magazines. So strange to love a design team known for their enchantress styles, dreamy fabrics and colors, when she herself held tight to straight, simple lines and dark colors in her work clothes.

As if putting on this dress would somehow change who she was.

How ridiculous. And she looked completely idiotic sitting here, refusing to try on a confection in satin and crystal when her fifteen-year-old charge pranced around in a six-thousand-dollar wedding dress she was too young to buy.

She stepped into the dressing room, and Jasmine followed to help fasten the complicated tapes and tug at the fabric so it draped correctly. Venus kept her back to the mirror. Not for drama, but because the less time she spent looking at herself, the less vain she imagined herself to be. She swept out of the dressing room to the mirrors.

Mika's jaw fell to the floor. Jasmine's smile made her eyes almost disappear. A few of the other saleswomen gasped.

This was who she wished to be.

The dress hugged her curves like water, swirling at her feet in a waterfall of satin. Ruby beads sparkled and winked, making her hair glisten as if more beads hid in the strands. She was grace and light, powers imparted by the nature of the dress. Every movement had an elegant swish of fabric, a bright flash of crystal.

The sight took her breath away, while at the same time a part inside her scolded for how much she enjoyed being beautiful.

Her head was *so* messed up.

She wasn't used to walking slowly, so her first steps tangled in the cloth. Then she took more languid strides—reminding herself of her grandmother—letting the dress carry her, versus herself carrying the dress. She felt like the Queen of England, or a cover model, or a bride waiting for her groom.

At that moment, she looked up and out the doorway of the shop, and saw Drake frozen and staring at her.

SIXTEEN

Her heart stopped.

Her breathing stopped too, but since her heart had stopped, it didn't matter if her lungs were working or not.

He was arrested mid-step, as if he'd been passing the shop and only happened to look inside. Why had he looked in *this* shop? Why had he been walking past it at *this* moment?

Someone called his name, but he didn't turn. His eyes, even across the twenty yards that separated them, captured hers as firmly as if his hands clasped each side of her head to keep her from looking away, from retreating. She couldn't move. She couldn't breathe. She was going to pass out.

Suddenly one of the high school boys ran up to him, and he dragged his eyes away from her.

Venus picked up her skirts and escaped into the dressing room.

"You spent *how much*?"

"Daaaaad." Venus shifted the phone to her other ear as she scrubbed at her toilet rim.

"For a dress?"

"It was a *Marchesa*."

"Do you intend to get married in it?"

"It's for Grandma's Christmas party." She swiped at a lock of hair falling into her eyes and inhaled deeply the nostril-searing cleanliness of bleach. She attacked a non-existent bowl ring.

"Grandma invited you this year?"

Not everyone in the family was invited, since it was a special gathering put on by the bank. "She's going to introduce me to some people for my company."

"Oh. And you didn't have anything else you could wear?"

Grandma's Christmas parties were always formal attire. She had a simple black number she used for evening parties — floor length, unadorned, scoop neck. The opposite of the Marchesa.

But how she wanted that gown. And she felt so guilty in wanting it that she thrust it in the back of her closet as if she could convince herself she hadn't given in to her vanity and laid down quite so many thousands of dollars for it. "This dress will make me memorable. Remember? You always told me to be memorable, especially when meeting important business contacts."

He sighed. "I guess." After a short pause, "Are you cleaning your bathroom?"

"Uh ... yeah. How'd you know?"

"I hear you scrubbing."

"Oh."

"Is, uh ... everything okay?"

Venus sat up on her heels and adjusted the cordless phone closer to her ear. "What do you mean?" She tossed the sponge into her bleach and water bucket.

"Well ... you always clean the bathroom when something's wrong."

Hmph. Dad knew perfectly well she cleaned when she was upset, but in all her years living at home with him, he never said anything to her about it. This was the first time. "I'm fine, Dad." She wasn't about to discuss with him what her counselor had told her, that she went on a germ hunt every time her life felt "out of control."

"Do you need anything? Money to pay for that expensive dress?"

Dad's fix-it side was showing. "No, I don't need anything."

"So how's work? It's a computer-based company, right?"

"I had enough experience with PC games that it hasn't been a problem." Not too much, anyway. "I've got a rhythm going by now."

"How's your software coming along?"

Venus poured the bleach water into the toilet and flushed it. "I've been working on it at night. It's still having problems with MoCap data."

"Oh. That's too bad." As if her father actually knew what she was talking about. But he'd always loved listening to her about work.

"The tool worked fine with our first batch. I need new data to keep testing it, but I need to rent a MoCap studio to get it. I'll have to look around for one."

"You're working with Drake Yu. Ask him for one."

No. She didn't want to ask him for anything. She didn't even want to put herself in the same room with him alone. "Um ... maybe."

"You don't want to ask him?"

Man, why was Dad being so persistent about this? "I'll wait for a good moment."

"Well, I'll let you go."

"Okay, Dad."

"Don't forget to ask Drake about that Momo-thing. Bye."

She clicked off. She needed to shove her attraction to Drake in the back of the closet, just like the Marchesa gown. She didn't want to like him. He might have changed, but that was like buying a refurbished computer—too risky. She had more important things in her life—his sister's company, her own. No time to waste on handsome, mesmerizing, possibly still-immoral men.

She had to admit to herself that she'd never been so afraid of a man before in her life. Afraid and excited at the same time.

She didn't fear what he'd do, but what she'd do to him.

The cold South San Francisco air flapped at her cheeks as she got out of the car. She shivered, but not with chill. No one walked the cracked street, and the tall industrial buildings blocked out any sunlight on this cloudy day, casting gloomy shadows on the dirty walls and browned windows.

She prayed as she set the alarm that her car would still be here when she got back. Which hopefully wouldn't be too long—she'd called in to Darla not to expect her this morning, but Mondays were always busy, so she could expect a mountain of work when she arrived that afternoon.

But it had enabled her to avoid Drake, because she couldn't yet face him when he'd seen her in that gorgeous dress less than twenty-four hours ago.

She entered the MoCap studio, a nameless old warehouse with boarded-up windows, which she'd only found because a remnant of the building number was still painted on the curb. The metal door creaked open. "Hello?" Must, sweat, and Lysol hit her in the face. Not a pleasant combination.

A woman with platinum blonde curls hurried into the open area near the door, screened off from the rest of the warehouse with tall partitions and a few ficus trees. "We're in the middle of a session." She motioned toward the back of the building, where Venus heard grunting, running, and bodies crashing.

"I'd like to speak with Jeffrey Stuart." Venus surreptitiously tried to peek through a crack in the partition, but she only saw a glimpse of some blue gym mats set up on the floor.

"He's ... in a meeting." The blonde's gaze flickered away.

Venus narrowed her eyes and flexed a muscle in her jaw. Her feet itched to turn around and walk out. Slapped in the face with his questionable work ethic, she certainly didn't want to work with this guy, even if his studio was the closest to San Jose.

But she was desperate and short on time to finish ironing out the wrinkles in this program. She only needed a few hours, and she could pay top dollar for them. "I'll wait." She crossed her arms and studied the blonde's face.

The woman gave a sharp inhale, and the whites of her eyes flashed against her blue eye liner. In the next moment she recomposed her face, although her hands smoothed her white button-down cotton blouse with fluttering fingers. "We ... don't have anywhere for you to sit."

Venus glanced around at the sparse reception area, if the ten-foot-radial semi-circle around the front door counted as such. She sighed. "If you bring me a chair, I'll wait here."

The woman gave her first smile and hustled away to return with a plastic garden chair. Venus sat to oblige her, but as soon as she disappeared behind the partition, she got up and kicked at the bottom of a partition to nudge it aside. She situated her chair in front of the crack to watch the MoCap session.

Looked like a game or a movie. Probably a game. A man ran over the blue gym mats that covered the concrete floor, dressed in what looked like a black diving suit covered with reflective sensors. Cameras had been set up around the blue mat area—Venus counted twenty. Hmph. The website mentioned thirty-two cameras, which was what she needed. Jeffrey Stuart better have an extra twelve cameras stashed somewhere in this warehouse.

She craned her neck to catch a glimpse of the computer setup in the corner. The technician sat like a king behind his wall of equipment. Venus squinted, but couldn't see it any more clearly. She'd ask Jeffrey to give her a tour later.

The actor in the MoCap suit now walked over to where a huge blue mattress lay in a corner. A few men directed him, discussing with the technician. Venus strained to hear but only got her earring tangled on a screw protruding from the edge of the partition when she leaned close. Good thing she hadn't punctured her skull on that thing.

They took forever to figure out what they were doing, to adjust cameras so they'd pick up the sensors on his suit better. Venus took her latest issue of *InStyle* magazine out of her purse and flipped through it while they discussed the action being recorded. After more gestures, they seemed to have decided what to do. Venus put down her magazine.

The man walked a few yards back from the mattress, then did a running leap. He held both hands out as if he were firing twin guns at a target to the side of the mattress, before landing in a heap.

Venus heard his shoulder pop even from where she sat. *Ouch.*

People ran toward the poor guy from all directions. Venus sighed. Game over.

She checked her watch. It had already been twenty minutes? She dropped her magazine back in her purse. The warehouse couldn't be that large. She'd go in search of Jeffrey's office. Everyone seemed to be focusing on the injured actor, so she could probably sneak around without being caught seeing anything she wasn't supposed to.

She peered around the partitions. Doors lined one side of the warehouse, while the majority of space had been used for the MoCap studio setup. No one in sight.

Most offices had the old-fashioned glass-paned doors, so she glanced in as she walked past. Some doors were ajar. Nobody home, in any of them.

Oh, wait. The last office held a man seated at his computer with his back to the closed door. He apparently hadn't heard the anxious calls from other people rushing to the injured actor. No name on the door. She drew up to the window in the door to see if he had a name plate somewhere on his desk.

She didn't *mean* to glance at his computer screen. In fact, she tried really hard not to, because she didn't want to view anything proprietary and hush-hush. But something about the movement on the screen reminded her of some animations she had seen done, and she leaned sideways to get a better view around the man's head.

Terrorwars III. No way! She hadn't worked on that game, but she'd known the other Game Lead at Oomvid, and she'd seen the animators and programmers working on it.

It wasn't out yet. Oomvid had paid megabucks to hype up the release, especially since it had been almost two years since *Terrorwars II* had come out.

This was an advanced copy. *Way* advanced. No one except Oomvid employees had access to this game.

Well, apparently not anymore.

Then she caught a gleam on the desk, and a tumbled name plate. *Jeffrey Stuart.*

And suddenly, Venus understood everything.

She turned the knob and slammed into the room. "You slime."

Jeffrey jumped in his ergonomic chair and whirled around. Confusion dotted his pale eyes for a second, but then they relaxed into a half-lidded perusal of her person, from head to toe. "What can I do—"

Venus stabbed a finger at his computer screen. "That's what Yardley promised to you if you'd refuse to rent the studio to me."

His mouth cracked open, making him look a bit like a largemouth bass, while his eyes darted from the computer, to Venus, to the computer again. "Uh ..." Then his backbone solidified, and he rose to his feet. He tried to stare down his nose at her, even though he stood at least six inches shorter. "I can rent out my studio to whomever I choose."

Maybe she could still get her way. "Look." Venus approached him, slowing her walk to something less intimidating. She casually propped a hip against the edge of his desk. "You've already got the advanced copy of the game. You could still rent the studio to me."

Jeffrey's eyes had wandered between her mouth and her chest, but he gulped before answering her. "They also promised ... overflow work." He tried to look brave, but only succeeded in looking like a rabbit about to be pounced upon.

"Oh for crying out loud!" Venus slammed her palm against the desk. "You're not one of Yardley's cabana boys. I only need a few hours."

Jeffrey had shot up almost a foot. He retreated from her fierce gaze by picking up a pen with trembling hands and fiddling with it, not looking at her. "We don't want your business, Miss Chau."

The way he said her name made Venus feel a hundred years old and senile. She leaned down and shot flaming crossbow bolts into his balding skull. "I am going to tell every project lead I know about how your studio does things." She had the satisfaction of watching his cheeks pale, then burn pink.

"Go ahead. I still won't rent to you." His voice quivered, but he managed to keep her gaze this time, albeit with lots of blinking.

She walked out before she decked him.

Her fists clenched at her side, making her manicure dig into her palms. The pain kept her from punching the wall as she passed the other office doors.

She shouldn't be surprised Yardley would do this. A man unscrupulous enough to try to steal her program would certainly want to keep her from using that program to create a rivaling game.

He was stupid if he thought she'd take this lying down. This would only fire her resolve. She slammed the front door on her way out. She'd show him. She'd create the best game and blow his sorry butt out of the water. She'd shove it in his face—

Wait a minute, where was her car?

She'd parked it right there. She knew she wasn't mistaken. Did someone steal her car? In broad daylight in South San Francisco? She ran across the street, each step like burbles of boiling water in her gut. *Where was her car?* She hadn't left anything important in it, right? No laptop, no papers. Nothing anyone would want to steal aside from the fact it was a BMW convertible left in a seedy manufacturing district.

Too late, she saw the dented pole with the faded, bent red and white sign, *No parking at any time.*

The boiling water went nuclear. Venus screeched and kicked at the curb.

All it got her was a broken stiletto.

SEVENTEEN

Venus, where have you been— "

"Not now." Venus almost knocked her palm into Esme's face as she limped through the doors into work. She didn't want to listen to Esme's perfectly reasonable questions when she herself felt as pleasant as if she'd gone dumpster diving.

She smelled like that oil-drenched, grimy towing yard. She also smelled like the tobacco the tow truck driver had been chewing as he talked (and spit) at her, giving her the paperwork to fill out. Limping on her broken heel had made her hips start to ache, as if the inferno headache frying her brain wasn't enough.

"Are you ok— "

"Not now." Venus pushed past her and wound her way down the hallway to her office.

Drake walked out of his sister's office, saw her and stared.

Venus glared back. *"What?"* She started to march past him but felt ridiculous in her heel-less state and pulled both shoes off before stalking down the hallway.

She sensed rather than heard Esme behind her as she turned into her office. No rest for the wicked. And she'd most certainly said and thought a lot of words God would not approve of while getting her car back.

Venus crashed into her desk chair and looked up at Esme, who was hovering but trying not to seem like she was hovering. "Esme, I'm not mad at you, I'm just a little stressed."

Esme sighed. "Oh, good."

"Go get a cup of coffee, and come back to me in twenty minutes. Not a second sooner. I don't care if someone is bleeding *and* burning. You will not disturb me. Understood? And shut the door on your way out."

She dropped her head and dug her fingers into her forehead. The click of the door released a pent-up breath, but her next inhale only got her a lung full of diesel fuel fumes from her blouse.

Why was this happening to her? She read her Bible every day. She prayed every day. She went to church every Sunday. She had even started working with the youth group—with *kids!*—and this was the circus her life became.

She bent to pick up her shoes from the floor. Three hundred dollars, but now only fit for the trash after walking all over South San Francisco. She would have wept, but the very sight of them reminded her of her aching hips, her aching feet, her aching head, and the gas-related smells that accompanied it all. She tossed them in the circular file.

Breathe, Venus. Get back in control. Except lately her life resembled Black Friday sale day with too many pairs of shoes spilling out of her arms.

Knock, knock. The door opened.

Venus slammed her palms against her desk. "I said, not even if someone is bleeding and burning—"

Drake stopped halfway into her office. He regarded her with raised eyebrows.

Venus kneaded her fingertips into her temples. "Now is not a good time."

"I gathered that." He came in and shut the door, tossing a file onto her desk. "How about bleeding, burning, and crashing?"

"What's crashing?" She opened the file.

Drake caught sight of the shoes in her trash bin. He picked up the heel-less wonder. "I'd hate to see the other guy."

"Very funny." She scanned the papers. "The system's not supposed to crash—"

"I'll tell it the next time we're out for coffee."

Venus checked to make sure he hadn't sprouted a flowerpot out of his head. "You are just begging to get decked, aren't you?" He had that infuriatingly calm look on his face.

He shrugged and dropped her shoe back in the can.

"Why did they use this patch for the code?" She stabbed at the paper. "EBF 4.0 is too new."

He bent over to look. "They said you told them to use that version EBF."

Venus resisted the urge to bark and growl. "Who are you going to believe, me or them?"

"Venus, stop being defensive." His neutral expression never changed, although his voice hardened.

She couldn't *not* be defensive. Whenever something went wrong in other companies, she was the first to be blamed as lead programmer and as a woman. She *expected* to be blamed, so she went on the attack instead. He knew this. He'd worked with her. She continued skimming the papers so she wouldn't have to answer him.

A tentative *knock, knock* at the door, then Esme's voice trembling behind it. "I know you said not to disturb you, but things are *crashing* . . ."

Venus wrinkled the papers in her fists to prevent her hands from flinging them up in the air. "No one is listening to me."

Drake laughed. *Laughed!* "You're CTO. Get used to it." He walked to the door and opened it.

Esme's cheeks bloomed English rose red at the sight of him. "Oh, I'm sorry, Drake. I didn't know you were having a meeting."

"We were discussing the *crashing*."

Venus started at his tone. Was he actually being sarcastic?

"Oh, good." Esme heaved a sigh and smiled sweetly at him, serene and beautiful, so relieved she didn't have to break the news herself to that horrible Gorgon, Venus.

Venus made an effort to cool down, be nice for a change. After all, it wasn't Esme's fault. Or Drake's, if she was being perfectly honest.

"Do you know why the programmers used this EBF version?" She held out the papers toward Esme and tapped her nail against the offending section.

Her brow wrinkled, and her pink lips parted. "You told them to."

"Why would I tell them to use version 4.0? It hasn't been through Q&A testing yet."

"But . . ." Esme's mouth formed a confused O. She flipped through the leather folio in her hand, and then showed her notes to Venus. "You told me to tell them this." She pointed to a line. *Use version 4.0j EBF.*

The perfectly legible handwriting instructed her to tell the programmers to use the exact EBF version they'd used. Venus grabbed the folio to look closer at the notes. Had she been half-asleep when she told Esme to do this? This was completely stupid. But it was right there in black and white.

Something inside her cracked like the melted sugar crust on top of a crème brulee. How could she have done something so incredibly wrong? She never made mistakes like that. Not on something so elementary.

Drake pulled the folio from her fingers and scrutinized it, brow furrowed. "You said this?" Even he couldn't quite believe it.

An icy boulder crashed in the pit of her stomach. "I . . . I must have." She braced herself. Drake was going to go ballistic the way he had done in past meetings, loud yet cold, like the roar of an avalanche against an arctic cliff. And it would crash over her while she tried to stand tall and proud and take it like a man.

He tossed the folio back on her desk, where it plopped and slid a few inches. Her tense muscles jolted. She wouldn't let herself close her eyes—she kept them trained on his expressionless face, waiting for the blow.

He cast her a cursory glance. "Fix it."

She kept her eye on his profile. She had expected it to come, and it hadn't.

He turned to look at her. "What?"

"That's it?"

"What's it?"

"I'm waiting for nuclear detonation."

A smile creased the corner of his mouth before his eyes slid to Esme, a wide-eyed onlooker, and he wiped his humor away. "Just fix it." He turned and exited her office.

Venus stared at the empty doorway. That's it? That's all he said? That couldn't be all. He was as much as, if not more of, a control freak than she was. Five years ago, he'd have exploded, then pored over the code with her, demanding changes as he went.

This man was a complete stranger to her.

Esme stood with lips pressed primly together, hands clasped in front of her. She exuded a faint aura of frustration, or disappointment. At what? That Venus hadn't gotten into more trouble? How ridiculous. Now she was being completely stupid.

She stood and handed the folio back to Esme. "I'll talk to the programmers. Is there anything else I need to see before I do that?"

Esme's face blipped back to her habitual cheer. "No."

She sighed. "Good."

She padded down the carpeted hallway toward the other end of the building, where the programmers held court. She stepped gingerly, even though she knew it wouldn't cause fewer germs to adhere to her bare feet. She almost wished she'd worn hose, if only to give her another barrier between the dirt and her toes. Maybe she shouldn't have thrown away her shoes ... no, her aching hips wouldn't have let her limp around much longer. She could have used the antiseptic wipes in her desk drawer or her purse, but what was the use? She'd have to walk somewhere else and would get dirty again.

Eeeek! Cold stabbed up the soles of her feet from the concrete floor of the large room where the programmers' cubicles were set up. It didn't help that the programmers kept the temperature sub-arctic because the computers ran so hot. She skittered to Macy's cubicle.

The Web director wasn't there. She peeked next door into Lisa's cubicle. "Where's Macy?"

Lisa looked up at Venus, then her eyes slid away. "She told Darla she had a doctor's appointment today."

Something about that wording made Venus a little uneasy, but her feet were getting frostbite and crashing programs had priority over strangely worded answers. "Esme told me about the wrong patch. Did I really tell you to use EBF 4.0?"

"Actually ..." Lisa swiveled back and forth in her rolling computer chair. "Esme was the one who gave us the instructions on that. At the time I thought it was a bit strange, and I asked her if she was sure. I remember thinking it was odd that she didn't consult her notes when she repeated her answer."

Venus stilled, feeling like the megawatt air conditioning had frozen her into an ice sculpture. Sometimes the fact she worked with all women made her suspicious of cattiness when there wasn't any. Cattiness, that is. Lisa's hazel eyes seemed earnest. Maybe she was a good actress? Because why would Esme do anything suspicious? Bananaville was her company too, not just Gerry's or Drake's or Venus's.

Venus put on her professional face. "What's important now is how long it'll take you to fix it. We need to use version 3.0p instead—Q&A just finished testing it last week."

"We'll start right now." Lisa hesitated. "Will you email Macy about the changes? That way she'll know it's from you."

Again, that odd wording. If Venus were a more touchy-feely boss she'd probably understand it. Trish picked up social cues better than she did—she made a mental note to ask Trish about it when she got the chance.

"We'd better go over this before I have you make changes." She leaned over to peek inside Macy's empty cubicle again. "I wish she were here. Maybe I should wait so you don't have to go over it again with her to get her up to speed."

"No, no." Lisa stretched a hand out as if she were afraid Venus would take off. "It's okay. I'd rather you go over it with me, anyway. Prevents ... um, miscommunication."

Okay, even Venus caught that one. "What kind of miscommunication do you have with Macy?"

"Nothing. I love working with her." But Lisa didn't elaborate, and what was more, she didn't even crack a smile. Venus stared hard at her, but she simply blinked up at her from her chair.

Well, if she didn't want to talk, Venus couldn't strap her to a rack and torture her. It was actually rather refreshing to talk to someone who didn't want to gossip.

They went over the code to be fixed, and Venus tried to contain her dismay at the scope of what needed to be done. Lisa cowered under Venus's scowls, despite the fact she repeatedly assured Lisa she wasn't upset with her. Lisa's spinelessness began to annoy Venus as much as the consequences of her mistaken instructions to the programmers.

They both winced at an entire screen of code. Venus finally closed her eyes, wondering if it would go away if she prayed really hard.

"Venus, there you are."

She jumped—literally had some hang time—at Drake's voice behind her. Not just because she was startled, but also because he'd take one look at the code on the screen and start yelling at them both. Lisa must have picked up on her anxiety, because she bit her lip and dipped her head.

Drake paused as he took in the page of code that had formed the posse crashing and burning the system that morning. The silence thickened like Jenn's egg drop soup when she added cornstarch.

He exhaled long and low. Venus didn't want to actually edge away from him, but she couldn't help shifting her weight to the leg farthest from him and leaning way back.

But his expression never shifted from curious and thoughtful. He leaned down. "There's an easy way to fix this." He opened another application.

Venus stared at the stranger bent over Lisa's computer. No temper? Not even an icy glance or a cold, sarcastic comment? Was he actually calmer than *she* was?

She straightened and frowned at his indecently broad back. They'd always both been driven, but she'd at least prided herself on the fact she had softer feelings than he did. Maybe that early heart attack had mellowed him in more ways than one. Had he really had a complete attitude adjustment?

Without turning his head, he remarked, "I left something for you on your desk."

Another emergency? More work? "I should probably stay—"

"I'll take care of this."

He couldn't have dismissed her more firmly than if he'd turned her around and given her a boot in the butt. Hmph. She glanced at Lisa. He seemed in a good mood—it might be safe to leave her with him. "Fine." She swiveled—hard to do dramatically in bare feet with toes about to fall off from the cold—and marched out. She missed the firm clacking noise she could have made with her stilettos to signal her displeasure.

She tried stomping down the hallway, but the carpet muted her striking heels, and it hurt, besides. *Stop being such a baby. Be grateful he didn't throw a fit. Why are you so mad?*

She didn't know. And she hated that she didn't know. She was angry at Drake for some unknown reason, and she was angry at herself for being so illogical.

She slammed into her office. What the heck was that on her desk? She flipped on the overhead lights.

A pair of Michael Kors pumps, glossy brown leather with gold metal trim. She'd seen them at Neiman Marcus last week.

Drake had bought her shoes.

EIGHTEEN

Venus arrived at church on Saturday night, ready to demolish a few egos. Most notably, Drake's.

That is, if her jeans button didn't pop off in the middle of the video game competition. Working with Drake had made her so stressed, she'd eaten way too many Reese's peanut butter cups lately. It was all his fault. Which was why she intended to play him like an iPod.

For once, all the kids had arrived on time because David had warned that no one would be allowed to enter the competition if they arrived after seven o'clock.

A couple high school boys were talking near the door when she entered. "Venus!" Timmy did a few shadow boxing moves. "Ready to rumble?"

Josh laughed. "Dude, Venus will take you out."

The door behind her opened and Drake entered. He saw her—specifically, he got an eyeful of her jeans—and paused.

Venus's cheeks heated faster than her coffee in the microwave. Drake rarely saw her in anything other than suits at work and slacks at youth group, and these jeans were a bit tighter than normal. Did she look that fat?

"You look really good, Venus."

She blinked. "What?"

"You were looking too skinny for a while, there."

"What?" Her hot cheeks prickled. She could swear she saw sparklers shooting out from her eyes.

He gave her a bland smile while the high school boys gaped. *No one* spoke to her the way Drake did. Well, no one spoke that way and *lived* except for him.

"I'm just saying you look sexy rather than twiggy."

"*Twiggy?* Sexy? We're at church—don't use the S-word in front of the guys." She flapped a hand in their direction and hit somebody's nose, eliciting an "Ow!"

Timmy spoke up. "I already know all about s—" Chris smacked him in the arm, hard.

Drake cast a casual eye over the guys. "If they don't learn at church about God's intention for sex, where would you rather they hear about sex—from their friends?"

Venus opened her mouth, but then closed it again. She was saved by David's call down the hallway, "All contestants gather in the Social Hall!"

As they headed toward the Social Hall, Drake leaned close. "Winner buys dinner."

His silky voice tingled at the base of her neck, but despite the prancing of her heart, she stepped away from him. He made her uncomfortable; she didn't want to like him, and this was just weird. "Winner buys *Xenon's Revenge* when it releases next month."

He didn't press. "You're on."

She felt safer, but a bit disappointed too. *Stupid.*

"Okay guys, here are the rules." David peered at the paper in his hand. "Everybody who signed up will be assigned a random opponent for the first round. This is single elimination"—his voice rose as kids protested—"because we have so many people playing. Quit yer whining."

The murmur went on for another few seconds before he continued. "Be careful with the game consoles. One belongs to the church, but five belong to me and the other guys." He nodded to some high schoolers and a few junior highers.

"There are six stations set up around the church. Each competition will be assigned to a station. No complaining about who gets the big TV here"—he jerked his thumb at the gigantic 73-inch HDTV in the Social Hall—"and the projector screen in the sanctuary. It's all random. *Comprendez?*"

He gave them a few seconds to vent their spleen, then continued. "We chose *Psycho Bunny* so the junior highers' parents won't throw a hissy fit, but it's challenging enough for the high schoolers. Plus, we could get six copies of it for the six stations."

He had to shout as the kids talked and the volume rose. "If you haven't put your name in with Kat, do it now!" Venus hustled over to where Kat sat with her laptop, ready to input names and randomly generate the first round lineup.

Venus played against Timmy for her first game in the 1st and 2nd grade Sunday school room. She trounced him in seven minutes.

"Veeeenus." He sighed and placed a dramatic hand over his chest. "No mercy?"

"Nope."

She had to wait for her next round, so she sat beside the high school girls in the sanctuary pews, where they watched two junior highers face off. "You guys aren't playing?"

"Naomi was, but she lost."

"We came for moral support."

"Except she doesn't need it anymore."

Venus glanced around the sanctuary. "Did Mika come?"

"She's outside talking on her cell with her mom," Naomi said in a hushed voice.

Venus sat up straighter. "Is she okay?"

"I'm not sure, they were talking in Japanese."

"But it sounded like maybe Mika was in trouble."

"But her mom drove her here tonight, so it must not be that bad."

And with that comforting thought, they turned their attention back to the game on the projector screen. Venus sighed. She'd never understand teenagers.

Well, even if they weren't concerned, she was. She got up a bit abruptly and aimed for the side doors, blinking in the darkness after the bright lights. From somewhere, Mika's voice spat out Japanese sentences like bullets.

Venus turned the corner of the building to see the slim girl pacing back and forth, head bent as she listened to her cell phone, other hand gripping her hip. She paused when she saw Venus, eyes wide, mouth stretched. She whirled away with a swirl of her ponytail.

Venus headed back inside. Who was she kidding? It wasn't as if she was motherly. What could she hope to do for a girl having parent problems? She barely remembered to be civil to her own mother most days.

She returned just in time to be called for her second match, this time against Chris. She demolished him in thirteen minutes.

He stared stupefied at the TV in the junior high Sunday school room as she set her controller down. Then he pointed a finger at her. "You are no fun." But he grinned as he said it, flashing his newly installed braces.

She passed several games on her way to report her victory to Kat. She was impressed at the skill of some of the other kids. It was a while down the road, but maybe testers for her game ...

One junior high girl squealed as she beat a high school boy. The boy good-naturedly groaned and flung himself backward on the ground while his friends ragged him with laughing and pointing. The girl giggled and crowed. Other junior high girls did Snoopy dances for her.

Venus paused, watching the innocent play. She couldn't possibly give her violent shooter game to these kids. Never. It would be like taking them into an NC-17 movie.

But she also knew kids their age would get hold of the game—via friends or relatives—and play it anyway. She'd make tons of money. While corrupting children.

She continued down the hallway. She couldn't control stuff like that. It was that way with any game in the industry.

The difference was, it would be that way with *her* game. With something she'd developed and brought into being. Her game concept of a *SOCOM* with sexy all-female players would fit right into the market, and she knew she'd make a killing, but suddenly the realization of what she was doing made something writhe inside her, like a dormant dragon. Her shoulders tensed as she shuddered.

Kat glanced up at her with raised eyebrows. "That was fast."

Venus buffed her nails against her shirt. "When you're good, you're good."

Kat laughed as she inputted the win in the computer. "Your next bout won't start for a while, sorry."

Venus's eyes turned unwillingly toward the side door. No, Mika was probably still on the phone. And what if she wasn't? What could Venus say to her—"Sorry your mom is being a pain"? Or some pat answer like, "Give your burden to God and He'll give you strength and peace." Oh, please. Trish or Jenn would know what to say, but Venus was used to barking orders, not comforting hormonal teenagers.

So what did she do? Headed out the side door, naturally.

This time, she followed the sniffling sounds around the corner. Mika leaned against the stucco wall, gripping her pink cell phone, head bowed. Venus hesitated. Would she want company or not? Venus herself usually wanted cave time so she wouldn't bite someone's head off.

Apparently Mika wasn't Venus, because she raised her head and regarded her through reddened, wet eyes. Her lips drooped like roses in the rain. She sniffed again, still regarding Venus, still not saying whether she wanted her to go away or give her a hug.

Ugh, maybe she wanted a hug. Venus was *so* not a huggy person. But this was a teenage girl, and she'd just fought with her mother, and Venus tried to imagine what she'd feel like if she were ... well, emotional. Like Trish—Trish was always emotional. Okay, if she were Trish and had stormed off the phone with her mom. Yeah, not a pretty sight. Mika probably wanted a hug.

Oh, man.

Venus forced herself to reach out a hand toward Mika's shoulder.

Mika sobbed and buried herself in Venus's generous bosom. The feel of bony arms around her and a damp face against her chest made her spine straighten and her arms to become like tree branches. *Breathe ... relax ...* She awkwardly put her hands on Mika's back and patted lightly.

Mika cried for a long time. A very long time. Tears soaked through Venus's shirt until her bra became damp, which made her cringe a little, but what was she going to do, pull away from this hysterical child and say, "Sorry, this bra is saturated"?

Finally, her tearful symphony began a decrescendo. "M-my mom hates me." She spoke into Venus's shirt.

Good, Mika was talking. Venus felt the earth right itself under her feet. Sane, communicative individuals she could deal with. She solved problems all the time at work. "She doesn't hate—"

"Nothing I do is ever good enough for her."

"I'm sure you're—"

"She told me I didn't practice enough violin today. I practiced for two hours!" Mika wailed and snuffled into Venus's shoulder.

Ew. Don't think about the snot. "Two hours is—"

"She doesn't make my brother practice that long, but that's 'cause he's a *boy*." She said *boy* like *idiot.*

"Well—"

A voice roared in her head—sounding a bit like Drake, to be honest—telling her, *Venus, shut up.*

She shut up. She wasn't sure if it was really a message from God, but if she was reduced to yelling at herself, she better listen.

Mika's tears grew stronger. "I hate first generation Japanese parents! They're so demanding, and they only want their own way, and they won't listen to you!"

Which sounded an awful lot like second generation Chinese fathers and second generation Japanese grandmothers (but not so much like irresponsible, third generation Japanese mothers). It probably would have been a lot like Venus's first generation Chinese grandparents, except she didn't know enough Cantonese to understand about 50 percent of what they were saying to her every time she went over to their house—she was lucky she knew enough Chinese to order at a restaurant.

"And I don't know why I'm taking violin lessons when I don't even like playing it, but my parents make me take lessons because my cousins all play in regional competitions."

Venus was about to say she could relate to that, but remembered to keep her trap shut.

"And they don't understand that this is America! Americans don't eat all that *tsukemono* and *gobo* and *tako.*"

And *tong sui*, and *bao yu,* and *lop cheong.*

"I can't bring home any of my friends to eat that stuff! They'd totally puke!"

Trust me, honey, if they're Chinese, they've probably eaten worse.

Mika started off on other things that sounded vaguely familiar to Venus, probably because she'd heard her Japanese cousins talk about them. Being raised mostly by her Chinese father had apparently spared her from horrors like *uni* and *takuwan* and *obon* dances.

She was getting the hang of this. All she had to do was provide a shirt-sized Kleenex for her tears, an occasional pat on the back, and ears to listen to sobbing and ranting. No advice or solution required of her.

She was starting to feel like a real *girl.*

She heard the side door slam, and she shifted to protect Mika from whoever approached.

Kat's voice sounded from behind her. "Venus? Your next bout is ready. It's against Drake."

The primary reason she'd come tonight, to serve him humiliation and defeat on a silver platter. Or at least on a 73-inch HDTV.

Mika shuddered against her sopping wet blouse.

Venus hesitated only a half-second. "I'm forfeiting, Kat."

"Are you sure?"

Venus wondered if she could get a friend who worked at Mega-Media to give her a free copy of *Xenon's Revenge* when it released next month. "Yes."

Kat's footsteps padded away. For a moment, Venus thought she heard a second set of footsteps. But then the side door closed, and she was left with Mika in the silence of the evening.

Drake followed Kat back into the church. Venus hadn't looked around—she had curled protectively around the high school girl who had been clutching at her like an octopus.

If he hadn't seen it with his own eyes, he wouldn't have believed it. Venus, with the nasty reputation of being the most difficult and most successful programming lead in the video game industry, comforting a young girl. Venus, who had *kahones* of steel that Drake couldn't even find in other men he'd worked with.

But hadn't he seen her change in the months they'd been working with this youth group? Hadn't he himself felt different as he sat and listened to the boys in his small group answer the Bible questions? They were typical teenaged boys, but their earnestness to do right, their inner confidence, was something he hadn't felt at their age. He hadn't even felt it in his early years as CEO of various gaming companies. Not until his heart attack.

He'd joined this church and this youth group to oblige Gerry, who had insisted he work with her church youth program rather than a local, non-Christian program. He didn't do much—Herman ran the small groups, asked the questions on the sheets typed up each week. All Drake did was listen as the boys answered. Yeah, the answers were painfully obvious, but the boys loved and respected Herman, loved and respected the words they read in those tattered pew Bibles.

Drake still couldn't understand why. What was there in those words that he couldn't see?

It had something to do with Venus comforting a crying girl, when she could have been inside waiting for their match-up. He wasn't surprised she'd forfeited, considering the circumstances, but he couldn't believe she'd been out there in the first place, giving a girl a hug when she barely tolerated being touched in a handshake.

He wasn't at the point where he'd answer the next altar call in Sunday service, but maybe he'd listen a bit more to Pastor Lester as he paced on the low dais at the front of the church. The man often spoke so fast he didn't finish his sentences, but he always had a point—and lately, those points had been uncomfortable barbs in Drake's side.

NINETEEN

"What do you mean I can't take the rest of the day off?" Venus, leaning against Drake's oak desk, smacked the heel of her hand against it. "I've handled three emergencies this morning. Three!"

"I need you here." He'd risen from his chair so that he also hunkered over his desk, his eyes darkening to teak and staring her down. Good thing she'd worn her four-inch heels today instead of her three-inchers.

"I need to take a personal day."

"To use your own phrase, you're not 'bleeding or burning.'"

"It's called a personal day because it's *personal.*" If she told him the real reason, he might blow the top off his salt-and-peppered head.

"It has to do with your company."

Busted. "The system is not going to crash in the next eighteen hours—"

"I need you here because of our sponsors—"

"They don't have to worry."

"I need you here today—"

"We'll go live in two months, right on schedule—"

"Venus, shut up and listen to me."

She shut up, but she also straightened and stuck her hands on her hips. It brought her eye level with him and a little farther away from his ire-filled glare.

"Nickelodeon is coming today."

"What? I thought they were supposed to come next week."

"They called today to reschedule. They have questions about the system and I need you there to answer them."

There were some things Drake couldn't answer for her. "How close to a decision are they?"

"They'll decide about sponsorship after we meet with them today."

Oh, no pressure at all. Venus walked to the large picture window and frowned at the leafless trees in the tiny parking lot. "Why do the biggest sponsors come on the rare days I actually have other things to do?"

"What is so important about your appointment?"

Venus glanced over her shoulder at him, mouth open. Maybe? No. She turned back to the parking lot.

His long-suffering sigh reverberated down her spine. The creaking of his chair wheels told her he'd sat back down. "I promise I won't get upset."

Maybe he wouldn't. He'd certainly proven enough times that his volcanic temper had gone at least partly dormant. "I'm meeting with an animator."

Drake tilted back his head so he could shoot sparks at the ceiling. "You can't reschedule *that?*" Maybe not completely dormant.

"She worked with Jaye before. We're thinking of bringing her on board to help test the tool."

"Is she coming from out of town or something?"

"No."

"Again, you can't reschedule?" Like it was the most obvious thing to reschedule a meeting with a potential business partner in favor of a multi-million-dollar sponsor for *his* company. Well, put like that...

"She might be able to get us MoCap data to test the tool with." Hopefully original data and nothing illegally obtained so they wouldn't face a lawsuit down the road.

Drake looked at her as if she'd sprouted a monitor instead of a head. "And that's important, why?"

"Considering how hard it's been for us to get MoCap data, she might be worth her weight in Intel processor chips."

A knock on the door. Darla stuck her head in. "Venus, Maria Kress is here to see you."

"Show her to my office—"

Drake shot to his feet. "Nickelodeon is scheduled to arrive—"

"I'm only going to reschedule, okay?" Venus flung her arms out. Her fingers itched to grab her shoe off and brain him with her heel.

A brassy voice sounded from the hallway. "I'm here to see Venus Chau."

Someone's soft voice answered, "She's in Drake's office, number twelve."

A second later, someone shoved Darla aside and knocked open the door. "Venus, I'm Maria."

She seemed to pose in the doorway, reminding Venus of her mother at dinner parties. The first thing she noticed was that Maria was practically falling out of her halter top. The next thing was that Maria's eyes had swept the office before riveting on Drake. Rose pink lips parted and smiled at him. "Hello."

Venus mentally flexed her claws. Maria had that indefinable confidence in her sex appeal that Venus had never been able to mimic, that absolute comfort in her own skin which Venus still couldn't achieve. Venus felt gawky next to her, plain-faced and trying to disguise it with makeup whereas Maria shone with natural color. Venus's rear end had suddenly expanded another few inches as she stared at Maria's slim hips and long legs. And Maria's fresh, friendly smile contrasted with Venus's dark mood.

Maria extended a graceful hand to Drake, which he automatically clasped. "So pleased to meet you." She made it seem like a caress.

Venus gritted her teeth.

Drake, however, dropped her hand rather more abruptly than was polite and coolly nodded toward Venus. "Your appointment's with *Venus,* not me." She could almost read his mind—*Do I look like a Venus to you?*

"Oh." Maria's eyes widened, and she touched the tips of her fingers to her lips, drawing attention to them. She laughed, a self-deprecating yet sensual sound. "So sorry."

Drake raised an eyebrow at Venus and jerked his head toward the door. *Intend to get her out of here anytime soon?*

Drake wasn't responding to this woman's hypnotic spell? Was that even possible? Venus broke from her stupor, but not before exchanging a bewildered glance with Darla. "Maria, something came up— "

"Actually, I already hired an animator and didn't tell Venus." Drake suddenly reached out to reclasp Maria's hand and gave her a warm, apologetic smile that didn't reach his eyes. "I'm so sorry. It was my fault entirely."

Luscious lips formed a petal-soft O. "Do you still need the MoCap data?"

"Nope." With an over-bright smile, Drake darted out from behind his desk and turned her toward the door with a firm hand on her shoulder. He nudged Darla aside as he ushered Maria out of his office.

"But I came all this way." Even Maria's pout was lovely.

"Sorry about that. I'm a jerk to work for, anyway. Good-bye!" He closed the door as soon as she cleared the threshold.

Venus and Darla both choked, trying not to laugh while Maria still stood outside the office in the hallway. Then Venus stuck a finger out at him and hissed, "I still need an animator."

"You didn't want her, right?" Drake made sure to pitch his voice low.

"I don't have any other candidates."

"I'll help you find one." He sat back down behind his desk.

She opened her mouth, but couldn't decide what to say.

"And MoCap data," he added.

She pulled herself to her full height, arms akimbo. "Why?"

He leaned back in his chair and crossed one leg over the other. "So that *I* can decide when you need to take a 'personal day.' "

Venus seriously considered telling him to take his MoCap data and shove it, but the sad fact was that the man had enough contacts to find her a great animator, and she hadn't had any luck getting a session at any MoCap studio without flying to the East Coast. She pressed her lips together, and her nostrils flared.

His bland expression told her he knew of his imminent danger of being strangled but didn't fear her. "Nickelodeon will be here soon."

"Oh!" Darla hustled out the door so she could be at the receptionist's desk. Venus took the opportunity to follow her out in a dignified exit.

Darla had barely closed his office door before smiling at Venus. "Wow, he really has the hots for you!"

Venus flushed. "Darla, don't spread rum— "

"Who does, dear?"

Grandma stood a few feet away.

"You look like you need a double-shot of espresso."

Esme's voice jolted Venus out of her reverie as she slowly headed down the hallway. "What?" She paused.

Esme stopped alongside her. "Are you okay? Did the meeting with Nickelodeon go well? You look like you've been hit with a two-by-four."

She sighed. "Almost. My grandmother is waiting for me in my office."

"Chieko Sakai?" Esme's eyes grew wide.

Famous, or infamous. Venus nodded.

She touched her shoulder. "Is there anything I can do for you?"

Her concern almost made Venus start crying. "No, but thanks for offering."

"It's nothing." She smiled. "I feel like we're … friends. Friends help each other."

The words warmed her more than coffee. Venus had never had a female friend outside of her cousins. The women in her workplace hadn't been interested in hanging out with her—possibly because of her aggressive work ethic, and later possibly because of jealousy or cattiness (several had insinuated she'd gotten surgery and was lying about her stomach virus).

But Esme actually liked her. Venus hadn't felt this way before, hadn't ever felt like she had a close (non-blood relation) girlfriend to count on or confide in. She returned Esme's smile. "Thanks."

Esme's cell phone rang. "Sorry." She checked the number. "Oh, it's Lisa, one of the programmers. Hello?" She waved to Venus and hurried down the hallway.

Venus stood outside her closed office door and sucked in a lungful of air. Maybe Grandma had gotten tired of waiting for her meeting with Nickelodeon to end and left. Fat chance.

She opened the door.

Grandma glanced up with a warm smile as she sat in the chair opposite Venus's desk, her legs crossed and a slender ankle bobbing up and down. Venus sighed as she sat down at her chair—Grandma hadn't kicked off her brown pumps, and Venus didn't quite have the courage to slip off her stilettos. Grandma's neat Chanel suit made Venus feel rumply in her Calvin Klein, especially since she'd been creasing her skirt under the meeting room table while talking with the folks from Nickelodeon.

"Did the meeting go well, dear?"

"Yes, very well." She tried to infuse cheerfulness in her tone, but couldn't quite hide her apprehension. "So, Grandma ..."

Grandma reached into her purse and handed her an envelope. "This is your invitation to the Christmas party."

Yes! Venus resisted the urge to raise her arms in a caveman gesture and instead gave a polite smile. "Thanks, Grandma. I'm looking forward to it."

"Hudson Collins will be there." She looked down, uncrossed and recrossed her legs. "I had lunch with him yesterday."

And hopefully chatted up her brilliant granddaughter and the breakout development tool she'll unveil in a few months.

"I mentioned your name, and he seemed a little concerned."

No! Venus folded her hands on her desk so she wouldn't pound them against it. "Concerned?" Her voice was pitched a bit higher than normal.

"Apparently your name came up a week ago when he'd had drinks with Yardley."

Rat slime fink turd worm scum cockroach. "What did Yardley say about me?"

"Hudson wouldn't say." Grandma's eyes found hers, hard as obsidian in contrast to her gentle smile. "I hopefully alleviated his fears."

"Thank you, Grandma." But she knew that wasn't all. Grandma had said something more, she could feel it.

"He seemed interested in your new position here." Grandma glanced around her spartan office. "He seems to hold Drake and his family in high regard."

Score one for me, right?

"He'd be impressed if the Yu family were also behind your project."

Venus frowned. "I don't know Drake's family as well as you do, Grandma."

Grandma waved a languid hand. "Oh, I wouldn't ask you to talk to them. I'm good friends with Paul and Diana." She regarded Venus with a steady gaze. "But it would certainly help you if Hudson could see that you also were friends with Paul's children."

Venus clenched her stomach against a twisting cord of nausea. "I go to church with Gerry."

"And you work closely with Drake."

Venus pressed her lips together for a moment. "There's nothing inappropriate, Grandma."

"No one's saying anything like that." She leaned forward in her chair. "But there's nothing wrong with being seen outside of work in social situations."

She didn't want this. She did. She knew she shouldn't feel this leap and heel-click of her heart.

Grandma positively beamed. "I think you should attend my Christmas party with Drake as your date."

Drake had never before been attacked as he approached his parked car, but Venus did a good impression of it.

"I need your help." She appeared out of the shadows and mauled him.

He grabbed her wrists and plucked her hands from his jacket lapels. Her scent—breezy, exotic amber, and very expensive—made him want to keep her close, but he also knew she'd slam her heel in his instep if she felt trapped. He nudged her away—but not too far. "Are you bleeding? Burning?"

"No."

"Car problems?"

"No."

"Am I going to like this?"

She opened her mouth, then closed it.

Not a good sign. "Just spit it out, Venus."

"I need you to be my date for Grandma's Christmas party."

The first word he heard was "date," but the unromantic "I need you to" made his heartbeat restore to normal tempo. "Why?"

"Grandma did some damage control for me with Hudson Collins."

"Damage control?"

"Yardley slandered me to Hudson. Grandma set him straight, but she also played up my relationship with you."

"We have no relationship." Although he'd like to change that.

"But Hudson doesn't know that."

He crossed his arms and took a step away from her, regarding her with narrowed eyes. "I'm starting to feel like a hired escort."

Venus looked at the ground. "I'm sorry. That came out wrong."

What had he expected? She didn't trust him. The woman had issues enough to scare away most sane men. The crazy thing was that he did understand her, and she drove him nuts.

"Drake, I didn't mean it to sound so callous. I just didn't want you to misunderstand."

"No chance of that." Venus always said what she meant. Sometimes he wished she were less efficient and more tactful.

"I really need your help."

She never needed anyone. The fact she approached him must be killing her. "Venus, we're not even friends."

"I don't hate you anymore."

"Is that supposed to make me feel better?"

"No, of course not. I apologize. I'm not good at this stuff." She sighed. "Mr. Yu, I have a business proposition for you."

He turned back to her, an unwilling smile tugging at his mouth. "Go on."

"I would like to request your escort for my grandmother's Christmas party. You are successful, professional, and good-looking, and I am asking you to allow me to use your family connections to impress a potential investor."

Good-looking?

"This is a business proposition, not a sol-solicitation or a favor." She swallowed.

"If it's a business proposition, what do I get out of this?"

She didn't speak at first, just stared at him with eyes dark and large in the shadows cast by the lamppost. Then her shoulders settled back. "What do you want?" she asked in a low voice.

Had he heard her correctly? He waited for her to laugh and say it was a joke ... except Venus never made jokes. Or she'd burst out and say she'd changed her mind. She did change her mind ... sometimes.

What did he want from her that she'd be willing to give? Because regardless of what she said, he wasn't about to dig up her resentment against him again.

"Nothing." He reached in his briefcase for his car keys. "Nothing. I'll do it as a favor."

She blinked at him.

He took a step closer and looked down at her. "Favors don't get repaid, Venus."

Her mouth tightened. "I know that."

At least he got a response. He would have sighed except she'd snap at him more, and he was too tired to deal with her. "Is there anything else?"

"No." She dipped her chin as she said it, and he almost didn't catch her reply. She seemed almost disappointed—it would serve her right if she was, although she'd probably deny it to herself.

She gave a little shake of her head and glanced back up at him. "Thank you, Drake."

"You're welcome."

"Good-night." And she disappeared into the evening darkness like a ninja.

He deactivated his car alarm and fumbled with his bag as he climbed into the driver's seat. Yes, he understood her, but he still wanted to wrap his fingers around her throat and squeeze. Yes, she didn't want him to misunderstand, but she'd sucked any enjoyment he could have had from an evening with her. Yes, he knew she was neurotic, anal, and driven, but he was still surprised when she pulled stunts like this.

He started his engine. She disarmed him, and he didn't like it. He should be more than a match for her. While he wouldn't do anything to hurt her, he also didn't want to roll over so she could walk all over him with her five-hundred-dollar shoes.

A thought occurred to him just before he backed out of his parking stall. He sifted over her gestures, her words, the things she didn't say in their conversation.

Yes, this would unnerve her. He knew what he'd do.

TWENTY

Venus couldn't have spoken to save her life.

She had opened her front door to Drake, but she wasn't prepared for the sight of his eyes darkening to mahogany when he saw her in the Marchesa gown. The vision of him in a black tuxedo made her want to grab his lapels and repeat that mind-numbing kiss. To prevent herself, she gripped her doorknob hard enough to make it give a faint metallic creak.

She made it to the car but stopped short at the sight of Esme's petal-fresh face in Drake's backseat.

"Esme."

"Hi, Venus. I hope you don't mind?"

Yes, I mind! "Of course not." She climbed into the front seat. "I didn't even know you'd been invited."

"Drake was so nice, he remembered a comment I made about the invitation on his desk. It was *weeks* ago, but then he called and asked me to come with you two as his parents' guest."

Weeks. Around the time Venus had accosted him out in the parking lot and demanded his escort to the party? She glanced at Drake as he got in the car, but couldn't interpret his look. "Uh ... Esme, you've been working so hard lately and done such a great job, I'm glad we're able to give you something special."

Drake coughed.

"Thank you so much, Venus. I couldn't ask for a better boss."

"It's nothing. You deserve it." Well, having Esme around would keep her mind off of Drake. He started the engine, and they headed toward downtown San Jose.

"I'm excited, but I'm also nervous," Esme said. "I've never been to a big business party like this before. You've probably been to tons."

More than she cared to remember, for more years than she cared to remember. "You'll do fine. You're naturally friendly and elegant." Whereas Venus still felt awkward when she was the center of attention. Maybe Esme's poise could rub off on her.

They arrived at Grandma's bank, gave the car over to the valet, and headed inside. As a woman took their cloaks, Venus caught a glimpse of Esme's dress.

A simple, but not cheap-looking black dress, in that clingy fabric Venus could never wear because it made her hips look out of proportion, but which made Esme runway-perfect. And how on earth did the woman manage to have a behind as tiny as the church high school girls?

Drake did a double-take at Esme, and heat rose in her chest. No, she didn't want to flush and clash with the ruby crystals on her gown. She visualized air-conditioned Nordstrom's, the lap pool at her gym, Hawaiian shave ice—stop it, she'd gain five pounds just thinking about shave ice.

Stupid Drake.

Then he caught sight of her in the Marchesa—again. His face stilled, his eyes darkened.

She didn't want to feel so cheery about it.

They entered the bank, flanked by strings of garlands. A gigantic Christmas tree dominated the far end, glittering like an emerald and diamond-crusted pendant—a rival to the jewels of the people gathered.

Venus entered the crowd like she was on her way to a board meeting. Essentially, she was. Despite the fact Grandma called it the bank's Christmas party, people came to gather information about business, learn and share gossip, and make handshake deals—not to party.

Esme hovered close to Drake, wide eyes taking in the clusters of businessmen and women standing and chatting. She looked charmingly overwhelmed, making Venus feel like a hulking gladiator in the Colosseum.

Drake suddenly reached into his pocket and pulled out his cell phone.

"You brought it with you?" Now Venus didn't feel so bad for having hers in her purse.

"I was expecting this call. Be right back. Hello?" He walked a short distance away.

Esme followed him with her eyes, and Venus—never the most sensitive person—suddenly realized the truth like a wooden staff *crack* to the side of her head. "Are you and Drake ... oh, I'm sorry. That's too personal." But a burning had grown in her stomach, like glowing *hibachi* coals.

Esme blushed. "No, it's okay. Yes, I've liked him for a while." Her freshness and openness made Venus feel like a pill for her flare of jealousy.

"I'm sorry, I didn't even know you were—"

"Oh, we're not dating." Venus added the implied "*Yet.*"

But Venus wanted Esme to be happy. And she herself didn't want Drake, right? Drake was the last man on earth she could ever be happy with.

She didn't have time to assimilate her tumultuous thoughts and feelings, because Drake returned to their side. "Sorry about that. Let's find Chieko—"

"Drake! How are you, m'boy?" A tall, slender man approached and shook Drake's hand. His moustache matched his accent—Southern to the core. "And won't you introduce me to your lovely ladies?" He bestowed a charming smile on Esme, who returned it with a delicate tilt to her chin.

He shifted his gaze to Venus, who tried to mask her face into something friendly and approachable, but the man's expression faltered. Really, it wasn't as if she scowled at him. Just because she didn't smile like a debutante . . .

"Esme Preston, Venus Chau, this is Miller Kendig. He's on the board of directors for Russo Graphics."

While Esme flashed her pearly whites, Venus tried to remember where she'd heard that name. Oh, that's right—the company Drake started after he sold TrekPaste.

"Esme is operations manager, and Venus is CTO for Bananaville, my sister's new company."

Miller shook Esme's graceful hand. "Hard to believe someone as pretty as you is smart as a whip too."

"Oh, Mr. Kendig." Esme had just the right amount of flirtatiousness, without seeming ingenuine.

"Call me Miller."

Venus realized she was pouting and relaxed her mouth. She'd always prided herself on the fact that she was efficient, but Esme's charm elicited a warmer response than she'd ever had. She happened to catch Drake's look to her. Amusement gleamed from his watchful eye.

"Well, Miss Preston, if Drake here gets to be too unbearable, you give me a call. I'll give you a job working for a nicer employer." He winked at Esme. She smiled and lowered her lashes.

He turned to Venus with a cooler expression. "You're Drake's CTO?"

His handshake seemed harder and more aggressive than the one he gave Esme, but Venus returned it firmly. "Technically, I work for Gerry. I heard you've taken Russo Graphics light years beyond what it was when Drake was there." Actually, when he *owned* it, but she had enough sense not to mention that to the head of the board of directors.

Miller gave Drake a mischievous smirk. "Shouldn't have sold out, m'boy."

Drake took it in good humor. "I received an offer I couldn't refuse."

Miller laughed heartily, glancing back at Venus. "Uh ... Nice to meet you, Miss Ching."

Chau. Oh, brother. She tried to smile, but it felt more like a sick simper. "Same here."

Venus turned from Drake talking with Miller, but she came face to face with another woman. She and the woman started, but then Venus recognized her. "Pamela! How nice to see you."

"Venus." Pamela Wyatt leaned in to buss her on the cheek in a puff of rose-scented face powder. "Who are you here with? By yourself?"

"I came with Drake Yu."

"Drake! Where is he? I haven't seen him in ages." Her gaze darted around.

Venus stepped aside to include Drake and Esme. Miller's tall shoulders were just disappearing into the crowd of tuxedos, so they were standing alone together.

Pamela danced up to him in a flutter of baby-blue silk and gave him a kiss. "Hello, Drake."

"Pamela! It's been years." His smile beamed down at the smaller woman, brighter than any he'd given to Venus. Or Esme, for that matter, which mollified her. *No, stop being jealous.*

"What have you been up to?"

"I sold Russo Graphics and retired, but now I'm temporarily out of retirement and working for Gerry. This is Esme Preston, Gerry's operations manager."

They shook hands. "And how do you like working for Gerry?"

The two of them chatted for a few minutes. Esme responded with friendliness and the right amount of deference, which Pamela warmed to immediately. They parted with "We should get together for coffee," and "I'd love that," as if they were old friends.

Then Pamela turned to Venus. "I'm sorry, I have to fly—I have to make sure I speak to Sandra before she leaves the party early. It was nice seeing you, Venus." And she disappeared in a swirl of blue silk.

Venus was starting to feel like Frankenstein's monster. True, she wasn't as charming as Esme, but she wasn't *that* difficult to converse with.

"I'm going to get something to drink. Do you want anything?" Her voice came out a bit harsher than she intended.

Esme didn't notice and simply shook her head. Drake, on the other hand, raised an eyebrow at her. She schooled her face into a neutral expression. She didn't have to explain anything to him. "Well?"

"Nothing for me, thanks."

An open bar had been set up at the far end near the Christmas tree. She stood in the crowd, waiting for an opening. She kept away from the tree, not wanting any fir needles touching her gown. One good thing about having it there was that it covered the awful dead chicken head painting Grandma had bought earlier this year from Trish's ex-boyfriend, in order to foster goodwill with the boyfriend's wealthy Japanese banker parents.

Someone jabbed her with an elbow. She moved away. Another hand touched the small of her back, and a spasm rippled through her muscles, making her skin shrink away. She jerked away and stepped on someone else's foot. She glanced over her shoulder. "I'm sorry."

A medium height man smiled back. "That's all right."

She'd thought she stepped on a woman's shoe, not a man's, but maybe she was wrong. She was about to turn and try to muscle her way to the bar when he spoke again. "Can I get you anything?"

"No, thank you. I'll get it myself." She might be at Grandma's party, with an exclusive guest list, but she wasn't stupid. She refused to drink anything she hadn't received directly from the bartender's hands.

The man's smile didn't falter despite her rebuff. "I'm Arnold King." He held out his hand.

"Venus Chau."

"My uncle is friends with Chieko Sakai. You're one of her granddaughters?"

He actually pronounced Grandma's first name correctly. She shook his hand. "Yes, I'm Laura's daughter." Venus speculated on his age. Her mother's, probably.

Arnold held onto her hand too long. Venus's smile cooled, and she yanked her arm to disengage herself. His faded blue eyes discreetly checked her out, and her stomach tightened. She felt a draft under her skirt and wished she'd worn hose.

"Nice meeting you, Mr. King." *Yeah, right.* Venus sidestepped around him.

"Wait." He grabbed her arm with one hand, while the other molded to her waist.

It was like being embraced by a dead squid. She tried to step away, but his hand gripped her arm harder, and while his touch at her waist wasn't so close, he still wouldn't remove his fingers from her.

She twisted around to make him let go of her, but this brought her face to face with him. His hands immediately latched onto her upper arms.

Venus's wrists snapped up to knock him away. "Keep your hands off me." Her glare seared through his limpid eyes straight into his lecherous brain.

But he was an octopus. "Venus," he chided, smile lines creasing his face. One hand cupped her elbow, the other one snaked around her arm to touch her waist again, this time higher up.

Concealed by the press of bodies and her skirt, she jabbed him in the instep with her heel.

He grunted, his face folding into lines of pain, but his masking tape hands wouldn't let go of her—he probably held on so he wouldn't collapse onto the floor. She knocked his hand from her elbow and pushed him away with a knuckle in his gut. He stumbled backward and his fingers left her ribcage.

She spat, "I don't care how good friends your uncle is with her. My grandmother is going to hear about this." And for the first time in her life, she was heartily glad that Grandma had those adamantine claws hidden under her respectable Chanel suits.

Venus shoved her way through the other party guests, although she slowed her pace when she reached a group with drinks in their hands. It was too early in the evening to spill something on this insanely expensive gown.

She elbowed her way to the bar and signaled to the harried bartender. "Soda water and lime." He hustled to get it for her.

Venus kept her head turned behind her to make sure no one sloshed into her. Suddenly a beringed hand popped up above people's heads and fluttered at her.

"Venus!" called a shrill voice. The small figure pushed her way toward her.

The woman erupted from the crowd, a little unsteady on her heels, but with a beatific smile on her Shiseido-powdered face.

Mom.

And she was drunk as a skunk.

Her mother, thankfully, didn't drink often, but she was a mean drunk when she did overindulge.

"Stop it." Mom slapped Venus's hand where it gripped her upper arm. Venus only tightened her hold as she pulled her unwilling body away from the bar. She had commanded the bartender to not serve Mom any more—hopefully the man would obey later in the evening.

A part of her realized she ought to leave now and take Mom home. But that would mean cutting short her evening, and she hadn't had a chance to talk to anyone, not even Grandma. Certainly not Hudson Collins, and she absolutely refused to leave before she had at least two minutes with him.

Her guilt warred with her selfishness, and she knew she was being selfish. And she was in this situation all because of her mother. Venus shoved her away from the bar with more force than necessary.

"But I wanted a drink." Mom scratched viciously at Venus's hand, making her drop her arm.

"Mom!" Venus rubbed her hand. Dark pink scratches, but no blood. "You've had enough. Grandma will kill you if you embarrass her."

That was only wishful thinking. Grandma, while ruthless in business matters, always bailed out her youngest daughter. No one in the family understood the illogic of it, especially since Grandma had no grace for anyone else.

Normally, Venus would just leave her mom to fend for herself, or for Grandma to take charge of, but tonight she needed to stay on Grandma's good side. Her company depended on it.

But how would it look to have her drunken mother tagging along? Would it be worse than allowing her to stagger from person to person throughout the room? And Venus couldn't get rid of the mass of worms in her stomach that wriggled and squirmed because she actually cared about how it looked. That these people and their wealth and connections mattered to her.

She'd played this game before—been to other company parties, schmoozed with other rich people, made alliances and gathered information—but she'd never had her own interests on the line like tonight. And she'd never had her mother with her.

Mom had turned a pasty mochi shade of white under her pink rouge. Venus whirled her around and pushed her to the restroom. She waited outside rather than going in because she freely admitted she didn't really want to watch her mom casting up her accounts.

The lighting didn't reach into this far corner, and the darkness cocooned her. She scanned the party—at least, as much of the crowd as she could see—searching for whom she might want to talk to.

There was the CEO of Giusti Graphics, a small gaming company, who had been Venus's coworker at one of the startup companies she'd worked at. She could go say hi, see how the business was going for him. And there was her grandmother's good friend, Mrs. Lee, whose children owned and operated various companies around the Bay Area. She'd ask Grandma to re-introduce her, in case Mrs. Lee didn't remember meeting her four years ago. Venus hoped to meet

Drake's parents, since she hadn't been introduced yet. Gerry was here somewhere too. And there was . . .

She suddenly felt hollow. Mercenary. Shallow. More concerned about her gaming company than her own mother—regardless of how irritating that mother was at the moment. She was certainly a wonderful Christian, honoring her mother so well.

Except God had been the one to drop her into her family as the fat only child of a beautiful, selfish mother. God had done all this to her. She pressed her hand to her forehead.

No, she wouldn't go down that road again. She'd struggled with this anger for so long, it was burning a hole in her soul. She knew she had to stop blaming God when all the choices she'd made were her own.

Like now. Her gaming company.

But didn't God want her to be successful? Didn't He want her to use the brains and talent He'd given to her? How could her gaming company be bad?

She knew she hadn't prayed enough about this. She would—later. Right now, she needed to concentrate on the party, on meeting the right people, on utilizing this opportunity Grandma had given to her.

"Hey, Venus." Drake materialized out of the darkness like Dracula.

She jumped six feet into the air. When she got her breath back, she jabbed him in the arm, creasing his jacket. "Are you trying to kill me?"

"What are you doing here?" He didn't even rub his arm. She must not have hit him hard enough.

"Waiting on my moth—"

"Drake." Esme approached like a faerie, bringing light to contrast the darkness cloaking Venus. "Your mother asked me to find you."

She'd already met his mother?

"What did she need?" Drake shifted his weight away from Venus, closer to Esme in a protective stance.

"Actually ..." Esme colored, roses and cream in her smooth cheeks. "She wanted you to introduce me to Ron Hinck."

Hinck ... Hinck ... oh, that's right. CEO of Blood Mechanics, the newest gaming company on the block.

Drake's face brightened, as if Esme's cheerful presence had saved him from Venus's dark mood. Which it probably had. "That's a good idea. I saw him by the bar." They walked away.

Venus wanted to grab her shoe and hurl it at the back of his head, but it would be a waste of a shoe.

She turned back to the restroom door and sighed. She pushed the door open. "Mom, are you okay?" Retching sounds echoed against the tile walls so she couldn't be sure where her mom was, but Venus thought she saw a shadow under the door of the last stall.

"Venus." The voice sounded right in her ear.

She gasped and whirled. Grandma stood beside her. That was the second time tonight—why was she so jumpy? "Hi, Grandma. Sorry, you scared me."

"Are you all right?" She eyed Venus, standing with one foot in the restroom and one foot out.

"Mom's inside."

"Ah." Grandma's lips pressed together. "Well, I need you to come with me. She'll be fine if you leave her."

"Leave her? She's sick." As if Grandma couldn't hear that quite clearly.

"Which means she's not going anywhere anytime soon."

Good point. "What do you need me for?"

"I was talking with Hudson Collins." Her lips spread into a rich smile. "He wants to meet you."

TWENTY-ONE

He *is not God. He is not God.*

He was just king of the entire fiefdom of gaming.

Venus had dealt with important men before—CEOs, CFOs, boards of directors, venture capitalists. Why would Hudson be any different?

Well, she'd never had her own company on the line before. She'd never had a development tool about to be unveiled that would change the face of game development across the country.

He'd understand the import of the Spiderweb. Venus just needed to charm him, to make sure he understood that she was professional, efficient, and someone he'd like to work with.

Um ... yeah. Charm. Compared to Esme tonight, Venus had as much charm as a box of cornflakes.

Grandma cut a swath through the crowd surrounding a short, robust man who reminded her of Reed Richards from the *Fantastic Four* comic. He had the dab of silver at his temples and the air of a scientist, not a businessman.

Grandma smiled at him as she guided Venus forward. "Hudson, my granddaughter, Venus Chau."

They exchanged polite nothings. Up close, she realized that although he gave off an air of casual friendliness, his eyes were as warm as a Minnesota winter, an icy blue. They regarded her now with speculation and a little incredulity. She lifted her chin, hoping to present a businesslike air despite the romantic Marchesa gown.

"Your grandmother says you're working on a development tool." He bestowed a gentle curving of his lips, dimpling his weathered cheeks, but Venus wasn't fooled. It was a *You're female and pretty, so I can't believe you'd have a brain* type of smile.

"The tool is completed. It's in testing right now." She battled him with her gaze. *What do you say to that? This little bimbo isn't just "working" on it; she's actually finished the tool.*

He blinked once, slowly. The disbelieving expression had morphed to one that said, *You've probably made something simplistic that doesn't live up to your assertions about it. You can fool your grandmother, but not me.* "Tell me about it."

"The Spiderweb encompasses all disciplines—designing, animation, programming. It's compatible with the different applications for all three areas of game development. We've established compatibility with most programming and design software. We verified 3ds Max, and we're verifying MoCap data and Maya right now."

Hudson had stilled, like a snowy mountaintop just before an avalanche. Venus wasn't sure if that was good or bad.

"Most programming and design software?"

"Yes." *Go ahead. Start rattling them off, as if I don't know what software programmers and designers use.*

He opened his mouth as if he'd do just that, but then he closed it again. A chinook wind blew through his icy gaze. "Tell me more—"

"Hudson, so good to see you."

Yardley! Venus's hands fisted at his unctuous voice. What was he doing here? She didn't think Grandma had invited him—she'd have told Venus if she'd been forced to. Venus glanced around. Where was Grandma? She needed one of her famous set-downs right about now.

Even Hudson's brow wrinkled at Yardley's rudeness in interrupting their conversation, which made Venus start breathing again. Maybe he'd foist Yardley off so they could continue.

"Hello, Yardley. How's your uncle doing?"

Bummer.

Yardley had transformed into a simpering idiot. Apparently his uncle and Hudson were good friends, and so Hudson wasn't about to treat him like the slimeball he was. So Yardley spent time—*her* time!—chatting about things and people she could care less about. Venus plastered a polite expression on her face and hoped they wouldn't notice her clenching jaw.

Yardley slipped her a sly side glance—yes, he knew exactly what he was doing and how Venus felt about it. She dug her nails into her palms to keep from winding up and popping him one in his sneaky, arrogant nose.

"I see you've met Venus." Yardley bestowed a gracious smile in her direction. "She, ah ... left my employ a few months ago."

The way he said it implied she'd been fired, not that she quit. She opened her mouth, but he beat her to it.

"She certainly lives up to her *reputation* in the business."

The most well-known aspect of which was how difficult she was to work with. The creep. "I simply wanted to spread my wings, Yardley. The people at Bananaville respect my opinions and expertise." In ways Oomvid never did.

Yardley's smile widened and sharpened. She was going to slap the challenge off his face right here in the middle of Grandma's party if someone else didn't do it first.

"Hudson, I thought that was you." A woman's voice, flowing like Chinese silk, entered the fray. A fragile Asian woman cut right through Yardley and Venus in order to take Hudson's hand. A stout Asian man with a naval commander's presence followed her, and then Venus saw Drake behind him.

His bland expression made her stand down. He'd brought the cavalry.

The woman gave a cool nod to Yardley, then turned to Venus with a shining face. "I'm Diana Yu, Drake's mother. I've been wanting to meet you. This is my husband, Paul."

She returned his firm handshake. His face was stern, but his eyes gleamed. "I've heard rumors about an innovative development tool you've completed."

"It's in testing phase."

He glanced at his son. "Drake says the program is excellent."

What was she supposed to say to that? She smiled and kept her mouth shut, aware of Hudson following the conversation even though Yardley attempted to distract him.

"And you're starting a game development company?"

"I'm forming my team now."

"Drake and Gerry have both been impressed with you while you've been at Bananaville. Gerry told me you have good business acumen and organizational abilities. Drake vouches for your technical expertise."

Whoa. Did Drake tell his father to say that? Hudson glanced at her, ignoring Yardley completely. She smiled at Paul. "Thank you." Her eyes found Drake's, just over his father's shoulder, and communicated a silent *Thanks.*

"I'd be curious to look at your business plan when you've finished it."

Oh my. Paul Yu had just set himself up to rival Hudson Collins in investment in her company. Dangerous, but clever tactic.

Paul turned to give Hudson a neutral gaze, while Hudson actually grinned. "You old dog."

Paul guffawed. "Not older than you."

Yardley's rather strident voice cut through the conversation. "That woman is going to cause a scene."

The crowd parted like a curtain to reveal Venus's worst nightmare. Her mother, laughing and sloshing a drink, flirting with the same handsy guy who had felt the sting of Venus's heel earlier. What was his name?

The man stepped in front of her mother, blocking her view, but Venus noticed immediately when Mom's wild cavorting toned down. Oh, no. Not a good sign. If Mr. King lived up to expectations, her mother was going to respond any second—

Slap!

The sound sliced through the murmuring of the crowd, Mom had hit him so hard. The man bent nearly double, his hand up to his face.

Paul Yu frowned. "That's Arnold King. Doesn't he own that art gallery in Saratoga?"

Yardley's voice in a pseudo-whisper carried to everyone around her. "Venus, isn't that your mother?"

Esme would not stop talking.

Which might be a good thing, since Drake wasn't really in a mood to talk. But her prattling grated like a car's steel frame dragging on asphalt. He pulled onto the freeway, missing Venus's presence in the car.

"It's too bad Venus had to leave early to drive her mother home. She looked so voluptuous in that gown."

The way she said it made Drake's hackles rise. Her tone didn't imply a compliment, exactly. He said nothing. Venus had completely knocked him out in that dress—his brain had dribbled out of his head when he first saw her—so he assumed Esme had some natural feminine jealousy.

"And I can't believe Venus's mother," Esme breathed in touching concern.

He gave her a side glance.

"Such embarrassment for Venus's grandmother. And poor Venus looked like she wanted the floor to swallow her."

Actually, Venus had looked like she wanted to slit Yardley's throat. His parents, who knew a little about Venus's mom from what he and Gerry told them, had been sympathetic to her awkward situation, but he wasn't sure what it had done for Venus's case with Hudson Collins. And after what he'd done to try to bail her out.

It had been such a coincidence. He'd *happened* to be with his parents, and he'd *happened* to see Yardley approach Venus and Hudson. Esme had *happened* to be occupied talking with Ron Hinck—when Esme said she wanted to meet the CEO, he had been relieved to foist her off on Ron after she'd clung to Drake all evening. And Drake's parents *happened* to hate Yardley's guts after working with Oomvid for their third level of funding a few years ago. So, after he explained what he wanted, his mother had practically charged over to Hudson, Venus, and Yardley. But the rescue mission hadn't done any good.

Esme sighed. "It's too bad Venus was so caught up in networking that she didn't notice her mother's behavior."

He opened his mouth, but then some check inside him made him close it. He remembered when he'd come upon Venus outside the women's restroom. Before Esme interrupted them, she said she'd been waiting on her mother—probably while her mother was being thoroughly sick in a stall. Since her grandmother had been with her and Hudson, he guessed Mrs. Sakai dragged her away from the bathroom in order to introduce her to Hudson.

Esme seemed rather catty tonight about Venus, especially when they hadn't spoken to each other much all evening.

"And how rude to slap that poor man."

Drake knew Arnold King. Gerry had complained about him after a party at his art gallery a few years ago, so he had a good idea what had made Venus's mother deck him. However, he wasn't about to enlighten Esme.

She dipped her head, fiddling with her clutch purse. She looked almost shy, except she'd been pointed enough in her comments since they got in the car. "I hope I didn't embarrass you tonight as your date."

No, no, no. He needed to nip this in the bud. "Actually, you were my parents' guest, since you took Gerry's place on their invitation. So send them a thank-you card tomorrow."

"Oh." She looked confused, then her face settled into a neutral expression. For some reason, it didn't make Drake relax as he glanced at her.

If anything, it had been an enlightening evening. While Venus was her normal cactus self—but flowering in that incredible gown—Esme had been cloying like his grandmother's perfume, and just as easily gave him a headache. He never thought he'd say it, but he preferred Venus with all her frowns and moods over Esme's smiles and not-quite-innocent remarks.

He needed a good swift smack upside the head.

The physical attraction had always been there, but he never thought there was more to it than that. Yet here he was, preferring Venus in all her snarkiness, snarls, and sharp edges.

However, despite all her barking, Venus was a straight shooter. From Esme's remarks tonight, she seemed to have an onion's acrid layers to be unveiled. He didn't like surprises.

He couldn't reach Esme's apartment fast enough. He pulled to the curb in front of her complex's gate and she turned to him with a sweet smile. "Thanks for such a wonderful evening. Would you like to come in for some coffee?"

"No, thanks. I have work that I need to finish tonight."

She patted his arm. "Poor thing. Don't work too hard."

His heart attack last year ensured he'd never do that again. He didn't answer.

"Good-night." She got out of the car and shut the door.

He waited until she'd safely entered through the gate—with a cheerful wave in his direction—before driving away. Had he been clear enough in his message to her? He didn't want Esme holding hopes when he wanted to focus in a different direction.

Maybe the fact he couldn't stop thinking about Venus meant that there might be more to this than just the physical pull. He'd kept her at a distance because he had never done something so unprofessional as an in-house relationship, and he hadn't wanted to waste time on something transient. But maybe this wasn't transient. Maybe this was worth a deeper look.

Lately she'd treated him with regard and politeness versus thinly veiled hostility. He could thank the stash of Reese's in his desk for that. And they might even be doing her good—she was less bony lately.

He'd have a chance to talk to her in a few weeks at the youth group ski retreat in Lake Tahoe. Four days in a cabin with twenty teenagers would make her eager to spend some time outside, alone with him.

Until then, he'd tread carefully. She'd be peevish at work on Monday after the disaster tonight.

He'd make sure to stick a Reese's on her desk in the morning.

TWENTY-TWO

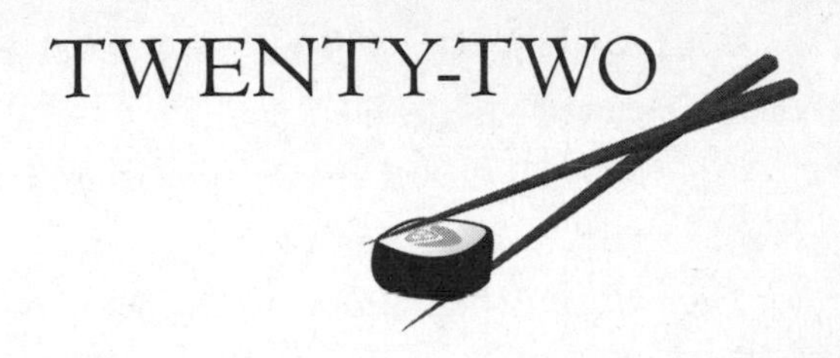

Drake wasn't a bad driver, but he was driving her nuts.

He'd change lanes to pass when she would have waited for the car in the other lane to zoom by and pulled in behind him. He'd wait behind a slow-moving vehicle when she'd have zipped left and passed him. He'd accelerate at first when merging onto the freeway, but then he'd slow down if there was a car approaching—supposedly to let it pass him before he merged into traffic—but the car would inevitably slow down too, because *most* drivers sped up when merging, and then the two of them would be going 45 mph on the freeway!

Venus slouched in the passenger seat, crumpling the maps to Lake Tahoe in her fists. She'd wanted to drive, but Drake's SUV took more passengers than her little BMW convertible, so she'd agreed to navigate. If she didn't grab the steering wheel from him before they even got to Lake Tahoe.

Drake gave her a sidelong look, as if he knew what she was thinking. Venus ignored him, concentrating on the U-Haul in front of them and the giggling of the high school girls in the backseats.

"I know what you're thinking," he said.

"No, you don't."

"Just shut up and let me drive."

"I haven't said a word."

"You're practically shouting when you grab the dash, or grab the door handle, or roll your eyes and look back."

She sniffed. "I look back to check on the girls."

It was his turn to roll his eyes.

Okay, so she was a little bit of a control freak. He already knew that. He should have let her drive.

She suddenly heard the scream from The Who's "Won't Get Fooled Again," made famous to her generation as the opening theme for *CSI: Miami*. She'd programmed her phone to play it when Jaye called. She opened her purse and fumbled for her cell phone.

"What ring tone do you have for me?" Drake asked.

"Darth Vader." The girls in the backseat erupted in giggles at that. She flipped open the phone. "Hi, Jaye."

"Venus, I'm at the airport."

"Airport? Why?"

"I—"

The girls in the back started chanting the *dum-dum-de-dum* from *Star Wars* that signaled Darth Vader's entrance onto Princess Leia's starship. "Jaye? What did you say?"

"And—"

"Quiet, back there. Jaye, repeat what you said."

"Mom fell and hurt her ankle last night. I'm flying to Arizona."

"She's okay?"

"Yeah, just a sprain."

"How long will you be gone?" Now the girls were chattering about *Star Wars* episodes two and three—specifically, about how hot the Anakin Skywalker actor was. "Will you guys keep it down? How long?"

"Probably a week. Got time off of work."

"Is Nancy home? I can stop by next week—"

Now the girls were pulling Mika's long hair into some Padmé-esque styles while Mika squealed.

Venus twisted around in her seat. *"Will you guys shut up?"*

Five pairs of eyes grew as large as mochi ice cream balls.

Maybe the phrase "shut up" had been a bit harsh. But at least she could hear Jaye now. "What did you say?"

"Nancy and Junior are coming with me."

Taking his family with him for only an ankle sprain? That seemed ... odd. "Well, I'll work on the testing until you get back."

"Sorry to leave you like this. If you need anything, just call my cell phone. Gotta go, Venus, we're boarding."

"Talk to you later." She clapped the phone shut.

Temporarily chastened, the girls kept their conversations low enough to wake only half a graveyard, and Drake didn't comment on what he'd overheard, so Venus had a few moments of peace. She suddenly felt so ... alone. An irrational fear of being abandoned rose up in her.

That was ridiculous. Jaye had created the Spiderweb with her. He'd never leave her.

"You'll be fine, Venus." Drake didn't look at her.

How did he always know what she was thinking? "Of course I'll be fine. Why wouldn't I be fine? I'm always fine."

"How long will he be gone?" His reasonable tone irritated her like her control top pantyhose digging into her stomach.

"Just a week. He's only on a trip to Arizona."

He gave her a sidelong look.

"I'll simply work on the Spiderweb while he's gone."

"Of course you will."

"I can even fix all the bugs. Without him."

"Of course you can."

"Besides, I'm a control freak."

"We all know that."

She glared at him. "You're not helping."

"You're stressing too much. Relax. We're on a ski trip to Lake Tahoe."

"I don't ski." She turned away to look out the window.

"You'll still be able to relax."

She stuck her chin out. "No, I won't. I brought my laptop."

Drake slid her a sideways glance. "Are you serious? You brought your laptop?"

"Of course I'm serious. I need to work. I have tons to do." Drake, of all people, would know she wasn't a slacker.

"What kind of work?"

"Emails."

"Oh." His face relaxed.

"And I need to log in to the server to check a few new applications."

He shot her a disbelieving look. "Venus. We're going to a cabin."

Had the altitude gotten to him? "And?"

"It's old. It's a rental."

"So?"

"Venus." He sounded like he was talking to a three-year-old. "You can't work there."

"What . . . what are you talking about?" A rumbling started in the bottom of her stomach. She was starting to see where he was going.

"There's no high-speed Internet at the cabin. There's only dial-up."

"Aren't you kind of young to be thinking about college?" Venus dumped another half-shovel of snow to the side and paused in her digging. Yet again. The junior high and high school girls' enthusiasm over digging in the snow made up for her lack.

"Come on, Venus, dig!" David called to her from farther down the run, where he and several junior high boys were digging a banked curve.

She wished, for the hundredth time, that she'd opted to go skiing instead of staying here at the cabin. David had conveniently forgotten to tell her about the annual sled run—the youth group rented the same cabin every year, and it had a long, sloping field between it and the cabin next door, which was perfect for a sled run.

She slid a few inches in the packed ice, making a shallow gouge in the steep initial drop to the run that enabled the kids to build up speed on the way down. Thank goodness for her expensive boots with specialty non-skid soles—well, not completely non-skid, but they'd been low-skid for most of the morning. They'd been a last-minute purchase the day before they left for the trip.

The high school girls had gotten positively clingy last night, their first night at the cabin. They'd never had a female staff worker specifically for the high school girls on the ski trip, since Keiko rarely went, and Kat worked primarily with the junior high girls. So they stuck to her like limpets and even listened when she did the nightly devotion before lights out in the large bedroom where all the girls slept on sleeping bags.

Including Venus. She hadn't known until arriving at the cabin, and the horror of it made David ask her if she was okay.

Drake had anticipated her lack of planning and brought an extra sleeping bag, but he hadn't had to look so smug about it when he handed it to her. She'd never "roughed it" before (and she knew this wasn't really roughing it). She'd been too busy the weeks before to find out more about the cabin, but she knew it was privately owned and rented out to the high school kids every year, so she assumed it would be like a two-star hotel. Even a beachside motel in Oregon where she'd once stayed had had bedding and *wireless.*

The high school girls clustered around her now, helping to dig their famous sled run, and chattering only a little faster than they dug.

Mika flipped some snow at Naomi, who squealed. "I'm thinking about colleges now because Mom is making me do it."

"But you don't have to apply for another two years."

Mika shrugged. "That's the way Mom is."

"I have to apply later this year, and it's hard to figure out where to go," Naomi said.

"Sometimes it's easy." Sarah flicked snow at Rachel. "You know you're not smart enough to get into Stanford."

"Hey!" Rachel tossed snow at her. "How would you know? My grades could magically improve in the next year."

"You also have to think about if your parents can afford it." Venus started digging again.

Rachel stuck her tongue out at her. "Well, Mika won't have to worry about it. She's got good grades and her parents are doctors."

Naomi nodded. "She can go wherever she wants."

"But that only makes it harder to know where to go." Mika tucked a strand of hair under her knitted cap.

"Yeah, how did you know where to go?"

Bright eyes turned on Venus like headlights.

"Uh ..." Hers had been a no-brainer. She'd been accepted at Stanford but gone to San Jose State since her father hadn't been making enough, but by the time she wanted to get her Master's, he—she suspected with a loan from Grandma—had been able to send her to Stanford for a couple years.

"Well, first you look at finances. Then you figure out how far away from home you want to go. Then you look to see what colleges offer classes in the major you might want." Hey, she was sounding like she knew what she was talking about.

"But how did you know where God wanted you to go?"

Oh. That's right. God's will. "Um ..."

"I mean, sometimes I pray about something, like which electives to take at school, and He doesn't answer me."

"Or like, which boy to ask to Sadies."

"Or whether to quit soccer and join track."

"And I don't want to make a mistake. It might change the entire course of my life." Naomi's eyes had grown large and fearful.

The girls were so in earnest, Venus wasn't even tempted to roll her eyes. Problem was, she didn't know either. "Well ..."

"And even if I kind of know what I think God wants me to do, sometimes it's so hard to do it."

"Yeah! Like, I don't really want to help babysit the kids for the summer adult Bible study, even if the church does pay me, but I know God wants me to do it."

"Oh, I like babysitting," Naomi said.

"Well then, you take it. I want to take more hours at my other job."

"Okay. Tell Mrs. Cathcart."

"Oh, but . . ." Rachel turned to Venus. "Like that! How do I know God wants me to do the babysitting instead of Naomi? Maybe He wants me to learn something from it. Or what if He sent Naomi to offer because He doesn't want me to do it, because I don't want to?"

"Things like that," Mika said. "How can you find out what God wants you to do, versus what you want to do?"

"And then make yourself do it if you don't like it?"

The girls looked at her and amazingly shut their mouths. Venus started to sweat even more than she already was. Knowing God's will? When was the last time she'd even prayed for God's will?

She had to say something. "Um ... sometimes ... you just don't know." Was that right? Knowing her luck, she'd advise them to do something completely wrong. Shouldn't her extensive Bible reading lend her an answer? Maybe she should have them talk to David about it, or Pastor Lester.

"It's getting dark; let's get back to the cabin." She waved to David. "It's four thirty!"

"We'll be right there."

They gathered up the shovels to store inside the toolshed. Kat would be making dinner for them all about now, and Venus could eat an entire pan of lasagna. Drake and the others who'd gone skiing would be back soon, and she wanted to make sure she and the other kids got some before the hungry skiing crew got their hands on the grub.

Suddenly Kat rushed out of the cabin and headed toward them, slipping in the snow.

Venus told herself not to panic, but her heart did a ski jump anyway. "What is it?"

"Rebecca," she panted.

"What about her? She's inside, isn't she?"

"She had a fight with a couple junior high girls earlier this afternoon, so I told her to go outside and cool off. She's supposed to help me cook, so I looked for her but I can't find her."

Venus handed her shovel to Mika. "Put this in the shed for me. Where could she have gone?" She hustled toward the cabin. Flashlight. And a map of the area. And an extra layer or two—it was getting colder.

"One of the girls said she saw Rebecca walking down the road." Kat pointed down the residential street, walled on both sides with snow shoved aside by the plows.

"I'll go look for her." Venus tried to sound cheerful, but only sounded rushed. They had snaked through a labyrinth of streets to get to the rental cabin. How could she possibly find a small, cold girl by herself? Maybe David could search with her? But that would leave Kat alone in the house with the fifteen kids who hadn't gone skiing—not a good ratio.

At that moment, Drake's SUV and Herman's van roared up the street, revving their engines as they strained up the steep hill. They eased into the driveway and kids spilled from the cars.

Venus had never been so happy to see Drake in her life.

TWENTY-THREE

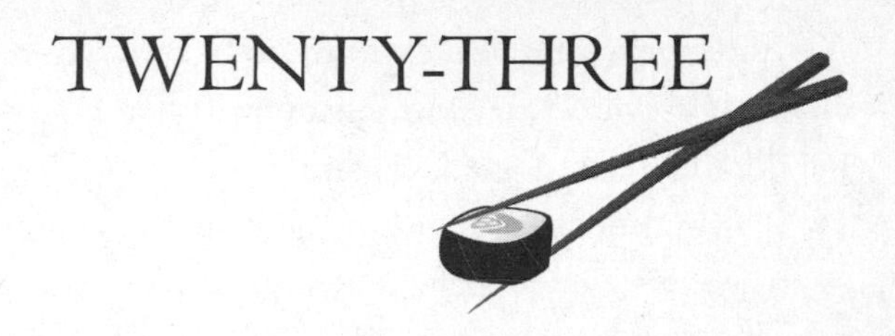

As soon as her fingers unthawed enough to move them, she was going to strangle Rebecca.

Venus walked down a lonely snowy road with houses standing as silent sentinels on each side. The skiing started early and most weekend warriors went to bed early, so many of the rental cabins stood foreboding in their dark silence.

Wait, there—lights! That cabin had lights in the window. She hustled toward it.

Ice Princess, she wasn't. Her right leg slid out from under her and she landed hard on her rump. Her jeans immediately sucked up the melted ice, wetting her panties and flash-freezing her cellulite.

Oh, man.

She considered sitting in the wet puddle and crying, but the fear of Drake happening upon her like that made her shoot to her feet, where she wobbled in the slippery road for a second. Granted, he'd gone to search in the opposite direction, but she refused to be caught crying. He might do something nice like fold her in his arms and kiss her. And considering how cold, wet, and hungry she was, she might kiss him back.

And what's wrong with that? a part of her wanted to know as she trudged toward the lighted cabin. She'd spent months dancing around him while accepting Reese's peanut butter cups. She'd originally kept him at arm's length, but he'd proven to her that he had changed. Dramatically. He even came to church with Gerry on Sundays.

She rapped on the door to the cabin, which looked as old as her own. Male voices from within stopped, then lumbering steps toward the door. It cracked open. "Hello?"

A rumpled, college-age boy. Quite high or drunk, if his slack face was any indication. Whew—he smelled like a still. Definitely drunk. "I'm looking for a young girl who ran away from my cabin a few streets over."

He perked up. His mouth propped open. "She cute?"

Her sharp glare slammed an icicle into his eye. "She's twelve."

"Oh."

Venus was heartily glad for her bulky ski jacket, making her look like an elongated apple. She caught sight of three other young men in the room beyond, two with beer bottles.

The boy fingered his bottom lip. "When'd she run away?"

"About two hours ago."

"We've been inside since two," one of the other boys yelled at her.

The guy at the door shrugged. "Sorry. Haven't seen anyone."

"Thanks." She had turned away before even finishing the word. The door closed almost as quickly.

She pulled out the walkie-talkie from her jacket pocket as she slid down the driveway back onto the road. "Drake? Any luck?" She had to admit he'd been thinking clearer than she had—he'd shoved the walkie-talkie into her hand just before they set out from the cabin, him taking the streets south while she took the streets north.

"Nope."

"Me neither."

"I'm about to reach the main highway. I'll turn back and meet up with you."

"I'm at . . ." She aimed the flashlight at a crooked signpost a few yards down the road and squinted to read it. "Mulberry Lane."

"Keep looking. I'll catch up."

What was that up there? A short figure without a flashlight. It had to be Rebecca. Probably sniveling and hysterical and as frozen as an *azuki* bean ice cream bar. "Rebecca!" She quickened her pace.

Rebecca starting running toward her. Actually, running rather fast. With a strange loping gait.

It wasn't Rebecca.

"Aaaaah!" Venus thrust her hands out, palm first, to stop the dripping, muddy, slimy, slobbery golden retriever from leaping up and depositing all that water, mud, slime, and slobber on her mostly dry person. So far, only her butt was wet. She did not need water down her shirt, thank you very much.

The friendly canine panted at her, then dropped and rolled in the muddy snowbank. "Don't do that ..."

He got up and started sniffing the air, his black wet nose coming closer and closer. As he (she?) beelined toward her jacket pocket, Venus remembered the chocolate bar wrapping one of the girls had given to her, which she'd stuck in her pocket to throw away later.

"No, stay away. Yuck! Your entire face is wet! No, stop. Stay. Stop! Not any closer! Ewwww ..."

If it were anything but chocolate and plastic wrapping, she'd have thrown it away from her and made a run for it. She wasn't exactly sure what chocolate did to dogs, but she knew it was bad—did they go into seizures or something? And it couldn't be good if Dog ate the plastic wrapping—wouldn't that twist up his intestines or something?

Stupid dog. He didn't deserve her concern for his health, the way he kept following her as she backtracked down the icy street. She was sure to twist her ankle any second now. She swerved toward the side of the road, batting away Dog's nose every time he came close to her jacket pocket.

"You are very disobedient! You ought to be ashamed of yourself!" She shook her finger at Dog, who licked it. "Ew! These are cashmere gloves, do you know that? How am I going to get your dog slobber out of cashmere? No! Stay away from my pocket—whoops!"

She stumbled over a chunk of ice and tumbled into the snowbank. Her jacket kept the snow from wetting her back, but ice from the top of the bank sifted onto her head, down her jacket, into her shirt, and soaking her bra. "Aaaargh!" Her jeans had become blue razzleberry twin popsicles, and her gloves had pieces of ice sticking to them.

What was worse, Dog trotted right up and rooted at her pocket, inhaling the chocolate scent in long, snotty breaths. Good thing the walkie-talkie was in the other pocket.

"Get away!" She swatted at Dog's head, who thought it was a game and tried to lick her waving hand. "No, no, no!" She had to get out of this snow, if only Dog would let her.

"Move!"

Dog backed away, tail still wagging.

Was that a dog command? Well, no time to question good fortune. She scrambled to her feet, dripping chunks of snow. Ugh, she had snow in her shoes! Cold wetness slid down her ankle.

A faint whistle carried on the brisk air. Dog's ears perked up, and then he dashed off.

Venus scowled as she brushed snow and water from her arms. "You were about five minutes too late," she groused to the invisible owner.

"Venus?" crackled from her jacket pocket.

She grabbed the walkie-talkie. "I'm here."

"We found Rebecca."

"Thank goodness." Followed by, "I want to be the first to wring her scrawny little neck."

Silence. She just knew Drake was laughing.

"Where did you find her?"

"I didn't. Ronald called my cell phone to tell me she showed up back at the cabin."

"What? You have coverage?" She pulled out her cell phone, which she'd brought along on the fluke chance she'd get a signal. Still no bars.

"Head back to the cabin. I'll meet you there with a cup of cocoa."

What she really wanted was a triple-shot latte, but cocoa would have to do. She juggled the walkie-talkie, the flashlight under her arm, and the map in her other hand. "Okay. I don't think I'm too far—"

With a flicker, her flashlight went out.

Venus dreamed of mochas.

Full fat milk, steamed until it was frothy with that microfoam the barista insisted was essential to a good coffee drink. Five pumps of chocolate — no stinting. With a heaping tower of real whipped cream on top.

Venti sized.

A whopping five hundred calories, with half of those calories from fat. Worth every single extra minute of her workouts for the entire week.

Well, almost. Worth it until she had problems buttoning her waistband or pulling up her jeans.

She huddled deeper into her jacket. She'd stop obsessing about her weight if she froze to death. Where was Drake?

After telling him her flashlight had gone out, she'd buzzed him on the walkie-talkie three times to demand — er, ask him where he was. He gave three different street names, but since she didn't have light to read her map, she didn't know how close he was. "Why don't Lake Tahoe residents need street lamps like normal folk?"

"Because then it wouldn't be considered 'rural' anymore."

Drake's voice shot out of the darkness from behind her. "Where are you?" She turned around and got the full glare from his flashlight. "Aah! Turn it off." She rubbed her eyes. "I didn't hear you coming."

"Your teeth were chattering too loudly."

"Were not." She clenched her shaking jaw.

He grasped her arm to pull her up from the fallen tree log she'd been squatting on. "You're soaked."

"Brilliant deduction, Sherlock. We're surrounded by *snow.*"

"Which is frozen. Why are you wet?" He sniffed. "And you smell like wet dog."

"You really know how to make a girl feel good about herself."

"Hey, I'm not going to lie to you when you smell like wet dog. What happened?"

"What do you think happened? I got attacked by a wet dog."

"Are you bleeding? Burning?" She could hear the smile in his voice.

She would have ground her teeth, except they'd already been shaved to nubs from chattering with cold. "Shut up. The beastly mongrel wanted Naomi's Snickers wrapper from my pocket."

"That's your fault for keeping chocolate on you. You're in the country. With raccoons and bears."

"Bears?" She looked around, even though all she could see was, well, dark.

"Why do you think all the trash goes in those enclosed wooden shacks by the side of the road?"

"Uh ... ants?"

"Tell me you're not that ignorant."

She bristled like a rather wet, icy porcupine. "Excuse me, you were never exactly Survivor Man yourself."

He stilled in a way she could sense even in the darkness. "Things change when you almost die."

She couldn't speak. She'd never forgotten it, but for him, it seemed to follow him around like a ghost, appearing in dark corners.

"Come on, let's get you home."

They walked in silence for a few moments, but the words spilled out of her mouth before she could stop them. "It changed you a lot, Drake."

"It didn't change me. It made me realize I needed to change things."

"That's why you retired." It wasn't a question. He didn't answer. "But that's also why you came out of retirement, right? To help Gerry? You two didn't get along well when I knew you."

"She hated me. I wasn't there for her when she miscarried, when her husband divorced her. So when she needed my help for her company, I wanted to make up for it."

They walked in silence. Venus could feel her legs again, although nothing below her knees. Then it occurred to her. "That's why you're helping me with my company."

Again, he didn't answer. He didn't have to, and she didn't want to embarrass him more.

A breeze rustled the tops of the redwood trees towering above them like God's armed guards. Maybe it was nice out here in the country. Quiet. Peaceful. A world completely removed from her normal life.

She'd never really asked God what He thought of her normal life. She usually figured that opened or closed doors were God's way of telling her where to go. She never asked before deciding on what to do.

Like her company. She hadn't prayed about it. Maybe God was telling her to stop and ask for His will, for once.

Do I even want to know?

She inhaled sharply, and the cold air cut her nasal passages, frosted her lungs. The reality was, she was afraid of what God would tell her. She was afraid of having her shortcomings held up in the light where she couldn't deny them anymore. She was afraid of being told she'd never reach that point where she would have "made it."

Could anyone blame her? She had echoes of her mother's censure all through childhood, of how hard she'd had to work to prove herself in the male-dominated game development industry.

She knew in her head that God didn't care about what she accomplished or failed at. But her heart still shrank back from asking Him.

She finally did what she'd been expecting to do all night—she slipped. One foot slid forward, the other slid backward. Her inner thigh muscles screamed. One arm windmilled in the darkness, the other thrust out but only brushed her companion's jacket. "Drake!"

She hung in mid-air an agonizing second. Then arms wrapped around her ribs while her feet skidded in circles on the ice. She grabbed onto his life preserver arms but couldn't get purchase for her feet.

He bounced her upward until she was more upright, and she finally was able to straighten her legs and stand. Only then did she notice the pounding pressure of blood in her ears. Her jacket had ridden up and cold air tickled her exposed waist. Her shoulders hunched from where she grabbed at him, and the scent of his cologne mingled faintly with woodsmoke from his jacket.

She wanted to kiss him.

How cheesy. She wasn't in a chick flick, and she wasn't as sweet and cutesy a heroine as Sandra Bullock or Anne Hathaway.

It didn't make her want to kiss him any less.

Esme. Esme liked him. He seemed to like Esme—had taken her to the Christmas party. Esme, her *friend*.

"No."

That sounded like her voice. Was she nuts? The man kissed like Casanova!

"No."

There it was again. Someone was controlling her vocal chords, and it wasn't her brain, because that was twisting like a psychedelic kaleidoscope.

"I can't. I'm too busy. You're ... *you*. Esme. This isn't a smart ... *thing*."

"What? Thing? Eloquent, Venus."

Considering he was still holding onto her tightly, her objections sounded rather stupid. But thoughts of Esme cooled her heated brain rather quickly. She was going to be nice for a change.

Also, even though his embrace warmed her better than a hot shower, it felt too strange. She'd gotten used to keeping aloof from men, striving to be more professional, less emotional, less feminine. She focused on nothing else but her own company, to set all else aside until she had it.

This was just too weird a ... thing. She really had no better word for it. And her entire body screamed with fear.

He let her go. She immediately missed his warmth as cold air refroze the water in her clothes. And a vast sea, still and awful, iced over in her heart.

She couldn't see his face, but she wouldn't have wanted to anyway. She turned and started walking.

"Venus."

She kept walking.

"Venus."

"I don't want to talk about it."

He sighed. "Venus, you're going the wrong way."

TWENTY-FOUR

Venus picked at her salad and considered flinging a radish across the table.

She was picking at it because Mom had asked her out to lunch, but now that they were at the restaurant, neither of them knew quite what to say to each other. She wanted to fling food, because despite Venus's attempts at small talk, Mom only answered in monosyllables, and she had a childish impulse to get her mother to say something, anything.

Venus hadn't talked to her mother in over a month—since driving her home from Grandma's Christmas party. She'd seen her at the family New Year's party, but they'd avoided each other successfully.

Well, what could she say? "Gee, Mom, you're looking better since you were sloshed and embarrassing at Grandma's party"?

"Venus, I'm sorry."

At first she didn't realize Mom had spoken, until she reasoned that even in her daydreams, Mom never apologized. She glanced up, but Mom wasn't looking at her; instead she poked at her pasta bowl.

Venus had to say something. The silence was going to stretch too long and then her mom would either get mad or start crying. "Uh ... about what?"

"I'm sorry about the Christmas party." Mom spoke to her linguine.

"Oh. Uh ... thanks. I mean, that's okay." What was wrong with her? Besides which, it wasn't okay. Who knows what kind of damage the whole fiasco did for Venus's reputation, maybe even Grandma's reputation? The memory of the night smoldered in her chest like lava rocks.

She ought to forgive and forget. She ought to honor her mother. The thoughts were only sprinkling drops that sizzled away on the coals.

Mom licked her lips. "I heard Yardley deliberately point me out after I slapped Arnold."

"You heard that?"

Mom straightened in her ladder back chair. "I was tipsy, not deaf."

Venus fought the urge to roll her eyes.

"Besides which, Yardley spoke loud enough for everyone to hear." She blinked a few times, then licked her lip again. "Why does he dislike you so much?"

Venus looked down at her salad. "I quit his company, Mom."

"That usually doesn't make people so malicious."

"Yardley doesn't like that I'm setting up a game development company. Rivalry and all that."

"Quite a bitter rival," Mom said dryly. "Did you steal something from him?"

"What? No!"

Mom shrugged. "Just wondering. Did he steal something from you?"

The question came at her so fast, she didn't have time to force out a suitable denial that wouldn't be an outright lie. "Uh ..."

"Ah." Mom's eyes gleamed. "I thought so. Your super secret software program, right?"

"It's a gaming development tool."

"So, something he'd be very interested in."

It wasn't a question, so Venus didn't answer.

Mom swirled a shrimp and some noodles on her fork. "I wouldn't worry, dear. Don't underestimate how much power your grandmother has."

Venus didn't like playing this social-business game. Why couldn't things be more straightforward?

"And don't underestimate Drake's parents either." Mom took a bite. "He seemed rather interested in you."

Venus set down her fork with a clatter. "He's my boss, Mom."

Her mother shrugged and chewed, and her innocent look said, *You can say what you like, but I know you have the hots for him.*

Venus hated when she did that. She sighed, breathing in pungent oregano and savory cheese from the kitchen. Another reason to pick at her salad—she had wanted lasagna but ordered the healthier option without even opening the menu, so she wouldn't be tempted. Her skirt waistband cut into her stomach when she sat down—too many Reese's peanut butter cups recently. Stupid Drake.

Why not date him? the insidious voice whispered.

No. Esme liked him, for one, and she wanted to focus on her company. Business relationships were easier than personal ones. Look at how well she did with her mom, with Grandma. It was too complicated, and she didn't want complicated.

That was why she had chosen to live with her dad when her parents divorced. He didn't show affection very much, but that also meant he didn't fly off the handle at ridiculous things or betray her with selfish neglect when she wasn't expecting it, like her mother did. Her relationship with her dad was simplistic—he was happy when she succeeded and unhappy when she didn't. Venus could understand him better than she could understand her volatile mother.

Mom reached for her water glass. "Are you still working with your youth group?"

"Yes."

"Do you ..." Mom regarded her speculatively. "Do you like it?"

"Actually ... yeah, Mom."

"Really? I wouldn't have pictured you enjoying working with teenagers."

"I wouldn't have either. But ... they grew on me." They made her laugh. They made her feel young. They made her so proud; they made her want to gather them to her and protect them exactly like a mother bird and her chicks. "Originally it was because of Gerry, but now I'm really glad she required it."

"I don't understand. It was for work?"

"I never told you? Gerry wanted us to connect with our user demographics better."

"Did it work?"

"Well, we just got a really positive report from our testers on the new version. Apparently the fact that everyone's been working with kids outside of work has helped quite a bit."

"That's marvelous."

"In fact, I have a presentation next week to a major investor."

"You always hated those."

Venus grimaced. She had no problem sitting at a meeting table with other people, but standing in front of them made her nervous.

Mom sipped her water. "It's because you were overweight for so many years. You don't like being the center of attention."

Why did she always have to bring that up? "We are not discussing that, Mother."

Mom pursed her lips but didn't pursue it. "Why don't you just have Drake do it?"

"He's driving his mother to Oregon for some funeral."

"Driving? Isn't it a long way?"

"His mom refuses to fly, and his dad's out of the country on business, so Drake volunteered." The timing couldn't be worse. Gerry was making only part of the presentation—the technical side was all Venus.

Mom gave a smile. "It says something about his character that he'd drive her himself rather than asking an uncle or somebody to do it."

"There is no one else who can do it." Venus thought Drake was nice to drive his mom, but she pitched her answer to squelch any of Mom's wayward romantic hopes. No telling what embarrassing things Mom would do if she thought there was a chance for something more.

Mom gave her another innocent look. Venus glowered at her.

Mom's eyes fell back to her food. Her voice was so soft, Venus almost didn't hear her. "You know I only want you to be well-provided for and cared for, right? I don't want to worry about you."

Venus's voice was soft too. "I know, Mom." Her mom's overtures lately—more than she'd ever done before—pleased Venus, although she didn't expect her to drop all her self-centeredness and turn into June Cleaver. And Venus was starting to learn how to respond to her with more love and grace.

A bustle at the door made her glance up as a waiter ushered in a couple to a table. A foot-long spike stabbed into the base of her stomach.

Drake, with Esme's pink-tipped nails wrapped around his arm.

The CTO candidate didn't look any better the third time she read his resume, so why was she bothering?

She knew perfectly well why—to stave off the feeling of drowning every time she looked at the PowerPoint presentation.

Well, not *drowning*, exactly. She refused to be beaten by a stupid presentation. But she was doing something that certainly needed to be done—looking for her replacement here at Bananaville—so it wasn't avoidance or procrastination, per se. Not really.

One candidate looked promising. She studied his resume again, as if that would make more experience somehow appear between the lines. Well, might as well call to set up an interview.

Ew, her phone hadn't been cleaned in days. She fumbled in her desk drawer for her purse, but pulled out her computer case instead. She hoped she'd have time later today to work on it. She set the case beside her desk, reached in for her purse, and grabbed a wipe-up. She even scrubbed between the buttons. And the underside. And the cord.

She called. "Hello, this is Venus Chau. I saw your resume—"

"Oh, no."

She blinked before answering. "Excuse me?"

"Not another interview. They're so tedious."

Did he really say what she thought he said? "I'm calling about a job—"

"I really can't do another job interview. They take up so much time."

Venus glared at her computer screen, closed his resume file, and emptied it into the recycling bin. "Since you're not interested—"

"Oh, I am. Interested." He yawned as he said the word, so Venus was guessing that's what he said. "But you'll have to hire me based on my resume alone. Or I might give a few minutes to you now on the phone."

"No, thank you." She hung up without saying good-bye.

Well, it was nice to be able to at least eliminate someone. Next candidate—even less experience, a little young, perhaps, but still worth an interview. She dialed.

The first thing she heard was someone shouting at the top of their lungs in the background, followed by a whispered, "Hello?"

"Um ... I'm Venus Chau, I saw your resume ..."

She heard the background voice raise to bellowing level. "And you messed everything up with your laziness and incompetence ... *Are you on the phone?*"

"Can I call you back? Bye!" *Click.*

What was up with these people? Did the hiring process change since she last looked for a job a year ago? She brought up another resume on her computer. Dare she try another phone call? She wouldn't have been surprised to get a chicken farm or a funny farm instead.

She flipped the screen back to the presentation, but that only made her want to lay her head down on the desk and cry.

Esme's hesitant knock sounded on the door.

"Come in."

She poked her head in. "Did you want more coffee? I'm going to make a pot."

"Thank you, yes." Venus held out her mug.

Esme peered at the presentation. "Do you need any help with it?"

Venus slumped in her chair. "Want to do it for me?"

Her eyes sparkled like black diamonds. "Really? I'd love to."

Venus sat up, blinking at her. The offer was like a life preserver—*no*, Venus wasn't drowning. Just ... stressed.

And as Operations Manager, Esme was qualified to give the presentation. Plus, Venus would be there in the room. It wasn't completely unheard of to have someone else present it. Venus wasn't averse to taking advantage of Esme's cute face and sweet smile.

"Do you feel up to it? It's the Amity Group—they're a pretty big investor."

"I'd love the opportunity. I won't fail you."

Venus glanced at the slides on her computer, now not so threatening. "I'll send you the preliminary slides. You'll need to organize them and figure out which others to add. If you're comfortable presenting it, I'll ask Gerry if it's okay."

Esme's sunbeam smile made Venus blink against the glare. "Thanks! I'll be right back with your coffee." As she turned, her heel caught Venus's computer bag strap. Her foot kicked up a little, and she looked back at the bag. "Oh! I'm so sorry. It's not damaged, is it?"

"No, it's fine." Venus returned it to her desk drawer. Esme's curious gaze as she turned the drawer key in the lock seemed a little strange. She shrugged it away as she dropped the key in her blazer pocket. "Thanks for getting me coffee."

Esme nodded and pranced out.

Venus paused before emailing the PowerPoint presentation to Esme. Was this really a good idea? She hated feeling like she was passing the buck. But if Esme would do a good, or even better job at it—be more enthusiastic, look charming and natural, and present the technical data in a competent light—why not? Besides, she'd email Gerry to ask if she thought it would be okay. If Gerry said no, then Venus would just do the presentation herself.

Esme returned and plunked the coffee cup down.

"Thanks. I just emailed the slides to you."

Esme looked down and bit her bottom lip until it looked like a raspberry. "I hope you don't mind ... I had already said yes ... I told him six o'clock ..."

"You have a date? That's fine." What was Esme's problem? Venus wasn't a monster, expecting her to stay late to work on a presentation that wasn't due until next week.

Esme's V-shaped smile and strange, direct gaze sent a bolt down Venus's spine. "I'm so glad you understand. When Drake asked me out, I was so excited. I didn't want to disappoint him." She breezed out of the office.

Venus wasn't sure how to feel. She liked Esme, and she—logically—knew she *shouldn't* be jealous about Drake. But even after a week, the memory of the almost-kiss in the snow burned into her brain, making her a liar.

But why would Drake want to kiss her if he was interested in Esme? That seemed out of character—he was never a flirt. Which meant he might be open to Venus if she made a move ... She quelled the surge of electricity that jolted through her heart. No, Esme liked him. Esme, the best Operations Manager she'd ever had, the nicest person she knew, the first woman outside of her cousins who seemed to like her. Venus would not go after the man Esme confessed to liking. That would be completely heartless of her. She reached for the coffee.

Ugh, Esme made the coffee strong this time. Venus went back to scanning resumes.

She jerked awake from a snooze. Too little sleep last night? She gulped down more coffee. The résumés blurred in front of her ...

A hammer was pounding on her desk. She could feel it through her skull. Which was strange, because she couldn't understand what her head was doing on her desk in the first place.

Venus opened bleary eyes to the sideways picture of her phone. She blinked, and it came into focus a bit more, but it still lay sideways.

She inhaled, only then feeling the hard surface of her desk pressed against her cheek. Had she fallen asleep? After all that coffee?

She closed her mouth, feeling the sliminess of—oh no, she'd drooled onto her desk. An attempt to raise her head brought the hammer pounding to a thunder. Her skull had cracked open.

Dizzy. She eased upright. Room spinning. How long had she been out? She creaked her head sideways to check the computer screen—the screensaver was on. Those psychedelic wavy lines made her close her eyes. Okay, well, the blinds were open and the room was dark. Must be at least past six.

Had she caught the flu? That was just great. She should go home and take something.

A note on her pristine desk caught her eye.

I told everyone to leave you alone—hope that was okay. –Esme.

So Esme had seen her sprawled out on her desk? Venus frowned and massaged her neck. Why would that bother her? It's not as if Esme took incriminating pictures or brought the entire company in to laugh at her. She'd even saved her further embarrassment by telling people to leave her alone. So why did Venus feel like she'd been lying here naked instead of just asleep?

The blood pounded in her head as if it would burst out of a vein any second. Venus fumbled for her desk drawer to get her purse—locked. She'd locked it? That's right, she had. Where had she put the key? Oh, that's right, her blazer pocket. Funny, her blazer was creased and twisted around in the opposite direction she'd been lying.

She unlocked the drawer and got out her Advil bottle. She gulped a couple tablets down with the bottled water on her desk. The liquid made her mouth feel less like a rat's nest, so she drank all of it.

Time to go home. She reached into the drawer to get her purse and computer bag.

The bag was upside down. It lay near the back of the drawer as it had been before, but flipped over. Such a trifle ... but she pulled it out and unzipped it.

A jumble of cords fell out. Rather than neatly coiled and tied up on itself the way it always was, the power cord lay in a haphazard nest on the laptop. She hadn't left it that way last night; she hadn't left it that way this morning when she had briefly opened it to make sure it had enough battery life to last the day in her desk drawer.

She only used this computer for one thing—the Spiderweb.

She was having a heart attack. A squeezing in her chest made her gasp and rub her breastbone with her shaking palm. She heaved to draw in breath, but the air came in reedy gasps.

Someone had seen her development tool.

TWENTY-FIVE

She didn't care who she had to run over, she was not going to be late to work today.

Venus slid around a slow-moving ancient Honda and revved her engine in the early morning traffic. A blaring honk followed her from the guy she'd just cut off.

Her phone rang. She answered with her Bluetooth wireless earpiece. "Hello?"

"Hello, dear."

"Mom, this is not a good time." She squeezed in between two cars so she could make the freeway exit coming up. More honking.

"Well!" Her mother's huffing sounded like hurricane winds in her earpiece. "That's a nice welcome."

"Mom, the presentation is today."

"What presentation?"

"The one I told you about last week. At lunch. That I was stressing over."

"Speaking of lunch, you should go to lunch with me today. There's this new restaurant I want you to take me to."

"Mom!" Venus jammed on the brakes before she rear-ended the minivan in front of her. "The presentation?"

"What presentation?"

Venus strangled her mother's imaginary neck until the car behind her honked to get going. She hit the accelerator, but not soon enough to prevent an SUV from cutting in front of her, forcing her to hit the brakes again. Her padded computer bag slid from her passenger seat and thumped onto the floorboards.

Aargh! She reached over to grab it and slide it back on the seat, enduring another round of honking from the cars behind her. She couldn't stop that rush of despair that blew up from her stomach like a typhoon every time she looked at her laptop—ever since last week. She knew it had been hacked into, knew the development tool had been copied. She hadn't had time to do much more than worry excessively about it.

One thing she did know—Yardley was behind it.

"So, dear—lunch?" Mom's voice had that distracted tone—she was probably making breakfast or something like that.

"No, I'm too busy today."

Tense silence.

Oh, brother.

"Mom, I told you I have a presentation today—"

"It's only a presentation; it takes one hour. You have eight hours in your workday. You can't spare an hour to eat lunch with your mother?"

"I still need to go over the slides with Esme"—she hit the brakes as she took the turn on the exit lane a bit too fast—"and set up the meeting room equipment"—she turned the corner and stopped hard at the sudden line of cars waiting for the light—"and go over the schedule with Gerry." Could this light take *any* longer?

"That's not going to take you *all* morning, is it?"

"Today. Is. Not. A. Good. Day. Mother." Finally the light turned green.

Click.

Oh, great. Just when things between them were getting better. Maybe she should have offered to have lunch tomorrow. Why did she always think of these things too late?

She screeched into the parking lot and grabbed her stuff. She wasn't actually late, but she wasn't as early as she wanted to be.

Darla came running out the doors of the building, heading straight for her.

Oh. No.

"Esme quit!" Her voice echoed off the concrete walls.

What? Without talking to her? Without warning? "Today?"

"This morning. As of an hour ago."

"Why?" Venus hustled toward the doors. "Is she still here?"

"No, she left!" Darla heaved. "She didn't even tell Gerry in person. She sent an email, and then flung the news over her shoulder at me as she left the building. I had to be the one to tell Gerry. She's having a cow, by the way."

Unnecessary news because Venus heard the shouting as soon as she got within a foot of the doors. Esme gone? What was going on? She clenched her jaw and inhaled, then yanked open the glass door.

The noise level sounded like a hundred cats in heat. She plunged indoors.

Darla followed. "We have another problem."

"What?"

"Macy crashed the server last night. A bunch of people have been here since four this morning trying to fix it."

"Where is she?"

"She quit!"

Naturally.

Darla clenched shaking fists to her stomach. Her eyes were wide, but her jaw was so tight, it could have been wired shut. At least she held in her fear and anger rather than unleashing it, which somebody was doing down the hallway.

"Does Gerry know about Macy?"

"Oh, yeah," she said dryly.

"When is the Amity Group supposed to arrive?"

Darla straightened, tugging at her modest silk blouse. "Not until noon."

Venus realized Darla had dressed the part of a receptionist today, and a tiny piece of stress melted away. "Good. Then we have time. Come with me." She marched behind the lobby down the corridor.

As she turned the corner, she discovered that not all the noise was emotional. Some of the voices were merely hurried as techs shouted to each other, trying to fix the system. So different from the first day, when they'd all been gathered in the breakroom.

The argument emanated from Gerry's office. Venus knocked and didn't wait before barging in.

Lisa, the website programmer under Macy, faced off against Gerry. Lisa stood as immovable as a stone Buddha while Gerry's white face had the skin pulled back like a corpse. Although she stood behind the desk, her shoulders angled forward as if she'd leap over the top and beat up the poor girl.

Lisa turned toward Venus as they walked in. She panted as if she'd run a race and her mouth was solid and mutinous, but her wide eyes had a frantic gleam.

She'd rescue the poor tech first. "Lisa, the system—"

Lisa turned to her with desperate appeal. "The system is a complete mess—"

Gerry slammed a fist down on her desk. "The system wouldn't be a mess if you hadn't—"

Lisa rounded on Gerry. "There was no way to know Macy would—"

"You're senior programmer under her—you should have been watching ..."

Venus gave Gerry an urgent, *Shut up and let me talk to her* look. Gerry's nostrils flared, but she turned and stalked toward the window of her office.

Venus had never met such melodramatic women in her entire life. Did they pump hormones into the air filtration system or something? The mess today was huge, but Gerry needed a serious chill pill, as the high school girls would say. Venus remembered how she'd dealt with Angeline on her first day here. Okay, that had been a bit harsh, but Venus had only worked with men before coming to Bananaville. She'd learned a thing or two about dealing with women since then.

"Lisa, it's not your fault." Venus heard her mother's voice. She'd pitched her tone exactly like Mom when she was being charming and soothing—which she usually did when she wanted something. But maybe that was the solution, since Venus certainly didn't have a nurturing personality.

She kept her voice quiet, in hopes Lisa would calm also. "We know you do your best. There's nothing you could have done . . ." And more repetitive, calming things, which seemed to work because Lisa's breathing slowed from offended heaves to a more normal rhythm.

Venus touched her shoulders gingerly, but it seemed to relax her more. She turned her gently and pleaded with Darla over the girl's head. Darla obliged by wrapping an arm around her shoulders. "You go with Darla, now, and we'll take care of everything."

As soon as the door closed behind them, Venus hissed at Gerry, "Do you have to argue with everyone?"

At the same time, Gerry whirled. "Do you know what the Web director that *you* hired did last night?"

They faced off, each breathing fire. But Gerry seemed to check herself, and she took a deep breath and backed off. A bit disgruntled, Venus did the same. Since when was volatile Gerry the calm one of both of them?

Gerry sat at her desk. "I'm sorry. When you hired Macy, you certainly couldn't predict what she'd do."

"Her résumé was stellar." Venus rubbed the back of her neck. "I should have followed her more closely. I would have known she was incompetent."

Gerry tapped two fingers on her desk. "Lisa said it was deliberate."

"What?"

"Sabotage. Why would anyone sabotage us?"

"I . . ." The thought of her tampered laptop made her pause. Was all this connected somehow? Was *Esme* connected with it? She couldn't breathe for a moment. "Esme didn't say why she left, did she?"

"No. Just polite nothings." Gerry gave a groaning sigh. "Well, we can't do anything about it now." She checked her watch. "It's seven thirty."

"So we have, what, four and a half hours before Amity shows up?"

"Do you have the slides for the presentation?"

"Yes. I'll do the presentation." The acid boiled in her stomach.

"We need the server up so we can demonstrate it for Amity."

"Lisa's working on it—"

"Lisa's smart, but she's just out of college. Can we call anyone to help us out?"

Venus snapped her fingers. "Jaye. I'll call him." She fumbled with her purse and grabbed her cell phone.

Gerry waved her out. "I'll call Drake."

Venus hustled down the hallway, trying to keep her computer bag from slipping from her shoulder. "Jaye, I need help. Our server is down."

"Venus … I'm in L.A."

"What?"

"Last-minute trip. Manager told me yesterday. Left last night."

She kicked open her office door and dumped her bags on the floor. "Well … what are you doing now?"

"In traffic. Talking to animators in an hour."

"Okay, I'm going to have Lisa call you."

"Now?"

"I need the server up. Talk her through it."

"Sure. 'Cause, you know, it's really easy to fix something you can't see."

"Just do something. It's not like I have a ton of options."

"Okay, okay." He clicked off.

Venus speed-dialed Lisa and gave her Jaye's cell phone number while she booted up her computer. No emails from Esme. Rats. The latest version of the presentation she had was the one Esme sent on Friday. They'd worked on a new version yesterday, and Esme had promised to email a copy to her—but apparently she'd had other things on her mind, like quitting and leaving them hanging out to dry. She'd have to get it off Esme's computer.

She swept into Esme's office. The pink stuffed bears were gone from her desk. A wave like an electric field passed through her, making her shiver and her stomach cramp. As she clenched her midriff, she fisted her hands, fighting a sudden desire to rip the stuffing out of those dratted bears if they were still here. And the computer was still on. She toggled the mouse to disrupt the screensaver.

Gone. Wiped clean of every piece of data that wasn't an application.

Venus collapsed into the chair, her stomach vibrating like a truck engine about to blow. This was deliberate. It must have taken Esme at least an hour. She knew Venus would need that presentation, and she'd purposefully destroyed it.

Venus said a few not very nice words.

Gerry had mentioned sabotage of the server. It was starting to sound more plausible by the minute. Was it connected to her laptop too? That bitter coffee, waking up as if she had a hangover ... She opened their Instant Messaging application and sent Gerry an IM:

Esme's hard drive is completely erased.

What do u mean erased?

She erased the presentation too.

Can u redo?

Yes. She hoped so. *Did Esme or Macy have anything against Bananaville? You? Drake?*

I'll ask. On the phone w/ Drake.

While waiting, Venus looked to see if she could recover anything from the hard drive. The vibrating in her stomach had moved to her hands, and she found it hard to type.

Running feet down the hall. Stopping, starting again. "Venus! There you are!" Darla grabbed onto the doorframe to stop herself before she ran past. She looked frantic enough to combust, but she seemed to be trying to keep her voice down.

Oh. Man. "What is it?"

"It's Amity!" Darla started to hyperventilate. "They've arrived early!"

TWENTY-SIX

What do you mean, she quit?" In the confines of the car, Drake's voice sounded like a roar.

"Drake," his mother admonished from the passenger seat.

"This morning." Gerry sounded close to tears.

"Did she say why?"

"No. None of us suspected anything."

"Well, Venus can do the presentation." Even though she was horrible at them. He'd actually been relieved when he heard Esme was going to do it instead.

"She's preparing right now. But Drake, what's even worse is that Macy crashed the server last night."

"You're kidding."

"Lisa's been here since four trying to fix it. She says it looks deliberate."

"Why would Macy do that?"

"I don't know. But with Esme quitting . . ."

And he was too far away to turn back. They'd started at four thirty this morning and were just past Chico. He glanced at his mother. Not that he could turn back—she couldn't miss her own sister's funeral.

She gave him a troubled look. "I'm sorry."

"Not your fault, Ma." He said it automatically, but his hands clenched the steering wheel. *Breathe deep. Calm down.*

Gerry gasped. "Esme erased her computer. The entire hard drive."

A programmer could not do that by accident. "That has to be deliberate."

"Venus just IM'd me. Esme erased the presentation."

Oh, no. Venus was bad enough at presenting when she was prepared. "Can she redo it?"

"She says yes. She asks if Esme or Macy had anything against us."

He barely knew Macy, aside from the fact she was Esme's friend and Venus had hired her. But Esme ... would she really do this just because he'd turned aside her interest in him? She'd seemed to take their talk last night rather well. It seemed so petty. It didn't seem like her, but then again, he was realizing he didn't know her well at all.

"Oh my gosh! Oh my gosh!"

"What?" Drake pushed his Bluetooth headset closer.

"Amity is here early! Gotta go." Gerry clicked off.

Early. They were early. He stared at the stretch of highway, empty and desolate. His mind felt the same way. He couldn't believe it. Venus wouldn't have time to prepare. They wouldn't be able to do a demo because the server was down. And he was a hundred miles away. He slammed his palm into the steering wheel.

"Drake," his mother breathed.

"Sorry, Ma." Automatic.

He had never felt so helpless in his life.

Breathe. He breathed. He couldn't do anything else. *Breathe.*

He remembered the song from church that Sunday. *This is the air I breathe ...* He'd been going to church because Gerry asked him. It seemed to have calmed her, and he wanted to please her, so he went. Same with the youth group—she'd wanted him to, so he'd done it.

Pastor Lester's sermons were okay. The worship music was okay. The people there were nice, although most of them had the typical Asian shyness and restraint.

But somehow it had all wormed its way inside him. He wasn't even sure what. Suddenly it didn't seem so impossible that there could be a God. That He'd care about the mess happening right now.

Breathe.

For the first time in his life, he prayed.

Venus exited the deathly silent meeting room, hounded by Gerry's silently howling gaze. As she closed the door, she heard one of Amity's VPs mutter, "Boy, Yardley was right about her."

Yardley.

She froze right outside the meeting room door. Everything that had happened—her laptop, Esme erasing the presentation, Macy sabotaging the server—had been bent on embarrassing and ruining *her.* Not Bananaville, not Gerry or Drake. Venus. Only one person in the world hated her that much, and that was Yardley.

She'd have time to think more about it later. Right now, she had to see if Jaye had helped Lisa fix the server. But she couldn't stop the ice water from running through her limbs, chilling her heart.

Yardley. Yardley had done all this to her.

It wasn't entirely his fault. She should have been watching Macy more closely—a quick chat with Lisa had revealed Macy had been slacking off since she started, and to the rest of the team, she hadn't seemed as experienced as she was supposed to be. They talked to Esme, who allayed their fears enough that they'd put off talking to Venus.

Apparently, the entire website team was a little afraid of Venus.

She sighed.

Venus should have insisted on Esme sending her a recent copy of the presentation. Should have called her back to work to send it or asked for her password to get it off her computer herself.

But she hadn't. She'd been so caught up in petty things like almost kissing Drake, she hadn't paid enough attention. She'd neglected her work at Bananaville, she'd been careless about her laptop.

A chasm had opened in her heart, yawning, empty, aching. It sliced deep within her. It cut through her organs, her muscles, her bones.

And Esme, one of the few people she'd allowed close to her, had done this.

The hammer fell three days later.

"Venus. Won't like this."

"Spit it out, Jaye." Venus shouldered the phone, clicked on her mouse, and closed the file she'd been looking at. Almost time to leave work.

"Esme is new Game Lead for the *Tortufa* project."

"What? At Oomvid?" She was glad she was sitting. Her legs had turned into the fatty, creamy almond Jell-O her Aunty Linda made.

Really, she shouldn't be surprised. She'd turned everything around in her head, and she couldn't see how Yardley hadn't been involved somehow. Esme's working at Oomvid—and as Game Lead, no less—just confirmed all her theories. "Yardley brought her in?"

"According to the grapevine."

Venus thought, but didn't say, some more not very nice words.

"Something else."

She already knew. "The Spiderweb?"

"Pete let me see a brand-new development tool they started work on."

Her gut ached. The acid in her stomach had been terrible for three days. "Is it ours?"

"Close. Not exactly. Won't infringe on the patent."

"Maybe they came up with it themselves."

After a long pause, Jaye replied, "Don't be stupid, Venus." He hung up.

The Spiderweb was his too. And now they both had nothing.

Esme had stolen it. Had been working for Yardley and waited until Venus brought her laptop to work. Venus had only done that a handful of times—but Esme had only needed her to bring it that last time.

Deceitful. But why had she erased the presentation? Why had Macy crashed the server? Much as Yardley hated Venus, would they really do something so malicious just because he wanted them to?

Somehow she knew it had been personal, at least on Esme's side.

And Venus intended to find out why.

The longer Venus waited for Esme to come home, the more creative she got in what she'd do to Esme when she finally saw her.

Esme's apartment complex looked a lot like Venus's condo—probably the same developer—but sat in a not-as-nice area of San Jose. Venus had parked near the apartment so she could keep an eye on her car.

Where was Esme? And Venus thought *she* stayed at work late.

Her cell phone rang. Drake. "What?"

"Where are you?" He sounded cautious—that voice people used when trying to placate a psycho.

"I'm waiting outside Esme's apartment door. Her welcome mat is filthy, by the way."

She thought she heard him groan faintly. "I just heard the news."

"She stole the Spiderweb."

"I heard about that too."

"Well, then, why are you calling?"

"What do you think you can do?"

Venus smiled grimly. "I have a lot of good ideas."

"Venus."

"She's not home yet, anyway."

"Just don't do anything stupid."

"I never do anything stupid." But she was starting to *feel* stupid. She clicked the phone shut.

Maybe Esme's zeal for her new position kept her after hours. Or maybe she had a hot date. Or maybe she'd come home already, despite Venus's vigilance in watching for her car. Maybe she'd seen and recognized Venus's convertible and made a quick getaway.

Drake was right. This was stupid. It had been dumb to even think she could catch Esme at her home. She'd just started a new, high-stress job that would probably demand sixteen-hour days from her for a few weeks, at least. Was Venus really willing to wait until midnight for her?

That would be a no.

She slunk down the apartment steps like a thwarted thief, cloaked in darkness and embarrassment. The burning under her breastbone just made it worse. It was one thing to want to deliver a slap to Esme, quite another when she deserved a good wallop herself. And one slap deferred didn't make the other one less mortifying.

She stepped out onto the street just as a sleek new silver Mercedes convertible slid past.

With Esme behind the wheel.

They saw each other at the same moment. Esme gunned her engine.

The street into the apartment complex dead-ended about five hundred yards down. It was also too narrow for her to pull around. She'd have to find a parking stall in order to pull in and do a three-point turn.

Venus raced to her Beamer, slamming her thumb on the button for her remote engine start. Her cousin would get a kick out of this. Originally when he'd convinced her to install the after-market feature in her upgraded security system, it had been intended to open her windows, start her engine, and turn on her A/C before she got to her Beamer oven on hot California summer days. Not in a race to beat a dashing Mercedes.

Thanks to the lateness of the hour, all the parking stalls near her apartment were filled, so Esme had to go down quite a ways before she could pull into an empty one and then jam out of it, headed back down the street. She was already roaring toward her when Venus got in her car.

Venus hesitated only a fraction of a second. This was a lot worse than a slap.

But Esme deserved it.

Venus threw the car into gear and backed out with a rush of squealing tires.

Shrieking brakes that seemed to go on forever. Then *bam!* Venus's car hopped sideways on impact. Her airbags erupted and slapped her with hard white hands. *Ow!*

All was silent for a long moment, which was nice because she needed time to make sure she was still breathing.

What had she done? She ached from the top of her head down through her spine. Rubbing the crown of her head, she wondered if she'd hit the ceiling. Good thing it was convertible cloth. Her chiropractor was going to kill her.

Oh, man. She took another deep breath. Maybe she shouldn't have done that. At least, not with her seatbelt off.

She reached over to open the passenger side door, then dribbled out of the car. She glanced at her front end. Luckily, she'd cleared the other cars parked on either side of her, so she hadn't dinged any of them.

She could walk at least. The airbags had hurt worse than the impact. She wandered around the car to the driver side door just as Esme's car door swung open.

Hmph. Not bad, considering. The damage to her door didn't look as bad as Esme's dramatically crumpled front end. She guessed Esme had been farther away than she'd thought when she first backed out in front of her.

"Are you crazy?" Esme had finally found her voice. She stumbled out of her car, eyes glued to the ruffled metal, mouth swinging open. Venus had never seen Esme completely unhinged, and the sight entertained her way too much.

Her horrified gaze rose to Venus, who could feel the smile pulling at her mouth. The sight of the unfortunate Mercedes gave her more satisfaction by the second. "New car? Bought it with your signing bonus, huh?"

Esme gave an inarticulate sound of rage and took a step toward her. Venus did a Billy Blanks and brought her fists up. "I wouldn't if I were you." She had a good ten inches and at least twenty pounds on

Esme's tiny frame, never mind that her only kickboxing experience was TaeBo Boot Camp DVDs.

Esme stopped, although she stood there fuming and flinging her arms around. "Why did you do this?"

"Why do you *think* I did this?"

"You're just jealous!" Esme stabbed her finger at Venus like a woodpecker at a tree trunk. "You can't stand the fact I've got the job you wanted!"

"If I'd wanted the job, I wouldn't have quit."

"You were stupid enough to quit Oomvid!" Esme screeched so loud that her voice cracked. "You don't deserve this job!"

"Yardley didn't offer me that job."

She stopped mid-breath. "What do you mean?"

"He offered me VP of Programming, you twit."

Esme's pouty bottom lip dropped full open. Her face darkened, and she trembled like a bowl of chili about to erupt in the microwave. "I can do any job you can do! I would have been a better CTO than you are!"

Ah. That was it. She'd finally dug out the root of her animosity. "Drake would have promoted you to CTO if he thought you were competent." It was true. Drake didn't play favorites when it came to his team. Venus had known that about him before, and she had seen that in him during the last few months.

"Competent? Ha! He just wanted to get into your pants."

Rather than your pants. But the girl might go ballistic if she said that, so Venus kept her mouth shut in a rare moment of tact. Drake had somehow told Esme he wasn't interested, whereas he'd been quite clear to Venus that he was more than interested. She felt rather warm and fuzzy about that.

Esme's attention returned to her car. She kicked at a tire. "You're insane!"

Venus crossed her arms. "You lose your sanity when your Operations Manager sabotages your company and steals your proprietary software."

Esme stilled. Her mouth twisted into an evil smile. "Prove it."

Venus frowned. Her sparkling apple-cider feeling at the destruction of Esme's personal property suddenly fizzled. She couldn't prove it. And the injustice of everything overshadowed this petty bit of revenge.

Make that an expensive bit of revenge. *Venus, you have reached an all-time low.*

Suddenly, headlights turned the corner into the parking lot. Oh, great. They were blocking the entire street and had to call tow trucks right away. Good thing one of her cousins owned a body shop and another cousin was her insurance agent. She left Esme weeping with her head on her door frame while Venus climbed into her passenger door to get her purse and her cell phone.

The headlights approached them and stopped. Why had the car turned toward them? Couldn't the driver see that he couldn't get through?

The car door opened, closed. A man's figure, but she couldn't see him because of the glare of his headlights. Venus had a flashing vision of a serial killer chopping off both of their heads. She flipped open her cell phone.

"Venus?"

She almost dropped her phone. "Drake?"

He moved into the light and surveyed the mess. "This is what you call not doing anything stupid?"

TWENTY-SEVEN

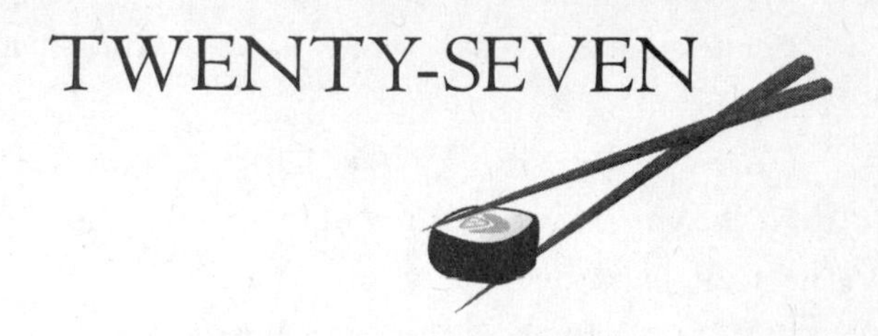

The rest of her world fell apart exactly two feet from her condo door.

Her cell phone chirped. She handed her keys to Drake so she could dig in her purse for it. He obliged by opening her door as she answered the call. "Hi, Jaye."

"Venus." His wheezing voice sounded like he'd aged a hundred years. "At the airport. Mom fell and broke her hip."

"Oh, no."

"Fell sometime this morning. Been on her kitchen floor all day. My sister didn't find her until tonight."

"How is she?"

"Doctors think she had a stroke."

"What?"

"Venus." The pause stretched out like a rubber band.

"Just tell me."

"We're going to move to Arizona."

She didn't answer. She was vaguely aware of her bag slipping to the ground from her shoulder.

"Nancy already called her boss to let her know she's quitting. She and Junior are coming with me to Phoenix tonight. In a couple days, I'll head back to California for a few weeks to clear things up."

"The Spiderweb ..."

"I can still help you develop it."

"The company ..."

Jaye sighed. "Venus, while it was *our* tool, it was always *your* company."

That wasn't true. Well, Jaye had been more excited about the tool than the game ideas, but the nights they spent thinking up applications and brainstorming …

"Talk to you about this later, Venus." *Click.*

Not have Jaye to help start her company? It had never occurred to her before. She still needed to find a strong core of people to form her team. She'd always thought Jaye would be with her in that core. But now, he wouldn't be there with her.

She was entirely alone.

Why did it suddenly feel like her entire world had shattered around her in raining panes of glass? They cut her, sliced through her skin, and she cried out in pain.

And then she was wailing. She couldn't open her mouth wide enough to unleash the despair that came rushing up from her gut. Drake's arm closed around her. She couldn't feel her feet.

Movement. The closing of her front door. Her knees hit the cold tile of her foyer. And then arms folded her close and she cried, her face buried in a warm shoulder. The tang of his cologne mingled with the salt of her tears. She bawled and unleashed all the pain, all the anger, all the frustration, betrayal, regret.

Her throat ached. Her lungs heaved. Her stomach cramped. She felt stripped and beaten, curled up on her tile floor. Gone. Everything had been wiped away. She had utterly failed. No matter how hard she had tried, it hadn't been enough. She was so tired.

She sat there for what felt like years. She became aware of Drake sitting beside her, cradling her body with his. She didn't want him here. She didn't want anyone here. She wanted to be alone. Her feelings were too raw, like an asphalt scrape on her knee, where the slightest breeze of kindness stung.

She pushed away from him. Her palms fell to the floor, propping her body up. She dropped her head, and loose strands of her hair curtained her face. She squeezed her eyes shut. "Go away," she sobbed.

“Venus.”

“Go away. Please.” She choked on the word.

“You need me now.”

She didn’t want him here, in her house—in the one place she was vulnerable, at this one point when she was most vulnerable. “No, I don’t need you.” Her voice echoed off the walls, the floor. “Just go.”

He didn’t answer.

Her words still hung between them. She cried because she couldn’t take them back. In the past few months, she had stabbed him over and over again with a dagger made up of her independence, fear, pride. But now, she’d reached a point where she didn’t care, because she had absolutely nothing left.

He rose to his feet, slow and silent. She didn’t look up at him, but her crying came harder and faster, heaving up from her chest. She didn’t want him to go, but she couldn’t form the words to make him stay.

His foot nudged aside her purse—he must have brought it in for her. She sobbed at his thoughtfulness. Why could she only hurt people?

He opened the door and left, closing it softly behind him.

Venus lay on the tile floor and cried.

She stared at the reflection of herself in her widescreen HDTV. Perched on the sofa, distorted and out of focus. Kind of like how she felt.

Indifferent morning light crept in through the blinds. She hadn’t closed them last night. She hadn’t done a lot of things last night.

She still made lists, even in her misery. She’d lost the Amity Group as investors for Bananaville. She’d lost the Spiderweb. She’d lost Jaye. She’d lost her car. Without help, she wasn’t going to get a demo ready for Hudson Collins anytime soon, so she’d lost him too. Grandma would be peeved, so she had probably lost Grandma. Mom was upset at her and probably wouldn't speak to her ever again, so she'd also lost her mother.

She'd probably tried Drake's patience and lost him too.

She didn't have anything left to lose.

God has failed me.

The rational part of her shrank at the words. God didn't fail people. People failed God. She shouldn't say such things.

"Well, I don't care!"

The walls didn't respond.

"I don't care." She didn't have any tears left in her. They'd all soaked onto the tile floor. "Do you hear me? I don't care."

When have you ever cared what God thought?

She stilled. It was as if a chill wind blew through the room, making her shiver.

She did everything a Christian was supposed to do—Bible reading, praying, going to church, tithing, serving with the youth group.

In all those things, did you care what God thought?

Wasn't He pleased? Weren't all those things what He wanted her to do? He wouldn't want her to neglect her Bible, or prayer, or any of that.

But have you ever cared what God thought?

About what? About . . .

About everything.

Her gaming company, which she could never seem to find time to pray about. She had prayed every day for her parents' salvation, but she'd never asked God if He'd even wanted her to create her own company. She'd assumed it was a good thing—she had the Spiderweb, the game premise had marketing potential, she wanted the control of her own company, she wanted the success and the glory, and so many people told her she ought to start her own company.

Since when had their opinions counted over God's?

Her chest tightened, and she bowed her head, curling herself around the pain. She didn't have an answer. She'd wanted it so badly, she had been reluctant to ask God because she didn't want to hear what He would say.

Well, He was forcing her to listen now.

All her dreams slipping from her fingers like water. Wouldn't it have been better to give it up willingly—even if it was grudgingly—rather than have God yank it away from her?

"Oh, God. I'm so sorry."

She did have tears left, and they burned down her face like liquid fire. Bitter, not salty, on her tongue. She folded in half, she couldn't curl herself up small enough. "I'm so, so sorry." How sad—how typical Venus—that God had to break her, strip her, shatter her before she came to Him.

"I'll trust you. I'll submit. I'll trust you no matter what happens."

She thought she felt a hand on her head, and then it was gone.

"What do you want me to do now?"

Arms folded around her that she couldn't see, couldn't feel, and yet she knew they were there. It didn't matter. Not any of the stupid things she'd done the past few months. Nothing mattered except that God still loved her. Had always loved her.

It was freeing, being in this place. She grabbed a handful of tissues to scrub her face. She felt cleansed, like when her mom took a scouring sponge to her, as a child, to get all the dirt off her hands and feet. Except . . .

God had never answered her question. What would she do now?

Venus had shrunk. Drake noticed it as soon as she opened the door to her condo.

"Thanks for driving me." She exited the house and locked her door, keeping her eyes away from his face. "I'll get a rental car today. My cousin said it'll take at least a week before he can fix my car." She turned to go but bumped into him. "What?"

He realized he was blocking her way. "You're shorter."

"Oh." Did her face actually flush? Venus did not blush prettily—red splotches rose from her neck and splayed unevenly across her face. But it made her attractive, for some reason—maybe because it proved she wasn't perfectly in control of everything about herself.

She didn't meet his eyes. "I didn't wear heels today."

Glancing down, he saw the metallic—and probably expensive—ballerina flats she'd worn instead. Weird. Venus without stilettos was like pizza without cheese.

"Thanks for, um ..."

He almost reached out to cup her cheek, but she kept her head down, as if to protect herself. "It's okay, Venus."

Her eyes flashed up at him, wide and more vulnerable than he'd ever seen her before. Then she headed down the stairs to the parking lot at a fast clip, quicker without her heels to slow her down.

He lengthened his stride to keep up with her. "Why the change?" He clicked his remote and unlocked the car doors.

She shrugged as she got into the car.

"Nope." He got in and started the engine. "No way. If I'm giving you a ride, I'm going to get an answer."

She glowered. The splotches on her face went from rosy to radish red. "It's complicated."

"We have a long drive." After everything that happened yesterday, he'd told her to come into work later—he'd insisted on nine or ten, but she'd negotiated for eight o'clock, which was still better than her normal seven—which meant the traffic would be bumper to bumper for a few miles on highway 85.

"It's about religion."

In the time they'd worked together, they'd never discussed God. "I go to church." He wasn't too happy with his Creator right now, but she didn't know that. He'd asked, after all.

"You never liked discussing religion before."

"I had a heart attack since then."

She went from radish red to port wine. "I had a talk with God this morning."

Drake had too—asking Him why He hadn't answered his prayer for help with Amity when Esme walked. The first time he'd really prayed to God—and a lot of good that had done. "And?"

"I think everything will be okay." She had a smoothness to her profile—the line of her skin flowed like satin. Her eyes were a little puffy but clear.

It irritated him. "What do you mean by okay?"

She caught his hard tone and frowned. "If I knew that, I'd be able to wave my magic wand and zap everything back to before."

Okay, okay. "What does that have to do with your shoes?"

"I don't ... need them anymore."

He suddenly knew exactly what she was talking about. "Your armor."

"They weren't *armor.*" She glared at him. "They just made me feel strong and tall."

"Venus, you're already five-nine."

"Tall-*er.*"

Tall enough so men couldn't look down on her or tower over her. So they'd have to look her in the eye if they said something disagreeable. And now—today, at least—she'd given it up.

Had she lost her drive to prove herself?

In some ways it was a relief—she was so contentious—but in other ways, it disappointed him. As if she wanted to be weak.

No, a woman who willingly caused a car accident in order to face off against her former coworker was not weak.

"Why don't you need them anymore?"

"Because it's all in God's hands now."

He shook his head. "I don't buy it."

"What do you mean?" She turned to glare at him.

"This holy-righteous act. You can't tell me you aren't pissed off about all of this." Because he sure was.

"I am. I was. I still am. But ..." She blew out a breath. "It doesn't matter anymore. I haven't exactly been following God."

Drake was a bit glad he'd never really tried to, if God was going to let stuff like this happen.

"I have to trust God's got it under control, somehow."

He didn't answer her. He didn't see any evidence of that control.

"That's why I don't need the stilettos. Not that I won't wear them again. But today, I needed to show that I trust Him. So I didn't wear them."

On the surface, it seemed an inconsequential thing, but Drake knew this was big for Venus. "I don't agree with your reasons for this, but I admire you for being brave."

She looked at him. She didn't smile, but her look wasn't hostile.

"Besides, I have to take advantage of the one day I can look down at you."

Her mother finally condescended to answer her call. "Hello?"

Yup, she sounded thrilled. "Mom, I've been leaving messages for three days." She closed her office door and sank into her desk chair.

"I didn't want to talk to you."

Well, Mom could be brutally honest when she wanted to be. "I wanted to apologize."

"So apologize."

"I'm sorry for brushing you off, but ..." No. No buts. "I'm sorry. Period."

Silence.

Hoo-boy. "I should have suggested maybe dinner that evening instead."

"I was busy."

"I really did want to—*do* want to spend time with you."

"You certainly didn't show it."

"A lot happened that day."

"More important than your mother?"

Same old argument. Well, she'd let her decide. "Frankly, yes."

Mom gasped.

Venus rushed on. "My operations manager quit that morning. So did the Web director. And before they left, they deliberately sabotaged the presentation to a *billion*-dollar investor. And then Esme stole my development tool off my computer—"

"Esme? The girl who was with you at the party? The one trying to catch the attention of that nice man you were with?"

"Uh . . . yeah."

"It was so obvious he wasn't into her, and she just kept trying. Desperate girls are so unattractive."

Venus had to grasp for something to say. "She was desperate, all right."

"You are well rid of her. She stole something from you? Probably revenge because she couldn't steal your man."

She would never understand her mother. "So . . . how about lunch today?"

More silence. But Venus thought it might be a more friendly silence than the one before. She was confirmed when Mom replied, "I suppose I can squeeze you in. I'm so busy at work today."

Venus's phone beeped. She checked caller ID—Grandma. "Mom, I've got a call on the other line."

"Oh! Well—"

"It's Grandma." Your *boss.* "Shall I tell her you're on the phone with me?"

"No! I mean, um, I'll speak to her when I get to the bank this morning. Bye!"

Venus clicked over. "Hi, Grandma."

"I just read about Esme Preston and Oomvid. Was she the girl with you and Drake at the Christmas party?"

Compared to her mother, Grandma was cake, but Venus still had to fight a heavy mantle of despair on her shoulders as she relayed everything—Esme, the Spiderweb, Amity, Jaye.

"I can't believe anyone would be so malicious. To actually sabotage the presentation when she'd already stolen the Spiderweb."

"I have to admit, I don't know for certain if she stole it. I don't have any proof."

"And you're not likely to get any."

How cheerful. Grandma was pragmatic, but sometimes she could use a little more glass-half-full mentality. "With Jaye moving and the Spiderweb stolen, I'm rethinking my game company."

"That's wise." Her complacent voice reminded Venus that one of Grandma's original motives had been to throw Drake in Venus's way. If she gave up her company, she'd probably stay with Drake. Today, that option sounded … nice.

"I'll let you get back to work, dear."

"Bye."

Venus brought up her schedule for the day on her computer screen. Despite Amity, she still had a lot of work for the public launch of the website, only a month away. If they could get an investor for round-three funding, that launch would be vital.

She should focus on work, for now. God had given her a good job, with a good boss and good pay. *Just trust in God. Trust in God.*

She stared at her computer. Right now, there wasn't much else to do.

Gerry met him at the door to Bananaville with a concerned look like when her kids came home with blood anywhere above the shoulders.

He stopped outside and stared at her through the glass doors. "What is it?"

"Are you okay? You weren't in church yesterday."

Was that all? "I was busy." He pushed open the doors, forcing her to step back and make way for him.

"You didn't go to youth group on Saturday either. One of the boys said he missed you. Well … in so many words. It was more like, 'I wanted to get Drake at *British Bulldog* yesterday.'"

He hadn't been able to face the kids, not with the bitterness boiling over inside him, burned and foul like an overcooked pot of rice porridge. He'd called David with a vague excuse for not being at youth group.

Gerry hopped alongside him, trying to keep up with his long strides. "Are you busy tonight? Come with me to prayer group."

"I can't. I'm trying to find a VC to replace Amity."

Her face fell into that maddeningly serene expression she'd had for a week. "Any luck?"

"None at all." He opened his office door with a bit too much force, and the door banged against the wall. Gerry flinched.

"None? What about Williamson? Or— " Her voice pecked at him.

He whirled and growled down at her, "Gerry, they're not returning my calls."

She licked her lips. "None of them?"

"We apparently stink like a sewer to everyone right now."

"Just from one presentation?" Gerry's hand flapped helplessly. "I don't understand."

"I don't either." More sabotage? Did Yardley have influence that rose that high? It didn't matter—there wasn't anything Drake could do about it, and the knowledge drove him into the ground like a tent peg, with each unreturned call hitting him as a physical blow.

It was worse that this had happened to Gerry's company, not his own. "I'd do something if I could." He turned to lay his briefcase on the floor and boot up his computer.

"You've done your best."

"That's not good enough, Gerry."

Something in his tone must have struck her, because she gave him a probing look. "What is this about, really?"

He looked away. "Nothing."

She regarded him in silence another moment. "Why is it not good enough?"

He didn't answer her at first, simply watched the icons pop up on his computer screen. He wasn't sure how to explain it to her. "I didn't come through for you." His admission squeezed out of him like the last drop from a lemon.

She leaned over his desk. "Why do you think this is all on you?"

In words like that, he sounded arrogant. "I don't." More silence, more shame. "I wanted to make this a success."

Gerry suddenly straightened. "For me." It wasn't a question.

He turned back to his computer. "Of course for you. You're my sister." Maybe he could just pass this off.

"You didn't have to make anything up to me, Drake."

Everything in him solidified, like marble veining into his muscles and turning him into a statue. He didn't want to talk about this with her. "Gerry—"

"You were different then. When I was going through the divorce. I understand that, now." Her eyes were too calm, too loving, too warm.

He had ignored her calls in favor of board meetings. He'd forgotten when he agreed to babysit the kids. He had let her go through that horrendous year all alone.

Gerry smiled at him, and it made his insides twist. "You didn't have to make anything up to me, but I'm glad you did. I couldn't have done this without you."

Done what? He hadn't come through for her then. He hadn't come through for her now. "Everything is going wrong." More like crashing and burning.

"You should come with me. The prayer group—"

"Gerry, I am not in a place to pray."

Her eyes grew soft, which only irritated him more.

"You're so bitter."

"You're so resigned," he shot back.

"I'm trying to leave it in God's hands."

"That's what Venus said." He stared at his computer screen. "It sounds like just blind faith to me."

"It's not blind."

He leaned his elbow on his desk and attacked her. "There's no way for you to know He's really there. That He's orchestrating all this—this mess."

She pursed her mouth and her eyes sparked. "Would you even see the proof if God gave it to you? Would you believe it?"

It made him pause. Would he? His thoughts paralleled Gerry's next words.

"Your unbelief might be what's *blind*." She stalked out.

He sat there, feeling the emptiness of his office, and wondered if he would ever feel the desire to see.

He didn't know how long he sat there, thinking and yet trying not to think. His computer had booted up long ago. He brought up an Internet news site.

The story was tucked away near the bottom of the page, after he'd scrolled down reading the other pieces of news, but he jolted as it thrust a spear into his gut.

"Amity Group under litigation for fraud."

He tried to breathe, but his lungs wouldn't respond; his diaphragm was pinned to his spine. No. This was ... this was ...

A sign.

He'd become a bug, suddenly aware of an overshadowing presence that could squash him. The air was thick with Him. He gripped the edge of his desk and closed his eyes.

He wasn't blind. He saw the proof. And all the while, in His awesome presence, Drake didn't feel terror, but power. Power far beyond what he could wrap his mind around. He wasn't *made* to be able to understand, which is why he just had to trust and believe.

I believe.

Running footsteps. Then Gerry darted into his office and slapped a piece of paper on his desk. "There's your proof." No triumph in her voice, but breathless awe.

He looked down at the printout of the article. "Gerry." He couldn't say more.

Opening and closing doors. A murmur of commotion. He looked up at his office doorway just as Chieko Sakai strode in, elegant in a silk suit, with eyes fierce and bright.

"Pack your bags. You're going to Japan tonight."

TWENTY-EIGHT

Venus would kill for a Reese's.

She eyed the Web director candidate balefully, although her testy mood wasn't his fault. He was qualified for the position—he just had the personality of a *daikon* radish. But Web Director didn't need to win Miss Congeniality.

At least this guy was better than the candidate she'd interviewed late last week. She'd been wearing flats to work since bashing Esme's car, and the candidate—the Dork, she fondly renamed him—had been about five-ten, maybe five-eleven. He'd taken great pains to look down on her as they shook hands, as they sat at the table (despite the fact her long torso and his short one put her a little above his eye level when they were seated), and as he left the building (none too soon).

She'd thought hard and longingly of the extra pair of stilettos in her desk drawer. But she wiggled her toes in her flats. *Remember why you wear them.* And she hadn't missed her aching toes and arches the past few days.

Under the conference table, she kicked her foot up and down. No, she didn't miss the pain and discomfort at all.

Her cell phone vibrated. Again. She discreetly checked caller ID under the edge of the conference room table. Mom. She'd called twelve times in the last hour.

Venus turned the ringer completely off and tried to look interested as the interviewee (whose name she'd completely forgotten) discussed his work ethic. She had to ask the question, but what was the point?

Most people lied anyway. Look at Macy's ability to deceive, the lying wench.

"So, say someone sabotages the system and it crashes, and it'll take twelve hours to fix it, and you have to do a demo for an important investor the following morning, but you have your son's birthday party that night. Do you stay at work to fix it?"

"Uh ..."

"I haven't got all day. Yes or no."

He blinked at her. "Is this a trick question?"

Er ... maybe that was a bit inappropriate.

The door burst open. Venus turned to deliver a scathing rebuke but luckily stopped short beyond uttering, "Erk."

Grandma stood in the doorway looking a bit like one of the Greek Furies, sans flaming sword. Her eye fell on the interviewee, and her blazing purpose dimmed a bit. "Oh."

Darla hovered behind her, worried eyes peering into the conference room. Over Grandma's head, she pointed at the old woman and mouthed, *I couldn't stop her.* Venus nodded—anyone who knew Grandma would understand.

"Mrs. Sakai, how nice to see you." Venus almost started at the sound of Mom's voice coming out of her mouth. Maybe she was learning feminine graciousness after all. She had to remember to thank her mother the next time they had lunch. "Would you mind very much waiting in Drake's office until I finish up here?"

Grandma of all people would know that this wasn't Venus's standard reply. She smiled and nodded, but in her eye shone a glimmer of approval. "You're doing well, dear." She turned and closed the door behind her.

Venus loosed a long, low breath and turned back to what's-his-name, the interviewee. "Do you have any questions for me about the position?"

"I'd really like to telecommute a couple days a week. Our son just turned three, and ..."

Venus lost the rest of his rambling as her mind grabbed that one word, *telecommute.*

Jaye telecommuting as Web Director.

Why hadn't she thought of that before? Was it feasible? She'd need to talk to Drake. And Gerry. And probably Lisa. "Thank you for your time." She flipped her folio shut.

The interviewee paused, mouth open. Oops, had she cut him off? Oh well.

She stood and held out her hand. "We'll be in touch."

He barely clasped her hand before she pulled away and opened the conference room door. She beat a trail to Drake's office, flinging open the door. "How do you feel about the Web director telecommuting?"

Gerry had joined Drake and Grandma. The brother and sister had mouths parted and brows furrowed, while Grandma's chin jutted out, and she turned her firm gaze at Venus as she entered.

Uh-oh. "What?"

"Amity is being investigated—"

"You're going to Japan—"

Venus froze, her eyes darting from Gerry to Grandma. She said what she felt. "I can't process."

Grandma sighed and gestured to Gerry to go first.

"Amity is accused of fraud." Gerry eyed Drake with a gleam and a half smile, which Venus didn't understand.

"Amity, as in our lost investor—"

"As in our close call."

The air blew out of her lungs in a rush. She *hadn't* screwed everything up with that horrendous presentation. Esme and Macy's efforts had been a godsend, not the sabotage they'd intended. This was too much for her. Relief made her legs weak. "I need a chair." She stumbled forward and sank into the one Gerry pulled out for her.

Drake looked implacable. Was he completely unmoved? No, maybe the expressionless mask hid emotions too deep for him to want to think about or address. She could barely grasp it herself. They'd escaped from even the briefest connection with Amity.

Grandma's fingers tap-tap-tapped against each other at her waist. She'd been patient long enough. "Grandma, you said something about Japan?"

"I spoke to Kenta Hoshiwara. His family owns the Hoshiwara Group, a Japanese VC that, so far, has only invested in Japanese toy companies."

And Grandma, of course, just happened to have his number in her PDA. *Hello, Kenta, it's Chieko. How are the wife and kids?*

"I told him about Bananaville, especially its partnership with American toy companies, and he seemed interested in discussing third-round funding. I also knew that some of Hoshiwara's toy companies are starting to expand and export to the U.S. I set up a meeting."

Gerry looked ready to bow down and kiss Grandma's feet. Venus wasn't far off.

"You three, pack your bags. I've made plane reservations for tonight to take us to Tokyo."

Just think of all those executives naked.

No, that would make me puke faster.

Venus leaned back in her seat. She'd been exhausted ever since the plane left LAX, but she couldn't sleep. The presentation tomorrow had to be perfect. This was her second chance, her last chance. She stared at her laptop, flipping through slides.

From the seat beside her, Drake muttered, "Stop worrying about it." He didn't open his eyes.

"I wasn't worrying."

"What happened to 'trust in God'?"

"Since when did you grow faith?"

He sighed and adjusted his shoulders. "Since we barely escaped being a fireball falling from the sky with Amity."

"If you put it like that, I suppose it was in the same class as parting the Red Sea."

"You have no idea."

She closed her laptop, unable to review the slides anymore.

"There's no reason to be nervous. You've done dozens of presentations."

"None of them have been set up by Grandma, in front of whom I really don't want to screw up. None of them had a company's funding riding on them." None had been while working for a man she liked more than a little, even though that liking made her want to hide in the closet and protect herself with her stilettos.

Drake snorted. "Stop it, you're psyching yourself out."

The truth was, she hadn't worked on the Spiderweb for a week. Since Oomvid, with more money and more manpower, was developing something similar, why bother? Where would it get her? She didn't have a team or even a partner for her own game company. She had nothing but Bananaville. That's why this presentation was freaking her out.

Each day in her time with God, she'd asked Him what she should do. She wanted to do something about the entire situation. Each time, the answer was the same.

One day, it had come from Psalms: "Wait for the Lord; be strong and take heart and wait for the Lord."

The next, from Isaiah: "For the Lord is a God of justice. Blessed are all who wait for him!"

She even tried to escape the Old Testament and any other admonishments to wait, but her reading happened to be in Colossians: " … being strengthened with all power according to his glorious might so that you may have great endurance and patience …"

The answer was the same now, an unexplainable check on her heart despite her desire to be moving. She gave way grudgingly, but she did give way.

Fine. I'll wait.

"You're not going to throw up, are you?" Grandma frowned at Venus from her side of the conference table.

"No." She'd hoped that moving the trash can closer to her wouldn't alert Grandma's "problem-radar," but she guessed wrong. She wouldn't know where the bathrooms were anyway—all the signs were labeled in *kanji* rather than English.

Gerry moved seats closer to Venus. "It's not all on you, so stop thinking it is."

"What?"

"The presentation. Trust God. You won't be terrible."

"Let's not talk about being terrible," Drake interjected from his seat on Venus's other side.

"Let's pray." Gerry grabbed her hand.

"Now?" Venus glanced at Grandma, who looked uncomfortable and turned her head away. "They're going to come in any minute."

"So then, I'll stop when they do."

"Fine. But don't hold my hand." No way would she show a sign of weakness like that to Japanese businessmen.

As Gerry prayed, Venus was able to breathe easier. *Who of you by worrying can add a single hour to his life?* God already knew how this presentation would go, if they would get funding or not. If Venus would make a complete fool of herself or not. Okay, that wasn't a pleasant thought.

She opened her eyes and listened to Gerry's voice, soothing in its cadence. She stared at the grain on the conference table, the pleats in her skirt (Grandma had insisted on a skirt suit instead of a pant-suit because she was presenting to Japanese businessmen), her modest black pumps, her—Oh, no!

"Amen."

"I've got a rip in my stocking!"

The tile floor of the women's restroom chilled Venus's stocking-less knees. As she hung over the toilet, she gave another round of thank-yous to God that Hoshiwara had Western toilets and not the traditional squatters. She'd still need a good disinfectant scrub when she finished, but she didn't even want to think how much worse it could have been to be sick over a squat toilet.

A knock on the bathroom door. "Venus? Are you okay now?"

"Yeah." The waves of nausea seemed to have passed. Drake must look a little ridiculous to be hovering near the women's bathroom door.

"You don't sound okay."

"I'm fine."

"The presentation went fine, you know."

It hadn't felt like it. Although to be honest, she couldn't remember most of the presentation.

"You weren't brilliant, but you got through it credibly."

"Gee, thanks."

"Gerry said you didn't do as bad as the Amity presentation."

"Are you *trying* to hack me off?" She flushed the toilet and rose gingerly to her feet. She swayed a little, but otherwise she seemed in good shape. Her efficient side loved how the fresh water filling the tank first ran through a faucet on top of the tank for people to wash their hands. She had to see if she could import one of these for her condo.

She cleaned up more thoroughly with the help of some wipes from her purse, and exited the bathroom, stopping short of bumping into Drake where he stood in front of the door.

He was very close. She still felt rather gross, but he didn't seem to mind she'd just been sick. His hand reached up, fingers cupping her face as soft as rice paper. A comforting gesture. And yet, lover-like too, somehow.

She stood still, not sure what to do. His gaze touched her with more intensity than his hand.

She closed her eyes to block out the sight. She sensed him withdrawing. "I don't know what I want."

He didn't answer.

She opened her eyes. He wasn't angry, he seemed to understand. Or maybe she just wanted to see that understanding in him, whether it was there or not.

She'd been striving for so long on just one thing—the Spiderweb. And now it was gone. Or maybe not gone, but probably useless.

What did she want? And would he still be there when she finally figured out what she wanted?

God didn't answer. By this time, she was getting used to it.

TWENTY-NINE

"Jenn, *I need a peanut butter cup.*" Venus pressed her Bluetooth closer to her ear to make sure Jenn heard her.

"You don't have to shout." Through the cell phone, she heard the *click-click-click* as Jenn turned on the gas range on the stove.

"Please tell me you made some." Venus took the exit off the freeway toward Jenn's house.

"Sorry. I made a batch while you were in Japan, but Lex took most of them."

"Aaargh!" She would have *words* with her cousin the next time they saw each other.

"I'm making raspberry truffles right now. Will those do?"

"Good enough. I'm five minutes away."

Jenn exhaled. "What if I didn't have any chocolate in the house?"

"Are you kidding? You always have chocolate in the house. *Homemade* chocolate."

"Well, you still need to wait twenty minutes before I start coating the ganache, so tough noogies."

"Ugh. Okay, bye."

Venus rang her mom's cell phone and almost ran into a stop sign when her mother picked up. "Mom! I've been trying to call you since I got back."

"Got back? From where?"

"Grandma got Bananaville an interview with a Japanese VC. I flew in from Tokyo yesterday."

"I've been calling you for days!" Mom's voice sounded like one of those seabirds.

"I called you before I left, and I called yesterday and today, but I kept being shunted straight to your voice mail. Was your phone off?"

"Uh ... my phone must have been malfunctioning." She was speaking rather fast.

Venus sighed. "Were you at the beach?"

"It's too cold for the beach, dear."

"Spa?"

"No! I was ... taking a personal day. Or two."

Venus's hands clenched the steering wheel, digging her nails into the leather covering. "If you needed to talk to me so badly, why did you shut your phone off?"

"Because if Grandma called me, I could say my phone was broken." Her voice sounded so calm and reasonable, Venus could almost ignore the fact her fiftysomething mother was playing hooky from work like a teenager.

"What did you need to talk to me about?" Venus turned into Jenn's parents' driveway.

"Where are you?"

"At Jenn's house."

"Stay there. I'll meet you. Bye!"

Venus yanked off her Bluetooth headset. Mom had been mysterious and melodramatic in her voice mail messages, and she still refused to just *say* what she wanted.

The heavenly smell of chocolate filled Venus's lungs and shot straight to her hips (she was sure she added an instant pound or two) when Jenn's mom answered the front door. "Hi, Aunty Yuki. How are you feeling?" Venus kicked off her shoes in the foyer as Aunty closed the door.

"Just had a checkup yesterday. The doctor says the cancer's still in remission."

"Great. Still feeling tired?" She loved Aunty Yuki, but she needed a chocolate badly. She nudged her aunt toward the kitchen.

"No, I walked a whole two miles yesterday."

They entered the kitchen, where Jenn stood stirring a pot of melted chocolate. Venus looked around at the countertops. "Where is it?"

Jenn gave her a sour look.

"Fine, fine. How much longer?"

"The ganache needs to cool another fifteen minutes before I can coat it."

"Where is it?" Maybe she could steal a little ...

"In the fridge. Don't even think it." Jenn brandished her spoon at her, splattering chocolate on the floor. Venus winced. Jenn cooked like a master chef but always made the biggest messes. She grabbed a paper towel to clean up the chocolate ribbons on the linoleum. At least the floor had been freshly scrubbed, from the smell of Pine-Sol.

Jenn went back to stirring. "And you still need to wait another minute for the chocolate coating to cool before you can eat it."

"Okay, I'll wait."

Jenn pinned her with a narrow gaze. "You don't know how to wait."

"I'm learning these days."

Jenn's eyes brightened with curiosity, but then slid to her mother, listening avidly by the doorway. "You'll never guess who Mom and I saw in Japantown today."

"Who?"

"Mrs. Matsumoto."

"Grandma's ex-friend?" Jenn had theorized that Mrs. Matsumoto, Grandma's only Christian friend—a very vocal Christian, at that—had said something to make Grandma uncomfortable. If it were true, it would explain why Grandma had suddenly stopped being friends with Mrs. Matsumoto, and why she had ripped on Lex and Trish's faith at various times in the past year. Venus had been steeling herself for something similar, but it hadn't occurred the few times she'd seen Grandma.

"Mrs. Matsumoto and Grandma are friends again." Aunty Yuki took a few steps into the kitchen and perched on a stool.

"And get this." Jenn waggled the spoon at Venus, causing more chocolate ribbons on the floor. "She got Grandma to go to a Seniors group a few weeks ago. A *church* group."

"What?"

"Mrs. Matsumoto is so happy to introduce Grandma to some new friends." Aunty Yuki smiled serenely as if it weren't anything special, but Venus and Jenn knew otherwise—Grandma had been so violently closed to Christianity for so long, her concession to a church activity spoke volumes.

Jenn glanced at her mother—not a believer, although not opposed to Jenn's faith. However, talking about religion with family had always been a dicey thing for the four cousins, since everyone else was at least nominally Buddhist.

Jenn raised her eyebrows significantly. "Mrs. Matsumoto is so glad"—*Translation: triumphant*—"that she and Grandma are friends again"—*talking about God*—"and she's spending so much time chatting with her"—*wearing down her defenses.*

Venus wasn't sure whether to laugh or feel sorry for Grandma. Both, probably. Mrs. Matsumoto was quite a character, but she and Grandma had been friends for a long, long time.

"We saw Monica Cathcart in Japantown too. The Cathcarts go to your church, right?" Aunty Yuki looked a bit dubious. "Jenn mentioned you were doing, er ... youth work?"

"Yes." For the first time, the admission didn't cause a twinge of embarrassment in her stomach. She didn't care what people thought of her—or rather, the incongruity of her working with teens when she had developed some of the most gruesome video games on the market.

She had come to realize that she loved working with those kids. The teen girls were like the sisters she'd never had. They made her feel lighthearted and young again. And the girls seemed to like her too—wonder of wonders.

"Monica said that her daughter *loves* youth group meetings on Saturday night since you started working with them."

"What?"

"That's what I said." Aunty Yuki laughed.

Venus didn't have time to react—Jenn propped her fist on her hip and said, *"Mooooom."* Venus counted at least three syllables in that one word.

Aunty Yuki sobered quickly. "Anyway, apparently the moms are very appreciative and think you're doing a great job, Venus."

Venus resisted the urge to preen. Who'd have believed game developer and Chief Technology Officer Venus Chau would be good with teenagers? Especially considering how notoriously bad she was at babysitting young children.

"How are you doing at work, Venus?" Aunty Yuki asked.

She couldn't exactly vent to Jenn the way she wanted to, not with Aunty Yuki—and her mile-a-minute tongue—sitting there. The news would be all over Japantown in mere seconds. "I just got back from a business trip to Japan."

"Oh, how wonderful! I remember my last trip ..."

Between eyeing Jenn's melted chocolate and trying to appear interested in Aunty Yuki's rambles about the forty-three Shinto shrines she visited, fifteen minutes never seemed so long.

Finally the timer went off and Jenn removed the pan of little chocolate balls from the fridge. She slapped Venus's hand when she tried to grab one. Really, considering how mild-mannered Jenn was normally, she became a monster in her kitchen.

Soon, soon ...

Venus's cell phone rang. Bananaville. "Hi, Gerry."

"It's Darla. I'm calling from Gerry's phone. Venus, I'm sorry, I know you just left work, but we have an emergency. This guy came in ..."

Jenn had started coating each chocolate ganache center with melted chocolate, then rolling it in cocoa powder. Venus lost Darla's words as her eyes followed each little truffle, lying helplessly in the cocoa powder, just begging to be eaten.

"Venus? Are you still there?"

"Sorry, Darla, what did you say?"

"This man won't leave, and in between his ranting, he insists he has an appointment with Drake—"

"Just call him."

"He won't answer his cell."

"Where's Gerry?"

Darla blew out a frustrated breath. "I just *told* you, she's out with her kids in Fresno for some basketball game."

"And he won't say what he wants?"

"He refuses to talk to anybody but Drake."

"Well, then, what could I do? He won't speak to me either." She reached for a truffle, but Jenn smacked her with the chocolate spoon. "Ow!" She licked the chocolate off her knuckles. Mmmmm …

"He seems to know you. He keeps taking your name in vain."

"What?"

"Calling you all kinds of things you probably don't want me to repeat."

The chocolate turned to ash on her tongue. "Did he give his name?"

Darla exhaled again. "I *told* you, no he didn't."

"Sorry, sorry. Tell me, does he have thinning yellow hair?"

"Yes."

"Acts like he's smarter than everyone else?"

"Yes."

"Big smile?"

"No, because he's been too offensive to smile at anybody."

Venus closed her eyes and rubbed her knuckles into her forehead to combat the raging headache that erupted there. Too late, she remembered the sticky chocolate remnants. Lovely—she now had brown streaks across her face.

"All right, I'm coming in." Never mind that it was seven o'clock and she still hadn't had her chocolate. She hadn't been able to discover where Drake kept his stash of Reese's that he kept surprising her with.

Venus called Mom.

"Hello, dear, I'm about fifteen minutes away— "

"Can you meet me at Bananaville instead? There's an emergency."

"Emergency? Is it Yardley?"

Venus stopped rooting in her purse for her car keys. "How do you know that, Mom?"

"I'll meet you at Bananaville!" she chirped. "Bye!"

Venus stared at her phone. Suddenly she couldn't wait to hear what her mother had to say.

Jenn handed her a plastic container with four truffles. "I'd give you more, but you'd probably yell at me for making you break your diet."

"I'm not on a *diet*, I follow a healthy lifestyle." Although her clothes had all been a bit snugger lately. However, her skin and hair had started looking better—healthier.

Jenn rolled her eyes. "Whatever. Eat and be happy."

"Thanks!" Venus headed out the door.

She eyed the container, sitting in honor on her passenger seat, while she drove to Bananaville, but she wanted to *enjoy* her chocolate when she ate it. It had been one thing to anticipate eating it in the comfort of Jenn's kitchen, another to gulp it down while driving to confront her mortal enemy.

Yup, it was Yardley. She recognized him, even from the back, through the glass front doors. He turned from harassing Darla as Venus walked in. "Yardley, what are you doing here?"

Darla saw Venus and dropped her head to her desk in relief.

Yardley's face turned the color of Darla's fuchsia twinset. "Your boss is not going to like the embarrassment to his company caused by your boyfriend!"

What? Her boyfriend? What boyfriend? Venus didn't think he could say anything to surprise her, but this made her mouth drop open. Darla also raised her head from her desk to stare at Yardley.

He stabbed a finger at her. "This kind of underhanded dealing just proves you can't play with the big boys. You always tried and you never measured up."

No one told her what she could or couldn't do. Venus shot lightning bolts from her eyes—she actually expected him to be struck and burned to a crisp. "Underhanded? You were the one who sent Esme and Macy in to do your dirty work for you."

"You don't know how to play the game, Venus. Thinking you could do as well as men with more skill and finesse."

"Because it takes so much skill to send a little girl to drug me and steal a program. The truth is, I was always smarter and better than you, Yardley, and it scared you to death."

"So arrogant. Wake up, Venus, you're not as brilliant as you think you are."

"Do you really think insulting me is going to make you look any less stupid and incompetent? You were threatened because you knew I could have taken your job." She said it just to irritate him, but as soon as the words came out of her mouth, she knew they were true.

"You can obviously do your own job quite well," he sneered.

"I can." She stared him down. "I presented to a Japanese VC two days ago. They're arranging for Akaogi Games—yes, the manufacturers of *Takoman*—to become a Bananaville sponsor."

At the name, Yardley flinched.

"Didn't Akaogi refuse to partner with Oomvid on a *Takoman* multi-player game? I think you were the one who spearheaded that." She took a step nearer to him. "So tell me how well I do my job, despite disgruntled ex-bosses who try to sabotage me."

Yardley's mouth opened and closed a few times, then he clenched his jaw and spoke through his teeth. "Talk about sabotage. Sending your little boyfriend into Oomvid to try to dig up dirt. You won't find any—I'm cleaner than a surgery room!"

That mysterious boyfriend again. Some guy had obviously done something to upset him, and he chose to believe Venus was behind it all. She pulled her shoulders back. "You're off your rocker."

Which only made him steam hotter. He looked like he might blow his thinning hair clear off his head. "I demand to speak to Drake—"

"He's not available, Yardley. You either deal with me or you leave this building." She pointed at the door. "Darla and I will kick you out bodily if you refuse. I warn you, we're in great shape." At least, she hoped Darla had some muscles under that slender frame. She didn't know if she could handle Yardley alone.

He ground his teeth, looking at her as if she were the devil himself, but not wanting to leave either.

Venus crossed her arms. "I have no idea what you're talking about."

Darla pointed out the glass doors. "Somebody's coming." Venus looked up to see Mom's tiny frame hop-stepping toward them.

She entered with a bright smile. "Hello, dear. Why hello, Yardley. We met at my mother's Christmas party. Do you remember?"

He looked down at her with a condescending smile. "You were a bit unwell that evening, as I recall."

Mom's smile grew hard, and her teeth gleamed. "You weren't invited, as I recall, but my mother allowed you to stay when you snuck in with the CEO of Oomvid."

Yardley's mouth pulled into a disagreeable line.

"I take it you're here annoying my daughter because of Brett?"

Brett? Who was that?

Yardley's face darkened. Venus moved closer to her mother.

Mom gave that false tinkling laugh that always used to grate on Venus's spine. It sounded like music to her now, while Yardley's back popped into a straight line. "Isn't Brett clever? He's an investigative reporter, you know. With the *San Francisco Chronicle*."

He paled. "A reporter?"

"Such a nice boy. His mother is my good friend. Venus, do you remember Mrs. Kawa—"

"Mom ..." Now was not the time for her to go tangential.

"Anyway, I told Brett about Venus's development tool, and how she thought that nasty girl Esme had stolen it and given it to Oomvid."

Venus knew the astonishment must be painted all over her face, but she couldn't close her mouth. She'd assumed Mom hadn't been listening when she told her about Esme.

Yardley ground his teeth. "Esme didn't steal—"

Mom's eyebrows popped up. "Esme? Not Ms. Preston? Know her quite well, do you?"

His lips disappeared as he pulled his mouth taut.

Mom smiled widely. "So Brett went to Oomvid for some interview and asked to use a company computer—all very official, nothing wrong with it—and well, Esme wasn't very smart." She spread her hands wide. "She used the company computer for all kinds of things."

"What kinds of things?" And would any of it even be admissible in a lawsuit?

"Brett just *happened* upon some emails Esme sent about how Oomvid's CTO hired her to *borrow* Venus's development tool. And other emails that were very specific about Esme handing Venus's program directly to you."

Email evidence? Oh my. Esme hadn't been smart at all.

Yardley's eyes darted around the lobby, as if looking for an escape, but he remained rooted to the ground. Venus couldn't figure out what was going through his mind.

"And wouldn't you know, Brett *happened* upon some emails among your programming team, about how you told them to work on a development tool similar to the one you handed them, but not similar enough to infringe on the other program's patent."

His nostrils flared. "All that was gotten illegally, and Bananaville won't look very good if I leak the information that the CTO's mother sent a spy into Oomvid to steal company secrets."

Mom's smile never faltered. "It won't be half as embarrassing as it would be for Oomvid to have yet another accusation that they steal technology. It's been a whole ten months since they were last in the front page headlines."

She had him. Venus knew the exact moment, because a muscle on his cheek jumped faster than a tick. Oomvid had been exonerated from that earlier accusation, but the company wouldn't be able to handle yet another accusation so soon with any kind of dignity.

Mom regarded him with cool eyes. "I wonder if you know something about that other incident too?"

His eyes flattened into slits.

Mom didn't back down. "It doesn't matter if it isn't true, as long as it's in the paper."

"That's libel."

Mom frowned. "Maybe." She brightened. "But Brett has many online connections."

Darla shot to her feet. Venus started—she'd forgotten she was behind the receptionist's desk. Darla's smile had the warmth of an arctic winter. "Sir, did you still want to speak to Drake?"

Yardley looked like an angry picture of Rumpelstiltskin that Venus remembered from a childhood book—she expected him to start jumping up and down in frustration. Too bad the earth wouldn't open up and swallow him too.

He glared at her. "I'm not leaving."

Venus shot him a look like a knife blade between the eyes. "You will leave now. I have wanted chocolate for *hours*, and if I don't eat my truffles in the next five minutes, I am going to *bite your head off*."

His fierce gaze had morphed into one that looked at her like she'd turned into a pink elephant.

Mom solved the problem by grabbing his elbow and pulling him toward the door. "So nice seeing you, Yardley. Say hello to your parents for me."

Mom pushed him out the door, but just before the glass doors swung shut, she opened them to call out. "Oh, I almost forgot. Silly me." She tittered. "I hope you don't mind ... When I drove up, I dinged your car a little bit ..."

THIRTY

Drake knew that if he told Venus the truth, she'd kill him. Painfully. But he couldn't deny that she had a nicer … silhouette since she'd put on a few pounds.

He admired her *silhouette* as she paced in his office, licking her fingers from her third Reese's peanut butter cup in the last half hour. "When Mom asked Brett to do all that, she wasn't thinking about legalities."

"I doubt the emails would hold up in court."

"Exactly. She thought social embarrassment to Oomvid would be enough to get what she wanted. What she wanted for me." She paused, her fingers tapping her thigh like she had the shakes—which she probably did, a massive sugar rush from the candy she'd been consuming. "I don't think this will get me anything but a libel suit."

"Have you looked into it?"

"Not yet. I wanted to ask you what you thought."

He almost raised his arms and shouted, "Gooooaaaaalllllll!" but restrained himself. "You'll need to consult a lawyer."

"Mom said she'd ask the family lawyer, but I don't know if he's versed enough in this sort of thing."

"It might not make a difference for you. Oomvid will continue to develop their own version of the Spiderweb."

She sobered and stared out the window of his office at the bare trees. "I know."

He didn't like seeing her like this—quiet, resigned. The Venus he knew never quit. Many times her pigheadedness caused him multiple migraine headaches, but this Venus—defeated, motionless, waiting ... he didn't like her so lifeless. "You can't lie back and let them walk all over you."

"I'm weighing my options," she snapped.

Her show of spirit cheered him. "I might be able to help."

She faced him, but her eyes were clouded. "I don't know what I want anymore, Drake." She paused, then resumed pacing. "I've never thought what would happen if this all were taken out of my control. I never considered not having the Spiderweb, not having Jaye. I should have. Maybe I just didn't want to think about it."

Her dream had died, and not at her own hands, but at someone else's. He could imagine how he'd feel in her situation.

"The strange thing is ..." She paused as if uncomfortable.

"What?" he asked gently.

"I'm getting along so well with Mom these days. Better than before, anyway." She grimaced.

"Maybe something changed."

"I think something did. She mentioned ... after Yardley left, she mentioned something about 'winning back her daughter.'"

He watched her face, not sure how she felt about it. Back when they'd worked together before, she had sometimes mentioned her father but never her mother, and from the small interactions he'd seen ... "Are you okay with that?"

"We'll never be buddy-buddy—she hasn't changed *that* much—but she's softer since the party."

She had a thoughtful look on her face. He speculated that her relationship with Laura Sakai might never be extremely close, but it wouldn't be as difficult as it had been before. That made him happy for her, for reasons he didn't want to dwell on.

A knock at the door, then Darla's head popped in. "Venus, your two o'clock appointment is here."

"I'll email you a list of a few lawyers," he told her as she left. She nodded and waved her thanks.

Bananaville might be on the upswing, but Venus had lost everything, with no way to get things back exactly the same as before. Maybe she'd be more interested in staying here. He wanted her to stay.

Logically, it didn't make sense—the woman was aggressive, arrogant, prickly, and argumentative. But somehow he worked easily with her, he trusted her. She was strong and armored for everyone else, but he found himself wanting her to open up and be vulnerable to him. And completely outside of the physical attraction between them, he liked her.

Was it right for him to keep her here? She could be CTO of a larger company, making more money, working toward her dream of CEO. Her talents were wasted here.

But if she had that better job, things would go back to the way they'd been before. She'd be driven, no time for relationships—she always made that clear. If she stayed here, she'd have more time, she might be more open to it.

That was selfish and self-serving of him. He was ashamed for even considering it.

And for the second time in his life, he prayed.

"I know you want what's best for her. I'm starting to want that too. You came through for me, even though I didn't deserve it. Maybe I can come through for her."

The problem was, there wasn't much he could do. He didn't have the same kind of clout as her grandmother, as his father ...

Dad.

Drake never asked him for anything. He'd raised his children to work hard and build their own kingdoms in the business world. He wasn't a magic genie to bail them out or give them a hand up.

But this he might do, as a favor to Chieko Sakai, who had connections with practically all the investors in the Bay Area, but no foothold in the game development community. Because of Drake, his father had some clout

He still hesitated to pick up the phone. A deep-rooted "obedient son" part of him warred with the desire to help Venus. Old versus new. But she had the courage to face an unknown future. He could face a potentially new chapter in his relationship with his father.

"God, Venus might not like my meddling this way. What do you think?"

He didn't get an audible answer, but he fancied God chuckling at him. That was good enough. He didn't think God disliked the idea. He picked up the phone and dialed.

"Dad? Are you still close to a few people on Oomvid's board of directors?"

If her lawyer pulled at his goatee one more time, she was going to reach over and yank it out for him. Clark fiddled with his facial hair every time he was thinking. Since he was brilliant, he thought a great deal.

Venus did not need the distraction today of all days, when Oomvid had specifically called to set up this meeting with her.

She sat at the spacious conference table and crossed her legs, bouncing her foot up and down and loosening her plain, low-heeled pumps. She'd been oh-so-tempted to grab her highest pair of stilettos for today's meeting—she even took out an old favorite, a pair of black and tan Valentinos—but her Bible reading time had been in Psalms again: "Though the Lord is on high, he looks upon the lowly."

The Valentinos went back in the closet.

"Stop it." She snapped her fingers and stabbed one at Clark, just as his hand crept up to his chin. "Do not touch your face."

He looked at his hand as if he just realized it belonged to him, then lowered it to his lap.

Her foot jiggled faster. She had arrived exactly on time. If they kept her waiting much longer, it would border on rudeness.

The door opened. Dean Logan Herne and Tip Connealy, both on the board of directors, walked in. Venus's shoulders eased back. She hadn't wanted to ask about Yardley when they'd called to arrange the meeting, but the presence of Dean and Tip meant lower executives like Yardley weren't invited.

They shook hands. Their eyes were firm and serious but not flinty or granite. Venus took it as a good sign. As they sat, Dean was the first to speak. "We'll cut right to the chase."

Clark sat with ruffled feathers, denied the pleasure of dragging the purpose of the meeting from them.

Tip passed folders to Venus and Clark. "We received the information you sent us about Esme Preston and our Chief Technology Officer, Yardley Yates. Your, er … mother, Ms. Sakai, contacted one of the board members directly, as well."

Venus wanted to sink through the floor.

"The board discussed the situation with the input of select advisors. We have terminated the employment of Preston and Yates."

Venus stifled a cough and ended up swallowing a bolus of air. Her hand rubbed her throat. They fired them? She hadn't expected anything like that, not when Brett's intercepted emails were useless in a lawsuit, and Dean and Tip weren't known for being pushovers or stupid.

Tip gestured to the folder in front of her, which she'd forgotten about. "That outlines our offer to you. We want to buy the Spiderweb. We also want to offer you the new position of CTO."

The edges of her vision started closing in. She grabbed the edge of the table. She would *not* pass out. She refused to allow herself to pass out.

Clark, who'd been reading the offer and rubbing his goatee, stepped in. "About the legal transference of ownership and further development of the tool …"

Venus followed with only half an ear. They wanted to buy the Spiderweb — not steal it. They wanted her as Chief Technology Officer of Oomvid.

Her first and foremost thought was that she'd have to leave Drake.

"You need a good slap upside the head." Lex glared at Venus, and probably would have delivered the needed blow had she not been holding baby Elyssa.

"Break it up, you two." Trish pushed her way between Lex and Venus so she could take Elyssa. "I need to feed her."

As Trish settled on the couch, Lex and Venus slid their eyes away at the same time. Even though they were cousins, once they passed puberty, they'd been uncomfortable disrobing in front of each other—put it down to old-fashioned Asian modesty—but since the birth of the baby, Trish had no qualms about her body.

She looked at the two of them, who were trying not to stare at her abnormally large chest as she undid her nursing bra. "Oh, for crying out loud. You guys are such prudes."

"You were too, at one point."

"Yeah, well, when you've had everyone and their sister gaping at you while you sweat and heave and push a seven-pound infant out of your nethers ..."

"You've gotten so crass!" Venus covered her eyes.

"I've gotten realistic. It happens when you discover bodily functions you never knew you had." She set Elyssa to suckle and covered her with a burping cloth. Thank goodness.

Trish's front door opened. "Hi guys." Jenn entered carrying a grocery bag and—more importantly—her pan-sized Longaberger wooden basket, which meant she'd baked something for dessert. Yum. She set it down. "Lex, can you get the rice cooker out of my car? And Venus, go grab the crockpot."

"You didn't cook it fresh? Sacrilege." But Venus slipped on her shoes to head outside.

"I cooked it yesterday, let it sit a day to meld, and heated it up in the crockpot. It's oxtail stew."

"Ooh, goodie!" Lex hustled out the door ahead of her.

They managed not to drop dinner as they brought it inside, just in time to see Trish make a face at the salad Jenn was finishing.

Jenn ignored her. "Greens are good for you, Momma."

"Yeah, well, Momma wants french fries." Trish grinned.

While Jenn dished up for them, Lex poked Venus in the ribs with a bony elbow. "Tell Jenn about it."

"What?" Jenn looked up, licking a drop of stew from her finger.

Venus related the Spiderweb offer and the CTO position to her steaming bowl of rice covered with stew. "Can we eat yet?"

"There." Jenn slid a bowl in front of Trish, who had come back from laying a sleeping Elyssa down in her crib. "Let's pray."

Jenn always said long prayers for grace. Venus suspected she did it just to annoy her cousins, who were usually raring to eat. Today, she asked for wisdom for Venus in her decision.

"Amen."

"What do you mean, wisdom for her decision?" Lex shoved some food in her mouth, but then started panting. "Hot! Hot!" She flapped her hand in front of her open mouth.

"I could have told you that." Venus blew on the rice and stew perched on her chopsticks.

"I have to agree with Lex, for once." Trish eyed her thoughtfully. "Why is there even a question about what you'll do?"

Venus chewed slowly, then swallowed. "I don't know. I don't feel ecstatic. I feel numb."

"Why would you feel numb?"

"Granted"—Lex swallowed—"it's not your own company developing the Spiderweb. Would you have made more by licensing it out?"

"Not really. They offered a very fair amount for it. I was surprised."

Trish gnawed on an oxtail bone. "Is it because it's CTO instead of CEO of your own company?"

"N ... no." Venus stared at her food. "I don't think it is, anyway. I mean, I still could work toward CEO in a few years, and besides, Oomvid is bigger now than my company would be, even in ten years."

"So what's your problem?" Jenn demanded.

Lex, Venus, and Trish stared at Jenn in amazement.

Jenn colored. "Er ... that might have been a little harsh."

"No, it wasn't." Lex stabbed her chopsticks at Venus. "What is your problem?"

Venus eyed the points in front of her nose. "Stop it, that's rude."

Lex lowered her chopsticks. "Is it Oomvid's work environment? But you'd be CTO, and Yardley's gone. Wouldn't that guarantee a little more power and respect?"

"I don't know. It would be hard to be a female executive, whether in Oomvid or my own company, but I already know that. Maybe I just like working for my team at Bananaville." That was an understatement. She'd even come to appreciate Darla—who'd toned down her wardrobe and now actually worked at the receptionist's station. And as for Drake...

"So you like working for Drake over the CEO of Oomv—" Lex suddenly smacked Venus's arm with her chopsticks. "You like Drake!"

"I do not. That hurt." But a prickling sunburn feeling spread from her ears across her cheekbones.

"Look! She's blushing!" Trish chortled.

Lex guffawed. "You like Drake!"

"You haven't liked anybody since ..." Jenn raised her shoulders and held out her hands, unable to remember.

"Since forever!" Trish laughed at her. "Oh, my gosh, this is great."

"I don't have time for a relationship." Venus burrowed into her food.

"You would if you didn't take that CTO position."

The three cousins all fell silent.

"You're thinking about it, aren't you?" Jenn said. "You're thinking of giving up Oomvid in order to *maybe* have a chance at Drake?"

"No! Well, yes." Venus sighed and dropped her chopsticks onto the table. "I don't know. This position is huge. It's even further up the ladder than I expected to be at this point in my life."

"You can't give this up. This is what you've always worked for." Trish gestured to Lex and Jenn. "We know because we've watched you sweat and toil to get to this place."

"Something about the job feels wrong."

"It is a lot of hours ..." Jenn said.

Lex shook her head. "But you've always worked long hours."

"And are you going to give up the Spiderweb too?" Trish asked.

"No, dummy." Lex rapped her chopsticks on her arm. "She'll still sell the Spiderweb, maybe negotiate for more money."

"But not take the job?" Jenn sounded incredulous, as if Venus had said she was going to become a park ranger.

Venus sighed. "It's something beyond logic. Something deeper than my feelings is telling me not to take this job."

Trish blew out a long breath. "That's pretty major. Are you sure?"

"I don't know." Venus dropped her head in her hands. "But I promised to submit to God, no matter what. To trust Him, no matter what."

"Maybe this is a test."

No one spoke. Venus could hear her blood pulsing in her eardrums. Was He really asking her to give up Oomvid? She'd be giving up her reputation and position in the game development industry that she'd worked on for years.

But had she really been happy developing games like the last one she worked on? Like the all-female multi-shooter game she would have developed for her own company—which she might still develop at Oomvid if she took the position—but which she was too ashamed to give to the teen boys she worked with at church? What kind of a job was that? All money, no morals. *That's lovely, Venus.*

So she'd give up Oomvid to do what—work at Bananaville? Was that where God wanted her?

With Drake?

Just the thought of him heated her chest like an electric stove burner.

It was nuts. This defied all logic. This was the ultimate risk of her career—but maybe this was God seeing if she'd really do what she said she'd do, and trust Him.

She didn't want to fail God.

"I have to call my lawyer." She scooted off her chair.

"Wait." Lex rummaged in her pocket.

"I don't need your cell, I've got my own."

"Er . . . It's not my phone."

"Huh? I don't understand."

Lex slammed her hand on the table with a faint clink and faced them all with a defiant look. "Now, don't freak out, okay? I didn't want a lot of hassle and fussing and this was the only way."

"What?" Trish paused with a fork halfway to her mouth.

"What are you talking about?" Unperturbed, Jenn reached for more stew.

Lex withdrew her hand. Sitting on the table was a gold wedding band.

Jenn choked on her food and Venus whacked her between the shoulder blades. Trish dropped her fork with a clatter into her bowl.

"Aiden and I went to Las Vegas last weekend and got married."

THIRTY-ONE

Darla's eyes bugged out of her head when she saw Venus. "I didn't think you even owned a real dress."

"Like it?" She sashayed in the front doors of Bananaville, enjoying the caressing swish of silk around her calves.

"I love the sash"—she pointed to the scarlet chiffon trails—"but isn't it a bit romantic for work?"

She actually felt romantic for one of the first times in her life. Maybe because she'd made a decision about what to do, maybe romance was in the air because of Lex—rather, *Mrs. Young.* It was so like Lex to elope. "I'm only in for a few minutes. I'm taking the day off."

Darla gave her a mock scowl. "Slacker."

Venus laughed.

"Well, that's both you and Drake, then."

Venus paused as she headed around the corner. "What?"

"He's out today too."

Oh, no! After all her careful planning. She tried to school her face in something halfway nonchalant. "Where is he?" Out with some other girl? On a business trip across the country? Or maybe he finally checked himself into a psych ward?

Darla shrugged. "Gerry didn't say."

Venus almost barged into Gerry's office, and last-minute remembered to knock first. "Come in."

"Gerry—" She entered, but Gerry's uplifted finger stopped her while Gerry spoke rapidly into the phone.

"So anyway, thank you for the cupcakes. I'm sure the kids will ... Oh, and your grandson likes chocolate that much? Yes, my daughter ..." Gerry gave a rather weak laugh. "Oh, Mrs. Howard, you're just so funny. Well, thank you for ... Your nephew's son eats too much chocolate too? How nice. Er, I mean, how unfortunate.... Oh, well, I'm glad he was okay. Anyway, thank you ... Oh, and he gave some to the dog too."

Venus and Gerry both sighed and rolled their eyes at the same time. Venus leaned against the doorjamb.

"Oh! I'm sorry, Mrs. Howard, I have to go ... No, really, I have to go. I'm at *work*.... Yes, it was nice chatting with you too ... I'm late for a meeting, have to run, bye!" Gerry slammed the phone down and smacked her head in her hands. "The woman drives me insane!"

"How'd she get your direct line?"

"Drake called her from my phone one time, and she collects phone numbers like normal people collect stamps or coins." Her voice was muffled as she burrowed deeper in her hands.

"Speaking of, where is Drake?"

Gerry lifted her head and saw the dress.

Venus's throat tightened as the silence stretched. She suddenly realized she didn't know how Gerry would feel about her decision. Well, it wasn't her business.

Gerry leaned back in her chair. "It's about time."

Venus straightened. "What?"

Gerry gave her a *look*. "Don't be stupid." She started writing on a piece of notepaper. "Here's directions to his house." She ripped off the sheet and handed it to Venus.

"You're ... okay with this?"

"Oh for goodness' sake, you have to ask?"

Gerry looked more irritated than thrilled to have Venus blatantly going after her brother, but Venus would take what she could get. She scanned the paper. "Where in the world does he live?"

Gerry sighed and raised her eyes to the ceiling. "Booneyville."

Gerry was wrong. Booneyville was the more populated suburb of where Drake's house actually lay.

As she wound down Arastradero Road—were those horses on the side of the road???—she called Gerry. "Are you sure he's home? He's not answering his cell phone."

"He just called me from his home phone."

"I think that's Stirrup Road ... It's a dirt track!" She'd almost missed it. She swerved onto the road, then realized it climbed at a steep angle up the hill. Oh my gosh, she was going almost vertical! She gunned the engine until she shot over the summit and almost hit a property hedge.

"Gerry, I am in the middle of nowhere."

Gerry laughed like Venus was the star of a comic standup night.

"What?" Venus wove down the curving road. At least it was paved, probably paid for by the multi-million-dollar homes on each side. Drake lived *here?*

"You think that's the middle of nowhere? Venus, you're still in Palo Alto."

"But ... that's a hawk flying there!"

"Have you ever driven south of San Jose?"

"Er ... I think I went to Gilroy once."

Gerry made a disgusted noise. "Venus, you're such a city girl."

"Don't any of these houses have numbers?" She squinted at a curb, but there were no sloppy red and white numbers painted on *these* curbs.

"It's the one with the red, circular front door. You can't miss it. I have to get to work, Venus. Bye."

Who the heck had a circular front door? What was he, a Hobbit?

She slowed to a crawl. Some houses had their front doors obscured by trees and hedges—because obviously, in a community like this, privacy ranked higher than curb appeal. A Hummer roared up behind her and latched onto her bumper.

For a second, the sight of it reminded her of Yardley's Hummer, and she wondered if it really were him and that he'd run her off the road ... No, it was someone else, a man with dark hair and expensive sunglasses. After a few yards, he pulled around her, jammed the accelerator, and shot off down the winding road like a NASCAR driver.

She turned the corner of the road.

Oh. My.

The view spread out before her. Okay, that's why he lived here. The land sloped downward to a lush valley, where a house or two stood regally isolated. Then the ground rose up in a forested area to the southwest, with houses dotting the ridge.

There! She almost missed it because she was ogling the view. The landscaped front lawn area looked welcoming as it sloped downward, and large windows broke up the stucco walls of the house where it rose three stories. Drake's car was no where to be seen, but maybe he'd parked it, oh, in the three-car garage. Imagine that.

She coasted down the driveway, wondering if she'd set off any security alarms. Nope.

Vigorous knocking on the very red, very round front door got her *nada.* Was he home? She peered through the round windows flanking the door, and had to angle herself in order to see through the spacious living room area to a back patio. Was that a thin plume of smoke? Barbeque grill?

She crossed the driveway to the side of the house. Oh, man. The landscaping ended with the front lawn. He hadn't yet done anything to the side, which had a dirt track. And she'd worn her strappy sandals with narrow heels.

She tiptoed down the dirt to the backyard, trying not to touch her heels into the mud—otherwise, it would probably stick like a golf tee and she'd go tumbling. Ugh! She got mud in her toes.

Apparently he had started landscaping the backyard, because green lawn rose up on her right. The road sloped below the back patio level, so she looked for stairs or a rising path to get her up there.

Suddenly, Cujo in the flesh came running at her, foaming at the mouth, eyes red like blood. She screamed and stepped back. Her heels sank into the mud up to the sole. Kicking out of them, she started backtracking. Mud sprayed up her calves.

"Brutus!"

The demon dog caught up with her. Jumped at her, saliva arcing through the air. Lethal claws landed on her shoulders.

Ewwwww. Big slobbery tongue licked all the makeup off her face.

She landed hard on her butt. In the mud. With Brutus on top of her. Apparently her makeup and her hairspray tasted good.

"Drake!"

At that point, she became aware of somebody laughing. Not just laughing—heaving and snorting and gasping for breath.

Good, because it was going to be his last.

Venus inhaled to loose another piercing shriek, but he forestalled her. "Brutus! Come."

Brutus hesitated, gave a last lick to her ear—ewewewew!—and trotted away, up a short path to the patio, just as she heard footsteps crunching through the gravel on the way down.

She flipped a slobber-saturated lock of hair out of her eyes and squinted up at him. The sun was behind him, so she couldn't be sure, but it looked like he was wiping away tears. "You are so dead."

He held out a hand, pulled her up and into his arms, and then kissed her.

It would have been more romantic if she hadn't still smelled Brutus's halitosis slobber. She broke away reluctantly. "Oomvid offered me—"

"I know."

He suddenly didn't look so dashing and romantic. "How did you know?"

"I called my father, who's good friends with Dean, and he encouraged the board of directors to go ahead with what they were already considering."

"They were going to buy the Spiderweb and hire me anyway?"

"They might have." He released her but kept hold of her hand and led her up the path to the patio.

Yuck, the backside of her dress stuck to her like a bathing suit.

The spacious patio had a 180-degree uninhibited view, due in part to a narrow infinity pool that would be heaven to soak in while watching the sunset. She caught her breath as she reached the top, but she was quick to grab the bar towel Drake handed to her.

"I knew you'd refused them when Gerry told me you were on the way here."

A perverse part of her didn't like being so easy to get. "I could have been coming to tell you that I quit."

A smile quirked his mouth. "Gerry mentioned you wore a dress."

Drat.

She scrubbed her face and tried to surreptitiously tug at her dress to remove it from her backside. She ignored Drake's laughing look. "If you wanted me to stay, why did you call your father?"

He sobered and looked away from her, scanned the trees on the horizon, the millionaires who lived there. "I wanted to give you a choice."

She stared at him. Actually, stared more at the mud streaks across his polo shirt and slacks, poor guy. "That's the nicest thing you've ever done for me."

"You're hard to please, Venus."

She smiled archly. "I know."

He reached out, grabbed her hand and held it, twining his fingers in hers, rubbing at dried flakes of mud with his thumb. "I'm glad you're staying."

"I am too." She slid her eyes to his and smiled. "Even though you don't pay me enough."

ACKNOWLEDGMENTS

Thanks to:

My editors, Sue Brower, Rachelle Gardner, and Becky Shingledecker, for being such an awesome team and making this book the best it can be.

My agent, Wendy Lawton, for being my cheerleader and mentor.

Diana and Steve Lee, for the, er, fascinating info about what pregnant Chinese women are supposed to eat. Also, huge thanks for helping me crash the Bananaville server.

Stephanie Quilao, for your info on women gamers and startups, for your company ideas, and for being a sounding board. Venus and this book would not even exist without your help.

Sarah Kim, for your info on startups, for great food, and even better wine.

Pamela James, for helping me name everybody.

Erin Kawaye, David Kawaye, and Randy Furuyama, for helping me find hapless victims to interview about video game development. Jon Okui and Chane Parker, for your invaluable help and letting me pick your brains.

To my critique partners and proofreaders Robin Caroll, Sharon Hinck, Ronie Kendig, Dineen Miller, Trisha Ontiveros, MaryLu Tyndall, Katie Vorreiter, and Cheryl Wyatt, for catching every magically healed sprained ankle and every car that transforms into a truck two pages later.

My church youth group and staff, for letting me cannibalize names, characters, and games for Venus's youth group.

The Seekerville ladies, for a good laugh and keeping me sane, as well as for more names when I was desperate.

GLOSSARY OF ASIAN WORDS (CAMY STYLE)

Azuki bean ice cream bar—(uh-zoo-key) (Japanese) Azuki beans or red beans are actually a common food throughout Asia, but the name *azuki* is Japanese. Red beans are often mixed with sugar to form a sweet dessert, sometimes as a soup (see *tong sui* below). I personally like azuki bean ice cream, which is sometimes sold as an ice cream bar like a creamsicle. Non-Asian people often think it's kind of weird, since azuki is essentially a bean, and no one would make garbanzo bean ice cream or kidney bean ice cream.

Bao yu—(bow [as in bow-wow]-you) (Cantonese) dried abalone, often used to flavor long-simmered soups.

Cantonese—the dialect of southern China (as opposed to Mandarin, the dialect of northern China).

Daikon radish—(die-cone) (Japanese) a plain white radish, very mild-flavored, which is probably why it's often pickled into *takuwan* (below). They also shred raw daikon as a bed for sashimi (slices of raw fish) at Japanese restaurants.

Gobo—(go-bow [as in bow and arrow]) the root of the Greater Burdock plant, often used in Japanese dishes. It's usually braised or pickled, but however it's prepared, I always think it tastes like flavored wood.

Hibachi—(he-bah-chee) (Japanese) a cast iron barbeque grill, usually small and heavy. Dad made the best steaks with our hibachi filled with mesquite charcoal.

Kanji—(con-gee) Chinese characters used in Japanese writing.

Lop Cheong—(lop-chong) (Cantonese) pork sausage, usually slightly sweet, often used in fried rice dishes or rice pouches. Very fatty but very delish.

Obon dances—(oh-bone) (Japanese) Buddhist festival of the dead. People will dance in a circle around a tower with musicians at the top. The dances are very repetitive and easy to learn, and it's a fun, time-honored traditional festival. But sometimes the teenagers who attend will make it like a high school dance, complete with girls crying in the bathroom by the end of the night. Ahh, high school.

Tako—(tah-koh) (Japanese) octopus. My dad, my uncles, and various neighbors always went spear fishing for tako and brought it home to eat. I only ever saw the small tako, not the massive ones you see on *National Geographic*. Grandma often made *tako poke*, which is an appetizer of boiled tako mixed with seaweed and sesame seeds, excellent when paired with beer.

Takuwan—(tah-coup-won) (Japanese) white *daikon* radish that has been pickled. I'm not sure why, but it's always radioactive yellow in color, like it's going to cause cancer just by standing within five feet of it. However, my grandma's takuwan was always just the right amount of sour and sweet, and I loved it.

Tong sui—(tong-swee) (Cantonese) sweet soup made from red beans or sesame seeds, usually served as a dessert at the end of a meal. Some people find it strange, but I *looooove* this stuff, especially the black sesame seed soup, served warm.

Tsukemono—(tah-kay-moh-noh) Japanese pickled vegetables. My grandmother usually made tsukemono with cabbage.

Uni—(ooh-knee) (Japanese) sea urchin. It's sickly yellow, slimy, and the most disgusting sushi ever prepared on the planet. My father is one of the few people I know who likes uni, and he enjoys his uni sushi with relish when we go to Kabuki Japanese restaurant in Pearl City (Hawaii).

Vietnamese iced coffee—Super strong coffee, dripped into condensed milk, then poured over ice. Major yum.

White Rabbit milk candy—This isn't really an Asian word, but it's an Asian candy that people might not be familiar with. It's similar to taffy, except it's white and packaged in smaller pieces than taffy. There is a big white rabbit on the package. I used to eat these like crazy all through school and into my twenties, until the sugar started rotting my teeth.

Sushi for One?

Camy Tang

"*Sushi for One?* is an entertaining romp into the world of multi-culturalism. I loved learning the idiosyncrasies of Lex's crazy family—which were completely universal. Enjoy!"

—Kristen Billerbeck, author of *What a Girl Wants*

"In Lex Sakai, Camy Tang gives us a funny, plucky, volleyball-playing heroine with way too many balls in the air. I defy anyone to start reading and not root for Lex all the way to the story's romantic, super-satisfying end."

—Trish Perry, author of *The Guy I'm Not Dating*

Lex Sakai's family is big, nosy, and marriage-minded. When her cousin Mariko gets married, Lex will become the oldest single female cousin in the clan.

Lex has used her Bible study class on Ephesians to compile a huge list of traits for the perfect man. But the one man she keeps running into doesn't seem to have a single quality on her list. It's only when the always-in-control Lex starts to let God take over that all the pieces of this hilarious romance finally fall into place.

Softcover: 978-0-310-27398-1

Only Uni

Camy Tang,
Author of Sushi for One?

Senior biologist Trish Sakai is ready for a change from her wild, flirtatious behavior. So Trish creates three simple rules from First and Second Corinthians and plans to follow them to the letter. No more looking at men as possible dates, especially non-Christians. Second, tell others about Christ. And third, she will persevere in hardship by relying on God. And just to make sure she behaves, she enlists the help of her three cousins, Lex, Venus and Jennifer, the only Christians in their large extended family.

But Trish's dangerously tempting ex-boyfriend, Kazuo the artist, keeps popping up at all the wrong moments, and her grandmother, who has her eye on his family money, keeps trying to push the two of them back together again. Then there's Spencer, the hunky colleague at work who keeps turning Trish's thoughts in the wrong direction.

It just isn't fair! She's trying so hard, but instead of being God's virtuous woman, she's going nuts trying to stand firm against two hunky guys. Trish thought following her three rules would be a cinch, but suddenly those simple rules don't seem so simple after all.

Softcover: 978-0-310-27399-8